As I watched, th... ...e. Whispers swirled in r... ...d, leaning against the window, to understand what they were trying to tell me, but they were too faint. I shook my head to clear them away.

Gasping, I struggled not to faint, not to give up. The cry that issued from deep within me came out silently . . . I don't want to see. *I don't want to see it again!*

The woods. The child's pathetic body mangled and bloody . . .

The past? Oh, my God . . . *the future* . . .

The vision was so vivid I could almost reach out and touch it. Little actors in a bloody play. No. *No!* I was sobbing now as I pulled myself up along the window ledge.

Far away on the edge of the woods *something* hovered. Something slithered across the very edge of my sight and my heart turned into a lump of ice. I followed it as it moved, something only *my* eyes could see. I heard an evil laugh echoing through space and I heard a child's broken wail on the air. I cringed inside. A child was being tortured and I couldn't help, couldn't lift a finger. I could not move; it was as though I were being forced to watch. Had it happened long ago? Or was it going to happen now?

And the hated, demonic voice penetrated the frailty of my conscience, forcing me to listen:

I have waited, Sarah . . . for you . . .

How could I fight it? How could I stop what was to happen?

EVIL STALKS THE NIGHT

Kathryn Meyer Griffith

LEISURE BOOKS ∞ NEW YORK CITY

*For my patient mother and father, who
never lost faith in my dreams, with love . . .*

A LEISURE BOOK

Published by

Dorchester Publishing Co., Inc.
6 East 39th Street
New York City

Printed in the United States of America

CHAPTER ONE

SUNCREST, 1960

I was ten that summer. I look back now through the haze of all the endless summers that came before and after and remember almost every second vividly. I can ask myself now—oh, yes, *now*—why didn't I see what was to happen? How could I have been so blind? How could I have been so innocent of the dark forces that stalked us?

But I was a child. Maybe you can't blame a mere child for all the sins of eternity. Maybe my innocence was what saved me. Heaven help me. *My innocence.*

We lived in a huge, drafty old fortress of blood-colored bricks. I used to think it stood so tall and proud, challenging the very skies, just to protect us, me and my family. There were nine of us who lived in that old rambling house that faced the woods. 707 Suncrest. Seven was my mother's lucky number. There were seven children. I smile now when I think of my mother and her superstitions. But I have turned out to be very much like her; seven is my lucky number, too. Or at least it was once, when luck counted. That was a very long time ago. So long ago when we all frolicked in the mysterious woods that ran the length of our street and disappeared among deep ravines and creeks that crisscrossed the land around us. So long ago when we were all safe and laughing in the old house . . . that summer.

It's a vicious circle I trample in; like life's a vicious circle, the ends always colliding somewhere. How insignificant and weak we are when we rush to try to escape what has to be.

That summer of 1960 when I was ten and my brother Jimmy was eight, the sun unmercifully scorched the land to a crisp brown and everywhere we ran the grass waved dry and brittle in the shimmering air. The soft greens and pale golds of early spring were long gone. Maybe that year there had never been a spring. I don't recall one. All I can remember is the swift, deadly heat that lasted way into October. It had been a strange summer.

Jimmy and I spent most of it trying to escape the terrible heat. We crouched together in the tall weeds next to our house and laughed at the silly world, hiding from everyone. Jimmy was a queer little guy even then and I would watch him as he stared emptily into space, or as he chased ladybugs through the grass. He would never hurt them; Jimmy never could stand to hurt anything—except Charlie. He would constantly tease our little brother Charlie with words, or lack of them, but never lay a finger on him, even though I'd be the first one to say that if any child on this earth needed the hand it was Charlie. He was as mean as they come. There were times I truly believed Charlie wasn't Charlie at all, but a demon in Charlie's skin. He could be so cruel.

But Jimmy wasn't anything like Charlie. Jimmy wasn't anything like anybody I've ever known. Jimmy was something special, but he never showed it to anyone. He hid it very carefully. It was many years later when I finally learned just why he had. Jimmy had light green eyes like me. I guess we must have looked a lot alike with our thin, serious faces and tow-blond hair, because a lot of people used to ask if we were twins. We weren't. It was just that I had a special feeling for Jimmy and we went everywhere together; we were inseparable.

I remember one hot day in particular. It was one of those

lazy days toward the end of August and we were brooding together out in the woods over the fact that in less than two weeks we would be back in school. Summer was so precious. We never wanted it to end.

"Sure is hot, sis. Whew!" Jimmy wiped a hand across his dirty face and smeared the grime deeper. He was grinning that mischievous grin of his and kicking the weeds into shreds with his brown bare feet as he was talking to me. He had this way of using his hands when he spoke, like a magician working at his sleight of hand. I asked him about it once and he just smiled weakly, but never said a word. I felt like there was always something he wasn't telling me.

"It's so hot you can see the heat waves rising in the air." I squinted my eyes and spread my sweaty hands before me. "You see 'em?"

He laughed oddly. "Of course I do, Sarah. Don't you know that I see everything? Don't you know that by now?"

I didn't reply. Silly boy, I thought. Silly child. No one could see *everything*. I truly believed that then . . . and I was the silly one.

"I think I'll go back home and see if Mom'll give me a fudgesicle," he said, and walked away into the sunlight. "It's been hours since we checked in with Mom. She's probably worried." His voice trailed back lazily on the wind.

"Probably," I said, almost to myself, frowning. I started to follow in his dusty footprints through the jungle of cockleburrs, scratchy twigs, and wilted daisies. My hands skimmed the growth as we went. I stopped to pick some of the healthier looking flowers, reluctant to follow my brother home. I was afraid Mom would corner us on the porch outside the ripped screen door and delegate a mess of new chores to do. Who wanted to go home and work? Not me. Summer was almost over and I had better things to do.

"I just hope that Mom doesn't remember that we never cleaned up that filthy basement yesterday like she told us to," I fretted out loud as our pace speeded up. And the

9

backyard was a junk pile. We had enough work to last us two summers if work was what our mother decided we should do. We were running then, the hot air rushing through our hair and our bare feet skimming the ground. I stopped, breathless and panting, to rest. "Come back, Jimmy! I'm stopping for a while!" A huge willow tree looked inviting and I lingered under it, waiting for him to notice I wasn't behind him and double back for me. I didn't want to go home yet. It took him a few moments to realize I was no longer in the race.

"Tired, sis?" He flopped down beside me, hardly breathing hard at all. The boy was a veritable cheetah.

I nodded, and I remember the feeling that came over me in that instant I looked at him, shading my eyes with my hand against the bright sun. I had the most ominous premonition that something was watching us, something very evil was . . . waiting for us. It nearly knocked me over, the feeling was so strong. It was the first time—*the very first*—that I was aware of it. *It was the beginning.*

Panicked, I jumped up and fled that place with a bewildered Jimmy screaming behind me, "What the heck is the matter? Sarah? Sarah, what are you running for? Will you slow down? Will you slow down!" He finally caught up to me and passed me. I never understood the meaning of what he said then until many, many years later. "You're *safe,* Sarah. You're *safe now.*" At the time I thought he meant tag. I was safe. We were home. He hadn't meant that at all.

I forgot the terrible moment as fast as it came once I reached the first step of our porch. We sat there huffing and puffing, wiping the sweat from our faces, and the run—or the fear—had soaked me. My shorts were wet and even the long braids that hung down my back felt clammy and damp to my touch. It was so darn hot. We sat there for the longest time just drying off and listening to the familiar sounds from inside the house. As usual, there were shrieks and cries of children; the strident voice of our mother trying to calm bedlam. "John . . . no, no, no! Leslie, get me the red bowl up there—yes, the chipped one." And a few seconds later, after the sound of the plates hitting the table, mother's voice again: "Has anybody seen Charlie? He has the forks and spoons . . . where *is* that child, he was just here . . . *Charlie!*"

Jimmy and I giggled on the back porch. It was as it should be; all was well with my world. It was a golden time I want to always remember and treasure.

"You know that if we stay out here any longer that old Charlie will come snooping and find us for sure," Jimmy warned me. "For sure. Let's sneak down to Satterfield's and ride the ponies!" His eyes lit up. "Come on!"

"Naw. I don't feel like it . . . and so what if Charlie finds us? He doesn't mean any harm."

"He's a brat."

"No." I stared him down. "He's just lonely. No one ever wants to play with Charlie and they run him off. How would you like it if the others did that to you all the time?"

"He's mean as an angry hornet, that's why. He bites. He hurts . . . things," Jimmy defended himself.

"That's why! You'd be mean, too. I told you, he's just lonely and fighting back any way he can. Why can't you all be nicer to Charlie?"

"Because he's a snitch and he's always whining around trying to get people in trouble. You know that nobody can have any fun when Charlie's around to spoil it. He picks his nose, for Christ's sake, Sarah!" He grimaced.

Why did Jimmy, of all people, have to feel that way about poor Charlie? Jimmy wasn't like that usually.

"Let's go catch the ponies," Jimmy begged.

I sighed, shrugging my shoulders at him and trying not to smile. I loved Jimmy so much . . . much more than any sister should. "Jimmy, first of all, we are not supposed to be sneaking off to ride those wild ponies at Satterfield's place. Mother would have our skins. Second, the last time we rode them, I got thrown in the thorn bushes at the edge of the creek and cut my legs to pieces, remember?"

He laughed, and I had to hush him because if Mother heard us out there she would recruit us for K.P. duty, pronto.

"Well, it was either the thorn bushes or the creek, and those rocks didn't look all that soft. I chose land." I held my chin up until it hurt. "That's just another reason why we should stay away from those wild animals. I could have broken my . . ."

"Rear, you mean?" Jimmy supplied the word. "You sure looked funny flying through the air when the pony ditched you! For Pete's sake, you should have been able to stay on it . . . it was such a *little* pony, Sarah."

"How do you know? I don't remember *you* riding one. You could never catch one!"

"I tried." He could be so stubborn when he set his mind to it.

"Did you? Did you really?" And it was my turn to laugh at him as I remembered the way he had desperately tried to run down one of the tiny ponies and been dragged through the brambles for his trouble. He was too afraid of them. Sure, I had been thrown—but at least I had caught one to be thrown from.

"They was wild!"

"They was *mad,* is what they were. Besides, Mother's right, they don't belong to us and we had no right. That was why I got thrown. God punished me." I said that last part so righteously. I lived the Ten Commandments and I believed. I truly believed in God and atonement for sins.

Jimmy tossed me a funny look. "There is no God!" He spat. It wasn't what he said that upset me so much; it was that he really believed it! I could see it in his eyes. It was as if he knew something that no one else knew, and he *knew* there was no God.

"Jimmy!" I was shocked, as I always was at his anger and his blasphemy.

"There is no God, Sarah, and you didn't get thrown because it was wrong and . . . I *still* think Charlie is a creep!" It all tumbled out like angry bees and his face turned red and ugly. Was this monster my Jimmy?

I forgot and became angry at what he had said about poor Charlie. Jimmy was lounging on the bottom step and I on the top one. I could feel the warmth of the wood under me from the hot sun. I could feel the splinters break away from the step as I bounced down to come even with Jimmy. Charlie needed a champion and I was the only one around. Not much, but Joan of Arc had always appealed to me — the romantic idealism behind it, not necessarily the flames. I squared my jaw at my younger brother and jumped in.

"He's our *brother*, for Pete's sake, and he's only six! Don't you have any heart?" I hissed, pinching his upper arm through the thin material of his plaid shirt to drive my point home.

"*Ouch!* Sarah, you rat!" he yelped, and lunged at me, finally laughing, and we rolled down the yard into the grass tumbling over and over in our mock anger. All a game. Always a game . . . I could never stay mad at Jimmy or he at me. We got up and started to brush each other's clothes off.

"You look like a dustball!" he teased, trying to make amends in his own way. He hung his head and shifted his eyes around to see if there were anyone around spying on us; then he dropped his voice to a tiny whisper. "But he's so *old* for only six! He hates everybody and everything." Then, even lower, so low I had to strain to hear: "He's a real pain in the ass."

"James Towers!" I turned away from him in disgust and climbed the porch steps. "You ought to have that filthy mouth of yours washed out with a bar of soap! Strong soap with lots of suds . . . Where do you ever pick up such language? It can't be from our parents. It can't be from *me*." I jumped up the steps three at a time, Jimmy trotting behind me like a hound on a scent. "What am I gonna do with you? I swear, you're gonna go to the devil one of these days if you don't clean up your act, brother. And that's one place I can't help you with." I gave him a penetrating look. "How can you hate your own brother like that?"

13

"I don't *hate* him—exactly." He was relenting again. "Well, he *is* a snitch. Even you have to admit that, Sarah. But I'll tell you what." He walked up to me, bright green eyes sparkling and a sudden grin on his face. "I'll try to be nicer to him, I really will—for you—for a while, anyway, Sarah. I promise."

We were standing in front of the kitchen door and Jimmy scooted past me and laid his hand on the doorknob, turning to look back at me over his shoulder. "You coming in?" he asked me. The house looked so cool; its familiar musty scent was cool. Even though it was a shabby old house with wooden floors and porches that leaned to one side and creaked in the summer storms, we cherished it. I couldn't count the times I'd scrubbed those wooden floors down on my hands and knees or helped brush a coat of much-needed paint over those old cracked walls, but I never minded the work—it was home.

The basement contained a pre-war furnace and the coal was stored in a tiny room with a trap door to the outside. One time Jimmy and I foolishly decided to make the coal chute our secret way into the house and sneaked in through its black narrowness. We came out looking like two black goblins and got caught—a spanking to boot.

The coal chute opened right above our mother's prized rock garden on the side of the house, and Jimmy and I spent many long hot summer days searching the whole neighborhood for sparkling treasures to stock it with. I loved to sit in the middle of it and lift the glittering rocks in the sun, reflecting their rainbows over the bricks of the house and the grass. There were small golden ones and huge silver-streaked ones with white frothy stuff running through them. Some of the rocks looked like solid glass, clear or milky white, even pastels as soft as a baby's breath. I have never seen a rock garden like that one in all my days since. Those rocks were poor man's jewels that we lugged near and far. Sometimes Jimmy and I took some of the prettiest ones up into the protective branches of our cherry tree that stood sentinel at the end of the sloped lawn; we played with them when we weren't too busy stuffing our mouths with the cherries when they were in season. From there we could also see Mother's collection of climbing roses. Red, yellow and pink blooms that filled the air with their thick sweetness. I took a deep breath of the perfumed air.

"Coming?" Jimmy's voice brought me back to reality in the fading pink light of the waning sun. The day was ending and I always fancied that at that precise time of day the world was standing still. It's the time of day when everything is bathed in that strange soft light that smooths life's sharp edge like the subtle kiss from a new lover.

We'd go in each evening and eat the big supper Mother slaved so hard over and then we'd all fight over who got the first hot bath. Later, we'd sprawl in front of the black-and-white television set, more than willing to be scared out of our wits by shows like *The Twilight Zone* and *Spook Spectacular*. . . and then, if the weather was nice, we older ones would sneak out and play hide-and-seek under the rising moon, wallowing through the deep gullies that ripped through the fields behind our house. We were like a pack of young wolves tracking the countryside, running the fences, trying not to make a sound and give ourselves away in the moonlight. Those were the good years, before I was shown the horror that was to be my life . . . and I forever froze those memories in my child's mind like flies in amber.

"Sarah? Come on in here and help me set the table for supper." It was my mother calling me. I ran down the steps, impulsively plucked a small rouged bud and went in and stood before her. "It's nice you could grace us with your presence, young lady!" she said sharply. "Where have you been?" It was always the same.

"Out playing, Mom . . . but here I am. See?" I smiled, silently, withdrawing and presenting my gift, then moved to lay out the plates for her.

"About time, too," she remarked, but not as sharply as

before. She was wearing one of her flowered sun-back dresses I remember so well and she was sweating from the heat of a stove on a summer's day. She twirled the rose in her fingers, then leveled steel-blue eyes at me; eyes that echoed Charlie's like a mirror, yet managed to hold a special warmth that was hers alone. She was still a beautiful woman, after seven children and years of broken dreams. She smiled a rare smile. I sighed, knowing I was off the hook, and dinner ran its usual course.

Mother once confessed to me that she always wanted to be a nurse. But we children had stolen that dream from her.

"But Mom, you *are* a nurse!" I smiled back at her, trying to make her see. "You get to nurse all of *us* . . ." She only smiled and planted a kiss on my cheek. Was it sadness I glimpsed in those blue eyes?

She had told me, "For you, Sarah, it'll be different. Just remember to follow your dreams to the end, girl; never give up. I let it all go too easily—but you, you never let go. You'll make it, I know."

"Are you sorry you had us all, then?" I asked, taking her work-worn hands in mine. "Do you hate us for it?"

She gave me that wistful smile of hers and shook her head. "No, child, I'm not sorry I had you kids. I love you children and, well, against dreams I suppose love wins every time. Love is more powerful than dreams—or anything. Don't ever forget that."

She looked at me as if she were trying to tell me some great secret. She loved us very much, I never doubted that. And I promised her I'd never give up my dreams. Never. "I'll be an artist someday, Mom—I'll be an artist or . . . or a writer. Truly! I promise."

And she had laughed then, and hugged me. I think there were tears in her eyes. "I just bet you will, Sarah-girl. You're one of those special ones that fate has laid a heavy finger on and you're *bound* to be something special, too."

Of course, I thought then that she said it only because I was her daughter, with no thought that she might have been foreseeing what was to come. Don't all parents say that to their offspring? And don't all parents hope for better for their children than what they have known? My mother and father had it rough, especially with all us children. It affected my mother, though, in more ways than my father. In general he was an easy-going kind of individual. My mother would worry and fret herself sick over money and bills.

My father was a salesman for a building company that did siding and small home improvements, and the money was sporadic or at times nonexistent. One day we'd be as rich as kings and the next as poor as beggar mice, and it drove my sensitive mother up a wall. If there were no food for the table or money to pay the bills, Mother was practically impossible to live with. Her fiery temper matched her red hair, and she sometimes vented her frustrations on us children, but almost always on our father. I would lie in bed half the night listening to their angry voices bouncing through the house, trying to block out the misery with a pillow squeezed over my ears. I loved them both, and I couldn't see for the life of me why they had to take out their anger that way on each other when they were supposed to love each other so. I always thought that it would have been easier if they'd pulled together at those bad times instead of pulling apart.

I usually sided with my father—I was always the champion of the underdog. I felt so sorry for him when he came dragging home late at night without the promised money from the big deal and had to confront my mother's wrath. I tried to ease his hurt a little in any way I could. I'd fix him the supper my mother was too angry to bother with and serve him like a condemned prisoner . . . he had failed, sure, but he had tried. He deserved something for that. But like with Charlie, I could help but I couldn't cure. It made me feel so helpless.

My grandmother hit it right on the head when she stated that my real problem was a soft heart. "You can't cure all

17

the evils of the world with a tender heart, child," she warned me. Grandmother was always sharp in her observations. She was undeniably Old German—Mary Elizabeth Summers, who'd come over a penniless immigrant when she was a child of ten. She married a hard-headed second-generation German and had only one child, my mother. Both my grandparents always wanted a large family, but had to be content with one child because Grampa was a frugal, practical man. He lived long enough to see his seventh grandchild, Samantha, born. He died before Samantha was old enough to call him Grampa.

It hadn't seemed to bother Grandmother much, though. Everyone knew we children were her whole life; she adored us. Grampa's frugality left her with a sizeable bank account, which Grandmother promptly lavished on all of us whenever our famine, or her fancy, struck—and she owned a monstrous old house with the mortgage paid in full. It was right down the street from us and Grandmother lived there the rest of her days.

Grandmother Summers was unusual, to say the least, and there were those in the neighborhood who said she was crazy . . . some thought she was a witch. Looking back, I understand why. I believe she had a limited gift of foresight. What really made her a candidate for unflattering speculation was her keen—if not obsessed—interest in the unknown. Her old house was as spooky a place as any child could dream of and she collected books on the supernatural. She truly believed in ghosts and demons and didn't care what the world whispered about her sanity. She conducted seances in her sewing room, and some swore they had contacted their lost loved ones. Everyone, but us, was deathly afraid of the old woman.

My grandmother, in the years before Grampa died, would visit us a lot and keep an eye on us; we never went without if she could help it. But in the later years of her life she became an invalid and a recluse. But she still saw us kids. She took to having us three older children overnight or for the weekend. Perhaps she was afraid of being alone, and wouldn't admit it, but we didn't care what her reasons were, because staying with Grandmother was a real treat. We loved it. I, especially, loved to help take care of her and listen to her strange stories.

"Have I told you the story about the girl who died . . . but wasn't really dead?" She'd always start it that way even though each of us had heard it since the day we were old enough to listen. No one could tell a story the way my grandmother could. She sat in her wheelchair huddled under a crocheted blanket and shook her bony finger at us. She had aged almost overnight. Her once beautiful blue eyes and lively smile had faded into shadows of their former selves, and her lovely red hair was nothing but ghostly wisps. Sometimes I'd see her staring out the windows or at the walls as if she saw something beyond them that we couldn't . . . and there was fear in her dull eyes. It used to frighten me. I thought, though, that it was just her age and Grampa being gone; her being alone and old. Helpless. I was wrong.

We all sat on the floor at her feet, our eyes wide and riveted on her as we silently urged her to go on and tell the story again. The lights were all off in the old house; it was late, and the television was turned down, casting its feeble, flickering light over the walls of the front room like tiny fingers. My oldest sister, Leslie, hung on her every word. I was more skeptical at times.

Grandmother smiled grimly, looking directly at me to catch my eye.

"You don't believe me, do you, Sarah?" Her voice crackled, the German accent still detectable, and she nodded her head at me.

I humored her. I wanted to believe. "Yes, Grandmother, I believe you." I whispered, hoping to God she wouldn't hear that boldfaced lie and strike me dead on the spot. "Go on with the story." I smiled at her.

"Well, child, it did happen . . . I know for a fact." Her thin

19

hand reached out and touched my shoulder, resting there as though she were afraid I would run off. "Back in those days, medical science wasn't what it is today and people were very superstitious. Things they couldn't understand got labeled as witchery or the like . . ." she crooned.

"Many people died, especially among the poor in winter, when there was no work or food to be had. Sometimes there were no doctors to say what they died of. Those were bad days. Ignorant people didn't know no better . . . they dropped their dead into pine boxes and lowered them into the cold earth to wait for Judgment Day. They were mourned and then forgotten. If you were poor, you lived, you died, and that was the end of it. It made no difference if you were a child or an old woman. You worked in the fields until death claimed you." She shrugged her stooped shoulders and paused for effect, her eyes far away.

"Sarah!" she'd suddenly snap, singling me out again.

"Yes . . . I'm listening, Grandmother."

She'd go on slowly.

"There was this girl, about fourteen, and the people of the town were afraid of her. She was a strange one, always keeping to herself. She heard and saw things that no one else could see or hear."

"She was a witch, Grandma!" Leslie piped in, smugly.

"No!" My grandmother seemed angry. "No, she wasn't. They—the stupid people—just thought she was. But she wasnt . . ." Her voice was sad. "She had a *gift,* that's all. They didn't understand. She had always been a frail child, and she had done only good to others. Yet one morning her brother found her at the edge of the woods near the end of town and she couldn't talk, couldn't move . . . she died a few days later. No one knew how or why.

"Her parents had loved her very much and their grief was almost too much to bear, but they dried their tears and buried her at the forest's edge, where she was found. She had always loved the woods and the open skies, and back then you didn't keep bodies around too long . . . especially in *her* case . . . the townspeople hadn't been easy over her strange death."

"Then what?" Leslie asked, her eyes bright as she licked her lips. We were all gluttons for punishment!

"They buried her in a shallow grave."

We held our breaths, shivering in the dim room.

"But her mother grieved for her daughter and she began to have terrible dreams . . . dreams that the child was calling her, begging for her to help her—that she wasn't really dead. People thought the woman had just gone mad with grief."

At that point I felt as if someone had brushed my shoulder, when there was no one there to do it. I felt as if someone had walked across my own grave and it frightened me. I wasn't one easily scared, and it confused me. Something caught the corner of my eye and I looked closely at the window. There was nothing there. I looked over at Jimmy, always so silent when my grandmother told her story. He was staring at the window, too. I shivered again.

"Tell us about the ring!" Leslie said, her face very wise.

"Ah, yes . . . the girl had this ring. It was a keepsake that her great-grandmother had given her for her birthday many years before and it was a pretty thing of tiny golden leaves. It was her treasure. Her parents could have taken it and sold it for money, for they were very poor, but her mother wouldn't dream of it and it was buried with the girl.

"But there were those who had no scruples. When the girl had been laid to rest, one of the gravediggers had taken a fancy to have it. A very poor man with six hungry little ones at home, the man was desperate. He had never done such a despicable thing before as to rob the dead, but one of his own six children was gravely ill and might not live to see the next sunrise.

"So that first night after the girl had been buried he crept through the dark woods to the grave. He would have the ring even though he had to dig up a grave to do it! He was sure God would forgive him. It was raining and storming that night and he was filled with great fear at what he was about to do. He hurriedly dug up the pitiful grave and opened the lid of the coffin and bent to slip the tiny ring off her little finger.

"But it wouldn't come off! Cursing, shaking with the wet and the fear, he knew the only way to get it was to . . . *slice off the finger itself* and flee with it. Later he could cut the ring free."

We were all quiet as the graveyard by then, waiting. Every noise and every strange shadow seemed endowed with its own unearthly sinister intention. It began raining outside and the wind moaned. The house grew chilly and we shivered under the blankets we had been given. Our grandmother had stopped to stare out the window.

"Go on!" we all begged. All of us that is, except Charlie. He would sit and watch us like he enjoyed our fear. He grinned when we grimaced, giggled when we gasped. Silently, he turned back to the sound of our grandmother's voice.

"He was terribly frightened by then, and cut the cold finger swiftly from the body. . . and then he heard . . ."

"What?" Jimmy demanded suddenly and strangely. The shadows stalked us, and the wind outside the house echoed the screeching of the restless dead in their shallow graves. The trees scratched the windows as if seeking entrance, and my grandmother's voice turned foreign to all of us.

It struck fear deep inside of me and I wondered why. It was only a story, after all.

"The girl began to moan aloud in her coffin and to stir. . . the gravedigger bellowed in fear. Not wanting to wait to see what would happen next, he fled the cursed place like all the devils of hell were riding on his coattails. He was terrified that the corpse was following him, crying for its missing finger, and in his haste he threw it back toward the body as he ran.

22

"She wasn't really dead, was she?" Leslie, the down-to-earth one of us, said softly, her pretty face white and her dark eyes glazed. We all knew how it would end.

"No . . . that's what they say." There was a peculiar note in Grandmother's voice. "It seems the mother had had such a vivid dream about her daughter that the father promised to go out to the grave himself at dawn and show the crazy woman that their daughter was truly dead. But when the father got to the grave, he was shocked to see it open and his daughter sitting up, weeping softly, in her coffin, her hand wrapped in the edge of her bloody skirt . . . alive after all. He took her home, thanking God each step he carried her and crying for joy—as his wife did, too. They nursed her to full health, just grateful to have her back, minus a finger or not!"

"God!" John gulped, gripping his little twin sister's arm. Amy sucked her thumb with a vengeance, her eyes like saucers.

"They call it the 'sleeping sickness,' don't they?" Leslie asked. "And when people have it they fall into a coma so deep that they look like they're really dead . . . but they aren't." She shivered, as we all did. "Ooh! That story still gives me the creeps!"

"Cutting her finger like that started the circulation back up and she woke up, right?" I said, solving the riddle. Jimmy and Charlie remained silent, listening to the night noises outside, thinking.

"Maybe . . ." our grandmother replied spookily. "Some said she was a witch, others said she was just lucky." She looked directly at me then and said, "But the town feared her after that and they shunned her like the plague. Her life wasn't a happy one. People hate the things they don't understand and they try to destroy them. They just don't know any better." Was that pity I saw in her old eyes—for me? I looked away, unable to stand her piercing gaze, and something fluttered inside me. A warning of things to come, perhaps.

"I don't believe she was bad. I don't believe she was a witch," I said firmly. "If the story's true at all . . ." I expressed my doubts every time I heard the story, but Grandmother never argued.

Many years later, right before she died, in fact, she finally made me believe in it. "The girl in the story, you see," she said slowly, "was your great-great-grandmother."

The truth in her eyes and the shock of it made me speechless. For some reason, I accepted what she said completely then and never asked another word about it. I couldn't. I didn't want to know the answers.

That was all a very long time ago, and I wish I could forget it. Oh, if I only could!

That was also the summer my visions started . . . just nightmares, really.

It was the first season of warning.

I often dreamed about the books I read. I went through so many at a clip it was no wonder that my head should be full of fanciful characters of this and other times. I loved to dream. My vivid imagination created bright pastoral worlds of wonder, with perfect rhyme and reason. I was a fairy princess, and Jimmy, my handsome prince. Together, we ruled a kingdom of eternal peace and magic, with Charlie as our faithful court jester of course!

And then my dreams turned dark.

I'd had trouble falling asleep that night. My room remained close and oppressive way into the dead of night, and my bedclothes tangled around me like hungry vines. I struggled out from underneath them and went to stand by my window, hoping for a moonlit breeze to cool my skin.

The lawn was drawn in shadows and the cloying sweetness of mother's roses seeped through the screen's tight mesh. The edge of the forest loomed jagged and forbidding, alive with the sounds of night. I fancied I saw movement there, and in spite of the heavy air, shivered with a chill of fright.

24

There was a thin wisp of wind playing with the tops of the distant line of trees, and I reasoned it was that and that alone that caused the shadow I swore I'd seen.

The breeze progressed up the lawn and met me at the threshold of my vigil. I shivered again, this time at the sound of voices, carried on the current of cooling air.

Children's voices. Laughter.

I strained my eyes and suddenly, I saw them. There were five in all, dressed in a fashion so unlike any I was accustomed to seeing or reading about, I couldn't place them. I just knew they belonged in a world that had long since passed into history.

They were playing some sort of game. One of them, a boy as far as I could tell with longish hair, played a small instrument like a flute or a reed. His music was masterful, but melancholy. The other children had formed a ring around him, laughing and singing and dancing, totally mindless of the shifting darkness that lay at their feet.

The breeze grew stronger and suddenly turned to wind. It whistled in the trees and then dropped to a low keening like I've never heard in my life. The children grew silent, stopping their game and uniformly staring into the woods as if waiting for something to appear.

And it did.

Again I caught that strange movement; a shift in the night. It came from the same place I'd witnessed it before. Fear washed over me, drenching me in an ice cold sweat. I felt the presence of evil, a strong, formidable power.

A shadow blacker than coal swooped down from the high reaches of the forest and scattered the frightened children. Terror filled their shrill, pitiful voices. One of the smaller ones, a little girl, tripped and fell crying to her knees. In an instant the shadow was upon her. I heard a terrible scream of laughter, and a flash of red gashed the darkness. My screams soon joined those of the doomed child and then drowned them out completely.

Something grabbed me and began shaking me, pulling

me from behind. I was being dragged away. I screamed louder and louder and finally awoke to the concerned eyes of my father. I collapsed into his arms and gripped him as tight as I could, sobbing like the world had come to an end. Over his shoulder I saw Leslie, and Jimmy, and Charlie all crowded in the doorway trying to see what had frightened their silly sister.

My father wiped the damp hair from my flushed cheeks and kissed the top of my head, crooning over and over . . . "it was a bad dream, sweetheart. Sshh! It was just a bad dream . . . a dream . . ."

As he rocked me in his strong arms, I felt so safe, so secure, I never wanted him to let go. Leslie finally came in and sat at the foot of my bed and patted my leg. Jimmy went to the window, glanced out very quickly and then stared at me. Charlie remained in the doorway, shifting his weight from one foot to the other, afraid to enter. His face bore one of the oddest expressions I'd ever seen. It all seemed so silly, with the lights on and my father stroking my hair.

He'd only been partially right that night. It *had* been a bad dream. . . . but it had been so much more. Sleeping or waking, my life would never be the same again.

CHAPTER TWO

On summer evenings the children of the neighborhood gathered to play hide and go seek. Because it was usually past our bedtime Jimmy and I had to sneak out through our bedroom windows to join them. How could we help ourselves? The summer nights were soft and warm and the moon was bright; the dark mysterious fields that flanked our house beckoned us and gave us no choice but to follow.

"Jimmy!" I hissed, reaching frantically for him. My hand felt emptiness and my brother was nowhere I could reach him. "Wait for me! You know I'm afraid of heights," I whispered from the edge of the roof. "Jesus!" It was a long drop. "Where are you?" We had slipped out of the window in my bedroom and scrambled out into the night to play in the fields with some other kids. Our mother wouldn't be happy if she caught us out climbing over the steep roof like monkeys.

It was still unbelievably hot for as late as it was. I guessed it was about ten or so, maybe later. All our brothers and sisters were sleeping and mother and father were watching television in the front room below us. We had to be very careful and very quiet or we'd alert them to our crime. I paused at the edge of the roof right above the

27

kitchen and, positioning my body cautiously, I sat down and dangled my feet over the precipice. "I'm not moving an inch until you show yourself." I was slightly angry and hoped my voice showed it.

Suddenly a small warm body edged down beside me and sighed. "Here I am. It's really beautiful out here, isn't it, sis?" he said meekly, swinging his skinny legs next to me. "Look, the moon has a blue ring around it. What does that mean? You read so much, you should know the answer." When we were children Jimmy thought I knew all the answers. He pointed, his eyes peering up through the murkiness and then deep into the yards below, searching.

"I think it means snow," I giggled. I felt like the queen of a magical land way up there, surveying my kingdom. Everything looked so different at night. I wasn't afraid of the night then. The katydids sang in the rose bushes along the side of the house. The vibrant blooms were faded by the dark and hid among the leaves, but their scent was strong and unmistakable; they were summer's sweet bouquet. I smiled, clasping Jimmy's sweaty hand tightly in mine, and took great gulps of the night air. I have only to close my eyes, even now, and I can still smell that night . . . those roses.

"Snow? In August?" He chuckled, swinging his feet wide of the gutters we were perched on. "I'd like to see that."

"So would I. That would be real wild."

"Silly."

I scooted just enough to lean over the edge and tore a stray branch off the old sugar maple. Jimmy grabbed hold of my waist tightly so I wouldn't fall. He could be like a mother hen.

"It won't snow tonight for sure." I gazed mesmerized into the skies as I fanned myself with the leafy switch.

"I love summer," Jimmy blurted out.

"I love . . . nighttime."

"I love the sunlight more . . ."

I laughed. "That's because you're afraid of the night,

28

that's why!" I didn't have to see Jimmy's face to know he was frowning.

He turned to me and I felt a shudder go through him. After a heavy moment of silence he said, "Aren't you afraid of anything, Sarah?"

"No. Why should I be? What is there to be afraid of, except bill collectors?" I tried to make a joke. "I read someplace once that you have nothing to fear but fear itself, or something like that."

"You read too many books, Sarah." His voice was strangely melancholy. "You ought to be afraid of the things that can hurt you."

"Like what?" I demanded. He sounded so old for his age. I thought he was teasing me, setting me up for the punchline as usual. But it wasn't anything like that.

"Like ghosts, demons . . . evil. It's out there, you know, waiting for you if you aren't careful . . . just waiting to trap you if you don't know the way. Evil . . . it's there, Sarah. It is."

"You're spooking me, Jimmy. Stop it! What are you talking about? The problem is you don't read enough books. Witches and ghosts are just superstitions, that's all. They don't really exist." I remembered the awful time Charlie had been walking the old wooden picket fence in the backyard and had slipped; we found him hanging upside down, screaming his lungs out about a thing pushing him off. He had ripped open his cheek and torn his britches where the sharp pickets had trapped his legs so he couldn't get down. A thing? He'd been terrified out of his mind and he still talked about it. But Charlie was always making up stories to get attention.

"I didn't mention anything about witches."

"It's all the same . . . rubbish," I huffed. A loud noise from the kitchen below made us both forget everything and freeze. We lowered our voices.

"Come on, Sarah, we'd better get down off here before Mom or Dad hear us," he whispered.

"Okay."

"Let's go!" Jimmy took a deep breath for courage and scrambled down the tiled roof right up to the tree we used to escape down. His hands grabbed out for the tree's wide trunk; his feet found the familiar branches. I watched, guardedly, as first his body then his head slowly disappeared down the side, hidden by the limbs.

"Last one down's a rotten egg," he yelled up at me. "Thanks!" I muttered as I jumped for the branch and bumped down the same path he'd taken. "And there goes Jimmy, faster than a speeding bullet and louder than a damn foghorn . . ." I told him when I safely landed. "The whole neighborhood must have heard that! Can't you do anything quietly? You'd make a lousy thief. Jesus!" He steadied me when my feet hit the ground.

"No cussing now, Sis. Remember what you're always preaching to me?"

"Well, just pipe down then, will you? If we're caught I'll never forgive you! You and your loud mouth." We listened for sounds of our parents but the chorus of katydids and crickets had abetted our escape. We were hidden by the shadows of the night.

"Where did you say the others were going to meet us?" I asked.

"The big pine tree, near the edge of the woods, if they got out."

"Let's hope so or all this was for nothing, and playing hide and go seek with just two of us wouldn't be much fun at all."

"You're right. Let's go see if they're there or not."

Our eyes growing accustomed to the dark, we made our way through the fields, cautiously skirting the treacherously deep gullies that sometimes gaped open in front of us. We knew the fields and woods well.

The wind suddenly picked up and I watched the faint line of black trees in the distance inch closer with every step. The closer we got to the woods the stronger the eerie sensation I had begun to have grew. There was something there . . . something hulking just on the fringe of the woods. Something waiting and wanting us to enter its domain.

I shivered even though the night was so warm. But it was a shiver of the soul that I felt that night; now I know the feeling well. I was frightened, but of what I didn't know. I was as skittish as a hare that smells a hound but can't see it.

"Jimmy?" I caught at his shirttail roughly and yanked until he stopped to stand and look back at me, his face pale in the moonlight. I discerned the strain, the irritation in his manner; the question on his lips even before he asked it.

"You feel it too, huh?" We were whispering. We were both shaking.

Gently I pulled him down into the nearest gully. "Let's just rest for a minute? I feel a little . . . strange."

"Me too," he answered, sinking down gratefully against the dry dirt that formed the crack in the earth.

We were silent for a long time. We listened to the night noises. The wind whimpering softly through the trees and the tiny humming of the insects that buzzed us. I thought I heard footsteps and the cries of forsaken children, their souls lost, their pain tangible. I laid my trembling hand on Jimmy's shoulder as if he were my talisman against the evil I felt so close that night. A scream ripped the air above us.

But it was not anything human.

"Did you hear that?" Jimmy yelped, his lips quivering. Oh God, was he going to cry?

"I didn't hear anything! What did you hear?" I slid my eyes over to meet his in the faint light. The forest was humming like a beehive. My heart pounded. I inched up to the edge of the gully and searched the gloom of the nearby woods. I felt a raindrop splash gently on my forehead and slide down my cheek. I touched it with my fingers and gazed at it in the dark. The substance was dark and sticky. I wiped it off in the grass. I didn't want to see it again.

"I don't know what it was. A scream . . . I suppose. You mean you didn't hear it?" He became nearly hysterical. I could hear his heart racing louder than a drum in the stillness.

"Maybe it was one of the other kids? Maybe it's Shep or Brian . . . maybe they've started without us?" I replied sheepishly, unwilling to accept any other explanation but what I could understand. "Do you see any of them down by the trees?"

He had climbed up next to me. "No. I don't see anything. Besides, that's the opposite direction." He pointed. "What would they be doing that far out anyway?"

"I don't know."

"Sis, it's still out there. It's still watching us—I can feel it!"

Another scream hit our ears.

"I'm not going out there! I'm going home!" Jimmy cried. He scrambled up out of that gully like a mountain goat and glared down at me as if to say *you're still down there?*

"What about Shep and Brian? They're waiting for us!"

"Let them wait 'til doomsday for all I care. I'm not going in there with . . . *that*! And if they heard that thing . . . they're home already! Where we should be! I'm going— you coming or not?" He reached out his hands for me, a gesture of real love at that moment. I could see his knees shaking. "Please, Sarah!"

I held back.

"Please, Sarah . . . I'm going to be sick!"

I tried to get his mind off his fear. I didn't want the whole night ruined. I wanted to wait and see what happened; wait until Jimmy was back to his old self. "Jimmy, do you remember last winter after that big snow? I think this is the gully that old Charlie fell into." I laughed, but it had a hollow, false sound to it. In my mind I could see that dazzling whiteness of the newly fallen snow around me in place of the warm moonlight, feel the cold wetness of it. It had snowed for days and we had all gone out to sled in it. Charlie ran off willy-nilly alone in the fields searching for gullies with deep snow to jump into. It was a game we all played. Except that time Charlie had outdone himself. The snow had been stiff with ice and way over his head. The hard crust had trapped him in its grip and he had screamed as he fought to escape. The funny thing was, I *knew* where he was . . . and I knew he was in trouble. Something had flashed in my mind just before we noticed he was missing. I never said a word, but led everyone to the spot where Charlie fell.

"We had a devil of a time pulling him out of that mess, didn't we? Remember the look on his face when we found him?" He'd been terrified, clawing at the snow until it was red with his own blood. "We almost didn't find him . . . remember." I gave another false chuckle. We had looked for that boy long after his voice gave out. He was buried so deep in the snow we almost hadn't seen him when we came upon him. Just his tiny bloodstained hands stuck out. I shuddered to think of what would have happened if we'd overlooked him and hadn't pulled him free. He was moaning about having chased something he heard calling him . . . until he'd tripped and fallen.

Chasing something in the woods. I stared up at Jimmy's pale face and realized he remembered that too.

"I'm going home! Now!"

"Wait!" But he had already turned tail and was running home, leaving me alone to decide what to do next. The woods were alive with voices. Faint, mocking voices that mingled in the wind that swept my face. Maybe Jimmy was right. I should run for home too. But what about Shep, Brian, and the others? What was out there with them?

There is nothing to fear but fear itself.

I was being silly. They deserved the right to know we weren't coming, so they wouldn't spoil their whole night by waiting on us in the woods. But as something vague and shadowy fluttered through my mind, I knew there was *another* reason why I didn't want them waiting in those woods.

If there was something deadly out there, I didn't want to be responsible for anything that might happen to them. It had nothing whatsoever to do with the supernatural, but with men. I knew there were evil men in the world that did evil things, even to helpless children . . . and there was definitely something or someone out there.

Nothing to fear but fear itself.

I scrambled up the side of the gully and started to run to the pre-arranged meeting place. I headed for the old, lightning scarred pine, not heeding the growing foreboding that increased with every step as I drew nearer to the woods. I kept on running. The tree loomed just ahead of me.

There was something in the woods. *Something.* I could almost see it out of the corner of my eye, but it moved too swiftly and I couldn't pin it down. My imagination was playing tricks on me!

I clung to the tree, breathing heavily and peering into the darkness. An unnamed fear pressed hard upon my heart and I fell to my knees from the sheer weight of it. Brian and Shep and the others weren't there. But something unseeable was. I could feel its rank breath on my neck. The moonlight cast eerie shadows everywhere and the wind began to howl savagely among the treetops and tear at my hair, wailing like a tormented soul lost in the trees. A sudden fierce rain began to fall, pelting me like sharp stones. The whole world had turned angry at me.

I was not alone in the forest. *It* was with me. Watching. *Hungry.*

Soaked and suddenly frozen by the sudden drop in temperature, I wrenched myself to my feet and started to run . . . for my life. The wind was gone, the rain stopped as abruptly as it had come, and I realized just how alone and vulnerable I was. The woods were my enemy and they glared down with dark, hateful stares. I had disturbed their peaceful sleep and awakened then to some unspeakable pain. The silence rang with warning. I stopped to catch my breath, leaning against a mammoth oak. I studied the black tree towering over me and listened to the silence of the woods as I waited. I felt like the last person on earth

34

after the final war. Alone. The only one left . . .

Blinking away the tears and shivering, I suddenly asked myself what nightmare had sucked me into the woods in the middle of the night alone and running from . . . what? *What* was I running from?

With paralyzing terror, I watched the huge black shape loom up before me. A scream rose in my throat but I kept it prisoner with my hands over my mouth. I stumbled over the debris of the wet forest as I slowly began to back away from the lumbering shadow that silently approached me. It reached out with things that were not quite hands that dripped with fresh blood. A wide, leering mouth and coal fire eyes full of hunger and hate hung suspended on the night wind. The hellish vision was all feeling and no substance . . . yet I knew it could kill me if it wanted.

"No!" I shrieked to the silent trees, to the monstrosity that was moving towards me. "NO! I will *not* give up! No, no, no . . ." I screamed as I stood up to it. A shadow fell across the moon, across my face. And it laughed like a demon from hell. I gathered my strength and ran from it again. Home. *Home.* Where I would be safe. I fled, stumbling crazily through the weeds and bushes in the night with it only one step behind me the whole way; but it couldn't touch me and I escaped it for some reason I've never figured out, unless it was to do what I was supposed to do someday. My innocence—or my ignorance—had been stronger than its evil . . .

I crouched, sniveling from fright, safe on the step of my porch. I crawled up the steps on all fours and huddled in the corner by the door, crying; afraid my sobs would wake my parents, my eyes tightly shut and my hands balled into fists at my mouth as if that would protect me. I didn't want to remember what I had experienced and seen in the woods that night. I never wanted to feel that sickening fear and helplessness again. The game was unbalanced, unfair; I didn't know the rules. But I would learn. I would learn and I would fight. I could hear the house settling and its old wood creaking around me and I knew I was safe within its walls and with all its love. *Love is stronger than anything.* Mother had told me that.

I remember praying that time would freeze that moment; I was terrified of growing up. Whatever was out there stalking, was waiting for me to grow up.

I'll wait for you, Sarah.

I lifted my head, my ears alert to the night, frozen where I huddled in the dark. I thought I heard faint laughter, too. I raised up slowly, wiping the tears from my face with the back of my hand, and turned my back on the voice that was more in my mind than out in the fields behind me. I quietly slipped into the house and carefully made my way through the dark and up to my bed, checking on the way to see that Jimmy was safe in his own bed. He was. I crawled into bed thankful and weary, with my wet clothes still on, and closed my eyes.

My hands searched under my pillow and found Spotty, my little stuffed dog, and clasped him tightly against my breast for reassurance.

Yes, I'll wait for you . . .

I steeled myself to ignore the voice and willed myself to sleep, a soft cool breeze from the nearby open window caressing my feverish face. There were whispers at the windowpane trying to get in; squeezing through the tiny holes of the screen. I refused to listen. *I was safe here.* It would go away. . .

Finally, I slept.

When the sun rose the next morning and I got out of bed, I wasn't sure what exactly had happened the night before. It was like the remnants of a hideous nightmare that eluded me no matter how hard I tried to call it back. Jimmy and I had a nervous laugh or two over it . . . had it really happened or had we imagined it all?

He wasn't sure, or so he said. In his own way he chose to forget the whole incident. The sun was bright and warm above us and like children can do, Jimmy put it away like an old toy he'd grown tired of . . . or so I believed for all these years.

But I never really forgot, even though I desperately wanted to. I couldn't afford to. I wasn't allowed to. I *knew* what had really happened. I had seen it in my mind.

CHAPTER THREE

The summer lazily wound itself to an end and we all trekked our ways back to school, fat and sassy from the long vacation; inches taller. None of our old clothes fit anymore, and Mother scraped together new wardrobes for all of us. Baby Samantha was growing, too, and she was now out of her playpen and crawling everywhere so that we had to be careful not to step on her as we ran through the house.

With the school year started, things went back pretty much to normal. Almost.

Except I noticed that Jimmy never went into the woods alone again. That in itself wasn't unusual because no one went into those woods alone for many years after that. The night after our strange experience we had observed all the police cars, sirens blaring and lights flashing in wide circles as they made their way through the woods all that day and the night to follow . . . searching for something.

I didn't need to be told what they were seeking . . . Shep and Brian had never returned home that night. And though the police and concerned neighbors scoured the woods for many days afterward, their bodies were never found. It would have ended there for Jimmy and me except that the burden I carried was too great for me to bear alone. A uniformed policeman knocked at our door a few days later and wanted to ask us some questions—did we know the missing boys—could we tell him anything? I couldn't turn my eyes away, as Jimmy did in silence.

Yes, I knew something! *Yes!* The young man with short blond hair and a shiny new badge listened eagerly to all I had to say, but his hope faded and his eyes betrayed him before my story was even finished. He didn't believe me. He *couldn't* believe me. I don't blame him for that. I can understand why he thought I was only an overimaginative child carried away with the gruesome excitement. He thanked me, his tired thin face nodding knowingly at my parents, who had listened with genuine shock at what I said, and then he went away.

I had tried. It wasn't my fault that they didn't understand. I tried to help. But I knew that they would never find the bodies—I knew that.

After that, Jimmy refused to discuss that night ever again—and me? I was cruelly labeled as a little . . . *strange*. Oh, people were nice about it, but all the same I was either crazy or just an out-and-out dramatic liar!

It was the first real lesson I learned and remembered. My face still burns when I think of the way that cop looked at me that day as I was telling my story. It was horrible. It would become a pattern that would be my destiny.

I heard my mother and father talking about me late one night when they thought I was asleep.

"Mary, I'm worried about the girl." It was my father's voice coming through the door. "Have you noticed how thin she's become, how quiet she is now? Sarah was never like that, Mary. Do you think we should take her to see a doctor or something? I mean, it's not normal for an eleven year old to be like that . . ."

My mother's voice was soft. "Sam, she's just going through a hard time since that . . . night. They were her friends. No matter what, *she* believes what she said. Don't worry, she'll grow out of it. Time will help her to forget."

"Forget what?" His voice was slightly irritated. I could easily imagine my mother gently laying a slender hand on his strong shoulder to ease his tension. They could be very close at times. They did love each other.

"Well, that nightmare or whatever she had that night. That dream, she thinks it *really* happened."

"You think so?"

"Dear, I know so. Children are like that. Something that's real and important today means nothing to them tomorrow, you'll see. I know our Sarah and she's got a brain in that pretty head and she'll snap out of this before you know it. She's a very special—*special*—child. Artistic. It's in her very nature to be so emotional. All children do it to an extent. Look at Charlie . . ." And then they laughed together.

I sat there at the top of the steps in the dark, my head hung in shame, and suffered their laughter. They, of all people, should have believed me. If they didn't, then who could? Who would heed my warnings; who could I go to for help? No one. *It was up to me.* I went back to bed with that hard truth humming in my mind, never to go away again. Never. But I still didn't suspect how hard it would all become someday. The visions; other people not believing; I had no idea then. I was lucky. At least some of my childhood was carefree.

"What are you reading now, Sarah?" my mother asked me one chilly autumn evening. I was curled up on the edge of my bed, alone, where she found me reading a very thick book. It was one of the few books I would allow her to find me reading. There were many books I would never let anyone see, books I read late at night, hidden under my covers with my light turned off and a flashlight in my hand as I turned the forbidden pages. Books that I could never begin to explain to my family. Books on ghosts, witches, and demons that were shocking because the authors were professed believers and renowned psychics with scientific facts to back their studies up. Then there was the trash written by those who only wanted to make a dollar by scaring you out of your wits with *invented* nonsense. I read all of it. Every book on the occult, scientific or entertaining drivel that was ever written. I set out to learn all there was to learn.

I had to.

"It's about witches and warlocks, that kind of spooky stuff, you know, Mom." I smiled my sweetest smile and held the book up for her to see the title. It was a harmless book that any kid my age would have wanted to read just for fun. I wasn't going to learn *much* from it but I wasn't going to skip it just because of that.

My mother just shook her head in fond exasperation and after laying a light kiss on my forehead to remind me it was almost bedtime, she went back downstairs.

The next morning as I was getting ready to go to school, she said to me in an offhand manner, "Sarah, if you're so interested in the supernatural, you should ask your Grandmother Summers about it. She's an expert."

"Thanks, Mom." I kissed her goodbye and ran out the door. I was late for school again. Too many midnight books that stretched their pages to the early morning hours. Sister Helen was going to kill me!

That was the year my parents decided that we all lacked religion and arranged to send us to a Catholic school. Mother patiently explained as we all donned those hated blue uniforms, that seven-year-old Jonathan and his twin, Ann, could both receive Holy Communion with their class while the rest of us heathens would take lessons after school and walk up en masse with the rest of the people.

"It's time you children learn what being Catholic is all about. It's time we put the fear of God into you. Your father and I have been remiss in our duties long enough. I've talked to Sister Helen up at Holy Family School and she's agreed to take you children in this year so you can become part of the true flock." What my mother meant was that the distasteful question of money had been settled. I knew how expensive Catholic school was and I imagine she'd gotten a discount rate because there were six of us in school with another coming up fast. We only stayed there a few years, but I've been grateful for that all my life. I'd always been very religious and devout in my own maverick way and for the first time in my life my hunger for religion was assuaged. I learned about God. I'd look up at the blue skies and pray He really existed. Someday I might need Him.

It was an ironic twist of fate that at the same tme I was learning about God, I was learning all about the Devil as well. I always felt that the two went hand in hand and that to be able to fight evil, you had to be able to recognize good. To know God, you had to know the Devil. They are just flip sides of the same coin.

As I walked to school that morning with Leslie and Jimmy grumbling ahead of me and the twins grumbling behind me, I thought about what my mother had said about talking to my grandmother. It was cold for October and I tugged my sweater tighter around my thin body. I'd grown so much that year that my uniforms, still almost new, were already short on me. My Grandmother . . . why hadn't I thought of her before? I think I had, but was afraid of what I'd learn . . . about myself.

In the years to come, I was *glad* I hadn't thought of it sooner. Maybe if I had she might not have lived as long as she did. A year is such a tiny part of a person's life and it had been just over a year since Shep and Brian disappeared and it was a year longer she had left to live because of it.

I could have learned a lot from my grandmother if time would have let me, but I never had the time. I saw her only three times after I decided to seek her advice and then she was dead, too. Another precious door closed to me.

The last time I saw her was a few days before her sixty-fifth birthday and I remember worrying over her frailness as she sat in her wheelchair listening to what I was telling her. In those last visits I disclosed all my secrets and she didn't laugh at me once. Instead, she closed her tired eyes and laid her bony hands weakly on my arm in silent grief. I saw tears glisten on her cheeks and when she spoke, it was with a whisper of a voice as if she were afraid someone would hear us.

"I was afraid, especially after that incident last year in the woods, Sarah. Oh, child!" She engulfed me in her weak embrace and held me close. "I was afraid and now I am even more afraid. If only you knew . . ." Her words died away as if words could not begin to explain what she knew she had to say to me.

"You might have the *gift,* child. I can't be sure, but you might. I don't have it, but I've known many through my life that have. They are to be pitied. They are rare . . . it isn't something I would have wished on you. It's a heavy burden. I think it's a curse at times . . ." She shook her white head and I noticed how old she had become, with her eyes so dull and her skin so wrinkled. When had that happened? Time . . . it heals wounds and opens graves.

"The *gift?*" I stammered.

"Yes." She stared at me and I could see how she fought with herself over what she should tell me and what she shouldn't. "Have you ever heard the word psychic or medium before?"

"Yes. In books."

"Ah, then you know about them?"

"A little." My eyes were guarded by then, my heart raced. I'd read about people who could see the future or talk to spirits and I also knew that sometimes they were considered freaks. I didn't want to see the things they claimed they saw. It must have shown in my face because my grandmother kissed me and soothed me with hugs. She understood.

"Your great-great-grandmother had it, though we don't talk about her much." My grandmother stared out the window again. "She was the girl with the ring."

"What happened to her . . . later?"

She sighed and kept her face away from me. "They burned her for a witch when she was thirty. So young. Those were terrible times." She looked back at me and smiled encouragingly at my look of shock. "It's better these days."

But *I* knew there were *worse* things that could happen and I also knew that I might find out what they were someday if what my grandmother feared turned out to be true.

We sat there in her huge, silent house hugging each other close that morning, each of us with our own private thoughts. Don't worry, *Sarah,* she told me lovingly. *Don't be frightened . . . I'm here. I'll help you. I promise.* And I kissed her goodbye that sunny morning in October of 1961 and went back home. They were the last words she ever spoke to me. It was the last time I saw her alive.

She was dead before the sun came up the next morning. They said it was a heart attack. Now who would help me?

Who would protect me? She *promised* me . . . and by dying she had broken that sacred promise.

I had loved her more than anyone in the whole world and when she died it was as if a part of me died, too. Her old house was never put up for sale, but boarded up and left to the mice and cobwebs. It fell into gradual disrepair. The weeds grew tall and wild up around the dusty windows and the paint flaked off. For years we would walk by it and mourn her being gone. We missed her so much.

The house remained silent and empty. We were never allowed in it once it was boarded up and my mother and father never talked about selling it. When I asked why it had to just sit there and why we couldn't just move in ourselves, I can still see that glimmer of fear in their eyes. I was told it was my grandmother's wish that it remain so. *Someday you'll understand. She wants you to understand, but not now.*

But I didn't understand. Why couldn't we live in the house? It would have been ours free and clear; no more rent. Heaven knows we didn't have any money. They could have sold it for something, white elephant that it was, instead of letting it mold away into dust.

"Ghosts . . . 'cause that's why!" Charlie chuckled to me one day. We were all outside watching him taunt the poor cat. Charlie had a mean streak through him and if he were in a real bad mood he'd take it out on anyone or anything that couldn't fight back. Our cat, Midnight, was a gentle old blue Maltese that wouldn't bring its claws out to save its life. Charlie taught it how. Once I had come across the boy swinging the poor animal around and around in dizzying circles by its tail. Then, when it was frantic and screeching in fright, he'd let it go to hit the side of the house or a tree. One time I was so appalled that I let my anger get the best of me and slapped him to the ground. From that time on, whenever I saw Charlie around the cat I'd keep an eye open so he couldn't hurt the creature again. He could be so cruel.

"There are no ghosts in that house," Leslie piped up right away. "Grandmother was too *good* to be a ghost!"

We all nodded like little puppets. Our grandmother was dead and all of us knew that. "There's no such things as ghosts," Leslie had said smugly.

Charlie just laughed that cold laugh of his and walked away.

I had looked towards our grandmother's house and thought deeply about life and death, and the thin line between the two.

CHAPTER FOUR

When I was twelve, in the early morning hours of a
sweltering summer night, I awoke to a soft hovering at the
foot of my bed. As I gazed at it it dimmed to a tiny pinprick
before my sleep swollen eyes, and as I fell back into
dreamland again I could have sworn I heard my grandmother's voice. It was too faint and too far away for me to
understand her message; if a message was what it was. The
next morning I puzzled over it and finally chalked it up to
an unusually vivid dream. I missed her so much since she
had died that unconsciously I beckoned her to wander my
dreams with me. That was all.

But the strange presence continued to plague me. For
months she wouldn't come and then, out of the blue, there
she would be. She was trying to tell me something. But I
could never figure out what.

I began to check old newspapers in the library each
afternoon after school, looking for articles on visitations
and psychics. I wanted real life experiences, not fictitious
accounts molded into profitable book form. I needed to
understand what was happening to me; what I should
do—or not do. There were times I wondered if I were going
crazy.

No matter what I did, my grandmother continued to

haunt my nights. Yet I couldn't reach her and she couldn't make me understand what she wanted.

The summer I turned sixteen, I finally came to understand.

One hot August night I awoke to distant sobbing. It came from everywhere; in my room, outside my dark windows, and high in the blowing treetops. I stumbled to the window and stared out into the night. It was then I knew from where the sobbing originated . . . in the hidden recesses of my heart. Outside the window, framed in light, I could see my grandmother crying . . . and I *knew*. I knew she was warning me . . .

I ran into the other rooms, waking everyone in the process. When I reached the twins' room, my heart almost stopped cold. They were *gone*!

Like the two boys six years before, they had simply disappeared.

Eventually their bodies *were* found in the woods—the awful woods. The whole town had turned out to search for them. But the woods remained silent and brooding and refused to give up any of its secrets for a long time. I never knew how they had died until many years later—and then I wished I had never found out. Poor John. Poor Ann.

Poor us.

It broke my mother's heart, and she was never the same. My father never laughed at anything again . . . the heart of our family died with John and Ann. The golden years were over.

We talked of moving away. My father talked my mother out of it. It could have happened anywhere—why blame this place? We had roots there. Moving wouldn't bring dead children back. It was inconceivable that such tragedy would strike twice. *No, we would stay.*

As the years went by, John and Ann's rooms were left untouched as if awaiting their return . . . growing dusty, and echoing with the ghosts of their childish tears, for they were dead and would never come home again.

The little Mustang was bright red and looked as if it had just rolled off the factory line the day my father and mother handed me the keys with big smiles. "You deserve it, Sarah . . . graduating with top honors from high school like you did. We're proud of you, girl. How much you'll never know." Dad made me pose by my shiny little car and he took one of those Polaroid pictures that developed itself in two seconds; then I insisted on taking one of both of them in front of the car, too, wanting to capture their rare smiles on film forever. I know they couldn't afford such an extravagant graduation gift for me and I knew of all the rest of the expensive items we'd ever had—all were eventually hocked, sold, or traded in. But for that moment in time it was mine and we all pretended to be happy. I did everything I could to make them happy in those days, for I knew it would only be a matter of time.

I had heard sobbing in the night again.

Charlie loved my car. I caught him hiding in it at all hours of the day and night, pretending to be driving it. He was thirteen that summer and all he talked about was turning sixteen and being able to drive it. He drove me crazy with his talk of it. Once he even stole my keys and drove it off; before my dad could run him down he drove it into a tree and smashed up the front fender. I wanted to kill him that night. I refused to speak to him for a week, I was so mad.

It was afterward that I remembered how badly I had treated him . . . and I couldn't look at that car and not remember Charlie.

That night it stormed so violently that the tree out back—the one Jimmy and I used to shimmy down from the forbidden roof—was pulled up by its roots and slammed to the ground. The storm whipped at our house and the sound of breaking glass was everywhere. We lost our electricity for the whole night and the yard flooded and water seeped into our basement. The next morning the water was three feet deep down there.

That was the night Charlie died.

No one knew why he went to the woods, but *me*. I knew he had been called there. In their grief, no one would believe my story. No one *dared* believe me. This time we found the body right away. I led the police straight to it.

I knew where he was because *she* had told me.

Poor Charlie ... his body battered and bleeding, all alone out in the angry woods. After his death you could smell the fear in the town and people had begun to talk about *us* ... about *me*. They avoided me and it hurt. They stared and pointed, whispering.

This time my mother had her way and we moved away from Suncrest and our home that summer. She believed there was a curse on us and we had to flee.

We left our home and moved far away to a new place for a fresh start where we were unknown and unfeared. If only it could have been that way ... that we could have forgotten it all that easily; could have escaped that easily.

Not even selling the little red car helped. Nothing helped.

What was to happen happened anyway. The golden years were gone forever and we were never to recapture them.

CHAPTER FIVE

I stood in the doorway with Jeremy's small hand in mine and together we silently murmured out last goodbyes to the apartment that had been our home for the last eight years. It was the only home my son had ever known.

"Don't cry now, Mom. You're doing real well," he said in a gentle voice. The pressure on my hand increased. I glanced down at his thin, freckled face and thoughtful blue eyes and offered a faint smile.

"Don't worry, son. If I cry now, who's going to drive? We've got a long way to go today and I'm afraid nine is still a little too young to be fighting the morning rush." I even threw in a tiny laugh and touseled his long blond hair. As usual it fell across his eyes and with an exaggerated gesture he pushed it back away from his face.

"Ah, Mom! Just give me a chance! I'll show you who can drive a car," he returned stubbornly.

"Sure you will—over my dead body." I bantered with him all the while my eyes kept sweeping the bare walls and the huge stacks of neatly labeled boxes in the room before me. All that was left of ten years of marriage—an empty apartment and an empty heart. The boxes looked like giant children's blocks scattered everywhere, forgotten and unwanted. I didn't want to leave, but I had no choice. On impulse, I knelt down on the familiar threshold and lightly ran my fingers lovingly through the rug's deep peach-colored pile. Jonathan and I had picked it out just last year. Was it only last year? As I laid my hand on the smooth wall for support to stand I could see myself reflected in the gold-veined mirror tiles on the opposite wall. Yellow sunbeams danced over their glossy surface and made the woman in them look golden; even beautiful with her long light brown hair and slim gracefulness. But looking back into my own green eyes I could see the great sadness there, see the drawn face and the lips that had forgotten how to curve into a genuine smile anymore. I'd lost twenty pounds since my divorce and still had no appetite. What I hungered for couldn't be found in a shopping cart.

I had again lost something very precious and not known why. I could help so many other people — strangers really — but not myself. The gift was like that. It applied to everyone but me, as if in the very gift of receiving I had had to shoulder all the ill luck that I saved others from. Someone else might take the lashes but I felt the pain. I smiled at the lady in the mirrors and took one last look at the apartment. I was flooded with memories as elusive as mist. Jeremy as a baby romping from one room to the next; Jonathan reading the paper in his favorite chair by the fireplace as I drew my pictures at the drawing table in the corner . . . so long ago. I put out my hand as if I could see him now, touch him; as if there was a magic door back into our past just waiting for me to enter and so undo all that had occured in the last six months.

Such a fool.

Quietly, I pulled the door closed and locked it. Inside I could hear the ghosts whispering and laughing. But I couldn't stay. I had to make a new life for us now that the old one was dead. I couldn't live in the past any longer. I couldn't remain bitter; I had to cherish the good memories.

I slipped the key under the door in the exact place I had told Jimmy he could find it. He was coming by in a few days to pick up the heavier furniture I had had to leave behind. He would fit most of it in his pick-up truck.

"Are we going now?" Jeremy asked.

"Yes. It's time to go." The sun was a huge bright ball overhead. "Here, you can take these bags." I handed him two carry-all bags and we silently walked out to the car together. Jeremy didn't look back once. We had planned originally to start out at dawn, but it was already after ten o'clock. All in all, a beautiful last day of March, even if it was as cold as hell. I slid into the front seat of the little red Pinto and closed the door. Jeremy thumped down in the passenger seat and for a few seconds we busied ourselves arranging the extra bags. I adjusted my seat and waited for the car to warm up. At least it wasn't snowing. This last winter had been terrible. I had never seen so much snow.

Whenever I remember that winter, I remember snow. Night after night lying alone in our queen-sized bed, contemplating the white darkness with a heavy heart. The sky was so bright with snow, it was like daylight. It was the worst time; the time right after Jonathan had walked out on me for another woman. For the first time in my life I was totally alone. For weeks, a terrible apathy held me in its grip and I'd go to bed early to muffle my tears in my pillow and watch the snow fall outside my window. I lived in my own sad world of make-believe and memories, purposely shutting the real world away. Over and over I kept asking myself what had I done wrong? How could someone I had loved so long and so much do what he had done to me . . . to all of us? How could he not love me anymore? How could he have just stopped that love—and more impor-tant, how was I going to stop loving him? It had been a time of painful rebirth for me, those few weeks. I worked in an ad agency as a commercial artist in St. Louis and I had taken a few weeks off. I couldn't face the world, I couldn't face myself. Who was I now? I slept, I read, I dreamed about the past, carefully wrapping it in the bewildered gossamer tissue of my tears to be tucked away forever like some priceless jewel. I sifted through my whole life and tried to make some meaning out of it all. All the work, the love, and the loss. And with every tear I mended myself; with every day I drew closer to that first light of a dark tunnel and made my way back to the world of the living.

Jonathan was gone. It was simple. I had to start my life again. In the space of a few months I had lost a husband, a home, and even a job. Before I could even go back into work I got a telephone call to tell me not to bother. The agency was folding. We'd lost two of our biggest clients and there just wasn't any work; what had been started so hopefully just three short years ago was no more. Blame the economy, God, or human fickleness; the result was the same. No money, no work, no agency. I wasn't surprised. In fact, I had expected it long before that, but the timing couldn't have been worse. I had no tears left when I went in to empty my desk and say my goodbyes. I would miss my friends more than the job.

Then there was the house.

The house that my grandmother had left me when she died all those years ago. The old house on Suncrest. It was mine free and clear. It had been for some time and I had run out of excuses to claim my inheritance.

There was nothing to hold me in St. Louis anymore. I'd be a fool to stay there. I had no job, no husband, and no way to pay the fancy rent on an overly big, plush apartment.

Yet, God, had I fought going back there ... *back to Suncrest* where the horror had begun. It was bitterly ironic that after all these years of trying to run away from the past I was now literally *trapped* into going back there. Heaven knows, I'd tried to sell the old place for years, but it would never sell for some reason. It had sat there patiently waiting for me. Waiting until I was forced by unavoidable circumstances to go back to it. I had never dreamed of going back there ...

But, we wouldn't stay there long. We were only going

back to fix the old place up enough to sell it, or rent it out, that's all. We'd use it as just a stopping place to someplace else.

If only . . .

I hadn't had any visions for many years. Perhaps I tried to talk myself into believing that *it* wasn't there anymore. That whatever evil had been there in the woods was long gone, its bloodlust long ago satisfied, and it had moved on. I hadn't felt it lurking in my dreams for so long . . . way before my mother died. That was more than six years ago.

I could hope. I could be a damn food as well.

But we were going back there. After almost thirteen years a dead woman would finally have her way and we would live in her house on Suncrest. At this moment, I had little choice.

Thank God for my brother Jimmy, I thought as I backed the car down the driveway and steered out into the muddy road. There was a thin crust of ice cloaking everything. Jeremy was making words with his finger on the frosted windows and humming softly to himself. I honestly didn't think I'd have the courage to go back there if it weren't for Jimmy. He was driving down in a few days in his pick-up to load up the rest of our furniture and meet us at our grandmother's house afterward.

It hadn't been easy to track Jim down. He wasn't usually an easy person to find, on the road with his country western band playing two and three night stands all over the state. It was hard to believe that the small intense boy picking over a used Fender guitar all those years now could play the best guitar in the state. Jim's genius had turned out to be his music. By the time he had graduated from high school he had caught the fever pretty bad and was already playing out with a band on weekends for extra money. He'd never had another job since but that. He'd gone through so many nameless bands since then I had lost count. Yet he loved playing and writing his music; it was his life and he was extremely good at it.

It was strange that he would call me last week like he did, as if he'd sensed in some way that I needed him. I found myself telling him everything about Jonathan, the other woman, the divorce, the ad agency folding, and finally how Jeremy and I were moving back to Suncrest to live in grandmother's house. *Our* house.

He was sorry about my job, but he was shocked at the divorce. "God, Sarah! You can't tell me that you didn't have some suspicion before this that he was fooling around on you? Big, famous psychic that you are? You didn't know?" He laughed trying to put some much needed humor into a lousy situation. Then, at my heavy silence on the other end of the phone, he had astutely switched tactics. "Oh, sis, I didn't mean it, I'm sorry. I couldn't help myself. You know how I've always detested that sacrilegious creep you married. A hunk of stone with a shiny badge for a heart wasn't for you . . . all he ever cared about was making collars, promotions, and how much of each of your paychecks you could stash away in his bank account. Good riddance to bad rubbish, I say. Cheer up, sis. He wasn't good enough for you and someday you're going to find . . ."

"No don't say it!" I moaned into the phone. My heart still felt like someone had taken a sledgehammer to it. Fresh tears froze in my eyes and my vision blurred. No matter what my husband had done to me, I still remembered how he *once* had been — all that love. Letting that image of him go was the hardest thing I'd ever had to do.

"I'm sick of people saying that one day I'll find someone who'll love me better. I don't care what he did to me. I loved him and as far as I'm concerned, there'll never be another man like him for me. Never." But somewhere hidden in my damaged heart I knew that what I really meant was that I would never be able to trust anyone like I had Jonathan. He had betrayed one of the strongest beliefs I knew; love. There was no greater crime than that and nothing would ever be the same.

56

I had lain in bed on those snowy nights and brooded over the future. Who was going to love me now? Where did I go from here? I had no idea.

"It's over, he's gone and that's all there is to it. I lost the game — in fact I never even learned the rules — and I don't want to talk about it anymore." I had Jeremy to love, and Jimmy. "I'll make it."

"I know you will. Aren't we two survivors?" he said softly.

"We sure are!"

"What about you and the boy moving so far away? Has Jonathan said anything about that?"

"To be truthful, I don't know and I don't care, either. I haven't talked to him in over two months. I don't know what he's thinking. Jeremy told him."

"You mean he hasn't seen Jeremy in two months?" Jim was surprised.

"No." I rubbed my eyes tiredly. If I had all the answers to the strange way my ex-husband was behaving, then I'd hold the secret to life. Psychic or not, I wasn't shown everything. When it came to my own life, my own personal danger, I remained in darkness. Maybe it was better that way.

"He's called him a few times, but he says he's been too busy to get over to see him. At first, before Jonathan moved in with her, he'd come over and spend time with Jeremy when he could. Lately, he hasn't even done that." It was hard even talking about it. It had happened so quickly, the alienation between father and son . . . I kept remembering my own childhood. The love, as brief as it turned out to be, had been the foundation of my whole life. Jeremy would be deprived of that; we were moving so far away. It would give Jonathan a plausible excuse not to see him now, one with little guilt attached to it because of the distance factor. Jeremy, I knew, could accept that easier than apathy.

"I'm sorry, Sarah . . ."

"It's not *your* fault."

"I feel bad anyway. . ."

"Well, don't." How could I convince him? It wasn't anyone's fault.

I'd gone over the same territory so many times . . . it had started two years ago. There was a day that I was allowed to see a scrap of future and frightened, I had told Jonathan. I warned him that he was going to be in an accident very soon. The vision was clear. A terrible accident. I begged him to be careful. He stared at me in the strangest way and then shrugged his shoulders, smiling sarcastically as he had buckled on his shoulder holster and walked out the door to another day's work. "What happens, happens," he said. He laughed and gave me a weak kiss on the way out. That very day he was involved in an awful collision in his squad car. His partner was killed outright and he was in the hospital for three weeks. His leg was broken in three places. But that was the least of the damage. After that, he looked at me with the eyes of a frightened, cornered animal. I'd turn to him at times and the smile would freeze on his lips and he would turn his head away as if my gaze could cripple or hurt him.

Nothing was ever right between us again. It was all right for me to help other people or write my articles on my psychic experiences for the whole world to read . . . but quite another cup of tea when he was the ultimate victim. We started to drift apart at an alarming pace. He began to act funny; he was gone a lot. There were times I was so lonely and I missed him so much I thought my heart would break. It would have been better, I often thought, if he had died in that crash, because to me and Jeremy he was as good as dead. Having been a cop's wife for ten years had prepared me for death, but not for what was happening.

I made up excuses for his cool behavior. It was his work, or the accident had made him realize that he was only mortal . . . everything but what it was. I knew he was unhappy and in time I learned the solution he'd found to combat his fear. He had fallen in love with another woman. A *normal* woman who wouldn't be able to pinpoint the day he was to die. She was divorced and had two boys. She was a barmaid. She was nothing like me.

He hadn't wanted to hurt me, he swore, as he had packed his bags that night. It was raining and I felt as if the whole world was crying for me. It was a week before Halloween and Jeremy stood, paralyzed, in the doorway to our room dressed in his new costume. He had wanted to show his dad what a pumpkin looked like.

Instead, he was watching his dad pack. His dad was leaving.

"I'm sorry, Sarah . . ." His eyes, bloodshot and tired, shifted between the wife he was leaving and the son. "Sorry . . . I never wanted to hurt you . . . but . . . I have to think of myself, you see . . . I love her and she's so special . . . please, forgive me!" The last a whisper as he opened his suitcase and cleared out his dresser. He packed his guns, the hand-carved jewelry box I gave him for his last birthday, and he rummaged through the closets looking for this shirt or that sweater. I had collapsed, sick and speechless, on the edge of our bed, my eyes not seeing anything but the items he was stuffing into bags and suitcases. How could he be doing what he was doing? He was cutting my heart out and he didn't even know it!

"Are you going to her?" Had that been my voice? So weak, so sad? My heart skipped a beat and then clunked on as he looked up at me with those piercing blue eyes of his. This wasn't happening to me, to us . . . it happened to other people—our friends—not to us. Never to us.

"I suppose so . . ." Guiltily, his dark curly head bent so I couldn't see his face or his expression.

"Will you call me?" I had a thousand things I could have said, a thousand pleas, a million tears were falling, silently, inside. Yet I couldn't utter a word in my own defense. I had nothing to say. *You might as well have taken a gun and shot me . . .*

"I don't know." He gathered his suitcases and started to leave. He couldn't get away fast enough.

59

"Can I have a number where I can get hold of you if I need you?" I trailed behind him like someone being left alone to die a terrible death. He was almost running by then; I reached out to touch his face one last time, my eyes unable to leave it. I had to memorize it for a lifetime. "What if I need you? If Jeremy needs you?" I was growing desperate. I hadn't taken him seriously and suddenly I realized that I couldn't stop him. Not with words, not with the love that I had always taken for granted; I was powerless to change what was happening and it was devastating.

"I'll call you." He was looking at his son with haunted eyes. He wouldn't look at me, I couldn't make him.

"Please . . ." But he slipped out of my hands and strode out the door, shaking his head. *You might as well have taken a gun and shot me, it would have been kinder . . .*

I watched him walk to the car and get in. He didn't look at us as he drove away, he was in such a hurry. Jeremy came and put his arms around me and cried. My tears came later. It took me days to realize that he was really gone. I remember as I held Jeremy and stood there listening to the rain the phone rang. It rang for a long time and when I finally went to answer it, they hung up.

I had never been a bad wife or even a nag as so many of his fellow policemen's wives were. I had worked so hard to make him proud of me. I had helped him with so many of his cases, and loved him enough to let him go when he wanted his freedom, no questions asked. But in the end, he wasn't even grateful for that. A few months with his new wife and stepsons had changed him into someone I didn't even know. Yes, it would have been better for us if he had died in that squad car last July; at least Jeremy and I wouldn't be feeling like losers. Jeremy asked constantly why his father didn't want to see him or call him anymore. Was he mad at him? Didn't he love him anymore? *What did I do wrong, Mother?* It broke my heart and then it made me angry. I wasn't allowed to even talk to Jonathan anymore, the doors were all closed. He was too busy with his job and his second job and his new wife and two stepsons to have time for Jeremy. *She* was jealous.

We were on our own, Jeremy and I.

I reflected on all of this talking with Jimmy that night. There was so much I needed to discuss with him, but it would have to wait until I could do it in person. I had to wait until I was ready.

"I can't believe you're really serious about going back to Suncrest." Jim had been genuinely appalled at the idea. "Isn't there any other way?"

"No." I'd thought he had understood. "I haven't got any place else to go, Jimmy."

"Christ . . ." I could see him rubbing his eyes and sighing. "That place must be a wreck and ruin by now. It's as old as the hills and hasn't been lived in for over fifteen years, girl."

"I know."

"All right . . . so we got our work cut out for us." His tone had changed from intense misgiving to begrudging acceptance. "What happens if the place isn't even standing anymore, then what do you do?"

It was something I hadn't thought of.

"I don't know, we'll cross that bridge when we get to it. I think it's still *standing* as far as that goes, but as to the exact condition it's in . . . who knows? Grandmother's lawyer wrote me just last year . . ."

"He's still alive! That old fart?" Jim laughed, interrupting me.

"Yes, he's still alive! A Mr. Largo wrote me last year, saying the house was still unsold and reminding me that if I came to live in it I could make it into a nice home. It needs work, but it is livable. He also mentioned some sort of letter or something that my Grandmother left me when she died; to be delivered in person, only. I've been curious enough about that alone to take the trip down there."

"He could have just sent the thing to you." His voice had been sharp. "I wonder what it is?"

61

"You too, huh? Curiosity killed the cat, you know." Then I had laughed. My brother couldn't stand secrets.

We talked about other unrelated things. I gave him instructions on how to get to my apartment and where I was going to hide the key; what he should bring and what he shouldn't. I didn't need to tell him how to get to Suncrest. He knew the way. The last thing he said to me before he hung up was: "You sure of this, now?" I knew immediately to what he was referring. I wondered how much he remembered. How much he knew about what had happened.

"Yes, I'm sure. I have no choice, really. Jim?"

"Uh huh?"

"We won't stay there long, I promise. Just until I get back on my feet or until the house is fixed up enough to be sold . . . I need the money. I don't know what else I can do. Property is worth its weight in gold and I can't just forget I have it, even if I could afford to, which I can't." Maybe he could see right through me. Maybe he already knew why we were really going back.

I think I did.

I couldn't run away any longer. I had to find out if it were still there.

"Fine. Then I'll meet you two there sometime next week." The phone had clicked softly. It had been a long time since I had seen my brother. It would be good to talk to him again. After all, we were all that was left of our family. Just us two. And now Jeremy, of course.

"Mom, did you remember to pack the sleeping bags, too?" Jeremy asked as we stopped at the last light on the edge of town. It turned green. The shiny Firebird behind us honked when I didn't hit the gas pedal fast enough. We surged ahead and I made a right onto the main highway.

"I'm pretty sure I did, son."

We passed the Quick-Mart where I did a lot of my shopping. It was open twenty-four hours a day and when

Jonathan worked the night shift and got home at odd hours, he'd have a craving for things I never had.

"You better have . . . I don't want to have to sleep on the hard floor," he grumbled, playing with the little furry bear I had hanging from the mirror. I threw him a warning look. Sometimes he got a little big for his britches. He'd been extremely obstinate lately. He carried a chip on his shoulders as big as a bowling ball. I guess he had the right.

"You won't. I didn't forget." I smiled over at him. It was hard to smile. We were passing the restaurant that Jonathan always took me to on our anniversary. There was the park we . . . I made a turn and I was on the edge of town, leaving it forever; leaving Jonathan and my past behind like a finished book. We passed his parents' house and I thought about how much I loved them. They were good people and would miss Jeremy terribly. Memories. Places. I hadn't thought it would affect me this way. My lips drew tight and I found I was gripping the steering wheel like it was a life preserver.

Then we pulled past another Pinto and there was nothing but highway in front of us and fields on either side. We were on our way. I turned the radio on and Jeremy and I fought, teasingly, over what station we were going to listen to. He liked hard rock music and I liked country. We sang along to the songs we knew.

It would be about an eight hour drive, I'd calculated, if we stopped for two meals and took our time. The roads were slick from the light rain that drifted down from the darkening skies and I wanted to be sure we got to the house in one piece. I had mapped out the route the night before and Jeremy held the map possessively in his lap and voice-fed me the directions as we drove. "Make a right here on Forty-four . . . yes, now . . . we want to watch out for the turn-off down the road ahead here somewhere . . ."

It had stopped raining and the sun was playing hide and go seek with the blue-gray clouds. I couldn't help but shift into a better mood. Just doing something to change my life, even if I wasn't sure it was the best move in the world for us, invigorated me after all these months of indecision and self-inflicted lassitude. It felt good to be on the move.

"Hungry?" I asked Jeremy a short while later as I noticed a Denny's sign to our right as we drove past it. We had been too busy packing that morning to eat breakfast and suddenly I was very hungry. Coffee sounded like a fantastic idea.

"Sure," he answered with a huge smile. "I could eat a horse! Where we going, Mom?" Jeremy had a man's appetite already and he was eating me out of house and home. I looked at him. He was small for his age, but in so many ways he reminded me of the way Jimmy was when he was that age. Yet my brother was six foot two now. There was hope for the runt, I thought fondly.

"We're going right here." I pulled the car off the highway and applied the brakes. "And you can have *three* horses to eat, if they have them on the menu," I teased back as I lined the car between parking spaces and turned the motor off. The little Pinto was almost nine years old and it still ran like a top. It was dependable and good on gas; it had never given me any trouble. I knew the trip would be made easily in it and as we jumped out of it, I mulled over the thought of getting its annual tune-up. I didn't have a lot of money left. I'd drained my savings account before we left and I was glad I had been building it up the last three years. I had been saving for a new car and now I was going to use it for something else: living. I'd had over two thousand in it and I wondered how long that could last me. The house wouldn't cost much, just upkeep and utilities. I'd always been good at redecorating on a shoestring and the trunk right now was full of cans of paint, wallpaper, cleaning lotions, brooms and mops. I figured the old house would be livable and attractive just cleaned up, painted and papered. I also figured that we could live a long time on two thousand and the child-support money I got every two weeks like clockwork from Jonathan. We would make it if we were careful, for as long as we needed to until I found another job. I wasn't sure where I could find a commercial art job around there. It had been so long since I was there that I had no idea what the job market was like. Suncrest was a world unto itself. It wasn't by a larger city, but located in a small town out in the middle of nowhere. How I would find work was in doubt. I just had to wait until I got there and started looking.

I'd had a secret desire for many years . . . to be my own boss, doing freelance artwork and writing. Before Jonathan had put his foot down I had worked for a newspaper—small articles on local topics of interest and illustrations to go along with the copy. I'd done small art shows and all in all I had scrounged up enough work to bring in some good money. The unpredictability of it was what drove Jonathan crazy . . . he wanted me to have a weekly paycheck so we could budget better, so I had finally taken a steady nine to five job in an ad agency. The job was boring and tedious. The pay was ridiculously low but I made more later. I hated putting my son in a nursery school and I detested clocking in half my life for a paycheck. But it was what Jonathan wanted and I always tried to please him. The beautiful brief days of my freedom were gone.

As I walked behind Jeremy into the restaurant I had hopes that maybe something could be arranged where I wouldn't have to work a regular job again. Maybe I could find enough freelance work to keep us in food and pay the bills. I had everything I needed otherwise, furniture, clothes, and the house was mine.

It seemed funny that the very thing that broke my heart had also given me my freedom. No one now could tell me what to do or what not to do. I felt like someone just released from prison and the realization that I could do anything I wanted, was a heady feeling. I was free!

We found a booth and, smiling at each other, ate breakfast. We talked about the trip, how we were going to find the house, and how we would find him a new school.

He was anxious to get there and start fixing it up. He was an ambitious child and in that he was like his father. I didn't have to worry about my son, I knew already that he would go far someday. He was smart as an owl and he loved to read. He was old for his age, just like I had been when I was a child.

Jeremy was a gift to me. I would never be alone again. As long as I had him, I'd have a part of Jonathan forever. But Jeremy was a person, first, and I wanted him to know that. I couldn't be pushy. He was all I had. I reflected on my own childhood and I knew that it wasn't going to be easy.

What would Suncrest and our new life be like? Was I doing the right thing in taking my son back there . . . *was it safe?*

I shook the ghosts from my mind and I made myself come back to the present. "You ready to go? Had enough to eat?" I asked him as I got the money out to pay the bill. I had splurged on this meal, but the next time I would have to be more careful. For the first time in years I was really worried about money and I had to be sure I didn't spend too much, too soon. As I left a tiny tip, looking around guiltily to see if our waitress had seen me, I felt like the poor country mouse in the big city. Only this time it was really reversed. I was the improverished city rodent scurrying home to the country. I fretted as I paid the bill, because I wasn't used to being poor anymore. When I was a child, maybe, but I had left all that behind years ago. But life is a circle inside a circle and I supposed we always came back to where we had started sooner or later. But I still would have to get used to it. That wouldn't be easy, either.

We drove the rest of the day and only wandered off the beaten path a few dozen times. I was terrible with directions and the maps never seemed to go exactly the same direction as the roads. Jeremy had no patience with my driving.

"Mom, you're a scream. I can't wait until I can drive." He

shook his head in mock disgust. "You need help."

A memory stirred somewhere deep inside me and I felt a far away shiver touch my heart as I listened to his words. Somewhere, sometime someone had spoken almost those same exact words . . . who was it? I couldn't remember. My mind had blocked it like it had blocked a lot of things. Sad, aching things that I simply didn't want to remember. Strange. Who had said that to me once?

"Mother!" Jeremy demanded my attention. "Wake up, will you?"

"I am awake," I bantered back, annoyed at the fleeting memory I couldn't capture.

"No, you're not!" he whined. "You're daydreaming again."

"No, I'm not. I'm just thinking."

"With you, it's the same thing. You better keep your eyes on the road or we'll be wrapped around a tree before you know it." And then I remembered. Charlie. I dismissed his aching memory, careful to side-step all the others that threatened to cave me in.

I knew Jeremy was right. I did daydream entirely too much and I lived in fear of the day I'd have a vision while I was doing something that needed all my attention, like driving. But I had been exceptionally fortunate in that I almost always experienced them when I was asleep, in dreams. I lived a strange life. In fear of them and hating them but proud of myself when I helped someone. I tried to live as normal a life as I could for Jeremy's sake and tended to forget my psychic abilities most of the time—when they let me. I'd learned to hide a lot, too. I didn't want to scare my son. But people always seemed to find out. It was as if I glowed with the power. Not everyone took my abnormality in stride.

It was bad enough that the dreams scared me.

The cranks and the letters, the telephone calls in the middle of the night, were harder to hide, though. Jonathan and I had lived in Benchley, a middle-sized town located just outside St. Louis where Jonathan worked on the police force. By leaving the place where my psychic reputation had become common knowledge, I had also left behind my fame. I liked the idea. Blessed anonymity. I was sick of the accusing letters and the quacks that called day and night. I realized just recently that I always felt safe, though, because I lived with a cop and felt protected; now Jeremy and I were alone and vulnerable.

Something inside warned me to stay anonymous and save us both a lot of unnecessary grief. I had decided for a lot of reasons that I would be more careful revealing my psychic powers. If I were smart I would ignore them and try to lead a normal life. I was going to try to forget what I had been. I had to, for my son's sake.

"Anything look familiar yet, Mom?" Jeremy questioned as the day wore on. He was taking in everything. "How about that?" He pointed at various local landmarks. "That?"

"Afraid not." I searched the passing countryside as anxious as he to start recognizing things. "It's been a long time since I was in these parts. I was only a child when we lived here and a teenager when we left. I guess I never paid much attention." I didn't tell him that I had too much else on my mind back in those days.

He was silent for a long time, his face pressed against the frosted window as his eyes devoured the sights. We stopped at a little roadside cafe for supper and ate hamburgers smothered in pickles and cheese. I was cautious with the money this time. Jeremy wasn't very hungry. I wondered if he was overly excited or tired. Maybe he was both. We ate quickly and went on our way. There was an unspoken urgency between us to get where we were going. He seemed as nervous as I the closer we got to our new home.

"I wonder what it looks like," he said. The sun began its

slow descent and the sky became tinted with soft oranges and winter pinks. I hadn't seen such a beautiful sunset in years. The clouds had turned from ugly greys and blacks to misty pastels that flew above the earth like tropical birds. The temperature hovered just below the freezing mark and thin coats of ice were forming over the tree branches and across the highway. Lovely, but dangerous; so I had to slow down. Random puddles had turned into glass.

"What *what* looks like?"

"Your old house."

It took me a second to fathom what he was referring to. "Where I grew up, you mean?"

"Yeah, can we go by it, please, Mom?" He grinned in the twilight, touching my hand lightly. "I'd love to see where my old mom grew up at." He was truly fascinated with the past. He loved old things.

I avoided his gaze. For reasons I could not explain, I had never spoken to Jeremy about the old place or about my family and what had happened there those long years ago. I'd thought in my own way I was protecting him. He didn't know about Suncrest. Sure, I'd told him about the happiest parts of my childhood and about all my brothers and sisters but I hadn't told him about the murders—not in so many words. He just knew that they had died; that there was no one left now but Jimmy and I. He'd seemed to understand my hesitation, the pain inside of me, and he hadn't pryed too much. He vaguely remembered my mom and dad. They had died when he was about four. They had both been killed in a car accident. I winced, remembering.

More than anything in the world, I was leery of going back to that rambling brick house on the edge of the woods. It was too damn close. At least my grandmother's house was a good distance away from the place where the bodies had been found; far enough away from the woods and the haunted fields of that terrible place.

I didn't want to go back there.

"Please, Mom?" he begged. "You've told me so much about it. I want to see it!" I looked over at my son and saw the stubborn set of his chin and felt my heart sink. He was so determined. He was just a child and he could never understand.

But I had to face it. I couldn't be afraid. Not if we were to have to live here now, even for a short while. I had to see if things had changed so I would know what to do. This was as good a time as any . . . it wasn't dark yet and I realized the house was right up ahead.

"All right," I said dryly. "We're going to drive right past it anyway, so you can see it, okay?" My mouth was suddenly cotton-dry and I heard my heart thudding wildly under my heavy coat. What would it be like, seeing the old place again?

I wasn't that child any longer. I could take care of myself — couldn't I?

"Great!" he yelped. "How much farther?"

"Should be right up ahead." I was stiff from all the hours of driving and I was tired. It was later than I had planned to get here. "We'll just drive by slowly . . . it will be dark soon and we need to get where we're going. We can't waste time gawking at an old house, you understand?" I knew my tone was icy, but I couldn't help it. I felt strange just being close to the old place.

It's all right. All right, I told myself. Drive by. The doors are locked. Drive by, fast . . . and nothing can hurt us. Nothing . . .

I felt suddenly nauseous as we came closer. The woods were all around us now and on the horizon an echoing nightmare began to take shape. The lay of the land was too familiar. I was cold, but I was sweating. The driveway. The fields . . .

I screeched the small car recklessly to a stop, spinning my wheels in the mud and ice, my eyes riveted ahead of me through the twilight. I couldn't believe it!

"Mom! What's the matter?" Jeremy had been thrown towards the dash by the sudden stop and he looked over his shoulder with wide confused eyes. "Why'd you do that for? I almost went into the window, for gosh sakes! Mom!" He shoved at my shoulder trying to make me hear him.

"We're here, then? Where's the house?" he demanded, staring at my white face. "Are you all right, Mom?" His voice was suddenly frightened. He knew about my visions, even if he didn't understand them.

"I don't believe it!"

"Mom!"

"It was here, son." I'd found my voice. "I swear it was. It's all gone. My God," I mumbled. Putting my hand to my throat I stared at the place where the old brick house had once stood. "It never crossed my mind that they could have torn down the old place," I exclaimed. *Or burnt it down.*

"Jeremy! No, don't . . ."

My son had shoved open the door and jumped out of the car. He was running towards the empty skyline and the spot that once held the formidable brick house. I was struck with a wave of fear at the discovery that the place of my innermost nightmares no longer stood. I was terrified that Jeremy was out there alone so close to the woods . . .

I slid from the car and followed him at a brisk pace, my hands shoved into my coat pockets, playing with the torn linings inside. I kept my eyes on the small bobbing shape ahead of me. Jeremy had stopped in front of the old cherry tree and had turned back around to face me, his hands held out and a tentative smile lurking on his lips. It was freezing out and the light rain had begun again but this time it was dancing ice particles that swirled around our heards. The wind howled and angrily whipped my hair across my face. I yanked a heavy woolen cap from my left pocket and tugged it down over my head, covering my ears. I walked up to where my son stood staring at the burnt-out shell of our old home . . . and the waving trees of the distant woods beyond. He was watching *something* . . .

I would *not* allow my teeth to chatter. I would *not* show my despair or the intimidating vibrations that I was violently feeling the closer I came to the ruins. I stepped up camly and laid a cold hand firmly on my son's shoulder.

He seemed troubled. He looked up at me with the most puzzled expression in his young eyes, as if he couldn't put what he felt into actual words; yet I felt the shock as our eyes met and inwardly I cringed. He had felt it, too.

He took my hand and we bucked the wind as it screamed around us. The sun was almost gone and the whole world glittered with its coat of ice. Without a word I led him back to the car where we would both be safe and warm again. For a second, I was afraid he would hesitate and pull back, but I smiled at him and the spell was broken. We walked carefully back to the car.

My bones felt like the dead branches and ragged lumps of burned timbers and bricks that littered the site, but my mind was vividly aware of the overpowering scent of fresh roses . . . and I was reminded of that long ago summer storm . . . the voices. I was bombarded and mesmerized by the memories. I had to fight to walk away. They tugged and nipped at my retreating back as I hurried towards the car with my son.

Sarah! Where are you? I froze, the whispers and giggles were so familiar. And far away in the distance as if it were frolicking with the treetops or the rolling, angry clouds above I could hear more childish voices: *Allie . . . Allie . . . come in free . . . Allie . . . Allie . . . all in free . . .*

Sarah . . . come home . . .

Then laughter drifting sadly all around me that only I could hear. I stopped, my hand on the car door handle; my other hand still tightly around Jeremy's. I turned to look at the burned shell of my old home—and I *listened*. Nothing. *Nothing.*

More than anything I had the strongest urge to run, to run away from this cursed place; to keep running and never look back or stop until I was hundreds of miles away. *Why had I come back?*

How could I have been so stupid?

"Mom?" Jeremy's face was ghostly pale in the fading light, his nose twitching like a scared rabbit. "What's that . . . smell?" he gasped. "Do you smell it, Mom? Do you?" he whispered.

I gaped at him. "Roses . . . son, they're roses."

I kissed him tenderly and swiftly on the cheek and shoved him into my side of the car, sliding in next to him. I started the car and turned on the lights.

"But it's only March, Mother," he insisted, shivering in his coat he had wrapped up around his face and nose, snuggling in the fur collar.

"I know. I know," I replied. I turned the car around and with a few false starts, returned it to the highway and back in the right direction.

"Let's go home." It slipped out before I could stop myself.

"Home?" Jeremy sighed next to me. He was exhausted and cold and bewildered by the shock of the last terrible months. Now this. "Home isn't here. We don't have a home, not anymore." The tone of his voice was tinged with defeat.

"We have a . . ."

"No, we don't! It'll be just like back there . . . nothing." Then he fell silent, brooding in his corner; cutting himself off from me like he had to do so often since his father had left. It was beginning to worry me, those sullen silences.

I was very tired and I didn't feel like fighting with him. I didn't want to admit that he was right. I didn't want to know. If my grandmother's house was in the same condition as the one we had just left, I honestly didn't know what in the hell I was going to do.

And pricking me with every breath I took was the

73

nagging, persistent suspicion that I never—never—should have come back.

That somehow, sometime, I would be very, very sorry I had.

CHAPTER SIX

The house was still there.

In the night's pale gloom I studied it as best I could. I sat in the warm car, lit up a badly needed cigarette and just stared. Jeremy slept beside me, curled up into a tight little ball that grunted and muttered occasionally. I debated if I should wake him to see it or not.

It was one of those bastardized Victorian styles that couldn't be comfortably squeezed into any category because so much had been altered and added through the years; my grandfather had been a good one for that. He could never tolerate anything in its purest form. Sitting there taking it all in, I didn't need bright light. I remembered the house very well. A huge, two-story frame with a ridiculously ornate, tiered portico in the front, held up by two, tall, white columns that made the house look like it belonged on a southern plantation. The tall, narrow windows were all made of rare curved glass. Pointed iron fences surrounded the place, making it look like a cemetery.

Rubbing my tired eyes, and leaning over the steering wheel, I wanted to go to sleep like Jeremy had and forget everything. The place was a dilapidated wreck. Weeds had taken control of the grounds, obliterating the first floor.

The paint had long since peeled off. There were loose boards everywhere. The doors and windows were all nailed shut with jagged wooden slats—to keep vandals away I supposed. I mused about the inside's condition. How many scrubbings would it take to get the wooden floors shining again? Were there any floors left to scrub?

If I weren't so disgusted and exhausted, I would have felt sorry for the old place. It reminded me of a very old helpless woman who had let time pare her away to nothingness. It made me want to weep. I couldn't tell who I felt sorrier for, myself or the house.

It looked like a hopeless case.

"Mom? We here?" Jeremy's voice was slurred with sleep. He rubbed his eyes and nudged me half heartedly.

"Yes, we're here. You want to look?"

"Do I have to?" But he was already peeking from under heavy lids. "Jesus! What I can see looks terrible, Mom. Do we really have to live in that dump? It probably has two million termites and they're all just waiting for us. You're not really going to make us spend the night in that spook house, are you?" he pleaded with me, still staring at the house, his eyes narrowed.

"I don't know . . ." I relented, giving serious thought. "It is a lot later than I had planned to get here. It's dark and the place doesn't have electricity or heat yet."

"Jesus, Mom . . ." He was wide awake now.

"And everything's nailed and boarded shut . . ."

"Mom!"

"Maybe we should find a cheap motel for the night."

"That's the best thing I've heard yet. Let's go!" he said.

"But, then, on the other hand . . . we have to watch our money and wouldn't you just love 'camping out' in a haunted house and 'roughing it'?"

The look he threw me could have been framed.

"I was just kidding! It's too late to start anything now. So you're off the hook." I started the car again and after one last glimpse of our new home to be, I put it into drive and pulled away. "As much as I hate the thought of spending money, I know we have to find a place for the night. It's too darn cold; anyway, even if we could get into the house in the dark, we'd freeze."

Jeremy was either sulking again or he had fallen back asleep. "We'll come back in the morning . . . things will look better then, you'll see." He didn't answer me. But what he would have said hung in the cold air like frost.

It was after eight and night had dropped its velvet curtain. I wasn't sure if I could find a motel this late. I had no idea where to even look for one. I steered into the first filling station I ran across and asked. They told me there was a reasonable place a couple miles down the road. What they meant by reasonable I never asked. If it had a bed and running water somewhere inside, I'd be satisfied. A hot bath was suddenly the most important thing in my life.

The motel I checked us into was about as large as the gas station. I marveled at the conveniences of electric lights and real hot running water once I had us checked in; by the looks of the place, I really hadn't expected them.

Jeremy was half asleep and I directed him to a bed and helped him to undress. That was something he never allowed me to do any more except under the most adverse circumstances. I tucked him in and went to take my bath. I ended up settling for a lukewarm shower because a shower was all they had and the water wouldn't get hot anyway. It didn't make any difference; there were so many bugs in the bathroom, I was glad they didn't have the time to mass and carry me away.

I slipped quietly into bed next to Jeremy. I'd tried the room's small television and found it didn't work. Laying there next to my son in the dark, I couldn't help but review the last few weeks and months of my life. Depressed, I'd decided not to read or anything else, but to just go to sleep. Depression affected me that way. If I didn't want to face life, I just went to sleep. Sleep was a great healer . . . when I didn't dream. Tonight I didn't want to face anything.

Tomorrow would be a long day.

But sleep played the crafty scoundrel and eluded me. After an hour of laying perfectly still and pretending to be asleep, I gave up. Propping my hands behind my head on the pillow, I stared down at my son's sleeping face. Some sort of flashing light across the highway illuminated his face in pale green and yellow rays. It made him look like a baby again and I couldn't resist brushing the long hair gently from his face and thinking of the past.

I missed my ring, my wedding ring. It had always reminded me of a daisy made of tiny diamonds. I rubbed my finger where it used to be and closed my eyes. It would have glittered in these muted lights and twinkled like it had a life of its own; it had always been a sort of a beautiful talisman for me, signifying security and contentment. The grand prize. Now it lived alone and abandoned in a special compartment of my purse. In that way it was like me. Put away. Forgotten. It had outlived its usefulness; it had no meaning now. I supposed that soon I'd have to bury it in my jewelry box. I smiled a tiny caustic smile into the emptiness encountering my blurred reflection in a cheap mirror that hung above the cardboard dresser across the room. I quickly looked away. It was an old silly superstition that my grandmother had instilled in my mind when I was a child and still stubbornly hung on. *You never look in a mirror in a dark or dim room because what might look back at you would be the devil or a demon, but not you.* Since the day she had told me that little gem I could never face my reflection in a dark room. I hated myself for my eccentricity, but I couldn't help it.

I didn't *think* it was true. It was just a childish game I continued to play. *Why?* I wasn't sure. Maybe it was like something she had also told me once. *There are more things in heaven and in earth . . .*

Disgusted with myself, I pounded the pillow into a round ball with my fist and slammed my head down. I needed to sleep. Why was I tortured night after night with old, dead words of an unsavory past? Why didn't they all just leave me the hell alone?

My body was so tired it ached in a thousand places. Arthritis at thirty. No wonder Jonathan hadn't wanted me any more, I was falling apart.

Jonathan! How I missed him, especially at night . . . I sent out a silent agonized cry to him: *Remember me. Remember I loved you!* The pain I felt was still so great, how could he not hear me? Even now, with so much time, distance and betrayal between us he should be able to *feel* it. I laid my hand lightly on my sleeping son's shoulder on top of the thin blanket, remembering.

No, I wasn't as bitter as a few months—even a few weeks—ago. I had always been a compromiser and it had always allowed me to accept things for what they were, no more. *You can never have everything you want in life.* I knew that and I tried to live it. *Just be damn grateful for what you do have.*

I had Jeremy. I had my talent and my intelligence . . . and I had a home. A real house that no one—*no one*—could take away from me. It was mine. Mine. *Mine!* I thought fiercely. I began to think about the house. As it was now and as it once was, or as I remembered it as a child, anyway. Amazingly enough, I found myself looking for excuses to stay and live in it ourselves. Not ever to leave it. I was becoming fascinated with the whole unique prospect of fixing it up and keeping it.

My own beautiful house.

It's a wreck. Just a pile of termite-eaten boards and weeds. Spider webs and age old dust.

The gift of a real house wasn't something to thought-lessly slough off. When would I ever be given another free house? I frowned, knowing the answer. As a divorced, unemployed woman with a child I couldn't buy a house on my own even if I sold my soul for one.

Mine. Free and clear . . .

There was no heat, no electricity. Did it have water? Yes,

there was a well in the back. Such bad shape it wouldn't even sell, remember? My mind kept striving to be heard over my heart.

You always loved it as a child . . . they don't make houses like that anymore . . . it's so big and the high, beamed ceilings, remember those? It has an upstairs and lots of ground for the boy to play on. Flowers and bushes . . . rose bushes . . . my heart cried.

If only . . .

I untangled myself from the sticky sheets and walked over to the window. Just what I needed: it was snowing outside. The flakes weren't large, though, and I had hope that they wouldn't even stick to the ground. I also hoped it would stop soon and the sun would oblige us tomorrow and come out shining. The thought of tackling that decrepit mountain of aged wood in the wet cold didn't appeal to me in the least.

I had to get in first, then execute an extensive junk-gathering campaign and a major cleaning. I was prepared for that, the car's trunk was loaded with what we would need. I found myself excitedly anxious over starting. Something else occurred to me as I stood in my nightgown surveying the snow outside; I had never heard anything mentioned in all those years about my grandmother's furniture. She had been an avid collector of antiques, and anything beautiful or just plain different. I loved old furniture and always dreamed of owning a house full of hand-picked antiques one day. I began to fantasize about my possible house full of treasures. I could clean and refinish them if I had to; rearrange them and clean the old rugs; I could buy plants to put on the wide window sills and hang some more with macrame from the tall ceilings. I could make it the home I had always dreamed of.

If only. The two big words loomed above me like messengers of doom. I had sensed that *thing*—or the dying shreds of a memory?—still lurking in those woods by the old ruins of my childhood home and I knew that to stay

80

here or even to contemplate it was playing with fire. It could even be suicide for all I knew. Was it only childish fears rearing long dormant heads once again, or was my fear grounded in some awful truth? Was *it* still here?

I weighed what I had to gain with what I had to lose. I glanced back at my curled up son and I shook my head. I had too much to lose! Yet, if I ran from Suncrest as my family had done so long ago, would it make any difference?

I had to face up to something I had never wanted to face up to before: *We hadn't hid all that well, had we? I mean, they had all died anyway.* Coincidences or destiny, if we were all cursed, did it matter *where* we lived?

I've been a practical person all my life. The bottom line was: If we decide to run, where would we go?

Sighing, I crawled back into bed next to Jeremy and willed myself to start feeling tired. I could think tomorrow. Even though it would be a waste of time. I was afraid I had already decided what I had to do.

I did know that we had nowhere else to go and that I yearned to put down real roots and that the house was what I wanted. I *wanted* to stay. . . if that *thing* would allow us, we would. For a while, anyway. We would stay and see.

"Breakfast. Breakfast." Jeremy merely muttered, rubbing his red eyes and yawning loudly. I prodded him again, sitting on the edge of the bed, fully dressed, waiting for him to come to.

"What do you want for breakfast?" I asked again, pulling the covers back from off his face where he had just yanked them up again. I was anxious to start.

"Jesus . . . it's so bright out there!" he mumbled again, covering his eyes with his dirty hands. I tugged them away, smiling.

"Gee, you're a regular dirt ball," I teased, turning his hands over in mine, studying them. "I said, what do you want for breakfast?" It was beginning to soak in. His eyes flew open now and he tossed the covers off him. He was a growing boy in one of those "eating stages." He attacked anything that wasn't tied down or wouldn't eat him first. It was embarrassing. People stared like they thought I never fed the kid.

"Food? Let's go . . . I'm starving." He was finally awake, his eyes feverish and his face flushed with sleep. He slid out of bed, gave me a quick stingy hug and lunged for his pile of clothes at the foot of the bed. "Can I have pancakes, Mom, with gobs of strawberry syrup? And biscuits . . . and coffee milk, please?"

"Hold on there." I pointed at his pile of clothes clutched in his skinny arms, motioning downward with my hand. "You need a shower first. Have you looked at yourself lately in a mirror?"

"Ah, but Mom!" he protested still holding his clothes. "Do I have to? No one's going to see me and I'll just get dirty again."

"Move! Bathroom's right behind you. I don't take dirty boys out to breakfast. I'd be ashamed."

"Mom?" He grinned sheepishly.

"Go!" I replied sternly and tried to keep from grinning back. He was a stubborn little cuss at times.

He dropped his clothes and ran for the bathroom like the place was on fire. A couple of seconds later I heard the shower running and a few moments after that it stopped and he was running back out with a wet towel draped around his thin waist. "Fast, huh?" He beamed and started to squirm into his clothes, his back to me, after I had turned my head. He was modest for his age.

"Uh, huh . . . Superman's got nothing on you." I said.

"Funny, Mom!"

I gathered the rest of our stuff and crammed it into our suitcases as he dressed. I had hardly slept at all. I couldn't stop thinking of our house and what I wanted to do. I had lain awake for hours and thought of my childhood at Suncrest and my family. A lot of the memories were golden, but many more were overshadowed by the terrible ones. Coming home had called them all out of their tiny cracks and crannies.

"You wouldn't believe this dumb dream I had last night, Mom . . . whew! was it wild!" He spoke to me with his back turned, still buttoning his shirt. When he turned, he still hadn't seen my reaction.

"A dream?" Something flashed through my mind.

"Crazy. I dreamed I was running through a bunch of trees, I think. Something was chasing me but I couldn't see it very good."

"Something?"

"Yeah, I don't know what it was, but I knew I didn't want it catching me, no way!" He looked up and met my eyes. "I was real scared. I remember that. In my dream I was real scared, I mean."

Inside of me, ominous whispers fluttered around my heart and I hoped that my son couldn't see the sparks of fear in my eyes. For a second, I felt frozen.

"Just a dream, son. That's all. I think everyone has those kinds of dreams. Symbolic. That's what it's supposed to be." I zipped up the suitcase and smiled up at him.

"What did it mean, then?" He cocked his eyebrow at me, waiting.

"Oh, well, I think I read somewhere that it's the fears you don't want to express during your waking hours . . . fears of the world and the unknown; you're trying to run away from the things in life that frighten you. It's pretty common so don't worry about it." I lifted the suitcase and swept my eyes one last time over the room to see if we had left anything. I wanted to move on and forget what we had just discussed.

"Oh," he said, following me to the door. I opened it and we stepped out into the bright daylight. "It was just so real, though," he added weakly, squinting his eyes up at the sun.

We loaded the stuff back inside the car after I had locked the door from the outside and returned the key to the office.

"It's warm out," Jeremy exclaimed, rolling down his window and leaning out, his face tipped up to the sun's warmth. It had to be at least sixty out.

It was the first of April. Snow last night and warm sunlight today. Life never ceased to surprise me. After what I'd been through, nothing surprised me anymore.

"By the way, what time is it?" He was peering up at the sun.

I snuck a glance at my watch. "About seven, I'd say."

"In a hurry, aren't you?" he said sarcastically, then softened it with an honest smile. "I only get up this early to go to school," he said. "Is this a school day?"

"No. It's Saturday." I parked by a sleek little Camaro in front of a truckstop that advertised EAT in huge red letters over the door. Underneath it said: *GOOD FOOD. OPEN TWENTY-FOUR HOURS.*

I wanted to see if the sign was telling the truth.

"Okay, I'll fill your belly with gooey pancakes before I put you to work."

But he was already out of the car and in the place before I finished the sentence. I followed him in and spotted him in a back booth, gesturing wildly to me, a tired looking waitress already standing patiently over him, order book in hand.

The pancakes weren't half bad. The coffee was fantastic. I ordered two large paper cups to go and a bag full of goodies to take to the house. There would be no food there, of course, and yesterday before we left the apartment I had fried up a mess of chicken and made potato salad to use in an emergency. With what we had in the bag, and the cooler, it should keep us happy all day.

When we drove up in front of my grandmother's house I had a chance to really see it for the first time as an adult. Maybe it was me or maybe it was my maturity, but it didn't look like it had when I was a child. Nothing looked like I had pictured it all these years. Suncrest was a little country town on the outskirts of a little larger town. It seemed strange not to see houses back to back, doorstep to doorstep like I had become used to. This was a sleepy rural town with a small population. Everyone knew everyone else and liked it that way. I wondered if they remembered my family. Probably. People like these don't forget tragedy that easily.

The streets were still narrow, graveled affairs that wound here and there like a skinny snake. People didn't lock their doors at night, feeling safe without such measures. The police department was small and probably wouldn't know what to do with a homicide if one fell into their lap. I'd noticed a few stores here and there, even a new, larger shopping center on the edge of town that hadn't been there years ago. A few new businesses dotted the main streets and some new houses had been built.

My grandmother's house sat all alone on a large square of land. The next house had to be almost a mile away. It was sheltered by towering trees and yards of black iron fence. To me, a recent city girl, it looked like a mansion.

Except for a few things, I realized Suncrest *was* pretty much the same as it had been when I was a child. *I* was the one that had changed.

I maneuvered the car up the weed infested driveway on the left of the house and parked. I took a deep breath. Here goes nothing . .

"Where's the hammer?" I turned to Jeremy. He always seems to know where everything was.

"In the trunk in that red box, remember? You jammed it in there yourself so you wouldn't forget where you had put it." He giggled and got out of the car.

I got out to unlock the trunk and rummaged through the assortment of boxes and bags until I found the hammer. I strolled up to the fence where Jeremy was waiting for me and swung it open. It didn't want to move easily and both of us had to push with all our might. Years of accumulated rust and weeds had frozen it in place, and the latch was broken. The corroded pieces finally slipped off and fell into the dried bushes. It opened.

"Well, I got to admit, Mother, you've done it this time." He stood there with his hands on his hips, shaking his head up at me. "This place is a real mess. It looks like a reject from the Twilight Zone." He grimaced as he walked up the front porch steps and craned his neck to scale the front of the house. Reject from the Twilight Zone . . . inwardly I wanted to laugh at the way children picked things up. After all these years they'd started reruns of The Twilight Zone again and Jeremy was one of their biggest fans. It had become a nightly ritual, watching that show. He was fascinated with them, and I found myself reluctantly joining him and remembering the twisted plots and twisted remarks Jimmy used to make about them.

"It's home, so respect it," I said, taking the hammer viciously to the ends of the wooden slats. They came away easily, rotted and broken. "Beggars can't be choosers." Jonathan had loved cliches and after all those years with him, some of them still popped into mind and out of my mouth before I could stop them. I hated cliches.

"And you're saying we're beggars?" Jeremy was taking the boards from me as I pryed them off and piling them neatly on the corner of the porch.

I eyed him seriously for a second over my shoulder and then grinned. "No man's a beggar who has love." Another cliche? Jesus!

"And we got plenty of that . . . pretty good, mom." He nodded, laying another board aside. I thought the porch looked well preserved for its age. The wood was only rotted through in a few places that I could see. It was standard slate grey. I was thinking more in the way of a warm chocolate brown. I might even go ahead and paint the whole house in shades of browns and tans. That always looks nice. It would be a job, though, because I could tell that there would be a lot of back breaking scraping to do first. The house looked like it had leprosy.

"There!" I yanked the last board off the door. Then I started on the windows. "There's no use in going in until we let some light in the place . . ." I grunted, already breathing harder at the exertion. "Otherwise, we won't be able to see a thing."

"Like a spook house, huh?"

"Something like that." We tediously went from one window to another until they were all open. I counted three broken panes. Which was nothing less than remarkable for how long the place had been left alone and untended. "We'll patch them with cardboard for now and fix them later." When I had known that we were going to come out here and claim the house and the lawyer told me what kind of shape it was in I had gone out and bought a set of those those 'fix-it-yourself' books. I figured we'd have to do most of the work ourselves and if it was written down in clear instructions, I should be able to do anything, or die trying. I was a great believer in self-teaching and learning by experience. I'd try anything once.

"Let's go in. After you." I waved my hand and bowed towards Jeremy. I handed him the little golden key the lawyer had sent me weeks ago and Jeremy twisted it until there was an audible click and the door swung open. We clapped. "Ladies first." He stepped aside after peeking in. Years of dust clung to everything like barnacles on the bottom of a sunken ship and long thick spider webs hung suspended in the stale air before us. I brushed them away with a wooden slat. I couldn't stand to touch them.

"Was this place *ever* clean?" Jeremy asked as we looked at the inside in awe. It was so big compared to what we were used to. There were white lumps everywhere . . . furniture covered with sheets and blankets. I began to shove the mottled, dirt-encrusted curtains apart, uncovering the windows. Some I just ripped right down off the rods because they were in such bad shape. Jim would be bringing all my curtains with the other stuff in a few days. I thought what a good idea it had been carefully packing away all the apartment's old curtains as I bought new ones. I liked changes and after a few years I could get tired of any color or pattern and the curtains would go. It was a good thing the apartment's motif had always been old-fashioned. Modern would definitely not look good in this house.

The dust could have choked a horse. "Yes . . ." I muttered as I went around the large room and yanked sheets off the old furniture. Memories came flooding back and I felt a lump rise in my throat. "My grandmother was an immaculate housekeeper when she was alive. This place was once a showcase, I'll tell you that. Nothing was ever out of place." I felt sad just looking at it now. Seeing her old home made me remember how much we all had loved her and I found myself missing her for the first time in many years. I found that the place wasn't the same without her.

I would have done anything to have gone back to those innocent childhood days. I ached for the old familiar smiles, the sound of stomping footsteps and the people I had once loved so much. I missed my family and coming here only made the ache and loss more acute; much more so than it had been in many years. What was I doing back here? How could I be happy here?

Silently, I made my way through the rest of the house, my mind full of memories as I rambled through the rooms, remembering this or that piece of furniture. Jeremy seemed to sense what I was experiencing and respected it by hanging back as we explored the large house.

It had eight rooms, three large ones on the first floor, a kitchen, a dining room and a living room in the front of the house. The upstairs consisted of five rooms; a bath, three bedrooms and a bright sewing room where my grandmother used to conduct her seances. I stood alone at the bay window and laying my hand on the cold pane, searched the scene outside. I could see for a long distance. All the way over to where my own house once stood, and the fields and the woods creeping along the horizon. I lifted the curtain away from the window. The light brightened noticeably across the room in a dazzling yellow shaft as the dust particles danced in the stream of sunlight.

My eyes were glued to the view as if mesmerized into a trance. My head began to hum and my hands turned very cold. I began to tremble with the feeling that something was coming for me—but too far away to really reach me, yet. The old cherry tree that Jim and I used to climb . . . the woods . . . the old house . . . the vision blurred and I wiped my eyes as if I had been weeping. As I watched, the ruins seemed to come alive. Whispers swirled in my head like angry bees. I strained, leaning against the window, to understand what they were trying to tell me but they were too faint. I shook my head to clear them away. My fingers feathered against the windows, down, down . . . I slid slowly, soundlessly, to the floor, my head slipping across the glass. I was having a vision as I had so many times before . . . but here it was different. I knew that if I let go I would fall into eternity. I would be vulnerable and unprotected.

Gasping, I struggled not to faint, not to give up. The cry that issued from deep within me came out silently . . . I don't want to see. *I don't want to see it again!*

The woods. The child's pathetic body mangled and bloody. . .

The past? Oh, my God . . . *the future* . . .

The vision was so vivid I could almost reach out and touch it. Little actors in a bloody play. No. *No!* I was sobbing now as I pulled myself up along the window ledge and my eyes swept the sea of browns and greys outside. It was April now, but the winter had left its mark.

Far away on the edge of the woods something hovered. Something slithered across the very edge of my sight and my heart turned into a lump of ice. I followed it as it moved, something only *my* eyes could see. I heard a laugh echoing through and I heard a child's broken wail on the air.

And far away I saw . . .

My fingers froze to the glass and my eyes flew open,

unable to pull away from what I was seeing. I cringed inside. A child was being tortured and I couldn't help, couldn't lift a finger. I wished I could hide it from my mind's eye, block the voice screaming out in pain, but I could not move; it was as though I were being forced to watch. Had it happened long ago? Or was it going to happen now?

Charlie! Charlie!

And the hated, demonic voice penetrated the frailty of my conscience, forcing me to listen.

I have waited S-A-R-A-H . . . for you . .

The trance broke like a crumbling dam and I screamed. One perfect scream that finally cut through the fog and released me. I was thrown back from the window and sprawled on the floor like a rag doll.

How could I fight it? How could I stop what was to happen?

When Jeremy came running up the steps and knelt down beside me, I had already composed myself and wiped the tears from my face. I was baffled, confused at the sheer power of what I had sensed. My hands were shaking so badly that I sat on them to keep Jeremy from seeing.

I had been challenged and I had been warned. It made no difference because I was also trapped. I had just been told I could not escape. *Would* not, this time.

"Mom! Are you all right?" Jeremy was blubbering all over me, his small angelic face as white as a sheet. "I heard you scream and I came as fast as I could. Mom?" He shook my shoulder, glancing quickly around the room to see what might have frightened me. I took him into my arms and held him tightly. I was afraid more for him than for me. The trap had been baited with honey and I had fallen into the thick of it. The door had closed and there was no going out the same way I had foolishly wandered in. *It* wouldn't let us leave now. *It* had us just where it wanted us; had wanted us all these years.

I took my son's face into my hands and looked into his eyes for a brief second. I saw the fear in them, the concern, and I sealed my heart. I pulled my courage back off the floor where I had dropped it a minute ago and took a deep breath. "I'm alright. Nothing to worry about. I just fell and, I think, I might have twisted my ankle, that's all." I lied. I never lied to Jeremy but at that moment I wanted to protect my son in any way I could. He mustn't know. He mustn't suspect. Until I could decide what we would do I didn't want to frighten him with ghosts and visions. He wouldn't understand. "I guess I slipped on something over there by the window . . ." I made a big show of trying to stand with his help and limping around a little to make my story believable. I had left visible slide marks in the dust on the window where I had fallen, supporting my story, and Jeremy accepted the fabrication as any child would. Such blind trust.

"You ought to be more careful, Mom," he clucked, helping me back down the steps. I braced myself along the walls and large chunks of plaster fell and clattered down ahead of us.

The color had once been baby blue like the kitchen and was now both faded and crumbling with age and neglect. The whole house was in a terrible state and I knew it would take a lot of elbow grease. Jeremy chattered away a mile a minute, oblivious of the heavier thoughts churning inside *my* head. We are like plowhorses with large blinders on sometimes. We only see what is right in front of us; especially when we know there is danger flowing on either side. My mind calculated how to put our *real* life into shape. How to fix up our new home and how to take care of bills and what to have for supper. What color to paint the living room. Where to start the extensive cleaning. How to stay alive from this morning to this coming night!

How to stay alive. How to escape or kill what surely wanted to kill us.

We worked almost all day cleaning the mess out of the house. Jeremy helped me carry some of the furniture out in the back yard and stack it up. The house seemed to contain everything I remembered, as if nothing had been touched from the day my grandmother died. Most of the stuff was still in good condition, even valuable because of its age, and I planned on refinishing it back to its original state. We swept the floors on the lower level and cleaned everything in sight until it shone. Jeremy had brought a portable radio and we turned the music up loud as we worked. I worked myself mercilessly and tried to forget what I had heard that morning; but only succeeded in making all my muscles ache like hell. The voice lingered in the back of my mind.

There was a well in the back of the house and I was surprised to see it hadn't dried up. The water spurted erratically from the pump, tinged with rust and sediment, but it was still usable and drinkable. Jeremy held his nose and made faces when he drank it. But it was still water and we needed it.

By the time the sun was sinking through the sky I had to admit that the lower floor was more than livable, even cozy, if you didn't think about how filthy the rugs and upholstery really were. We'd taken the rugs outside and shook them but until the rest of our stuff came that was about all we could do.

We'd come prepared in some ways. Jeremy lugged in the sleeping bags and lanterns from our camping days, and we cleared a space in the middle of the living room to sleep. It had warmed up some and Jeremy begged to stay in the house all night. I didn't argue. I was so tired we could have been in Alaska in the middle of an ice floe and I wouldn't have cared. Anything was better than that bug trap down the road we had spent last night in.

We devoured the chicken by lantern light and crawled into our sleeping bags side by side; arms around each other. Jeremy fell right asleep in my arms but I lay awake for a long time, clicking off an invisible list of things done and things yet to do.

And I listened. I listened to the creaking sounds of an old house that was surely objecting to our disruptive presence.

I listened to see if I could hear the voices, but the night was deathly still and only our breathing echoed through the rooms around me. *It* was sleeping as we were trying to do. Or was it only waiting?

From the moment I had first seen the ruins of my old home, I knew that someone, or something, had deliberately burned the old place down to the ground.

"They burned it down, didn't they?" I whispered to the silent house. "It was blamed for the evil and was their sacrifice, wasn't it?" A tear settled in the corner of my eye.

Something was with us in the house. I could feel it. But I wasn't afraid of it. It wasn't what lived in the woods. I knew that. Something shifted in the room behind us and faint murmurs wavered just beyond my sense of hearing. "They burned it down to the ground . . . after we left, didn't they?" I asked again.

No answer. But the feeling of condemnation was strong.

I understood what it wanted. "Yes. Yes. After we ran. Fled. Yes, we were afraid!" It was a confession and it was a revelation. A truth that had gnawed at me for thirteen years. "We should have stayed, right, and fought it?"

For one second I could have sworn something soft and faint had settled on my shoulder and whispered agreement. Something as light as fingers from the grave . . .

"Would it have helped if we would have stayed? Would more of us be alive today?" I asked the room, closing my eyes and sighing. Can a ghost touch the living?

My mind was suddenly filled with images of the woods and the dark hulking shape that abided and brooded there. Something had put it there in my mind; something was trying to tell me something. Who? I sat up and strained my eyes searching the room.

Grandmother? I said softly. *"What does it want?"* There was a scurrying of shadows and sighs trembling through the rooms. Finally it faded away back into the night and the house was empty again.

I began to drift off to sleep feeling safer than I had in a

long time. I had lerned the secret of the house. It was not a trap, it was our sanctuary. My grandmother had promised me all those years to help me. She had loved all of us with a very strong love and she hadn't forgotten me. She had been dead a long time . . . but she was going to help me just like she had promised.

Content, I went to sleep.

CHAPTER SEVEN

Jeremy wasn't there when I awoke. Enveloped in a sleepy fog, I studied his empty sleeping bag, afraid to think of anything else. It was chilly in the house and I crawled out of my own cocoon, shivering, and went to look for him. We'd both slept in our clothes last night and they felt damp to my touch.

As I walked slowly up the stairs I told myself that I was silly to worry. I couldn't keep Jeremy by my side every second of the day; we couldn't live like that. I listened and heard a suspicious shuffling above me.

"Jeremy, is that you?"

The house seemed so strange all of a sudden. My nose was runny and I wiped it with the back of my hand. How many weeks, months before this home for spooks became a real home? I was beginning to have doubts if this house could ever fill that bill. "Jeremy!"

"Here, Mom!"

He was lounging at the end of the porch, his feet dangling over the edge of the rotted railing, a left-over piece of chicken half way to his mouth. He turned to wave it at me.

"Neat, huh?" He meant the porch. We'd never had anything quite like it. "I'm just enjoying the morning. It's so pretty out." I could hear the birds chirping in chorus all around us. The sky was a cloudless blue. "You were so tired I just tip-toed out so I wouldn't wake you." He gnawed at the chicken.

"I was a little tired." I pulled him gently off the railing. "If we're going to sit out here, let's spread a blanket and sit where we can't fall off . . . I don't want you splitting your skull. Hear?" I peered down at the drop and all the concrete and stairs below.

"Yes, Mom." He nodded his head, crossing his legs and squatting down on the floor. "You worry too much. I can take care of myself."

"Sure you can." I didn't tell him that he was all I had. A child could only take so much of that. I was at the railing taking large gulps of clean country morning air. There was the scent of rain somewhere. It smelled like my childhood. I couldn't believe a place this beautiful existed anymore. In the April sunlight I could believe in anything, even fairy tales. This was our new beginning—nothing was going to steal it from me.

"It's late. We've got work to do." I smiled up at the sun, shading my eyes. He thought I hadn't seen him wipe his greasy fingers all over his blue jeans. I kept smiling and turned to look at him. "Ready to work . . . or do you want more to eat?"

He grinned. "No. I'm full now. What do we do today?"

"Well, I guess what we should do is go and enroll you in the neighborhood grade school."

"Are you kidding? It's Sunday!" He stood there defiantly. He had no sense of humor, Jonathan's child.

"Easy." I put up my hand. "Can't take a joke?"

"Sure."

He didn't see the glint in my eye. "But that is something we should take care of in the next few days."

"Mom? Let's face it, you need help here . . . and what's a few days anyway? Didn't I make all A's and B's last time?" His look was a plea.

"No, a few days couldn't hurt anything, you're right."

"Good! Let's go paint the house!" Everything was forgotten and he ran ahead of me down the stairs out to the car to get the paint out of the trunk. I found I wasn't very hungry. I tied a scarf over my hair and started to get out the paint brushes. We brought in water from the pump to scrub down the walls first.

We were working on the third wall in the living room and white paint was splattered on the sheets I had spread over the floors as well as all over us. There was probably more paint in my hair than on all the walls. I fell to the job with relish. It helped me forget all the unanswered questions that were squirming away in the back of my mind.

"Mom, there's someone at the door!" Jeremy yelled and ran to answer it.

It was the lawyer.

"I saw the car outside and I suspected it was you .. or else very gutsy burglars. I'm Clarence Largo." He put out a small hairy hand for me to shake. He was a small man. When I stood up and took his offered hand, I towered at least six inches over his silvery white head. He had one of those serious, thin faces typical of an old-time lawyer. No laugh lines, yet his grey eyes shone with intelligence and humor.

"I'm Sarah Towers." I smiled, aware of the paint cracking on my face. He merely nodded, looking me over first and then my son. He finally smiled and reached out to pat Jeremy's head fatherly.

"This is my son, Jeremy," I added.

He looked past us to the now white walls. "I gather you're staying awhile then?" He seemed nervous, but extremely curious. His sharp eyes ate everything in sight.

"Yes. But there's a lot of work to do, as you can see. It would help," I dropped a hint, "if we had electricity and heat."

His bushy white eyebrows rose and he seemed to be studying me closely. Too closely. "I'll take care of that. My sister-in-law works at the power company and she can pull a couple of strings here and there. I promise you, everything will be working tomorrow. I even have a handyman in mind to check up on everything. Plumbing, wiring . . . general condition of the house." He winked at me.

"Thank you. That's very kind of you."

"No. I'm just doing my job." He pulled a pen out of his tweed jacket's breast pocket, and then a small white card. "I'll just leave you my number so you can call me if you need something." He look up at me with those piercing eyes of his and I had the feeling there was something he wasn't telling me. "Don't hesitate. Any time."

"I don't have a phone yet . . ."

He smiled, already backing towards the still open door. So he was in a hurry to leave, was he? I realized then with a start that he was frightened. Frightened of what?

"I'll take care of that too," he said quickly. "I have an appointment." He glanced at his watch to make it look good. "I'll be dropping by again. I have that letter for you." I caught actual distaste in his tone. "I don't have it with me now. You see, this was a surprise visit. I didn't know I was coming myself." His smile was genuine but weak. His hand was balanced on the door, his face very white suddenly. Could he feel it, too, then? "I'll be sure to have it next time I come."

I couldn't resist asking him: "Did you know my grandmother, Mr. Largo?" His reaction shocked me.

"No! She was my brother's client many years ago and when he died I took the case over for him like I did all the rest." He spread his hands. His voice was almost a whisper. "I thought you would never come to claim . . . your inheritance." He cleared his throat and tried to smile. "I knew your family, though." The words froze in the air between us and neither one of us could say another word. Now I knew why he was acting so funny. "You look just like your mother. Remarkable." His eyes darted around the changing room. "You have your work cut out for you." I knew he had changed the subject on purpose and I knew better than to ask any more personal questions. If the rest of the neighborhood reacted to us like he was doing, we were going to be two very lonely people. He looked at me as if I were a ghost.

"But it'll be beautiful when we're done. My brother's coming to help." I was trying to be friendly anyway. We'd need a friend.

"Your brother?" His face was blank.

"Jim. He's coming to help, too."

"Anyone else?"

"No, we're all that's left," I replied. I shrugged and shook his hand goodbye. "I appreciate your help. Thank you."

"No bother. No bother. I'll be seeing you again." He was suddenly in a very real hurry to get out of the house. I was beginning to believe that the people around here must just take for granted that the house was haunted, or worse. That was the only explanation for his unusual behavior. He seemed like a nice enough man otherwise.

Jeremy walked him out to his car, a sporty blue Mercedes. So business wasn't too bad around here, I thought, amused, as I watched from the window until he drove off. It had been a short visit.

Jeremy came back in and picked up his brush. "Mr. Largo said that his wife's gonna send over supper for us. Some kind of noodles and . . . something." He scratched his head and clump of white paint ran down his wrist. "Chicken, I think he said."

"That was real nice of him." I was surprised. Maybe he was trying to make up for the shabby way he rushed in and just rushed out—or maybe he just felt sorry for us. "Ah," I teased Jeremy, "just when I was going to make the biggest, best supper . . ."

"You *hate* to cook. It sounds good to me. A good home cooked meal, *finally*." He stressed the last word and kept painting. He had more on the sheets than on the walls. But he tried: "The stove doesn't work anyway."

We didn't finish the whole room that day. The supper came, hand-delivered by Mrs. Largo, a sweet little woman with bright red hair. She practically dropped the food on the porch and ran. I hardly had time to say thank you before she was gone.

Was everyone going to react to us like this?

CHAPTER EIGHT

I stared out the window that night as Jeremy slept behind me in his sleeping bag. I would be glad when the heat was on, I shivered. Maybe, Jim would come tomorrow.

Once Jim came I knew I would feel better about everything.

It had been years since I had seen my younger brother. It had been too long. I had missed him even though he was always on the edge of my thoughts. I wondered how much he had changed. The last time I saw him he was still in the throes of the rock cult, complete with shoulder length hair and wire-rimmed glasses. The glasses weren't just for show, though, he couldn't see a thing without them. I always told him it was because he stayed up all night writing his music and lyrics. I wondered if he still dreamed of being a songwriter. He had informed me years ago that the traveling life wasn't for him. I wondered how he felt, still being bounced around from one town to another with a group of rag-tag musicians, playing what they wanted and how they wanted it. There was more to it I believed. If Jim wanted to just write music he would have found a way. There must have been another reason why he traveled with the band and did dives and one night stands like he did. I didn't see how he could stand that nomad life. He had always put such store in a real home.

Had he been running in his own way, too, all this time? Maybe, he knew what was waiting here for us? Then why was he coming back?

I was tired and freezing. I finally crawled into my sleeping bag next to Jeremy, trying to share his warmth. Tomorrow the electricity and heat would be turned on and then we'd see if that old relic of a furnace downstairs still worked, if the plumbing would hold out, and the wires in the walls wouldn't catch fire and burn the house down! I fell asleep envisioning Jeremy and I crazily plugging leaks in the rusted pipes with hunks of rags and fighting flash fires in the archaic wiring system. It was a deep, dreamless sleep; so deep that it was with a terrible start that the unwelcome noises roused me. Someone was pounding frantically on our door and I felt that old familiar chill start at my toes and spread throughout my whole being. Loud, angry echoes boomed throughout the house and the smell of roses was choking me. In that first second of wakefulness I entertained the tiniest of hopes that it was Jim knocking at the door, but almost in the same second I new it wasn't.

I stared at the door and slowly got up, walking on eggs all the way across the floor. I laid my hand on the knob and felt the hairs on my neck stand on end. Something was behind me! I spun around and the same drowning sensation that had overwhelmed me in my grandmother's seance room attacked me again, only much stronger.

Behind me the horrendous pounding vibrated through the house. I clapped my hands over my ears. "Who is it?" I cried, turning to gape at the trembling door in terror. My mouth was as dry as cotton and my heart was doing a rain-dance in my chest.

DON'T OPEN THE DOOR . . . SARAH . . . DON'T OPEN IT! A cold whisper of warning came from somewhere behind me.

"Who is it?" I hissed at the door. "What do you want?" Was I dreaming? Was this all a nightmare? No, I was awake and it was real. I pinched myself and tried to clear my wild thoughts. What should I do? Jeremy was still asleep; didn't he hear that noise? How could he *not* hear it?

The pounding grew more insistent. Louder. The whole house was shaking. But I obeyed the voice behind me and didn't open the door. "My God!" I whimpered, leaning up against the wall, trying to keep from screaming or fainting with fear. Jeremy slept peacefully through the god-awful racket.

He couldn't hear it then.

I clung to the wall and prayed. The whispers swirled behind me and the pounding trickled into ghastly laughter. Laughter I had heard in the woods all those years ago.

I was safe here. I told myself over and over like a protective chant. I am safe! *It can't get in the house . . .*

Oh, how it wanted to . . . but it couldn't. It never could because it was not allowed.

"Go away then . . . just go away!" I told it, angry for the first time. How dare it terrorize my son and me? How dare it destroy and kill with its evil? "Go away!" I ordered, my mouth up against the door and my head leaning against it. Suddenly I was so angry. . . and the laughter trickled slowly off into the night like a train whistle fading into the distance.

"Go away!"

The pounding stopped abruptly, faded away into the night, until there was nothing. Silence. Blessed, empty silence.

Like a whiplash the vertigo came and I clung desperately to consciousness with all my strength. Something was pulling at me and willing me to follow until the sensation was overpowering.

I turned and reached out my fingers to what stood guard behind me. *"Grandmother!"* I shrieked as I was sucked into eternity. *I was no longer Sarah; I was someone else. I was no* longer in the house but far away . . . in time.

A long woolen cape clung to me and flapped softly against my ankles and I was a young boy running through the woods. Stunned, I hid behind a tall tree and fought to keep from screaming. Who was I? Where was I? It was night and the wind was cold and rain splattered my hair. I stared down at myself. Loose fitting peasant shirt and heavy britches. My fingers followed the strange lines of a stranger's face. I began to run, hearing the laughter and the footsteps rustling behind me. So close . . . I ran, stumbling and crying away from my tormentor. The shirt was spotted with wet blood . . . a child's blood. There was blood all over my hands and my bare feet. There was blood on the ground!

The boy ran, twigs breaking under his feet until he came to a tethered horse rearing and pawing at the wind. He tried to calm the badly frightened beast but still it rolled its eyes until only the whites showed as if it were in great pain.

"Hush, now, hush!" The boy soothed the horse and gathered the reins trying to gain control of the animal. "It will be all right. I promise." The boy threw himself up on the horse's bare back and its huge hooves whipped the angry air around them. "Back. Back!" he screamed. The wind rumbled with laughter as the horse battled an invisible foe whirling itself around like it was possessed. As the forest was. The boy grew angry and slapped the reins against his mount and turned it to face . . . something! His eyes flashed with brilliant fire. He would not be beaten! He would not lose this time!

Josiah . . . this time you will not escape. NOT THIS TIME!

Far away, Sarah recognized the voice and screamed.

The boy on the thrashing horse screamed at the same instant and the vision began to blur and fade. The death screams of the horse and the boy rose together to one high screech and the horse went down in its own blood, white teeth bared in a gruesome mask of agony. And the boy . . . torn to pieces.

Sarah screamed and hid her eyes as the horse went down

under her and her bones began to break under her skin, her blood showering the leaves and the trees.

Then there was blackness. Nothingness for a long time.

It could have been hours later or minutes that I moaned and felt out into the darkness. A wall, a floor . . . I opened my swollen eyes and tried to sit up.

I was back in my house. It was still night and Jeremy still lay sleeping, undisturbed. I was huddled up against the silent door, sobbing in the dark.

What had happened? Where had I been? I shook my head and wiped the tears from my face and crawled back to my sleeping bag, trembling. There had to be answers somewhere to what I had seen and experienced and I knew I had to find them.

It might have been another time or another life . . . but I knew the boy on the horse. It was Jimmy. He had died in that horrible way that night long ago.

I lay awake trying to understand what it all meant. I sat guard next to my son for the rest of the night and as dawn's thin fingers crept into the house I finally felt safe enough to close my eyes.

CHAPTER NINE

I must have fallen asleep because I awoke again to a soft knocking at the door. But it was clearly a human knock this time. I stumbled to the door. The clear light of day all but obliterated the terrifying episode of the night before. I found myself doubting it had ever happened; surely it had just been a nightmare? No, I knew better...

I first peeked out the window and saw the old battered truck with the U-Haul behind it and with a relieved smile, I flung open the door. "Thank God! It's you Jim! I thought you'd never get here!" I laughed and threw my arms gratefully around the man standing in my doorway—only it wasn't Jim.

"Oh, I'm sorry!" I snatched back my embrace, red-faced. "I thought you were my brother!" A tall, dark-haired stranger was framed in the doorway, blocking out the sun. I looked up into his laughing eyes. He still had his arms around my waist, and wouldn't let go. I firmly withdrew his hands, angry that he was so amused by my error.

"Do you always greet strangers like that?" His deep gruff voice had the tone of authority. "I'll have to come more often!" He was tall, at least six-five, with rugged good looks. He was rakishly dressed in a faded leather jacket and blue jeans. His strange, piercing eyes examined me as if I were something he was thinking of buying.

"Not usually," I got out somehow. I was a mess. I had slept in my clothing for three nights running and I hadn't had a bath or washed my hair in days. Suddenly I felt highly embarassed and a little angry that he'd caught me looking so ragged.

"Well, it's not often that a pretty lady greets me like that. Usually I get the cold shoulder. But I liked it. I liked it a lot." Something in the set of my chin and my angry eyes must have stopped him. He put up his hand in a conciliatory gesture. "I know—you thought I was your brother."

"Yes. By the way, where is he?" I peeked around the stranger's shoulder to look outside. "That's his truck." I stated, careful not to go near him again.

It was then I saw Jim fooling around with something on the back of the truck. "Jim!" I yelped and ran past the stranger into my brother's waiting arm's.

"Sis!" He grabbed me and planted a brotherly kiss on the top of my head. Then held me away from him to get a good look at me. "You're so thin, Sarah!"

"That's the fashion, isn't it?"

"For what?" He grinned. "Toothpicks? You look terrible."

"Thanks . . . still the same old Jim, so damn truthful it hurts." Then it was my turn and hands on hips, I looked at him. The hippie of a few years ago was gone. His hair was no longer shoulder length and scraggly, but neater and shorter; the wire-rimmed glasses, however, remained. He wore cowboy boots and new blue jeans. A stetson was clutched in his hand. I thought he looked thinner, too. His shoulders drooped and there were circles smudged lightly under his eyes. But they were the same flashing green eyes I remembered laughing up at me when I was a child. Melancholy eyes that held something hidden in their murky depths that I could never understand; they were an old man's eyes. My brother looked like he was forty, instead of younger than I. A chill passed through me just looking at him . . . something was very wrong. Though Jim was

107

smiling, I could sense something struggling inside of him that reached out to me like an electric shock.

"You look pretty tired yourself," I said. "I thought you'd never get here!"

He eyed me over his thin shoulders as he jammed the tail gate of the U-Haul up and with a loud thump the whole back of the trailer came down suspended on rusty chains. "Thought I'd never get here, either." He turned and looked at me and then past me. I looked, too. "Had some trouble."

"By the way—if it's not asking too much, who is that?" I asked. The stranger was lounging against the door watching us. Something about the way he stood or the square set of his jaw reminded me insistently of someone else. It unnerved me. He casually gave me a mock salute and smiled.

"Oh, him? He's just a good samaritan. The old truck died on me about five miles back and if he hadn't come by and offered to help, I'd still be crawling around under the hood without the slightest idea what was wrong. You know how I am about engines, Sis. Don't know enough to fill a thimble. Now . . . this guy," he aimed a thumb at the nonchalant stranger, chuckling. "He knows all about them."

I sighed and turned to the man. "Seems I owe you thanks, also. That's all my furniture in the truck there. It'll be great to sleep in a real bed again. Thank you . . ." I put out my hand to shake his. He took it and I was surprised that his hand was so warm against mine. "Mr. . .?"

"Detective Raucher." Jim supplied, amused. It was a big joke to him.

I yanked my hand away immediately. I should have known . . . a *cop!* I should have recognized the stubborn set of the jaw, the arrogant stance that cried out cop. Just like Jonathan . . .

"Oh, you're a police officer?" I said coldly. "Anywhere around here?"

"Yes. Here." He smiled boldly.

"You don't look like a cop."

"What's a cop supposed to look like?" He raised a bushy eyebrow at me and threw Jim a conspiratorial glance. What had Jim told him? I wondered.

Jim chuckled and I gave him a small shove.

"Apparently not like you do, Ben." Jim shrugged. "And—oh, my—you even ride a motorcycle." He shook his head, horror in his voice.

It was only then that I happened to see the shiny black Yamaha parked in front of the house. I studied the tall man leaning against my door and was aware again of how I must look. I inched my way closer to my brother, lowering my head and trying to pull my fingers through the tangles in my hair. I felt his eyes appraising me.

"Mom?" The voice was Jeremy's. He swayed in the doorway, still half asleep and rubbing his eyes. "Who you talking to?" He looked at the detective and then over at Jim and his face lit into a smile and he was out the door in a flash and in Jim's outstretched arms. It had been years since he had seen his uncle but he seemed to know him instinctively. He threw his arms around his neck and hung on like an octopus.

"Is this Jeremy? I can't believe it! Last time I saw you, kid, you were sucking a bottle and playing with your rattle." They laughed. The Detective stood behind the two smiling. He reached out a hand and ruffled the boy's hair until he got his attention. Jim introduced the two and sent Jeremy off with a playful swat to his behind. "Get in the house. It's cold out here." But Jeremy had seen the morotcycle and headed right for it. The detective walked up around the other side and showed him his bike, explaining how it ran. The motor roared suddenly into life, disturbing the early morning silence. I marveled at how I could have slept through its arrival.

Jeremy looked up in awe at the stranger as they talked over the loud hum of the machine. He had made a friend. I looked on in displeasure, knowing full well that once my son knew the stranger was a cop, he would idolize him—a sort of surrogate father, you might say. I heard Jeremy ask him for a ride.

The detective glanced up at me and the sunlight streaked through his wavy hair. He was very good looking. "Maybe sometime . . . if your mom says it's alright, that is," I heard him promise. Jeremy's pleading eyes focused on me.

"Maybe sometime. Later. We have work to do." I motioned towards the loaded U-Haul and the full truck in front of it.

I hadn't meant to rope in the detective but he started to roll up his sleeves with a huge grin. "Well, let's start moving in this stuff . . . I haven't got all day." He tapped his watch. "I have to be on duty in two hours." I tried to protest, looking first at Jim and then at him, but they both ignored me. "Don't look a gift horse in the mouth, Sis." Jim nodded and jumped up on the tailgate of the U-Haul.

"Detective . . . you don't have to help. We can manage," I said stubbornly.

"Sarah, right?" He stated more than asked as he grabbed the end of the couch and started to pull, pushing me rudely out of the way. "Call me Ben. I'm a human being, too, you know. And I'd be a fool if I didn't take advantage of helping a pretty woman out, now, wouldn't I?"

I gaped at him. I didn't much care for his pushy manner and I was liking him less every moment. He was just like all the rest of them. Pushy, arrogant, and probably a wolf. It was disgusting. I glared at him as he helped Jim carry in the couch, but he seemed oblivious to my growing hatred. The angrier I became, the more he smiled and winked at me. I figured the best way to discourage him was to just simply ignore him. Maybe, he'd go away, like a headache.

"Mom, he's a neat guy!" Jeremy was next to me. "He said he'd give me a ride on his motorcycle next time he came over. Wow!" Then he was climbing up in the back of the truck and dragging things out. *Over my dead body,* I vowed wordlessly.

I debated a second, standing in the bright daylight and

then, giving in with an audible groan, I started to help unload. Every time I turned around, Ben was either right behind me or in front of me. Too close. It was bad enough he wouldn't stop grinning at me, but even worse, he was a cop and I wanted none of his kind anymore. I knew what they were like and I was determined to hate every last one of them. No exceptions.

By the time he climbed up on his shiny motorcycle and roared off in a cloud of fumes, I had learned to detest him and, I'm afraid, he knew it. Usually I wasn't a rude person but I was in no frame of mind for fun and games. I had been burned too many times. A man put on a badge and a uniform and he thought he was God's gift to women. Well, this was *one* woman who wasn't going to fall for it. Not again. Not ever again. It made no difference how charming he could be.

"Thanks for helping, Ben." Jim shook his hand before he left.

Everything was in the house, not in its final place, but at least inside. Jim gave me a disappointed look and then said, "She's not always this rude, Ben. I guess she just got up on the wrong side of the bed this morning." He was making excuses for me. My own brother!

"Well, next time I'll remember to come over in the evening," Ben kidded back, smiling at me, as Jim looked on. "Is she any nicer when the sun goes down?"

"No," I threw in sarcastically not being able to resist it. "At night I'm a real bitch." I knew I shouldn't be acting this way but something in his cocky manner ticked me off. Something about him made me boiling mad. It was his attitude, I guess.

"She's kidding, Ben. Come back anytime." Jim threw me a warning look and slapped Ben on the back.

Jeremy just listened, watching the two of us.

"Nope, I don't think she is," Ben replied without even a ghost of a smile. When he looked at me, in that second, I saw something different in his eyes that hadn't been there before. Suddenly he was being serious.

"You treated him like dirt," my brother said as soon as Ben was gone. "Why did you do that? After all, he helped me get here and then he helped carry in all that stuff when he didn't really have to." Jim wasn't really mad at me but he was confused.

"He's a cop," was all I said and walked back into the house. Behind me Jim was silent.

CHAPTER TEN

We began to put things in their place or at least where I thought they should be. It seemed strange to see all my old stuff from the apartment rearranged in the huge house. I'd always liked the look of solid wood and was so pleased to see most of the furniture fit in. As we worked, Jim kept going on an on about Ben Raucher. I couldn't seem to understand why he kept cramming the man down my throat. Then he said, "I have a feeling he'll come back."

"Oh, now you're the psychic?" I purposely was trying to keep my mood light because after all I was glad that Jim was there beside me helping us and I was appreciative that Detective Raucher had helped him get here, but truthfully I just didn't like the man. I didn't want to talk about him anymore. If he was half as smart as he had pretended to be then he would have gotten the hint and we'd never see him again.

"He seemed like a real nice guy to me. The strong and protecting type. You just took him wrong."

"What you're saying, in effect, is that I need a strong and protecting type, huh?" I put the last chair on the tapestry rug we had laid in the living room. The house was shaping up so fast I couldn't believe the changes we were producing. In just a few days a wooden shell had evolved into a stately home. Against my will I found myself becoming possessive of it. It was mine and it could be beautiful. I knew I didn't want to leave it.

"You need someone, Sarah." Jim was looking intensely at me.

"You're wrong. I don't need anybody," I snapped at him. "Especially an arrogant, smart-mouthed cop!"

"Is that what you have against the guy? You hate his guts just because he's a cop like Jonathan was?"

"That's not the only reason." I put the coffee table in front of the couch, a solid squat dark wooden table that I had always loved. "I need another man like a hole in the head and I need another cop like *two* holes in the head. Forget it!" I looked him straight in the eyes. He looked so tired but there was a brightness glittering in his eyes that I had never noticed before. Relenting, I said, "Jim, don't get me wrong. I'm not a man-hater, not by a long shot, It's just that I need time to find myself first. Before I get tangled up with another man, I need to please myself for once." I sighed into the space between us as he watched me with thoughtful eyes. "I don't know who I am yet. Let me find myself first, alright? Men can wait."

Jim placed my little dome-glassed lamp on the edge of the coffee table. "This where you want it, Sis?" He had mercifully dropped the other subject.

"That's fine." I smiled. Almost everything was in place and half the day was already gone. "I think it's time to take a break. How about you? You hungry?"

Jim rewarded me with a grateful smile. "Very hungry. I ran out of money two days ago and I haven't eaten since." He pulled the linings of his pockets inside out to show me that they were empty. "See—no money."

I felt instantly guilty. In all the excitement of moving I had entirely forgotten to leave him any money for the U-Haul or the gas to get it down here. Apparently he had had to shell it all out of his own pocket and, being Jim, he would never have uttered a word about it, either.

"Jim . . . I'm sorry!" I clapped my hands together silently and pressed them against my mouth for a second. "I forgot! I was in such a hurry," I confessed sheepishly. "I'll pay you back, don't worry."

"I'm not worried." He seemed disappointed in me. "And you don't have to pay anything back. I insist! I still got a week's pay coming from the last place we played, only I didn't stick around to collect it. The band's going to send it here as soon as they get it. I had to leave a day before our engagement was formally over."

"You didn't tell me you had to run out on the band to do this for me! I never would have asked you to do that."

"Wild horses couldn't have kept me away, Sarah!" he swore. "You know that. Anytime you need me, that comes first. The band can do without me a few nights. They'll get someone to fill in and cover for me. I'm not worried about it so don't you be."

"I'm still sorry and I'm still going to pay you back."

"Great, then pay me back in food. I'm starving! Some of your home cooking is all the paying back I need. I'm so sick of one-night stands, and whiskey smelling bars with their greasy food, I could just go to sleep and never wake up. Good riddance!"

"Well, sorry again, the home cooked meal will have to wait for a day or two until the electricity gets turned back on, but then, I promise, I'll stuff you until you're fat as a pig. But for now I can get you a good breakfast. There's a fairly good restaurant down the road and I'm sure I can get carry-outs. How does bacon and eggs, biscuits and steaming hot coffee sound?"

"Fantastic! You haven't left yet?" He gently pushed me out the door after shoving my purse at me. "Get plenty of biscuits and pints of coffee!" he yelled at me as I jumped into the car. "Make sure the coffee's hot . . . I'm freezing."

On the way there I casually thought to myself, Freezing? It must be at least fifty outside now. How could he be so cold? I hoped he wasn't sick or anything. But then, he really

115

didn't look too well.

Maybe it was the long trip or the lack of food that made him appear so frail and gaunt . . . or maybe he hadn't slept much the last few days. Yes, probably that was what was wrong with my brother.

But I knew it was more than that. I knew, I just didn't want to face it. My brother was very sick and I didn't think a couple of good meals would help him any.

Later in the afternoon, we all sat on the porch talking over old times. Jeremy avidly listened to all our adventures as children. He'd taken an instant liking to my brother. It didn't surprise me because they were very much alike in many ways. Jim gulped down his food and stared out over the neighborhood. He seemed to be brooding. "Hasn't changed much, has it, Sis?" He motioned at the land and the distant housetops. "It's as if we'd never left. It's all the same."

"Not exactly. The old house burnt down. There's nothing left but a black rim of bricks and the old cherry tree."

He turned stricken eyes to me. "Have you seen it?"

I squirmed uneasily under his penetrating eyes. "Yes. Jeremy and I stopped there the first night." I found myself shivering just remembering. "There's nothing left."

"Nothing," he echoed in a tight voice. He rubbed his eyes and laughed, but his laugh was anything but light-hearted. I wondered if he was thinking about all our dead brothers and sisters. Our poor family all buried in heavy boxes six feet in the soil. I wondered if he suspected what had happened to the house.

"Ah, but you're wrong." He suddenly startled me when he whispered as if only to me. "There is something here . . . still. And for always." There was so much raw sadness in his voice that it took me off guard. I didn't know what to say but just nodded my head at him.

"You know, don't you?" It was all so clear now.

"Know what?" He was being evasive and he knew it.

"It's haunted, that's what." I didn't want to beat around the bush. Jeremy had gone to get his Match Box Collection of small cars to show to Jim and I thought it was the right time to level with my brother. But it was as if Jim hadn't heard what I said. He went on reminiscing out loud. "Do you remember that old clubhouse we used to have?" His eyes were half closed and he seemed far away. Even though I was known as a psychic there were times that I could not see those things I needed to see. This was one of those times. I would have done anything to have been able to read Jim's mind or to know what the future held for us, the sole survivors of our family. But I couldn't. It was too close to me and for some reason I wasn't allowed to glimpse it. My fate and Jim's were sealed in the mists and I could not see through the greyness.

"I remember it."

"I wonder if it's still there."

"We could look for it. Sometime. If you want to," I offered.

"Yeah, let's do that one day, Sis." He sat quietly for a while and then went on. "Do you remember that summer I slashed my foot on that broken bottle and we ran through the rain to Grandmother's house ... I wanted it to stop bleeding and you made me walk through the warm water in the culvert on the side of the roads to clean my feet off?"

"It wouldn't stop bleeding, though, I remember that. We finally had to go home and Mother was so upset ..." Visions of Jim and I no taller than Jeremy passed through my mind, splashing around in the flowing streams of sun-warmed water that traveled the gulleys across the hot roads. The water rippled gently over our hot feet and we'd play in the swirling eddies. Those days seemed so long ago. Something inside of me registered the loss. "We had to go home and you ruined three towels before it stopped bleeding."

"It hurt so much when the doctor sewed it up. It took ten stitches."

"You remember that?" I was awed at his memory. I had thought all these years that Jim had forgotten all that. I had thought that there was little of our childhood that he remembered. Maybe I had been wrong all these years. I looked at my brother closely and I saw the fright in his eyes and the strain around his mouth.

"Yes, I remember. I also remember the times I raced my bike across the street trying to beat the cars. You'd always get so mad at me for being careless."

"I just tried to protect you." I said. But there was more to it and we both knew it.

"You mean, you always knew that something was going to happen. You tried to keep me alive." He turned a tired gaze on me and gave me a weak smile. "You succeeded."

I put my head on my knees and closed my eyes. "I fell out of the cherry tree once and you were there to catch me. When I was nine my appendix burst and you cried until mother couldn't stand it anymore and made Father take me to the hospital . . . should I go on?" I bit my lip and rocked my head on my hands. "We've always looked out for each other."

"That's why we're still around I guess," Jim confessed. "But it's going to be different this time, isn't it, Sarah?" He was very calm as he slipped his shoes and socks off so he was barefooted like I was; like we had always been as children when we ran the streets of Suncrest, so wild and innocent.

"Yes, it's going to be different this time."

He shook his head as if he was very sleepy and trying to wake up. "It's this place," he said. "It seems to bring back all those memories I thought I had buried too deep to ever trip over again. I'm sorry I'm such bad company, Sis."

"You're just tired, that's all. Have you had any sleep at all in the last few days?" I asked him, concerned.

"I haven't slept well for years. There isn't a night I don't dream about . . . them. There isn't a day that doesn't pass that I don't miss them, or wonder if this is *my* last last day, or if you and Jeremy are alright . . . still alive." He stopped abruptly.

He was haunted just like me. I should have realized that he would shoulder the guilt, too. That he would feel it licking up his scent right behind him on his trail, too. We were both potential victims, living on borrowed time.

The sun had slid behind a threatening black cloud and the shadows gathered across the porch and Jim's face was hidden. I felt his hand slowly take mine. It was hot and thin and I held it tightly.

"Jeremy's just like you," he said. I couldn't see it, but I knew he was smiling. "He's some super kid. I don't want anything to happen to either one of you. That's why I'm here. I'm not going to run away anymore. I can't."

"Neither one of us can. It's called us home . . . now we pay the piper." I heard Jeremy shouting to us. It had gotten so dark all of a sudden and the stairs were probably black as pitch. I could hear him bumping around upstairs trying to find his way.

We knew we didn't have much time to talk.

"Do you know who Jeremy reminds me of?" my brother asked gravely, turning to me in the dimness. "Charlie. He looks like Charlie. Haven't you ever noticed it before? I did, right off." There was defeat in his tone. "He's not like Charlie in any other way except that. It scared me when he first came to the door downstairs when I got here . . . seeing that face framed in that doorway."

I froze because I knew what he was going to say next and I really didn't want to hear it. I put my fingers up to his lips, but he pushed them away and the grip on my hand tightened even more. "You see, I *saw* Charlie. I've *seen* Charlie lots of times over the years, but even more often lately. . . *he follows me everywhere*. He's here with me now, somewhere . . . I don't know why he haunts me. What he wants."

I gasped and whimpered, staring around into the dark. Afraid to look but more afraid not to. What Jim was telling me was frightening me more than anything that had happened to me had. Charlie and his pitiful soul belonged to *it*, the demon in the woods. We couldn't trust anything Charlie did. But Charlie was dead. Dead! Was Jim going mad? Was I?

Jim saw the way I was searching our surroundings with my eyes.

"No, I don't mean he's actually here with us this very minute. I meant he's here at Suncrest. Right before the truck died he waved at me from behind a tree down the road there. Smiled that silly smile of his, you remember, don't you?

"I've tried to trick him—catch him—for years, but he just evaporates into thin air like smoke. He's a little kid, about so high." Jim lifted his hand about three feet off the ground. "Not more than six or seven. About the age he was when he had fallen in that snow drift that time, remember?" But my brother couldn't stop the flow of words. It was as if he was afraid to stop, afraid of the silence. "Maybe he's trying to warn us? Maybe, he's trying to help us?"

"What does he talk about?" I asked carefully.

Jim laughed then and lowered his head into his hands. I thought he was crying at first. But no, he was only choking on his words. "It's always the same thing, Sarah. Always the same exact demand . . . he wants me back here . . . back here with all of them!"

I looked away. My next words came hard. "We can't trust him, Jim. Don't be fooled by him. Until we know for sure what he wants, we don't dare trust him. We need to be extremely careful." Jeremy hadn't come back yet, so I went on in a calm voice and told my brother what had happened since I had arrived. I told him about the pounding on the door and my vision. I did *not* mention my dream about him, but I told him what I was afraid of.

"We've got to get away from here, Sarah!" he exclaimed when I was done. There was terror in his voice. "Until now, I had had doubts . . . but not any longer. All three of us have got to get out of here. We were fools for even thinking we could come back." He was deadly serious and listening to him I had to consider the possibilities of what he was saying.

I looked back at the house I had hoped to make a home and something moaned deep inside of me. I belonged here. Jeremy and I belonged here in this beautiful old mansion. I didn't want to leave it. I didn't want to lose it now that I had it. Where would we go? I tried to explain all this to Jim, but I could see it wasn't getting through.

"Sarah, listen . . . I'm not sure it's safe here for any of us. You have to think about your son," he urged me making me feel guilty. After all, I was the one who wanted to stay so badly. What if I were putting Jeremy in danger by staying? If something happened to him I would blame myself. Just the thought of Jeremy in pain or threatened made my heart thud inside my chest.

"Let me think about it?" I smiled trying to make him see the silliness of it all. The late afternoon sun made the thoughts of ghosts and death much closer than I cared for.

Jim shook his head. "Can we beat *it? It* wanted us back here . . . what does *it* want now? What does *it really want?*" But his words sounded strained. Untrue. I wondered if there was really more. He sounded like he already knew all the answers.

"I know it can't touch us as long as we're in the house. We're safe here," I told him.

He eyed me suspiciously. "Or so *it* wants us to think."

"You have a point there I hadn't thought of." It upset me the second he uttered it. If he was right . . .

"Oh, Jim! How can I leave this place! I love it already. It's mine. The first real thing that's all mine . . . how can I just walk away from it?"

"You might have to, that's all," he replied dryly. "What's more important—this house or your life . . . Jeremy's life? We can't fight what we don't understand." Again I caught a hollow tone in my brother's voice. What was going on?

Somewhere far off in its forest lair, *it* must have heard those words. A cold, clammy breeze swooped down on top of us and left us shivering. It must have been listening, waiting to discover the weak link in my armor.

"You're right," I conceded. "Now we have to decide what to do. No matter what, though, I have to finish fixing this place up. No one will buy it like it is and I sure could use the money. Besides, I'd like to see this old place full of happy people again even if it isn't us. I don't want it to be alone any more. Does that sound silly?" I laughed, and was relieved to see Jim smile the first real smile since our discussion had begun. He was handsome when he smiled, I thought. He still had those freckles across his pug nose and he looked like he was ten when he smiled like that.

"No. Not coming from you. You always were so darn soft-hearted, Sis. I don't know what I'm going to do with you." He teased me, tugging a loose strand of my dirty hair like he used to do when we were children. Still the same old Jim.

"But you'll stay and help us fix it all up, won't you?"

"No doubt about it." Jeremy suddenly was coming up behind us, his arms full of cars. "I'll stay to help and to keep an eye on you two until you do leave. I promise. You two are too precious to me to let anything happen to you." He meant every word too.

Jeremy's show-and-tell was interrupted by another visitor. A squat, roughly built man in grey overalls, he quickly mumbled that he had come out to check the furnace and the wiring. He clopped around in the basement with his immense flashlight for the longest time before he threw some switches. We had electricity! But before he left, he insisted on checking everything out again thoroughly. "Don't want you folks having any fires or anything here." He winked at me. He was older than he first looked, but his eyes twinkled with youth. If he had qualms about being in a so-called haunted house, he didn't show it. He went about his business and emerged some time later with a dirt smudged face and a satisfied grin; tipped his cap and was gone. That's all it took and we had all the comforts of home. Lights. Heat and water. Just in time.

The sun had gone down in a blaze of glory and we watched the shadows gather from a warm, well-lit house. The handyman had thought of everything, even light bulbs. I was to call him if anything went wrong or if I needed anything else. He had said that the telephone repairman would come the next morning. The lawyer had done his job well. I wondered when he would come by with my letter. I shrugged it off because it really wasn't that important. The letter had waited all these years, it could wait a few days longer, I supposed. I had more pressing matters on my mind.

Jim had slept after the repairman came and I decided to go upstairs and see if he would wake up long enough to eat something. I still had to go out for food because Jim hadn't connected the stove yet, besides the fact there was no food in the house. Tomorrow, I would have to go shopping, something I usually hated doing, but this time I was going to enjoy it. I refused to think about leaving. I could think about that tomorrow, I told myself.

I was half way up the stairs and on the landing when I felt the vision coming. Soft and gentle like a small wave; thoughts coming at me that weren't mine. They made me listen. Tiny whispers of warning.

I steadied myself, my hand trembling on the stairway wall, knowing that in a few seconds it would be over. Then, my legs still trembling under me, I continued up the rest of the stairs almost in a trance. The vision had been short but not sweet. It was deadly.

I knelt down next to my sleeping brother in the twilight and shook his shoulder until he sat up, opening his sleepy eyes to my pale face. "Jim. Jim . . ." I said softly.

"Sarah? What's wrong?" he mumbled in a leaden voice. He was still only half awake as he stretched and yawned, peering worriedly into my tilted face. "What is it?"

"We can't leave. Not ever!" I whimpered, beyond tears. I would have done anything to turn back the hands of time and start all over again. The trap had been sprung and we were sheep led to the slaughter house.

"What the hell are you babbling about?" He grabbed my arm. I could feel the tension growing inside him as he studied my face trying to read what had happened. "Why can't we leave?"

In a cold voice I answered slowly. "Because it will take Jeremy if we even try. . . I had a vision . . ." I winced at the look that crept into his eyes at my revelation. My legs gave out and I collapsed in a heap next to him. "It'll kill my son if I try to leave, Jim. We're trapped!"

"Who says?" he spat angrily. "How can we be sure that will happen? Maybe it's one of *its* tricks?" He rambled on and on, but the look in his eyes said more than his words. He believed *it* existed; he believed, then, that *it* could harm us. He knew.

I put my hand up to stop his words. "It's no use. We'll have to think of some other way to escape it . . . but if we leave . . ." I cried, fighting tears that were lurking just behind my eyelids, "Jeremy dies."

"Sarah!" He held me in his arms, speechless. He believed everything I said. He knew I heard things no one else could.

"But that's not the worst of it!"

He just stared at me. "Don't say anymore," he begged. But I couldn't help it, it was too much for me to bear alone. "Please." I didn't listen.

"To prove *it* has the power to do that . . . *it's* going to kill tonight. A *child!*" I couldn't look at his face. I turned away, crying. All the horror of my childhood was returning with a fresh vengeance. We were helpless against *it,* still like children.

"Oh, my God. . . ." he raved, jumping up and dragging me behind him down the stairs. "We have to do something!"

"What?"

"Go to the police, of course!" he shouted as we went through the kitchen. I pulled him up short as we got to the front porch.

"How are we going to do that? Answer me that?" I demanded to know. I had stopped crying. It wouldn't do any good.

"Why . . . we tell them about the murder. When. Why. How. You know!" There was something else very wrong and it was just dawning on him. He stopped dead in his tracks and turned to me, something registering besides his blind anger finally. "Sarah?"

"We can't." I choked out the words. *"It hasn't happened yet!"*

Jim just looked at me. He slumped down tiredly on the top step and I sat down beside him. The katydids were starting their nightly songs and I could smell roses heavy in the warm air. The moon was rising full above us and I could smell summer everywhere. It was as if we had gone back in time.

It was a while later, as we sat quietly in the dark on the steps, that I realized that there really weren't any katydids or roses blooming. It was too early in the year, and I shivered in the reality of the cold night air.

"When?" he finally asked.

"I don't know exactly. I only know it will happen sometime tonight."

"And we can't do a bloody thing to prevent it." It was like he already knew that. I waited for him to say something else, but it never came. He sat there staring out into the night world. The stars were coming out. I watched them glitter and pulsate above us.

"No. Not unless you want to go out into the woods . . ."

I felt him freeze beside me. He didn't say another word for a long time. Together we watched the moon climb up into the heavens and each, in our own way, prayed.

There must be something we can do, I thought. I kept

telling myself we had to fight it. Everything couldn't be allowed to happen again.

"There must be a way *to fight it. Stop it!*" He pounded his fist on the wood of the porch. I had the strangest feeling that Jim knew more than he was saying. We could hear Jeremy back in the house searching for us. He came out on the porch.

"Hey, here you two are," he said, breathless. "I've been looking everywhere." He plopped down beside us and I gathered him in my arms.

"Yes. Here we are," I said. "You found us." And so had something else.

CHAPTER ELEVEN

As the cool night fell and the slinking shadows came to greedily reclaim the world, the woods grew still and brooding. The trees were thick and held hands like ill-fated lovers criss-crossing the length of the valley. The trees had lost their childlike appearance and the narrow gullies were now rock-lined streams that etched themselves deep into the clay of the earth. The large benevolent house that used to smile down at the woods no longer caught the warmth of the sun in its shiny windows. Instead, the sun baked a crumbling pile of rubble and ash.

But at night the house was still there . . . and the children still played and laughed as they once had. The evil existed too. Forever's evil. The years that had died had not killed it. The woods mingled with the transparent images.

It didn't have to stay there, in the forest. It was not chained to the trees and the streams, but it liked being there. Time had no meaning. It liked the drooping trees' lush coolness. It thrived on the quiet and the desolation. The trees bloomed and died, preying upon themselves to fulfill the cycles of nature. It was at home. Here, it could think and scheme, remember—and gloat. It had come many years ago because that was where they were. It wanted to be near them and watch them grow. It had taken so long this time to find them. It had ponderously searched scores of years until it had discovered the child with the melancholy green eyes and the glow. It had finally found the child. It could always recognize the one when he was near . . . when it saw the child, it knew.

The brightness, the inner glow could not be hidden, and through the long lonely centuries its destiny and duty was to track down and destroy . . . that was its sole reason for existing.

It brooded alone in the forest, its eyes like burning coals and its shape large and powerful. Blacker than the shadows from which it sprang, it knew only the hunt. Its hatred had aged with the relentless centuries. Pacing in unconcealed anticipation on the soft, wet earth, it couldn't really remember when the hunt had first begun . . . or why, anymore. If it had had a face, it would have frowned in puzzlement. Why did it trail that one mercilessly through the long dusty ages? It stopped its movements. It thought, but the memories were firm distant towers and could not be budged. It couldn't reach them. It couldn't remember.

But it hated that one! It wasn't allowed rest or peace until it had found that one each time and snuffed out his goodness. Raw, primeval laughter rang through the trees standing guard around it. There was no uglier sound on earth than its laughter. It bespoke the very essence of evil. Its quarry was, after all, the best adversary it had ever faced—cleverer each and every time.

Yet, never clever enough. The evil had always won the game. Always!

It squelched the growing feelings of foreboding by summoning up the wind. It rose to a screaming pitch of sound that gave cover to its own roars of rage, howling grunts like an animal. It laughed in madness as huge branches and trees were ripped apart as it roamed the dark forest bellowing out its challenge. Come to me! Come and face me again and let us finish the game. It is time . . .

Come to me!

No. It couldn't go in that house! *Why? That had never happened before! And wasn't it strange . . . the child had recognized it so soon in the game. So soon. That had never happened before either! And that one had grown up sensing—knowing—when it was around.* It mulled over everything.

It had never lost before. What would it feel like—to lose?

One had tried to escape and it had punished them all! It gloated in glee remembering how it had taken revenge on all that one loved . . . almost all. The best was yet to come. That one always ran and the evil always had to punish . . . it was the most exciting part of the game. Humans were so pitifully weak, so easy to kill.

They were really no match for the evil.

Like the one's sister called Leslie . . . in the car. Far from these woods it had searched, found her, and had been enraged. She had fought and it had taught her the meaning of pain. She had taken a long time to die. Why did they fight so? Didn't they know that death could be sweet? It laughed and the ground shook.

Or the snotty little runt they called Charlie, and his puny little friends. It had tried not to kill so soon in the game, but couldn't stop. The smell of blood was so enticing him. Their throats were so frail and white, their faces so bloodless. They had overwhelmed the creature with blood lust. It had been so good.

If it had a mouth, it would have been grinning. But there was no mouth because there was no face . . . not a real one. It was nothing . . . nothing but the wind and the trees crying in the night. Nothing. Evil. Was it all so long ago? When had it started? Time had no meaning.

It should have been easy this time! It grew so angry that the earth and sky felt it and cringed. It had been thwarted! For the first time . . . someone or something had interfered and helped them. Something was protecting them. The evil couldn't enter the house . . . that *was* strange.

Who was aiding them? What would dare defy its power?

It raved to the sullen sky and sped through the woods as if it were a prison. It must be smarter than they . . . must lure that one away. There must be bait, though! Think. Think! It flew above the ground, bouncing heavily against the trees. Think. What bait? Suddenly it craved more blood. The game had gone on too long. The forbidden was the most craved. It wanted, but couldn't have.

It pictured their house shimmering, far away from the lush woods, his haven. The house was dark. Yet the center glowed. They could not be touched. Unless . . .

The thing must find their weakness. They were such selfish, frightened creatures when faced with pain. It had always been able to manipulate humans to do his dirty work. It recalled fondly one time a girl had been dragged to a stake. Her people had thought she was a witch and had burned the flesh from her bones, gawking at her agony. It had been so easy to arrange back then. Humans had been even more vulnerable and stupid then! It gloried in that victory of long ago. Weak, puny humans! There was a way to get them — there always was.

Sightless eyes looked and saw the child sleeping peacefully.

A child . . .

The laughter was vicious. It knew how to bring that one to his knees, knew now what to use as bait.

It would kill a child. Turning it flew into the night, becoming a wispy cloud that crawled across the huge pale moon. In the house a woman shivered as if someone had walked on her grave. A small child tossed and mumbled in his sleep. Sweat beaded his brow as his dreams turned to fitful nightmares.

The presence looked closely at the people in the house, and saw a smile flicker ever so lightly on someone's lips. A haunting smile as light as a feather. The one smiled.

There was just enough of the old power to protect them all . . . just enough . . . for now. But the evil knew it would

130

not hold out much longer, and when it did . . . there would be no stopping its wrath.

CHAPTER TWELVE

"I never should have come back here," Jimmy said as we sat on the porch watching the late stars. The wind had picked up and screamed angrily through the trees around us. "I came because you did . . . and," he added hesitantly trying to find the right words, "I was just sick of running away all the time. I was tired of the fear."

"And *I* came because Jonathan didn't want me anymore," I said dully. "Ever since the accident, it was never the same."

"What accident?" Jim was suddenly alerted.

"Didn't I ever tell you about it? I thought I did."

"No. Tell me."

"Last year Jonathan had a terrible accident in the squad car while he was on duty . . . right after I warned him that something might happen. I think that was part of the reason he started turning away from me. He couldn't stand the waiting."

"Waiting?"

"Waiting until I saw something else happening to him, I suppose." I shrugged in the moonlight, shivering from the cold breeze coming in. "He treated me oddly after that, like I wasn't there anymore or something. That was the beginning." I tried to keep the bitterness out of my voice.

"When the love's gone for some people, it's gone . . . he found someone else, that's all."

"Sarah! Can't you see the pattern? It's right there in front of you and you haven't seen it?" Jim exclaimed.

"See what?"

"All this!" He spread his delicate long fingers around us symbolically. "We've been manipulated like mindless puppets — our lives, our loved ones — until we were forced to run to the only place we had left to run . . . home." But his voice was sarcastic and brittle when he said the word. "And like good little puppets we obeyed our master. We came home."

"You're saying *it's* been behind everything that's happened to us? Jonathan's accident . . ." I was stunned and yet in another way I wasn't surprised at all. "I was stupid not to have seen it." The pieces of the puzzle were fitting together. Suddenly everything else made sense. What had it done to Jonathan? "Oh, Jim!" I was no longer angry at my ex-husband. He had almost died because of me and somehow he knew it! No wonder he had run so far away from us.

Jim stared into the night as if he were trying to see our adversary that ravaged out in the woods. To know it was out there, still waiting and planning more evil, sent shivers through my soul.

"Can't you see we've been torn from everyone we've ever held dear?" There was an intense hatred in his low voice as he tented his fingers and continued to glare towards the dark woods. I felt the presence of malevolent whispers lingering on the night air. *It* was there, plotting and polluting the whole forest.

"Everything," Jim intoned.

"There was someone you loved, too?" I asked. Even though it was dark, I saw a tear glisten in his eye. There was no one else he could bare his soul to. All of them were dead, so he turned to the last person on earth he truly loved and poured out things he had kept to himself for so long.

133

"I fell in love with a girl named Amy." He paused, whether from old pain and grief or something else, I didn't know. "Oh, she was sweet. You would have liked her, Sis. I was on the road. I saw her as I was getting into my truck after I'd gone grocery shopping. I don't know why, but I looked up just as I was turning the key and there she was. It was the strangest thing . . . I felt compelled to follow her back into the store." He smiled a brief, sad smile. "You know how shy I am. Well, you wouldn't believe what I did just to meet her. I walked right up to her and introduced myself and asked her for a date. She was the prettiest thing I've ever laid eyes on, but it was more than that. She was good. She had a good heart. It was like she was my soulmate from the second she looked at me . . . I loved her."

I smiled back at him. "Well, did she go out with you?"

He didn't answer for so long I thought he hadn't heard me. "Yes, as a matter of fact, she did—many times. I married her, Sarah."

I had always thought there was nothing my brother could do to surprise me, but this bit of news left me speechless.

"I loved her very much. Too much."

"You're married?" I had finally found my tongue. "You married and didn't tell me? Should I forgive you for this?" I laughed cautiously because I could sense that he hadn't told me everything.

"Yes, I married . . ." His voice faded away.

"Wow! You don't sound very happy. Where is she?" My brother had a wife and hadn't even breathed a word of it to me and now he was beating around the bush. I was so happy for him, even with all our other problems. I wanted to know all about her, and of course, couldn't wait to meet her. "Is she coming here?" I asked, excited.

"Amy . . . is dead," he replied quietly and fell silent.

I could have said a lot of things at that moment, but that silence was all I could manage.

We sat there for a long time wrapped in our own little

worlds. It was too much for me. Jim and I always shared everyting . . . even our greatest losses. I touched his cheek and pulled my hand back when I found it wet.

"It's alright, Sarah," he said, brushing off my pity. "I learned to live with it a long time ago. It's been a long time now — years. I've accepted it."

I wouldn't have asked him but he offered and I had no choice but to listen. "I've no doubt that she was murdered. *It* killed her. I feel it!"

"You don't know how she died?"

Jim stood up and walked to the railing on the porch. "No. One day she just disappeared . . . she never called, or wrote, and she never came back."

"Did you fight?"

He spun around to face me and I could tell he was angry. "No. At first, I racked my brain trying to decide if I had done something to send her away like that. But there was nothing. We loved each other, we were happy. And anyway, she wasn't like that. She never would have just walked off without a good reason. I searched everywhere. I looked every place she could have gone. She was nowhere. I nearly went crazy with grief. But I never found her. I still call her parents to see if they've heard anything . . . but it's hopeless. I know she's dead. I know what happened to her." He was looking towards the woods and our old homestead hungrily. "And I'll get even. I'll get that goddamn thing. I swear!" The words were daggers, sharp and lethal.

"It can't win all the time. It must have a weakness."

And we had to find it. The human mind has an uncanny way of tucking distasteful realities away in dark corners until the last possible second of confrontation. My mind had done that all my life. It was doing it again. I couldn't face the ugly truth until it pounced on me and sunk its teeth in. My mind had erected a brick wall in front of all the horrors. They lay there imprisoned, seething and rioting. I was safe on my side . . . so far. I knew I had to open those gates and let them in . . . and soon.

"We *have* to find a way to destroy it," I cried.

"No one else will."

"I still can't believe this is happening to us. It's the twentieth century, and we're stalked by a ghost—or whatever the hell that thing is!"

"That's why we're losing, Sarah. Something is eating us alive while we sit in awe that it's happening. We can't believe it. We want explanations, a reason for it, when there simply is *none*. We're cursed someway and it doesn't matter what it is out there . . . it's killing us and we have to stop it."

"If we can," I said tiredly. We were going in circles over the same ground looking for clues and not finding anything.

"Oh, I know we can. I have a few tricks up my sleeve. It doesn't have us beaten yet. Not by a long shot!" As Jim bravely uttered these words the air around us was ripped with the pitiful screams of a child—a terrified, dying child.

And laughter . . .

We clung to each other frozen in fear and when the screams continued, Jim took my hands away and walked off the porch and into the night.

"I can't stand it!" he cried. It only took me a second, glancing up at Jeremy's window, and I ran to catch up with him. We ran . . . to the woods, the screams guiding our way.

We had run non-stop for about ten minutes, when my courageous brother dropped to the ground.

"Jim? What's wrong?" I was breathing hard as I crouched next to him. I shook his shoulder to get his attention, but he acted as if I weren't there. After running towards the sounds for what seemed like an eternity, we seemed no closer to them. We had run this way, then that, our ears alert to any change in the haunted crying. It would stop and then start again, but always in a different place. When I saw Jim collapse against the roots of a tree and bury his head in his hands, I was about ready to give up.

"I can't run anymore, Sarah." His unsteady voice was

136

barely audible over the night wind. "I have to rest . . . besides, I don't hear it now. Which way should we go?"

I shook my head, pushing the hair from my face. I was as tired as he was, even more so . . . and scared. If I had to run for my life, I wouldn't stand a chance! "I don't know which way. . ." I tried to see his face in the dark, but I couldn't. The moon had cunningly hidden itself behind the gathering storm clouds.

"Listen," he whispered, grabbing my shoulder so hard it hurt. "Do you hear anything?"

"Yes, I heard . . . laughter." But I didn't need to answer his question for him to know that I heard exactly what he heard. I also had the uncanny feeling that we had been through all this before, long ago. It was as if we were those scared summer children all over again, running through the night woods all those years ago. A pattern was laid and we were following it again, though I desperately wanted to change it. What could we do now that would break that spell?

"Maybe it's a trick." Jim's voice was a faint whisper. "Maybe, it's tricking us. Maybe it just wanted us out here in these woods!" I could smell the sudden fear in him, just like that time when we were children. "Maybe there's no child in danger at all . . ."

Jim stood up and I could feel his body shudder. "It's lured us out here. There is no child!" he spat, as he spun around, a silhouette against the tall waving trees. There was only silence now, deadly silence. *Something* out there was watching us, and waiting. I could feel it.

Our moment of anger had passed and we were left defenseless—two frightened people remembering horrors from our childhood. "You could be right, except . . I *know* someone's going to die tonight. I know it!" I didn't know what to do. We could walk in circles all night through these cursed woods and still not find what we sought. I had a terrible premonition that whatever was to happen had already happened and no power in heaven nor on earth could change it now. We had heard those cries but it was possible that they had never originated from the woods at all. We had gone on a wild goose chase, in the middle of the night running like crazy fools. Why?

I had been a fool for thinking we could save that poor child in the first place. We weren't supposed to.

Jim spoke stealthly, as if he was certain we were being spied on. "Sarah, do you know what a bull's eye is?"

I thought he had gone crazy. "Yes, the center of a target," I answered stupidly. He took my hand and we started to walk away from the woods, back the way we had come. I had no idea we had gone so far from the house. But something deep inside of me didn't want to go. I turned my head and looked yearningly back into the darkness. I knew a child lay there somewhere in a pool of his own blood and even though I accepted the fact that he was probably dead, I wanted to help him.

"Yes, the center of a target . . ." Jim was saying as our walk evolved into a trot and then into a dead run. "That's what we are right now, I bet . . . a bull's eye!" It was then the fear struck me and almost threw me to the ground. I slid to my knees. Jim yanked me up and we ran on.

I could hear hideous laughter and I knew it was close behind us somewhere, stalking us . . . closing the distance. This had happened before . . . and many times before that.

A voice screamed inside of me to stop. Turn and fight! Change the pattern . . . and change the outcome. Do it this time! Do it and win or do it and end it all! But what about Jeremy, back at the house, waiting?

The second time I fell, something knocked me down. We were so close to the house then that when I looked up I could see the lights shining just ahead of us.

"Sarah! For God's sake get up! We're almost there!" Jim screamed and started to drag me. He was crying.

I couldn't answer because suddenly I cried out in pain as something tore through my leg. I head the laughter ringing in my ear and with one last burst of energy I raised myself to my one good leg, dragging the other. "Jeremy," I moaned as I hobbled on. I wasn't even sure if I still had a leg and I could feel my salty warm tears flowing across my lips as I tried not to think of the pain.

The house was so close!

Then something dug into my shoulder and for the last few seconds of consciousness, I was aware of a terrible struggle going on between the thing that had its claws in me and my brother. Then everything went black.

The next thing I knew I was sprawled on my own couch and Jim was placing a bandage around the lower part of my right leg. The pain was only a dull ache now.

"What on earth happened out there?" I said in a voice that couldn't have been mine. It sounded more like a mouse.

Jim looked up at me, patted my leg, and gently laid it down in what he thought was a more comfortable position. "There, it isn't a real bad cut . . . but it's deep. I want you to stay off that leg for a while, Sis." His face was very clear in the lamplight. I was shocked at the tiredness and misery in it. There were very dark circles all around his eyes and even though he was smiling at me, I could tell he was pushing it. "Now, I want to look at your shoulder."

"It almost had me, didn't it?" I felt numb, as if it had all happened to someone else. It wasn't real. I could remember the fear out in the woods but I couldn't connect them with here and now.

"It was too damn close, Sarah, is all I can say." Jim was peering at eight little holes in the top of my shoulder. My blouse had been torn away and the punctures were large, but clean; they weren't bleeding anymore. He rinsed the washcloth he had used on my leg and came back to clean my shoulder. Then he carefully put antiseptic on it. "Does it hurt much now?" There was guilt and concern in his face as he studied me.

"No, very little, really." I stretched my leg and then rolled my jeans back down over the bandage. You couldn't tell I had been attacked. The wounds didn't bleed anymore. The fact was strange to both of us. But we chose to ignore it.

"Sarah, I thought you were psychic. Didn't you see what we were walking into?" Jim seemed almost angry at me for not knowing. I flashed him an annoyed glance and went to put on a clean blouse. I could hear him pacing around downstairs as I slipped into a sweater. I ambled down the hall and looked in on Jeremy. His breathing was deep and regular. I slowly hobbled down the stairs a minute later and limped over to the couch. I couldn't have lost too much blood, but I was still weak from the strain and shock of it all. I slumped down on the couch and looked up at my brother and simply said, "I've told you before . . . it doesn't work that way, Jim. Yes, I'm considered a psychic, but it's a strange phenomenon. I don't see *everything*! And if it's too close to me, I sometimes never see anything! I can help other people but I can't seem to help myself. When I die, I'll die like everyone else . . . unexpectedly."

"I'm sorry, Sarah," he suddenly blurted out. Slumped on the couch, he looked like he was half asleep already. His head kept nodding. I stuffed a cushion under it for him and he sighed in weariness.

"You have nothing to be sorry about, Jim. You just did what you thought you had to do. It took courage."

"I endangered you, that's all I did! I didn't use my head. We can't fight it. We can't win . . ." His voice dropped off. "I don't know what to do anymore."

I sat down next to him. "Oh, you're wrong there, Jim . . . we'll find a way. Somehow." I was thinking of Jeremy. "We *have* to find a way." But I was sure that we were all doomed and that it was just a matter of time. Then the whole family would be gone, wiped off the face of the earth without a trace.

"Why am I still alive anyway?" I asked of the empty walls, but they remained silent.

I felt a cold chill as I tried to keep from falling asleep

too. I was so tired . . . I shivered as it got colder.

I'll help . . . I promised . . . the words were spoken inside my head but I knew it wasn't I who spoke them. It was my grandmother.

Maybe she was the reason I was still alive. I wasn't sure. I found a cover for Jim who was sound asleep on the couch, and made my way back upstairs. I slipped into Jeremy's room. I stared a long time at his innocent face and finally, exhausted, I lay down next to him. I gathered him into my arms and closed my eyes.

A child had died tonight. Tomorrow would come too soon. I didn't know what it would bring, but I would face it when it came. I was too weary to think anymore. My son was safe. There was nothing else I could do.

As I fell asleep I thought I could hear children's voices and laughter, distant and haunting, and my mother's voice calling us all home for supper. I thought it was real and we were all safe still. I smiled, remembering.

I wished I could go back, before it all began, and be happy again . . .

CHAPTER THIRTEEN

There was nothing in the morning papers about any mysterious child murders and as the day wore on I lived in a sort of daze. Jim stayed outside with Jeremy, scouting the area, and I finally settled on cleaning the yard. It would be hard, dirty work but maybe that was just what I needed to get my mind off the night before. Work was sanity and I was in doubt of mine, so I threw myself into the yard work with a vengeance. I pulled weeds and picked up old dirt-encrusted beer bottles and rusted soda cans old enough to go to a museum. Our yard must have become the dumping ground for the whole neighborhood. I put on old gloves and dug hunks of glass out of the dirt. I threw stray rocks out into the street until I thought my arm would literally fall off. By afternoon, I was caked with dirt and sweat and every bone in my body ached, but it felt good. There was always satisfaction in doing a hard job well. The yard was shaping up. I got out the lawn mower and started pushing. In all these years I had forgotten how immense my grandmother's grounds really were. It was almost palatial.

After a quick iced tea, I went back to work rearranging my grandmother's greatest pride and joy. Like my mother, she had her rock garden and we had always collected pretty rocks for her. But it was all but empty now. The rocks had long ago been scattered and lost. There was nothing left but weeds and crumbled dirt. I absentmindedly wondered where all those exquisite hunks of stone had disappeared to.

I was unceremoniously squatting in the rock garden, digging my heart out like a kid in a sand pile, when a shadow fell across me. I raised my head and there was Mr. Largo, our friendly lawyer, standing over me, an amused smile on his thin lips.

"I didn't know women still did that," he teased, putting out a very clean hand to help pull me to my feet.

"Oh, this?" I motioned to the mounds of dark rich earth that lay around me. "I'm trying to get the rock garden back into shape . . . it used to be so . . . unique." I smiled. "It's going to take a lot of work."

"You said that about the house, too. And I see you're meeting the challenge admirably." He was staring at the house and the grounds. "It's starting to look like a home again." From him that was a compliment and I accepted it as such. I thanked him and he followed me into the house.

Again I noticed his reluctance to stay inside too long. From the minute we entered the kitchen his attitude became one of restrained nervousness. He covertly glanced at everything in the kitchen and commented on the fresh paint and how nice everything looked. His hawk eyes never missed a thing, but I knew he was here for something beyond idle curiosity.

"The letter." He pulled a long, fat envelope from his suit's inner pocket and handed it to me like it was a fragile piece of glass. "I brought it this time."

The look of self-satisfaction on his face should have smothered him, I thought. Did he already know what was inside? Possibly. He must have read my mind.

"It's never been opened. It's been in my brother's safe all these years, undisturbed. We respect our client's trust."

Handling the bulky thing, I knew then why he was smiling. I knew what it felt like and suddenly excited like a

143

child with a gift to open, I tore the end of it and pulled out the contents, a thin, folded letter yellowed with age and a stack of old wrinkled bills—fifties and twenties! My mouth must have fallen open because I heard Mr. Largo laugh in unsuppressed glee at my good fortune.

"I don't believe it! There must be thousands here!" I exclaimed, stunned. I sifted the flattened bills through my trembling fingers. I felt like someone who just had discovered a hidden treasure. Imagine! All that money!

"Quite a windfall, I'd say," Mr. Largo commented, eying the money as I counted it, still gaping.

That's when it fell out of the envelope—a tiny wad of old, wrinkled tissue paper. That was all I thought it was too, until I picked it up and the weight gave me a clue that it was something more. I picked up the crudely wrapped bundle and began parting the paper. Mr. Largo watched like a hawk circling a henhouse with the roof ready to fall off.

I felt the form of the object and realized what it was long before either of us saw the glint of dull gold.

My great-great-grandmother's ring.

Its tiny leaves, once engraved so finely and carefully, were almost worn away with age. My smile faded just as faintly when I suddenly thought of all the history the ring brought with it. History best forgotten.

Something intangible whispered behind me. A presence.

"The gift," I murmured out loud.

"What?" said Mr. Largo.

"Huh?" I asked intelligently. I suddenly became aware of the lawyer's anxious figure. "I'm sorry, what did you say?"

"I said, the ring is beautiful. Then *you* said something about a gift." He looked at me expectantly. Did he know the ring's story?

"Oh, yes. Yes. It was given as a gift to my grandmother from her grandmother. And now from her to me. It's sort of an heirloom, I guess. It's worth my weight in sentimental gold." I laughed stupidly and before I knew what I was doing, I slipped the delicate circle over my left pinkie. It fit like a glove ... like a ring actually; a ring that had been forged in the fires of Hell just for me.

I finally turned my attention back to the letter, after I had slapped the money into a neat pile in my hands. "Five thousand and fifty dollars! Boy, will this come in handy!" I breathed, laying the money down on the table so I could read the letter.

Mr. Largo stood there while I swiftly read the letter to myself. I knew he was dying to know what it said. But I kept him in suspense.

I have had a few *good* surprises in my life, but that money and that letter had to take the grand prize. The money more than the letter, though, and the ring more than that. The letter was a different sort of surprise. Another story altogether.

The past was jumping out to grab me.

Dearest Sarah,

I know that when you finally read this letter, I will no longer be on this earth. I hope you and the rest of the family don't grieve over me too long. Believe me, I've had an interesting and exciting life. We all have a limited time here on this planet. Well, enough of that. I'm writing you to let you know something that I've been sure of for a long time now ... you have a special gift, child. Maybe you know what I'm talking about—your unique psychic ability. It is a gift with awesome responsibilities, I know. My grandmother on my mother's side had it but not as strongly as I see it in you.

It's one of the reasons you have always held such a special place in my heart. Your life will not be easy. I have read the cards and I forsee great trials and heartbreaks for you. So I am trying to help. The house has always been for you. It has always been a haven for me as it will be for you if you want it to be. I have a feeling that you will need a haven someday. It is a good place; a place where evil dares not enter. It was built that way. The ring is also a part of the

145

legacy. The money is a bonus. Call it future upkeep for the house, though you may use it any way you see fit according to your needs.

There isn't really anything else important enough to put down in this kind of letter; I feel strange writing it, but something stronger than myself has compelled me to do these things for you, my sweet Sarah. I wish you a happy life and I can tell you that I grieve more over the thought of leaving you here alone on this earth than anything else. I'm not afraid to die. You must face whatever hand life decides to deal you. The cards never lie. I have but one word of advice:

Never doubt, child, that there is terrible evil in the world and never say anything is impossible. I wish you luck . . . and remember me with love.

> *Always,*
> *your grandmother*
> *Elizabeth Summers*

There was no date on the letter. With a sigh, I folded it up and stuck it in my jeans pocket. The look of disappointment that spread over the lawyer's face was apparent.

But I wasn't going to share my grandmother's letter with a near stranger. I treasured it and Jim was the only one I wanted to show it to—maybe Jeremy someday when he was older.

Mr. Largo, when he realized I wasn't going to appease his curiosity, muttered his goodbyes in record time and left. I was glad he was gone. I needed some time alone to savor my letter and the gift.

I went back outside to work some more on the rock garden and to feel the warm sun on my shoulders. For a short time the horror of the night before and the horror I was waiting for seemed far away. I hummed an old tune my grandmother once taught me when I was a child. I let my mind flow with memories of this place and my grandmother when she was still alive. What would she say if she

146

knew that all the rest of her family were dead? Maybe she knew. She was dead as they were—maybe they were in paradise together. I hoped so. I pulled weeds and dug up a few old rocks that I rinsed carefully in the kitchen sink until they glittered as they had years ago. I pieced together fragments of my grandmother's face and her joyous smile . . . it was as if she were there with me. I had no doubt she was. She had never left this house.

I let my eyes travel the length of the newly cut lawn and dwell on the worn frame of the old house. It was strange that it was at that second that I first saw the similarities in my grandmother's house and my childhood home.

Was it my imagination, or was there something different about my new home? I stared up at the yawning windows, wiped the dirt from my fingers on my jeans and walked closer. Why hadn't I noticed it before?

The houses did resemble each other.

"Sarah! What are you staring at?" Jim's voice caught me gaping at the upstairs windows.

He had come up behind me and had surprised me so that I jumped. Jeremy was climbing the tree behind us. I looked up and watched his progress, tearing my eyes away from the house reluctantly. "The house," I answered, still following Jeremy's skinny body crawling through the branches. The tree was very old and very big. It reminded me of the way Jim and I used to sneak out of the house when we were children.

Jim was studying the house now. "What about it?"

I caught his eye and that suspicious appraisal he was giving me. "Oh, nothing, really. I was just thinking about what bad shape it's really in," I lied slightly. I was over-emotional after last night and I really didn't want to go into it at that moment with Jeremy so close and Jim so jumpy. Why give him anything else to worry about? He had enough on his mind. He was still staring at the house, his face very pale, and when he turned his eyes on me, they were full of questions I couldn't answer. I was afraid he had noticed it, too. After a second or two his gaze shifted to the rock garden and he smiled faintly. "Like mother, like daughter... you going to collect rocks now?"

I walked back over to the clearing and picked up some of the dirt in my hands. "I don't know, really. Do you remember that beautiful rock garden our mother used to have back at the old house?"

"Of course I do. There was this one gigantic gold-veined hunk of white stone that I used to hide my little cars under so you wouldn't find them."

"You're kidding?"

"No. You always thought you were one of the guys and you were forever taking our toys. I hid a lot of stuff, especially from Charlie." This last he said with a touch of real guilt. How we had all hid things from poor Charlie! Even our love, until it was too late.

Jim was kneeling down next to me. "I used to love looking for fool's gold. You know that yellow stuff that looks like real gold?"

I remembered.

"I wonder where all those rocks are now, Sis? Do you think there's any of them out there just lying around?"

Neither one of us was aware of how closely Jeremy was listening to every word we were saying, sitting up there in that tree like a timid squirrel, all eyes and ears.

"There might be ... but I don't think either of us want to go snooping around that place." A shadow fell across us and I looked around. There was no one there—no one that I could see.

"We'd be crazy to ... and, besides, I wouldn't let you!" Jim's eyes narrowed. "Not after last night! Not even in the brightest daylight."

"I understand," I said, and I did.

"If I wasn't such a coward..." But he didn't finish because suddenly I remembered the letter in my pocket and the money in the kitchen, safely hidden behind the canned goods I had picked up this morning at the nearby

148

store. I guess I had been so intrigued by what I imagined about the house that it had completely slipped my mind.

I grasped his arms and shook him to get his complete attention, I was so excited. "Wait until you see what I got special delivery today! You're not going to believe it!"

"Hey!" He grinned back, my excitement catching. "Since I've come here I'll believe anything." But behind his grin I could see the apathy that our situation was creating in him. In other words, he would pretend he cared—for my sake. As if nothing really mattered anymore. The roads all led to the same lion's den.

I was hoping the money and the letter would cheer him up. I couldn't help but think that the letter held a key for us; for our salvation. Maybe Jim could shed some light on it all. When he read the letter, perhaps he would see something in it that I hadn't.

I yanked the crumpled piece of paper from my pocket and waved it tantalizingly in front of his nose.

"What is that?"

"It's a letter . . . from Grandmother."

"But she's dead," he reminded me, his eyes following the scrap of moving paper, nevertheless.

"Of course," was all I said about that subject. "This is the letter the lawyer was saving for me. I had to actually move into the house to get it. Well, I got it this morning. The lawyer drove over a little while ago and gave it to me."

"Oh, *that* letter." He seemed disinterested already. "What does it say?"

I handed him the letter.

When he finished reading it the first thing he asked about was the money.

"It's in the house. I didn't feel like carrying it around in my pocket. You won't belive it . . . over five thousand dollars in cash! A stack of bills as thick as your hand! You want to see them?"

He followed me towards the house. "You think there's something in that letter that might help us, don't you . . .

149

with our . . . dilemma?" he said abruptly. His tone was not enlightening.

"Yes. What do you think?" My hands were behind my back, fingering the old, golden ring on my left hand. I was waiting for the right moment to show it to him.

"I don't know . . . by the way the letter is written, I don't think she had any idea what was to happen. To our family, I mean. Even though she was a very perceptive old lady." He leveled his gaze at me as we climbed the porch steps to the house. I was poised at the top step, by the door, my hand starting to touch the door knob. I turned to Jim, brushing the loose dirt off the ring. I tried to pull it off, but it stuck fast.

"But I don't think she had any of the answers we're seeking," he said dismally. He looked back at the tree Jeremy was still crouched in. Some inner uneasiness made him raise his hand to signal the boy to come in too.

I waved the ring, finger and all, in front of him. His face was void of expression, but something was going on inside his head.

It was then we heard the car drive up. We couldn't see who it was. Without a word, Jim went back down the steps to greet our guest. I absently toyed with the ring, still trying to pull it off, then followed my brother outside.

CHAPTER FOURTEEN

Jeremy peeked through the branches of the old tree. He was watching his mother and uncle talking. He broke off a nearby branch and twisted it around and around until it broke, then tore off the leaves. His eyes settled on the old mausoleum that they now lived in. He'd hated it at first. Hated it. Now . . . now he wasn't so sure. He missed the city all right and, yes, he missed their old apartment but even he had to admit he'd never had so much room to himself. He'd never been out in the country. There wasn't another house in sight. And their new home was so big . . . all those rooms.

His mother was having a ball redecorating the place. If this was what it took to make her happy again, then he could stand it. He knew she had been sad since the divorce and at least she wasn't crying in her sleep anymore. That had to count for something. He cocked his sun-bleached head, trying to hear what they were saying, but he couldn't quite make out their words. They were walking away now. He traced cracks in the tree's bark with his fingers and played make-believe in his head. He pretended there was no one else in the world but him . . . no house down there, no mother and uncle. He was adrift in this tree, deep in a forest where he could see no sky, only other trees. And it was dark, oh, so dark . . . and he could hear children.

Children playing . . . He shook his head and smiled. There was something strange about this place, though. He could feel it. It was keeping secrets. Secrets he wanted to know.

Just like those woods over there. He shivered up there all alone in the tree and thought about that ruined place his mom had shown him when they had first come. Her old home . . . the place seemed to *cry*. He wondered why. His mother wouldn't talk much about her mysterious childhood even though he had tried to weasel it out of her countless times. He was sure she was hiding something . . . or maybe trying to protect him for some reason. He knew there had been a lot of them at one time, but he didn't know where they all were now. Maybe she hated them and that's why they never saw any of them.

Then again, maybe something terrible had happened back there at that old ruined place . . . he hadn't thought about it much. It was only coming here that had reawakened his curiosity again. His eyes looked hesitantly towards the forbidden woods. He was thinking and a smile flickered on his lips. The thought crossed his mind that maybe some of those old rocks his mom and uncle were talking about before were lying out there somewhere just waiting to be found.

She'd never know he had been there if he didn't tell her.

Humming, he retrieved his Slinky from his pocket and, still grasping the last end coil, he let it unwind down through the thick branches. He jiggled it slightly when it got stuck. It bounced, and sunlight glinted off the metal links, golden and bright. His mother had given it to him a long time ago. He remembered her casual remark as she handed it to him that they didn't make them like they used to when she was a child. Too thin, too cheap nowadays. But he loved it anyway, cheap or not. He let go of it and watched as it collided with the ground below and recoiled back into a tight little circle like a shy snake.

It was more fun when it tripped down steps all by itself,

propelled by its own locomotion ... *clump* ... *clump* ... *clump*. He never tired of watching it do that. It fascinated him, the way it would go down every step dutifully until it reached its predetermined destination. So predictable. It reminded him of certain people he knew. Not his dad, though. He frowned ... never like his dad.

He slowly worked his way through the branches until his feet could touch the ground. They wanted him to come inside.

He was suddenly very sad. He always felt sad when he thought about his dad these days. Worried, too. He hadn't heard from him in weeks. No letter, call, or anything. Jeremy couldn't help but feel sorry for his father. There were things his mom didn't know and he had promised not to tell her. It would only hurt her more.

He had long ago accepted the fact that his mother and father were divorced and that they would never all live together again. It was a lousy shame, too. He'd been over at his dad's new place a few times when *she* was there, and he knew that his dad wasn't really happy, not as happy as he pretended to be. Jeremy was sure of it! There was something very wrong there and he could feel it, even if his dad was acting like there wasn't. That woman treated him bad, not the way his mom had treated him. When Dad had been around, Mom had always been happy and smiling, where that woman nagged all the time. She never shut up the whole time he was there and she rarely smiled at him.

Jeremy never stayed long. As much as he loved his dad, he couldn't stand the woman and her sharp tongue. She didn't seem to appreciate him too much, either. Her two boys hated him and were always trying to pick fights with him. He was glad to come home. At least, his mom loved and needed him and there wasn't that constant bickering that he hated.

He truly felt sorry for his dad. The last time he saw him, he'd looked terrible. His father gave him some stupid story about it just being his second job that he had just started. He was tired, or something like that. *She* wanted a bigger house, so he needed to make more money, that's what it was. She was never satisfied. Jeremy had noticed her new furniture and the fancy clothes and jewelry she wore and heard her bragging on the phone to someone about how much his dad bought her and about the new house they were thinking of buying. Money! All she cared about was money, and his dad was miserable trying to get it for her.

Jeremy felt sorry for himself, too. Things weren't the same without Dad around. Nothing was the same. As he strolled towards the house he thought about that Ben guy—the cop—who had helped his uncle the other day, and his eyes lit up. Now *he* would be perfect for his mom!

Mom ought to like him! Heck, he was just like his dad, wasn't he? A cop and everything. Jeremy sure wished his mom would start liking the guy. He had seemed interested before his mother had snubbed him that day. And that motorcycle of his . . . boy, Jeremy would sure love having a ride on that monster! It was something!

Thinking how he could arrange things to get the two of them together somehow, he took the porch steps two at a time. Suddenly a shiver went through him as if someone were watching hm and he spun around to look back at the tree. Nothing. But he could have sworn something was watching! He thought a child had scampered quickly away in the very corner of his eye when he first turned. Was it . . . no. He shook his head and turned back to the house. It had been his imagination more likely. Everyone said he had a vivid imagination, whatever that meant. Anyway, he had it.

The kitchen always smelled like coffee, a good smell that he had come to associate with love and home. Sometimes on cool evenings when it rained outside or in the winter when they were snowbound, his mother and he would bake cookies or homemade bread. The remembered delicious aromas tickled his nose and made his mouth water. Those were the days, such wonderful times that they had in the kitchen, the coffee perking noisily while they waited for the bread to bake—those were the times he wondered if his dad remembered. His mother was a darn good cook and she put a lot of love into it. He looked at the freshly painted kitchen and the rolls of flowered wallpaper and realized his mother put a lot of love into everything she did. His mom was just like that.

Jeremy was glad he had the mom he had. Even if his dad didn't see how special she was, he sure did. And nothing was ever going to hurt her again, if he could help it!

He suddenly heard a car drive up and without a pause he ran past his mother and uncle to find out who had come to visit them.

"Mom, it's Ben!" he yelled, though he didn't have to because by then she was right behind him.

"Hi, sport," Ben said. But there was no smile and no jokes as he looked over the boy's head into Sarah's frightened eyes. This time he was all business. He all but ignored Jeremy.

Jeremy felt left out and disappointed. Apparently he was in the way or something was wrong. Ben wasn't acting like himself.

"I need to talk with you, Sarah. I don't know exactly how to put this . . ." He was stuttering slightly like he was nervous or unsure of what else to say or how to say it. "I mean, what I have to say isn't going to be easy." His eyes were dark and troubled and continuously shifted from her face to Jim's in the background. He stared at Jeremy like he had just realized he was still there in front of him. "I need to talk to you . . . alone." Of course, he clearly meant without kids.

Jeremy shuffled his feet and threw him a dirty look. He glanced back at his mom to see what she thought of all this nonsense. The time was long past when he would be sent to his room so the grownups could gossip. He was too old for that now.

"Jeremy. . ." Sarah started to say something but he finished it for her before she could say it.

"I know . . . get lost. Right?" Jeremy smirked and rolled his eyes up. He knew exactly what he would do! He'd go upstairs to his room and then when they had forgotten him, he'd sneak down the steps very, very quietly and eavesdrop . . . just a little. By now, they were all acting a little funny and he wanted to know what was going on. But his mother read his mind. "Jeremy can go outside and play," she said, leveling a steely gaze at him. He knew that look. *No back talk. Just do as I say.* She laid a firm hand on his shoulder and gently directed him down the porch steps. He could feel her shivering just by her touch. Startled, he looked up at her face and it was as white as a ghost. Suddenly he was frightened and it made him shut his mouth. For once, he knew words wouldn't do any good. His mother was upset and it was clear that it had something to do with Ben.

He nodded, his head down, and slipped out the door. "Don't go too far away. . ." Her words echoed in his head as the door closed and he stood there staring at its solidness. Alone.

He shrugged his shoulders and went to sit on the porch steps, his chin in his hands. What was he going to do now? He wished he was an ant . . . he'd crawl back under the doorjamb and listen to their conversation. He hated being left out! Or if he was a puff of smoke . . . his mind started concocting little fantasies on that subject as he watched the clouds fly over the house. The sky was a soft blue and the clouds were pinkish. There was a rosy glow everywhere and darker shadows teased the light in the yard before him.

He suddenly found himself staring at the bushes at the edge of the yard. Something was hiding in them . . . something. He thought he saw a human smile, and just as suddenly it was gone—like that crazy cat in *Alice in Wonderland.* Jeremy bounced up from the step and walked up to the bushes cautiously. He didn't want to scare away whoever it was. Children needed playmates—maybe he was about to meet his first friend. He hoped it was another child, maybe a boy he could show his car collection to. Until that second, he hadn't been lonely, and now just the thought of meeting another child filled him with delight.

The bushes were thick shades of the deepest green, a huge wall of leaves and branches he could barely get into. "Hey, come out—whoever you are!" His hands touched the branches and spread them apart before his body wriggled through them. "Come on!" He laughed, his eyes bright. "Don't hide from me. I won't snitch on you for being here . . . where are you?" Jeremy was a little angry now. For days he had had the strange feeling that someone was watching him, usually from a distance. What did they want? Why wouldn't they come out and show themselves? What was wrong with them! He was getting tired of their games.

He was tired of being alone; playing alone.

"We could be friends!" He sighed. But the bushes were still silent. He'd gone through all of them . . . and there was no one. Nothing. Puzzled, he slumped down at their edge in the tall grass. He felt sad and angry at the same time. How could there be no one there? He saw someone just a minute ago. He lay back in the grass and studied the sky, his fingers fanning over the soft grass, caressing it. As he lay there and closed his eyes he thought he could hear a child's giggle somewhere far away. Whispers haunted the air around him. Sometimes they were so loud that he was sure if he opened his eyes, someone would be right there next to him. But when he finally did, the whispers and laughter faded away into the sunlight and were gone. He was still alone. He sat up, his head spinning. Light dazzled in sparks before him.

"Wow, this place is weird!" he muttered, his face sharp in the shadows of the bushes. "I wonder if it's haunted." He uttered the words to himself. There was a feeling around the place that made him aware of every tiny noise. He was as jumpy as a flea on a dog's paw.

What could he do? His eyes skimmed the distant line of mulberry bushes that circled the side of the yard and he got up, brushing grass and dirt from his clothes. He made a beeline toward a small gap in them. A second later he had pushed through the hole and out into another yard. There was no house to be seen, just grass and a stretch of weeds that seemed to go on forever. In the far distance, he spotted a tall narrowly built brick house that was a monstrosity. Did people actlly live in that barn? He ran across the field towards it. Cats of all colors and sizes scattered before him and ran to hide or crouch behind things where they could glare back at him. He was intruding in their territory.

One of the smaller cats ran right out in front of him and he had to jump to avoid stepping on him. It threw him off balance and he nearly stumbled. The house seemed empty. Nothing moved, except a curtain at a side window. It fluttered a second, as if a breeze had played with it. To him it meant that someone did live there, but they were just hiding from him . . . or spying. A bunch of old ladies with white hair and watery eyes, alone and afraid, hiding from the world. Jeremy smiled and waved cheerfully at the staring windows. He wanted to run up to the front door and pound on it, demanding to see them.

Come out, come out, wherever you are! Come out!

He was lonely. . . he'd never admit it to his mother or to his uncle Jim, but he really missed all his friends from his old home. He had no one to show his cars to, no one to play with and tease; no one to be taller or smarter than. He hadn't seen one child in all this time. He had a new BB gun that his dad had given him for his last birthday. Who could he show off his shooting to? He could hit a bull's eye at twenty yards!

But who cared?

His uncle Jim wasn't a gun lover like his dad was. Uncle

Jim hated guns, even toy guns.

Jeremy came to a dirt road that seemed to wind around the neighborhood like a snake. His mom said that nothing had changed much. He dragged his tennis shoes heavily through the dust, thinking about that. It must be true, nothing looked like it had changed in ages. He looked up at the tall trees, shading his eyes from the hot sun. The whole place had an unreal feeling about it, as if he had stepped back in time. Nervously, he wandered farther and farther away from his new home, knowing his mother would have a fit if she knew where he was heading.

He began to whistle as he skipped down the dusty path, the same dusty roads that his mother and uncle had once also wandered down when they were his age. But he wasn't thinking about his mother. He was hearing the painful echoes of past promises in his mind as he worked his way toward a place he had only been to once. He hoped he could remember where it was now.

I promise . . . I promise . . . the words beat in his head like a drum as he began to run over the ground. *Promise! I'll never leave you, son. I'll always be your dad and I'll always love you. If you need me, I'll be there. Always, son.*

Jeremy's face was angry as the thoughts hummed along with his quickening stride. Where was his father now? Tears glittered in the boy's eyes and he wiped them angrily away with the back of a dirty hand and kept on running. But his feet couldn't outrun his thoughts, no matter how hard he tried.

He would never cry in front of his mom like this and he was angry at himself when he acted so childish. His mother had accepted the divorce—why couldn't he? He guessed his mother was right when she said he'd feel better when he was finally enrolled in school. It would keep him busy and keep his mind off the past. But then she didn't know that; she didn't know that he still thought about his dad so much. He couldn't help it. He missed him. It was like part

159

of him was gone. While his mother cried outwardly, he had always hid his tears. In the mornings, sometimes his pillow would be damp.

He walked past a group of boys playing football in a field and he stopped to watch them for a while, plopping down in the dirt, his face suddenly eager and interested. None of them noticed him; none of them talked to him. He waited. He watched. "Hi there!" he said at one point to one of the boys when the ball was tossed accidentally near his foot and he picked it up and threw it back. The other boy merely nodded silently and resumed playing with his friends as if Jeremy weren't there at all.

They went on with their game oblivious of the lonely newcomer. He was an outsider and that was the way he would remain. Dejected, he finally accepted defeat and got up and slowly trudged away, peering over his shoulder every once and awhile to see if they would miss him. But they didn't. "So what!" he muttered under his breath as he went. "They're all bigger anyway. They don't want a little kid messing up their game." They just didn't want him around. He didn't belong, he didn't fit in. And to dwell on it too much might find him an answer he would like knowing even less. Even back home he hadn't had too many friends. Jeremy knew it had something to do with his mom. The same reasons that made his dad leave. Mom was different, too.

He wasn't sure, but he thought he heard laughter somewhere behind him, mingled with the sounds of the game. Let them laugh at him! Who cared! He didn't need them. He didn't need anyone.

He picked up a stick and dragged it, making tracks that wound along behind him like a scratchy tail.

He walked under the hot sun past strange houses and strange places until he came to his mother's childhood home. He had been drawn to it ever since the night he had first seen it. It seemed to beckon him as if saying . . . come.

Come. Here is something you have lost. Something you may treasure, may be here . . . come.

Maybe it was all those ghosts from so long ago. Maybe it was all that love still hovering there that lured him to the place. He meandered over the ruins, careful not to trip or to fall over the sharp bricks of the old foundation. There was the cherry tree. Something whispered through the breeze by his ear as he climbed the brittle branches and settled in on a top one like a contented cat. It was as if he were home. The place felt so familiar to him, as if he had been there before, long ago. The fields stretched out for endless miles before his narrowed eyes and he felt a twinge of guilt for being there. His mother had never asked him to promise not to come here, but in his heart he knew she didn't want him here.

She was afraid of the place. The woods. She didn't tell him so in so many words, but he had sensed it that first night by the fear in her eyes as she had scanned this same view. Something bad hung over this spot. He could sense it. But because he was aware of the danger, he knew to be careful.

As he sat up in the branches and listened to the wind, he wondered again why he had come. But the answers never came. The sun lowered itself slowly like a reluctant bather into cold water. The shadows weaved fantastic shapes around him as he watched. Then the wind came, suddenly cool on his face. It was coming in from the woods. He had only been here twice but he felt as if he belonged here . . . among the ruins . . . as if he had never left. The eerie sensation only lasted a moment, but when it passed, Jeremy let out a gasp.

Someone was whispering his name.

Jeremy gazed down and saw a small boy peering up at him through the shadows. The same steel-blue eyes as his, and the same smile. It was like looking in a clouded mirror and seeing himself. Even as he calmly accepted it, he knew that he did it too easily. "Hello. I'm Jeremy," he simply said, gnawing on a twig absent-mindedly. A small voice in his head whispered that he should run away. *Run . . .* "I knew I'd meet you someday," the boy on the ground replied. He was holding a big gray cat tightly in his arms. Jeremy noticed something funny about the cat right away . . . it never moved. Was it asleep? It remained so still. "It's a Maltese." The boy with the familiar smile indicated the cat he was cuddling as if he had read Jeremy's mind. "It's such a bad cat, sometimes, and I have to punish it. It's a pretty blue color though, isn't it?"

"More gray than blue," Jeremy corrected.

"*Blue!* I say it's a blue cat and I should know!" The boy's eyes had narrowed and he seemed angry.

Jeremy put up his hands in front of his face as if to ward off the other's anger. "Alright! If you say it's a blue cat, it's a blue cat!" He thought the other child was being stubborn on purpose. He smiled and teasingly threw down a few leaves on the other boy's head. His mouth fell open as he watched them simply go right through the murky figure and fall to the ground. Jeremy shook his head in bewilderment. "What the. . . ?"

"You must be her son." The boy's voice was like a dry rustle of autumn winds. Jeremy cocked his head and wondered . . . had the boy actually spoken, or were the words only thoughts? Jeremy's heart began to beat wildly inside his chest and his eyes grew huge. His fingers clung tightly to the branches as if he were afraid they would slip away. . . like reality was slipping away. "Who are you?"

"You don't know?" The strange boy's eyebrows rose and a cynical smirk spread across his face.

"No."

The eyes betrayed surprise and then unexpectedly, boredom. "You really don't know who I am." It was a statement. "She's never told you about me, then, has she? I would have thought *she* wouldn't have forgotten me so

162

easily." The voice was noncommital. The boy was stroking the cat again, thoughtfully.

Jeremy felt another twinge of fear. "Who are you?" he repeated. He didn't realize that he had begun to inch his way up higher in the tree as if distance meant safety. The boy below noticed it with a mirthful grin and glowing eyes. Jeremy was suddenly very afraid.

"I might tell you—someday—if you're good." He winked. For one moment Jeremy could have sworn that the image was fading . . . maybe it was the play of the light and shadow? Yes, that had to be it!

"I've waited a long time. You don't know, Jeremy." The cat never moved. Not even an inch. Not even the tail. In fact, Jeremy could have sworn that the thing was as stiff as a board. A shiver went through him as the boy seemed to waver like a dim figure in a thick mist.

Jeremy was speechless. It was beginning to get dark and he knew he had to get home. Darkness was not the time to be in this place, especially with this "thing" below him. He wasn't sure exactly what it was, but he didn't really want to find out, either.

He wanted to go home.

"I've been so lonely. You don't know!" The thing below him was whining. But only the voice was real now . . . the child had disappeared into thin air. "No one ever comes to play with me anymore. Everyone's gone. I used to have so many brothers and sisters . . . now they're all gone."

Jeremy felt a crazy urge to laugh at the words, but he was too frightened. He looked around the tree, everywhere, but the boy was gone. At least his body was gone. The voice continued to drone on first from one place and then another. ". . . so lonely. ." Jeremy was terrified. He had to get away.

"Oh, I know what you mean . . . why, I've been pretty lonely myself." Jeremy searched for a shadow or a hint of the person he had been talking to just a moment before. It was unnerving to talk to thin air. He had wanted a friend so badly he would have talked to an animated scarecrow if one would have talked to him. He would have taken what he could get and not complain. So what if this boy was a little strange? A branch cracked sharply next to him and suddenly the boy with the cat was sitting there, grinning at him. *Solid.* As real as Jeremy himself. Jeremy tried to convince himself that his eyes had played tricks on him and this boy was no different than he was.

Fat chance! A tiny wicked voice teased in his ear. Jeremy shook his head and smiled nervously back at the other boy. He was so close, Jeremy could have reached out and actually touched him. But for some reason, he didn't. If Jeremy was making this all up in his mind, he didn't want to know.

"I told you my name. So what's yours?"

The other boy remained silent. He was looking towards the woods like he could hear something Jeremy couldn't.

"What's your name?" Jeremy insisted.

"Haven't I told you who I am?" The face was suddenly a mask that hid something unspeakable.

"No." Jeremy was indignant. "Come on, you can tell me. Why is it such a secret?"

"Because." The boy's eyes were puzzled, his features twisted. For a second Jeremy wasn't sure he was even looking at a human face any longer. He had just about decided he'd had enough of this cat-and-mouse act and was going to high-tail it for home before it got dark. This kid was giving him the shivers. "Because I'm not supposed to be talking to you. I could get in trouble." Red-rimmed eyes floated in a ghostly white face and the voice sounded like a wail. "But . . . you're *her* son. *She* was nice to me. Nicer than all the others. *I liked her.*" He smiled a wan smile, his eyes glued to something off in the distance that only he could see. "I want to help her . . . but *he* won't allow it. *He* would hurt me terribly if *he* thought I betrayed *him.*" The stench of fear and some other indescribable odor almost gagged Jeremy. It was engulfing him, coming from everywhere at once.

Jeremy slapped a hand over his nose and mouth and tried to keep the contents of his stomach intact. "Whew! That smell!" It was the worst thing he'd ever smelled . . . like someone had died.

"I know. I know. Poor Jeremy." The boy giggled.

"It's not funny!" Jeremy scrambled down to the ground. That kid was *bad* and suddenly he wanted to be home more than anything. The shadows were lengthening and the sun was low in the darkening sky. When Jeremy looked up at the tree the boy was gone. He rubbed his eyes, but he was definitely alone. There was no other child anywhere. There was nothing. His mind realized what he had seen but rebelled. Spooks and goblins weren't real. They weren't! He started back the way he had come, whistling to keep up his shredded courage. He refused to look left or right and made darn sure he didn't turn around. It shocked him when a voice suddenly spoke right into his ear. "You want to see something neat?"

It was the boy! Jeremy jumped and felt his skin crawl. He threw a guarded look over his shoulder. The boy was standing quietly behind him.

He was too afraid to run. No telling what the thing would do if he did . . . if it *was* real. The best thing to do was act natural. Talk to it.

"Only if you tell me your name. I don't go with anyone who won't tell me his name." Jeremy shook like a leaf inside.

"Charlie. My name's Charlie." He waited for a reaction.

Jeremy just stared at him. Why did that name sound so familiar? He racked his brain but couldn't come up with anything. "Charlie . . ." He tried it out. "O.K. Charlie, follow, I'll lead."

Charlie led him into the field. Jeremy hung back for a

while, afraid, and then plunged into the weeds to where Charlie was standing and pointing at something hidden in the undergrowth.

Jeremy was very surprised when he saw what it was. Rocks. Dozens of sparkling rocks piled in neat little mounds. His grandmother's rock garden, or part of it.

"I've been saving them. Taking care of them . . . for *her.*" Charlie was grinning. "She always loved Mom's pretty rocks. You can take them back to her. Do you think she'll be pleased?" The voice was eager.

Jeremy was stunned. He stared at Charlie through half-closed eyes. He could only nod. He dropped down and started to gather the rocks. He knew it was expected of him. He'd collect an armful and run . . .

"Thanks, Charlie." The whispered words almost choked him. He wanted to *run* so bad, he could taste it. Something was terribly wrong here. "Charlie . . ."

But Charlie wasn't there anymore.

Jeremy shivered and got up. He had stuffed rocks in his pockets and his hands were full. He walked, faster and faster.

"Wait . . . I have something else to show you!"

Jeremy glanced back and saw Charlie *floating* over the gullies coming after him. Jeremy moaned and began to run. "Sorry, I can't! It's getting late and I promised Mom I'd be home before dark! I have to go home now." His voice had risen to a very high peak as he started to run. The sun was almost down and he felt the cooler air coming in as the light slipped away. His senses were on edge. The night was coming alive. Jeremy began running for his life.

"Wait, Jeremy!" The boy floated along behind him, close on his tail. No matter how fast Jeremy ran, the thing was right there at his shoulder, laughing. He couldn't be shaken. "Wait! I have so much more to show you. Out in the woods . . ." it cried. "You have to come! *Please!*" The voice sounded frightened and Jeremy liked that new development even less.

It wanted something. Jeremy was gasping for breath and his chest felt like it was about to burst. Yet he kept on running. Faster. Faster! The *thing* hovered constantly at his shoulders, pleading with him to stop and come into the woods.

Jeremy glanced back only once and saw hatred glowing red in the boy's unearthly eyes and he saw the woods shimmering hungrily back in the distance. The ominous shadows within swirled into human-like shapes that seemed to beckon him back. *Come. Come here to us!*

Charlie, the boy, suddenly disappeared. The thing that he really was floated near the edge of the woods, glaring at him. Spitting and hissing, it was angry that Jeremy had got away. For one crazy second, Jeremy even had an impulse to turn around and follow the thing into the woods. It seemed such a peaceful, soothing . . . lovely place.

Come . . .

NO! Jeremy had been torn for just a split second and he had turned to gaze back at the line of misty trees. Now he smiled and his eyes flashed defiance that mocked the power of whatever lurked in that forest. He knew better. As he turned and started to run away again, the woods began to hiss like a thousand tiny snakes and Charlie dissolved into the trees.

Don't you dare go! Don't you dare . . . go! The wind seemed to scream at him. The air around him turned into a fury and something began to wail.

"Goodbye, Charlie!" Jeremy yelled. The rocks were clunking in his pockets and his arms ached from the weight of those he carried. He lost a few as he jumped the gullies.

Something whipped across his face and he felt a terrible sharp stinging sensation down his left cheek and across his throat. He yelped, but never faltered a step. Terror and pain seemed to make him fly.

By the time he reached his back door and knew he was

safe, he collapsed in a heap on the bottom step. It was only then that he allowed himself to check his face. When he took his fingers away and looked down at them, they were covered with blood, as was the whole front of his shirt. It was a miracle he had made it home!

Something had scratched him nearly down to the bone.

CHAPTER FIFTEEN

I told Jeremy to go out and play. One look at Detective Raucher's face and I knew why he was here. Later, I realized my mistake in letting Jeremy out the door. I should have known better than to let him go with what I knew was lurking out there waiting to get its claws into us. But at that precise moment I cared only about the worry in the detective's face as he turned to me for help.

I was too close to the fire to try to fool with it. I knew too much, all of it unbelievable, and I was scared to death . . . for all of us.

"Let's sit down first. Can I get you a cup of coffee or something?" He had already seen Jim in the doorway between the front room and the kitchen and nodded. I supposed that when he had meant alone, he had simply meant no children. I didn't need to guess what he was going to talk about. I felt sick inside and when I looked back at Jim he was slumped against the wall, his fingers rubbing his temples as if he were in pain.

The detective's eyes smiled for the first time since he had walked in the door. "A cup of coffee sounds real good. I need it." He sat down on the couch across from me and I noticed the tiredness in his movements. "Maybe it will help me to stay awake. I've been up most of the night . . ." He let out a soft sigh. He smiled, trying to lighten things up a bit, but did a lousy job of it. I got up to get him his coffee. I had decided to dislike Detective Raucher, but today he wasn't the same arrogant man he had been when I first met him. Today he was only a deeply troubled soul and my heart went out to him. "Have you eaten? I can offer you a sandwich or something, Detective."

"Call me Ben," he said in a grateful voice. "And a sandwich sounds great, thank you." I fancied he was looking at me differently, considering something. For some reason, maybe his outright humbleness, I replied, "I'll get you some coffee and a bacon sandwich . . . and call me Sarah." I went into the kitchen and prepared it, my heart pounding wildly against my chest. I knew why he had come and exactly what he wanted. I was frightened and I didn't know what to do. I could hear Jim and him talking in low tones in the other room. I found myself silently formulating little lies and half truths to get out of helping him. But no matter what I came up with, it was going to sound bad. He'd want to know why I wouldn't help. I stopped myself, thinking I might be jumping the gun. Maybe he wasn't here to ask for my help. Maybe he didn't know about me . . .

When I reentered the front room they were both sitting on the couch in silence and they looked up at me.

"Here's your sandwich, Ben." I smiled, a little uncomfortable at using his first name when I hardly knew him. They were both staring at me as if I were a bug under a microscope and Jim's eyes said more than a thousand words. I set a mug of hot coffee down on the coffee table. "I hope one sugar is enough, because that's what I put in it." He had told me once how he took his coffee but that was when I hadn't liked him very much and I hadn't listened very closely. Ben nodded and put the coffee to his lips. I sat down in the chair in front of him, waiting. Ben ravaged the sandwich in record time.

"It's all right! I've got more, if you're that hungry!" I was trying to put off the confrontation, just as he was. With a sheepish grin he handed me his empty coffee cup. I refilled it and sat back down. Now was the time. None of us had any small talk left.

"Well, I guess, it's down to business," I said. Jim seemed to be off in his own little world so it surprised me when he suddenly inserted, "Sarah . . . Ben knows about you . . . your gift, that is."

"You do, do you?" I addressed Ben. Why did I always feel guilty when someone found out about it? Always the thief caught with his hands in the till or the child who's caught in a blatant lie. Over the years, I came to think it was better to pretend that it didn't exist. It was easier than facing it. Sitting there looking at Ben I remembered back to after Charlie's death, and the way the police looked at me when I had told them everything I knew. They acted like I was crazy. It was the way everyone usually reacted. It was always the way. I suddenly hoped Ben wouldn't look at me that way. I didn't want *anyone* to look at me like that anymore.

"The first day I met you, your name rang a bell, but I didn't make the connection till much later. You're that famous psychic that made all the papers some years ago with those murder cases." It was not a question, it was a statement.

I raised an eyebrow at him.

"I know, I checked it out." He continued, "I have friends in Benchley in the police department, so I had access to all your files." He raised his hands as if to defend himself. "I'm sorry, Sarah. But I had more than enough reason to pull those files. I wanted to know more about you."

"And that's how you found out?" My voice was perhaps a little too caustic.

"Yes. In the beginning I was just curious about you— mystery woman suddenly shows up to reclaim an old dilapidated house that's been rumored to be haunted . . . I've been a detective too long to pass that up." He tried a small smile then and I found myself thinking that he really

171

was a handsome man when he wasn't acting so macho. "Then one thing led to another and your name was mentioned by one of the old-timers down at the station who remembered you as a child. He said he talked to you once about something that happened here about fifteen years ago." He was hesitating, a guilty edge to his voice. His eyes were glued to my face, probably waiting for a reaction.

I looked over toward Jim who was standing there as still as stone. I knew I was on my own. "And. . .?"

"The guy told me the whole story of your family and then, later, through the computer and old records, I tracked down the rest of it. You two are the only ones left," he said softly. "I'm sorry to pry. It just happened."

"Why are you here?" I blurted it out, unable to wait a moment longer.

"Sarah, there's been another murder. . ."

I shut my eyes so he wouldn't see the pain. I heard Jim whisper, "No. Oh, no!"

"A little boy about ten years old. They found him this morning at the edge of the woods out there." He waved his hand towards the trees. "He'd been reported missing yesterday evening and we'd all been out combing the area for him since. We found him this morning. He was mauled to death." Ben seemed to be choking on his words and there was both grief and anger in his voice as he talked.

"And you want me to come in on the case and help—as a psychic, that is?" I was trying to sound a little indignant, as if he were bothering me. I didn't let him answer my question. "I'm sorry about the child, Detective Raucher. But I can't help you." My eyes slid to Jim's for support, but he was off in a dreamland somewhere and I wondered for the second time if he was really all right. He never seemed to be here anymore. "If you read my files, you know that I don't offer my help to police departments any more."

Ben interrupted me abruptly. "Oh, I know about your few bad experiences, Sarah! But that shouldn't stop you from helping again, when you can. On the whole, you had an unbelievable track record. So what if you made a few mistakes? You can still help. Think of that little boy."

"You don't understand. I don't do that any more." I started the lies, feeling uneasy as I always did when I avoided the truth. "My life was turning into a three-ring circus and I couldn't take it anymore. Do you know what it's like to have people calling you all hours of the day and night wanting help? More help than one person can give? Crazy people calling me a freak, people wanting to cash in on my gift, others wanting to lock me up in a little room and tap my brain. I was sick of it! I *would* have turned into a freak in a side show. I have a son, Detective! I'd had enough! I have to start thinking about myself and my son. That's one of the reasons I came here. I had to get away from all that!"

"You don't understand!" He was going to start begging me now and that, coming from someone like Ben Raucher, was almost more than I could stand.

I stood up angrily. "Oh, but I *do* understand! You want me to start all over again. Blow my cover and start the circus all over again. I won't do it!"

"A child, Sarah! A poor child . . . just like your Jeremy out there." Now he was getting angry. He stood up and looked over to Jim for support. He found none there. Jim was staring at the wall. A chill crawled up my spine, seeing him like that. Ben turned back to me and there was ice in his dark eyes when he spoke. "Yes, a child just like Jeremy . . . a child just like your brother Charlie all those years ago." There was a threat there and I glared back at him, something sinking somewhere in the pit of my stomach because I knew what he was going to say next even before he said it.

"Why are you bringing ancient history into this?" I demanded.

"It's not ancient history anymore, Sarah. I think there's a connection between this latest murder and that murder all those years ago. Fifteen years ago, right? I believe they were both killed the same way. And I believe you know more than you're telling. I don't just want your help; I want your confidence. That little boy last night died just like your brother and the others died. It's just a hunch *now*, but I'm going to prove it, I swear! You're already involved and you can opt to be on my side or you can run away again . . . like you did all those years ago."

I looked at him and my eyes smarted with pain and anger. He had me trapped and we both knew it. He was one smart man and a darn good cop. He'd done his job very well.

I sat down slowly and rested my chin in my hands, my face turned away from him. I had to compose myself before I could say anything else.

"We're not running anymore, Ben," I said quietly. I was so tired. So sick of the games. The lies. I had to protect my son. And then, I was angry, again. Like a rat in a maze, I wanted out! And like that rat, I was getting angry at the person who had trapped me in that maze and wouldn't let me out. We were all prisoners of the thing in the woods. I'd show it! I'd give it a hell of a run for its money before it pulled *me* down. I wasn't going to be as easy a prey as the rest of them. By God, I wasn't! I was going to fight!

Ben came over and took my hand, no longer the cop, just a friend. He tilted my chin up and looked into my troubled face.

"Sarah, I know you aren't involved in these murders in any criminal sense . . . but I pray you can help us find some answers. I'm afraid there'll be more murders. It's a pattern, don't you see?"

I looked away and nodded. He gently brushed the hair from my face and gave me a reassuring smile. "You'll help me then? Not just as a psychic but as someone familiar with the case by past experience, and as a friend? Both of you?" He was asking Jim, too.

I found myself feeling sorry for all of us. All of us lost,

pitiful, tiny people up against something we didn't understand. I wanted to lay Ben's head against my shoulder and soothe him. He seemed so upset by the child's murder. In a start of recognition, I had to stop myself from doing just that.

"Ben, I'll help all I can," I finally promised, pulling away. "But in confidence between us two—not officially."

I'd help him, but that was all I'd do. I wasn't going to get tangled up with another macho, self-centered cop again! No matter how sweet they seemed or how sincere, they were all alike. Men. All alike. They wanted you until they had you . . . then they wanted someone else. Oh, I'd help Ben all I could. As long as it didn't harm any of us, I'd help until it became too dangerous.

"He's right, Sarah." It surprised me when Jim spoke up. "We can't do it by ourselves any longer. Three against something is better than two." He looked at Ben. "Where do we start?" I threw a meaningful glance towards Jim when Ben wasn't looking. *Be careful,* I warned him, and he understood. There was only so much we could tell Ben. If he thought we were crazy, it wouldn't help us at all.

"You start with the truth. Or anything you know that might shed some light on what happened last night." Ben talked about the murder and everything he knew about the case. He asked me or Jim a question once in a while as the story unfolded.

I told him about the vision I had had about the child's death and told him all he wanted to know about our family and Charlie's death. There was a lot that computers and dusty files knew nothing about—the human side of the whole tragedy all those years ago. I told him as much as I thought he could swallow.

We sat there talking for a long time. I could see he was very upset by all the unsolved deaths. It wasn't very pretty and I felt sick to my soul, knowing that I was the reason for it. *This* I didn't dare tell him. I was at fault somehow, and I couldn't figure out why. There were so many secrets I had

175

to keep. My whole life was a grave—full of them.

And there were times I had to say things that I wished I could have kept secret. "You're right about one thing, though . . ." I had to tell him as he was getting up to leave. "There will be more murders, unless we can find a way to stop . . . them."

His face fell. "Are you sure? I mean, have you had another vision or whatever?"

"Not exactly. But I feel there will be more murders . . . I don't know when, or how. I might never know. I can't plan these things." As I spoke, I watched his reaction closely. He was guarding himself very carefully. "I never asked to have this so-called gift, Ben. I never wanted it. I hate it. There are so many times I can't understand what's going on . . . or I can't help anyway. The crime's already been done." I shuddered and for a second I thought he was going to break the rules and put his arms around me. "Sometimes it's torture," I whispered sadly.

He cleared his throat and touched my hand gently. "I understand. Believe me, it's not easy asking for your help, either. I had to think a long time before I came over here today. It's not that I didn't think you *would* help; it's just that . . ." He stopped, embarrassed at what he was trying to say.

I finished for him. I had seen that look too many times not to identify it. "You never believed in this kind of stuff before, right?"

"Right." He was talking to both of us now. "I've been a cop for ten years and believe me, I've seen it all. Crazies. The whole nine yards. I can honestly say that in all that time I've never really run across anyone I thought was a genuine psychic. A lot of quacks or con artists pretend to have the power, but they're just pretending. I used to laugh my socks off at 'em, or not so politely kick them out of my office." He gave me that scrutinizing look again. "But in all my years, I've never seen a time when I needed help before more than I do on this one. That boy was the most pitiful thing I've ever seen . . ." His voice trailed off.

"Then why do you believe I'm the genuine article?"

"Your track record." He smiled again. It seemed to break the spell.

I wondered if he really accepted my gift and thought that I could truly help him, or if Jim and I were just two suspicious characters to be put on his list and watched because there were too many unexplainable coincidences to tie us to this latest murder. I couldn't be sure, but Jim was right. We did need help.

"Ben, I have to tell you that I can't promise you I'll see something in time. I mean, like I said, I can't *make* the visions come. They do or they don't."

"I understand." He tried one last time to convince me to come out into the open. "You're sure you won't come on the case officially, Sarah? There is more evidence you'd be given access to if you were. If you'd just come down to the station . . ." He was hardheaded, I had to say that for him.

"No," I said firmly as I walked him to the door. "No, I couldn't. The newspapers would smell it a mile away and then — poof — I'd be the center attraction again. You must promise," I reminded him, urgently.

"Maybe that's one of the reasons I think that if there *is* a genuine article, then, you my girl, are certainly it. You aren't like most of those charlatans who are out to get all the glory. You're not a headline seeker. Publicity, that's what most of them want. They love having names in the papers and getting on talk shows. You're not like that, are you?"

"No, I'm not. I just want to be left alone. I've had too many years of all that. I just want to live in peace."

"And none of us will let you," he answered dryly. "I'm sorry."

"I'll call you . . . if anything happens," I finished. Drained. I noticed that the sun was beginning to go down and I didn't see Jeremy anywhere.

"I'll keep you posted on what's happening with the case. I have to go home and get a couple hours shut-eye and then I'll join the men out in the woods again. We're still searching for clues . . . anything. Looks like it will be a long drawn-out procedure. They're bringing in experts from all over the state to help us. We haven't had anything like this in a long time."

Fifteen years, his eyes said to me.

"Here's my number at the office and here's my home number." He handed me a small scrap of paper with two numbers scribbled on them. "Home number is the bottom one." And then he was gone. I looked out the door, my eyes seeking Jeremy's bright head. When I walked back into the house I peered out the windows to see if Jeremy was on the side of the house or playing in the bushes.

"What's the matter, Sis?" Jim asked, trailing on my heels as I walked to the kitchen and looked out the back door. The tree was empty.

"I don't know . . . I have a funny feeling." I looked at Jim. "I don't see Jeremy anywhere, do you?" Jim shook his head and then went out the door at a brisk walk. I stood by the door and watched him disappear around the corner of the house. He didn't come back for awhile and when he did, he was alone.

"Don't worry, Sarah." He tried to comfort me. "He'll be back soon, you'll see. He's just out playing somewhere. It's not dark yet."

He was right about that. But it was late afternoon and the sun was weakly shining. "Maybe you're right. As long as it's not dark and he's close to the house somewhere. I *did* tell him to stay close." He could be out hiding in the bushes somewhere.

"He'll be home before dark. He knows the rules," Jim said. "Besides I don't think *it* can hurt him unless he goes into those woods." He was staring out the window.

Part of me wasn't sure of that, but part of me refused to accept what had happened the night before, as well as this new murder. It didn't seem real because it didn't touch us. Then I remembered those screams we'd heard last night in

178

the woods, and it seemed all too real.

Jim sensed my anxiety and he seemed to be sharing the same memories of last night. I could see it in his face.

"If he doesn't come back in a little while, I'll go looking for him," he stated.

I started making supper as if nothing were wrong. Jim sat in the kitchen chair with his guitar and strummed a bit, trying to work out the words of a new song he was writing. His voice soothed me. I loved to listen to him make his music.

Jim had a lot on his mind. There was so much he wanted to say, but nothing he would. We knew each other so well. He was worried about Jeremy, and frightened like me, even guilty about that poor child last night.

But Jeremy was just outside playing . . . like so many other children . . . outside playing . . .

CHAPTER SIXTEEN

I was standing by the sink, washing the supper dishes, rinsing them meticulously and setting them in the plastic rack to dry when I first felt that familiar tingling. I kept my hands busy, but my eyes were glued to the fading scene outside the window. Twilight. It was growing dark. Jim had stopped strumming the guitar and his untouched plate was still waiting in front of him. I kept looking from the phone to the door to the window. Back and forth. Listening, watching and waiting. I was not going to panic, not yet. Jeremy had only been gone a few hours. His plate, covered to keep it warm, sat on the counter next to me. Chicken, mashed potatoes, gravy and corn. I'd made homemade biscuits especially for him. He loved my homemade biscuits, and there was chocolate pudding for dessert.

I watched the last rays of sunlight seep away into eternity. No matter how we tried to deceive ourselves, this wasn't normal. I threw the dish towel down on the counter and turned to Jim.

Before I could even speak he said, "He should be home by now. How could we have been so stupid to let him out unsupervised after what happened last night? I blame myself," he whispered vehemently. "How stupid could I have been . . . I know better than that!"

"It isn't your fault, Jim. It's hard to believe this is happening to us again," I offered. But I realized we had been incredibly naive to let the boy go out like that. I was staring out at the dim empty yard. When would we ever get wise? We were cursed. "I'm going out to look for him. I don't care how late it's getting or how dangerous it is. I'm going."

"Sarah!" Jim came up behind me as I stepped out on the porch and peered down the winding street. It looked like it did when I was a child and I smiled for just a brief moment, remembering all the games we used to play when we were children, so unsuspecting.

"Sarah!" Jim repeated at my shoulder. "You can't go out there looking for Jeremy alone. We'll go together." It took courage for him to say that. "Does he have any friends here?"

"No, not that I know about. He hasn't started school yet. Oh, I know I should have registered him long before this," I went on guiltily.

Jim picked up the phone. "I'm going to call the police, Sarah."

"No! Not yet! We don't even know if anything is wrong. He's only a little late," I interjected lamely. I couldn't stand the thought of dragging the police into this so soon. Jeremy might waltz in any moment.

"I'm going to call Ben," Jim declared as he dialed the number that was on the scrap of paper by the phone.

I almost protested and stopped him, but thought better of it. Ben had offered to help and he'd be called in sooner or later. Shades of the past and Jonathan . . . I mused on that for a second and then gave in. It didn't really matter. All that mattered was my child.

Jim mumbled a few words and then handed the phone to me. "I'm afraid I got him out of bed. He wants to talk with you."

I felt silly waking an almost total stranger. What right did I have to bother this man in his own home?

"Hello, Ben?" I tried to keep my voice steady.

"Sarah? Didn't I just see you?" It took me a second to see that he was teasing me. His voice was groggy, and distant, but somehow reassuring.

"Yes." I liked his voice.

"What's the problem?" He already knew what the problem was. Jim had told him and he was uneasy. His sixth sense was alerted, even if his voice was frayed around the edges.

"Jeremy went out a few hours ago, and he hasn't come back. Usually I don't worry, but after last night and that child . . ." I broke off. Outside it was growing dark. Inside I was screaming.

"Any friends?"

"No. We're so new here. Ben, I don't know what to do! I don't want to be an alarmist, but he knows the rules and this just isn't like him. I'm really worried."

"Listen, Sarah, I'm coming right over. We can talk about what to do when I get there if he isn't home by then. All right?"

"Yes, Ben. And thank you."

"No problem, Sarah. Try not to worry too much. I'll be there as fast as I can." I hope that's fast enough, I thought. The phone went dead in my hands.

CHAPTER SEVENTEEN

It began the moment the receiver settled in its cradle.

"Do you feel that . . . cold?" I asked Jim. And then my throat closed up. I was choking. The hair on the back of my neck prickled.

"Cold?" Jim seemed baffled. "I don't feel a thing. Are you all right, Sarah?" Suddenly he was beside me and I felt him take my hand. "Sarah?"

My mind fumbled, as an unnatural darkness invaded the house. With a cry of dread, I squeezed Jim's hand even tighter. "Jim . . . why is it so dark? *Jim?*" I felt his arms come around me, but that was all I could feel. The darkness and the cold had taken me into another world and I was wandering there, confused and alone.

I wandered, but yet I knew I still held Jim's warm hand. It served as a lifeline and if he hadn't been there, I might have slipped into oblivion. I gripped it harder.

"I'm all right. I don't know what's wrong. I don't know where I am," I told him. I was in a misty twilight world, almost like a trance. It had never happened like this before and I was frightened.

"I'm here." Jim said from far away.

"The boy is not in danger. Sarah, child . . . your son is safe." The soft voice whispered in my ear and in slow

motion I spun around to see a tall, willowy white shape in the distance. I could barely distinguish the features, but I knew the voice.

"Grandmother?" I hesitated and stepped closer. The figure rippled and shrunk.

"Safe . . . he's safe."

"Where is he?" I begged her. She was shrinking to a pinpoint of light and I knew that soon she would be gone. Why was she leaving? "Stay!" I ran after her only to find nothing. Nothing.

"It doesn't want him." The emptiness chanted. The misty world hummed and thumped around me and the light flooded the world like something had opened a great door. I awoke like a deep sleeper. Jim was shaking me and there was so much noise . . .

It was everywhere.

"Sarah! Sarah!" He was livid as he shook me. His face was white and his eyes were full of desperation and pain. "Wake up! For God's sake wake up!" There was a horrendous pounding and screaming—moaning—at the front door and Jim was shaking.

It had come for us!

"Wake up!" he cried again and slapped me across the face. It stung down through to my feet. I was still so dizzy I swayed like a frail tree in a strong wind.

"Thank God," he whimpered, as I stared at the door in horror. Jeremy was coming home . . . how could he if that *thing* was still here?

"What is it?" Jim was staring, too. "What does it want?"

We stared, frozen. The door began to actually move. It vibrated and shook as the onslaught continued. Whatever it was, was outside. "What ever *it* is . . . *it* wants in. And *it's* angry." I said, too placidly. I was living a nightmare again. The wood splintered into a thousand sharp pieces and splattered across us. We hid our heads against each other and I screamed. Just once.

Then it was silent. Gone to whence it came.

The relief was so great I wanted to laugh. "It couldn't get in," I said in awe, running my hands over the shattered door. "It couldn't break all the way through!"

Jim slumped in the chair. "What happened to you, before? Was that a kind of trance?" He was trying to understand.

"Yes. It was a trance. It was also a message."

"From who?"

"Our grandmother. She told me that Jeremy was all right."

"But she's dead," he exclaimed. When he looked up at me I could see the whites of his eyes, the lines in his face that had never been there before. "Why would she want to tell us anything?"

"So we wouldn't worry. But she left in such a hurry, I didn't have a chance to really talk to her. Now I know why." I nodded at the wrecked door.

"Do you think it's given up?" His mouth framed the words but never really spoke them. He seemed to be retreating further and further away from me.

"No," I said, laying a hand on his shoulder, "but it won't come back tonight." Jim nodded and the color came back into his face.

"I'll fix the door tomorrow," Jim said.

"Tomorrow is fine, Jim." A child. He was a small child again and I had to soothe him.

The door opened and I turned to see Jeremy standing there. There was blood all down the front of his shirt. I ran and held him so tight, I thought I'd break him. I tilted his chin up. Something had dug into his face. He was being the brave little soldier. "How did you do that?" I asked.

"I fell. I'm sorry I'm late. Are you mad at me?"

"I should spank your butt for that hare-brained stunt, young man!" I scolded, holding him at arm's length. "But I'm too glad to see you. We were ready to call the cops. Another ten minutes and we would have, too. You know you're supposed to be home by dark, don't you?"

Something glimmered in Jeremy's eyes and when he talked to me I had the uncanny suspicion that he knew a lot more than he was letting on, things we would never know. A shiver went through me and I wondered if my grandmother had felt like this when she had looked at me as a child.

"I know, Mom, Jim. I'm sorry. I ran home, that's how I fell, honest. It's just that the dark beat me." He widened his eyes as he noticed the door for the first time. "Wow! What happened to our front door? How'd it happen?"

I had to bite my tongue so I wouldn't spill the beans. Of course, Jeremy didn't know about the thing in the woods and he didn't know the real reason he had to be home before dark. We had never told him. Yet, as he inspected the battered door I saw that glimmer in his eyes again and felt that he was keeping something from us.

"Don't really know. Someone—we don't have the slightest idea who—tried to break in. I guess pranksters or someone who just doesn't like us," I lied, my eyes on Jim.

"Mom!" Jeremy's eyes narrowed. He didn't believe that. "Who would hate us that much?" He was giving me a thoughtful frown. "I mean, this door's a mess. It must have taken something pretty strong to mess it up this bad. But it didn't get in, did it?" His voice was full of guilt. He was trying to hide it, but I knew it was there.

What did he think had tried to break in? He used the word "it", not "he" or "they". Did he already know what had happened here since we'd come? I studied his face but could not tell. I checked the cut on his face with gentle fingers. He didn't flinch. It wasn't as deep as I'd first thought.

"No. It didn't get in," I said to him finally. How was I going to explain this? I didn't want to frighten him, couldn't bring myself to tell him what was going on. "It could have been worse." I put my arm around his thin shoulder and hugged him close. I could hear his heart racing. So he was afraid, after all? What was I doing to my son? I had brought him here and now he was in terrible danger.

"Sure, Mom. It could have been worse. It could have knocked the house down," he replied sarcastically.

What he said startled me even though I realized he was teasing. But it made me ask myself the question: Could it have? What would we do if it decided to try?

"It's late. First, supper, then bedtime, son," I said maybe too harshly. "Tomorrow I'm enrolling you in school. I think you've had enough of a vacation." I gently prodded him away from the door and towards the stairs.

"Ah, Mom!" He protested. "I'm not tired. Can I stay up a little longer?"

"No. And you're filthy. I want you to take a bath before you eat and then I'll tuck you in . . . after I doctor up that nasty cut of yours."

"A bath? Ah, mother!"

"No back talk. Look at you, you're a mud ball, not to mention all that blood." Then the one nagging question I'd held in since Jeremy came home, popped out. "Where were you all this time?"

His eyes looked away. I caught that. He *was* hiding something. "Oh, out exploring. Mom? I'm sorry about making you and Uncle Jim worry so much. I promise I won't do it again."

I saw that he was trying to make it up in some way.

"I'll go take a long, hot bath. I'll get so clean, you won't even know me."

"No way! If I can recognize you under all that dirt then I can spot you no matter what you do," I said.

Jeremy was just about to go upstairs when someone knocked loudly on the door. This time I knew it was a human. "It's Ben!" And then I felt foolish. Jeremy was safe and I had gotten Ben out of bed for nothing.

I opened the door.

"Ben." I smiled guiltily. "He's home."

Jeremy peeked out from behind me. The cut had began to bleed again and I tried to dab off some of the blood.

"I see." He seemed relieved and stepped inside. "It's all right, Sarah. I don't mind being dragged out of bed if there's a happy ending. I'm a sucker for happy endings. I'm just thankful that the boy's safe." He reached out to ruffle the kid's hair. "Looks like you fell in with ten pounds of wildcat, huh?" Jeremy laughed as Ben looked at his cuts.

"I'll see to it," he said, and took over. I went for bandages and antiseptic as he asked me to and then watched as he carefully attended to the wound.

It made me look at Ben Raucher in a whole different light.

"How did this happen, son?" The question was inevitable. Jeremy gave me a quick glance.

"I . . . fell . . . on some rocks." Ben looked like he wanted to believe the story, but didn't.

"You be more careful, okay?" Ben reprimanded.

"Yeah, okay. Thanks, Ben."

"Jeremy, your bath?" I reminded him. After he went upstairs, I turned back to Ben. "Thanks for coming like that. It meant a lot to us to know you were there if we needed you. You're right. Better safe than sorry." The shadows under his eyes were more pronounced than earlier. The worry and lack of sleep had taken their toll. "I don't want my son to turn into a statistic."

"Well, under the circumstances, Sarah," he spoke my name softly as if he liked the way it sounded, "I'd be sure to lay stricter ground rules from now on. Keep your son closer to home until we can catch this nut who's responsible. Will you do that for me?" He smiled wearily then and I felt sorry for him, knowing what I knew — and he didn't. "I don't want to have to jump out of my bed like this too often." He yawned.

"You look tired . . . you need to go back to that bed and get some sleep. I'm sorry I woke you." I blushed brightly, and Ben noticed. His expression changed. He looked at me with tender eyes. His look made my face turn a shade pinker. "It was really no problem. That's what I'm here for. If

188

you need me again, for any reason, just call." His eyes twinkled.

Was that an invitation? I wondered.

"Well, I'll try not to drag you from dreamland next time." I promised. "Would you like some coffee?" I was just being polite. The man looked like he was about to literally fall in his tracks.

"Thanks, but I think I'll pass on that for now. Can I take a raincheck?" He was perfectly serious. "I'm bushed to the bone. I'm going home and get some more sleep. The first dose wasn't enough."

"Sure, you deserve it. Happy dreams." Under the circumstances, I was immediately sorry I had said that. No one could have happy dreams after what had happened.

I thought he was going to leave. But he stood there in front of me expectantly as if he were waiting for me to add something. We stood that way for what seemed a long time.

"What's wrong?" I finally asked.

He grinned that half-serious grin of his as if he knew a funny secret. "Isn't there something you want to tell me?" he insisted, studying me. Then I saw his eyes shift sharply towards the door.

"Oh! You mean what happened to the door, right?" Should I tell him the truth? I appraised the whole situation. It was about time I did. I was tired of lying.

"Bingo! Give the lady a prize! You're going to tell me what happened?"

Jim walked up. "I'll tell you what happened. *Something*—not some*one*—tried to break it down. As you can see by the damage, whatever it was almost succeeded. But it didn't get in and we don't know what it was or why it was doing that, except," and here he glanced over at me. ". . . something has had it in for us ever since we came here. Something wants us out of the way, or dead." Jim's voice was cold, his eyes haunted.

"You expect me to believe that? You mean to say that

you don't know what it is or why it's trying to kill you? Only that it *is* . . . and you've never seen it?" Ben said incredulously.

"You've got to believe us, Ben." Jim sighed, looking very old and tired himself. "We haven't got a prayer unless someone does, and helps. Just look at the odds we're up against . . . we're the only two left out of nine. Not very encouraging, huh?"

"What do you think this thing is?" He turned and asked me point blank.

"I can tell you what I *think* it is, but you'll probably think I'm nuts. I know I would think you were if you told me the same thing." Well, I thought: here goes nothing.

"Go ahead . . . I'm listening."

"You better sit down, then," I warned him and gestured to a seat. "It's a long story and not a particularly pretty one."

After he'd sat down, he said, "You sure you want to tell me this?"

"Yes. It's about time. We need an ally. Even if you can't accept what we believe has been happening to us since we were children, it'll do us good to confide in someone else."

Jim lowered himself to the rug and sat cross-legged. He looked like a ghost of the Jim I knew and loved.

I began to tell Ben about our family and our childhood, about the terrible being we believed lived in the woods and what it had done to all of us.

I told him everything from that first summer's night in those woods until a few minutes before when the door had been battered. Ben stared at me until I was finished.

"You think I'm just plain crazy, don't you?" I sighed when I'd said everything.

"No—I don't know what to believe, Sarah. Everything inside of me rebels at the whole idea of a supernatural creature that kills children out of evil spite. It doesn't make any sense. I'm a realist. I've never been faced with anything quite like this. If it hadn't happened to you, would *you* believe it?" he accused.

190

"I guess not. But you asked for the truth and I gave it to you. Or the truth as I've seen it. It's the only truth I know," I apologized. I knew it had been a mistake to try to explain our lives to a stranger. There were still so many times that I still couldn't believe all that had happened to us—and was still happening. So many times I was afraid I was just crazy.

"On the other hand," Ben said cautiously, "I can't argue the fact that you do have this psychic ability. It's in the records. It's real—as fantastic as that seems. I don't think you're lying to me or trying to con me. What I think," he said, rubbing his chin absentmindedly, "is that some very disturbed person has had a personal vendetta against your family all these years. And he's clever enough to have tricked you into believing all this supernatural phenomena, so you are too damn afraid to go to the police. That's what I think."

"You don't really believe that?" I asked, pitying him for his ignorance. How long did I try to believe that it was just the evil manifestations of a deranged mind and not anything unearthly? Too long. By the time I had awakened my family all were dead and what was left of us were trapped, right where it had always wanted us. Here.

"You really believe that a person arranged all those freak accidents to my family that to this day cannot be explained? My father died of a heart attack. They said, *off* the record, he had been frightened to death. *On* the record it was a massive heart seizure. His heart couldn't take the strain anymore and I'll tell you why! Leslie, the oldest, died in a horrible car accident on a sunny, beautiful spring day. *It* arranged that somehow. Our mother was brutally murdered by 'person or persons unknown' with a baseball bat. No arrests were ever made. Samantha, the baby, was found dead in her crib one morning . . . and . . . I can't go on," I moaned. "You know the rest. I can't stand to think about it anymore! This wasn't done by anything of this earth. That's the truth. And we don't know why it's doing this or how to stop it."

Ben just stared at me, a thousand conflicting thoughts warring in his mind.

"It's too fantastic. I still think it's just a very clever psychopathic murderer. And so what if you did go to the police? Apparently they had a hard time swallowing your stories. There *are* cases we can't solve. It doesn't mean it's been done by supernatural means."

"What you think doesn't matter. The only thing that does matter is that they're all dead. This child, now, too. There'll be more. This thing isn't human. It has such power—you don't understand!"

"Maybe, because of grief, you truly believe that."

"No!"

"Sarah, you've gone through a lot. But it can be fought. This killer can be stopped." Of course, he still thought of it as a person. Killable.

"*If* you know how to fight it. We haven't been able to find the secret combination, yet, to that little mystery. But we will," I said, looking up towards Jeremy's room. "We'll have to find a way to get it . . ." I was thinking of Jeremy and the other innocent victims that might be its next prey. ". . . before it kills again."

"You leave that end of it to the police, Sarah." Ben was solemn. "You're in grave danger the way it is. I want all of you to be extremely careful from now on. Promise me. Stop this nonsense about evil manifestations and leave it to us. Keep your head down and lay low for a while. He's clearly out to harm you." He tilted his shaggy head towards the mutilated door. "I'll make a report on this tonight."

I was shaking my head slowly. He didn't understand. Perhaps he never would. "Can't you see that what we're up against isn't . . . normal? Just look at the condition of the door. Imagine the strength it must have taken."

"It's human." He ground out the words, trying hard not to waver. Something I had said touched home, but he still couldn't believe what we believed.

I felt sorry for Ben. At least, though, he was out of danger and because of that there was no real need for him to believe the truth. Enough that he was forewarned of the danger; maybe that would save him, if not us.

"I have to believe it's a human foe that we're facing, Sarah. I have to believe it's human, and beatable, or there's no sense in going on. I can't fight shadows and bugaboos. I'm just a down-to-earth cop. I know criminals and I know insane people that are cruel and clever in committing their crimes. Ghosts and demons, I don't know anything about. If I can't see it, then it doesn't exist." He was firm, but gentle, too. "I think it's somebody very clever and very cruel who hates your family for some unexplainable reason and has been out to get all of you. I've seen things *you* wouldn't believe! There are things done to human beings that you'd never think was done by a human hand. Terrible, gruesome atrocities that make your heart want to cry out against the unfairness of it."

"Like that child last night?" I reminded him.

"Yes. Someone very evil, I'll admit, did that . . . but he was a human, not a thing." Ben stood up. I could tell he felt sorry for us, for what we'd been through. Sorry we'd been terrorized and butchered over the years. But he wouldn't allow himself to believe that the thing was not of this earth.

I wished more than anything in the world that I was still as innocent as he was, that I didn't know the bare truth. I wished that I was a child again. Better yet, I thought, I just wished I were someone else. There are times in my whimsical moments that I think our whole lives are just a dreamed up fantasy and our dreams are the total reality. Lately, in my dreams, I am a child again and running with my brothers and sisters, all still alive and smiling. Could *this* be the nightmare? I was tired of it. Maybe, I had to die to wake up.

"Ben, you can believe what you want. It doesn't make a bit of difference one way or another. What will happen, will happen. You can't stop it, but you can be warned. I feel better that I've tried."

"I appreciate it, Sarah." He seemed thoughtful for a second or two and then touched my hand lightly. It was like an electric shock that ran down the length of my fingers and jumped off. He calmly took his hand away, his eyes widening. He had felt it too. Then he collected himself and said, "I'm going to get this maniac off your back. I'm going to track him down and put him away in a tiny, dirty cell somewhere—the farther away the better. I'm going to get him if it's the last thing on earth I do. I promise you that, Sarah." His eyes were like black ice under his dark brows. "He's not going to cause you any more grief. He's not going to cause *anyone* any more grief. And any help you can offer, I'll be more than glad to take."

It was then I realized that he merely saw us as poor, misdirected victims. We weren't responsible for what we chose to believe, not after what had happened to us.

Wasn't it better that way? Looking into his concerned gaze, I understood that he had really tried to understand. It just wasn't acceptable to his nature as a cop.

After he had left, with one last hard glare at the splintered door on his way out, I laughed sadly. "See, Brother," I sighed, "no one believes in ghosts and demons but us."

"You can't say you didn't try, sis." His voice was brighter than I would have expected from the disconsolate look on his face.

"Nope, you can't say that I didn't try. So where are we now? Back where we started. Square one." I was studying the door. For some reason, in my mind, a clear floating picture of a dead child among wet leaves dyed red with blood arose unbidden before me.

At first, I thought it was an image of what had actually happened. Then with an inward moan, I knew it for what it was . . . yet to come.

And another image superimposed itself over that one. Jim . . . his band . . . a man laying very sick in a motel bed . . . and the images formed themselves into a certain order

194

until I could read them like a message.

"Jim, in a second, you're going to get a telephone call." Was my voice strained? I was still grasping for an understanding of what I had just seen. "You have to go away for a while."

He stared at me dumbstruck. "You're kidding! You think I'm leaving you and Jeremy alone now? I'm not going anywhere!" He watched me intently. "What else do you see? What's going on?" His eyes fluttered and I thought how little he had changed since we were children together. Always so protective of me, but a coward at heart. How he tried to be brave. He could just never seem to quite pull it off.

"You'll go." I smiled at him. "You have to go . . . and nothing's going to happen to any of us while you're away." No, not to *us,* my heart cried, remembering the other thing I had seen. No—not to us. Not this time. Not now.

"You mean it's safe?" He couldn't fathom what I was telling him. "What. . .?"

The phone rang, its cry shattering the silence of the house. Jim never took his eyes off of me as he picked up the phone and talked to the person on the other end. When he hung up, he was staring at me. I hated the way he was looking at me. "How did you know?" It was a stupid question and he waved his hands at me. "Forget I asked." He sat down. "I guess you know as much as I do."

"No. Enlighten me."

"Well, it seems like the substitute lead guitarist I arranged for the band to use while I took some time off, is very sick. Apparently he was pretty heavy into drugs and the guys found him zonked out of his mind this morning . . . he can't hold a guitar now, much less play one. They want me to come back—immediately. They got a heavy gig starting next week in a fancy resort upstate. The money's the best we've ever been offered. Too good to turn down. Rich's wife, Beth, is about to have their first child and if there's no work, there's no money . . . and if there's no lead guitarist, there's no job. They can't find a replacement. They're counting on me, Sarah. What am I going to do?" There was panic in his eyes.

If there was anything outstanding about my brother, it was his loyalty. He couldn't stand to let anyone down, if he could help it. He'd been with the band for so many years, he thought of them as family, too. He was going to be Rich and Beth's baby's godfather when it was born. And one of the other guys, the drummer, I thought, had a sickly mother to support.

They needed him and he had already been gone too long.

"You do what you have to, Jim. You go and help them." Was it fear I felt, as I said that? Fear of being alone, or fear that I would never see Jim again?

"You sure it's safe?" he probed. Safe? Was anything safe anymore? In my heart, I knew if it wanted to kill us it didn't matter where we were. The house was safe . . . but for how long? The rest of our family had run as far away as possible and had it done any good? No. Grandmother's house seemed to be the only haven. I toyed with her ring. Did the power I so often cursed give us some protection? Was that why I was still alive? Had it been me all those years it *really* wanted? Was I the cause of my own family's murder? My head whirled and my stomach churned. If I walked out into the forest right now and let the thing kill me, would Jim and Jeremy be spared?

"Sarah, are you sure it's safe?" I heard my brother's voice raise an octave.

"It's safe. Or at least, I don't see anything *un*safe in your going." I was telling him the absolute truth, too. "I see all of us back here again."

"Alive?" It was a cheap shot of him, I thought.

I frowned. "Yes, of course, alive."

"You've been wrong before." How little he knew of the gift. "Are you sure? I don't want to leave you two almost defenseless."

"We have Ben." Ben. My mind wandered off the track a little. Should I call him to tell him I had seen another child in another vision? It was about to happen again. Then the million dollar question would be; what good was the little information I had gleaned to even bother him with it? I had only gotten a small glimpse of the vision, not enough to have any real facts. It had happened like this many times before. A sneak preview of coming events. Often in such a case I would see more as time went on. I dreaded that.

On the cases I had helped the police with back in Benchley, the first vision had come like that. Faint. Sometimes a catalyst was needed to develop the rest of the message. Ben, I suddenly comprehended, had been the catalyst in this case. Just sitting next to him had produced it. The image was like a lead line, gossamer thin, to the completed vision to come. Somehow Ben had touched it off.

"Thank God for Ben," Jim said.

"Right. There's nothing you can do that Ben can't," I offered tamely.

"But he doesn't believe . . . it's not the same."

"Does it really matter, you think? If he believes or not?"

He shook his head. "Yeah, you're right. But I still don't really want to go. Not after all that's happened. I don't trust it." His eyes shifted to the windows uneasily.

"So? Are we going to live entombed in this old house for the rest of our lives until we die of old age?"

"No." He smiled faintly, and yawned. "Well, that's that. I'll call them tomorrow and tell them I'm coming. But only till they can get another guitar player. Sarah? I've decided to quit the road for good. Settle down here with you and Jeremy, if you'd let me. I'm tired of being rootless. I've had it and I want to have a real home."

I wasn't all that surprised. I had known it was coming. It was the way it had to be. The trap closing in, gathering us all here.

"What will you do, then? Playing has been your life. It's

all you ever wanted. It's all you've ever known."

"I want to."

"Jim, you don't have to do this for me, you know. I won't ask you to give up what you love just to stay here and protect us."

"No, Sarah. It's partly that, but it's a hell of a lot more. I'm tired of running. I want to stay in one place. There are a lot of reasons why I'm quitting the band. I'll stick it out just long enough until they get a new guitarist, and then it's home I come." He was pleading with me to let him stay.

"Jim, it's home, too. What will you do then?" I repeated.

"What I've always wanted to do. Write my music and try to sell it to other artists. Maybe, do some local nightspots as a solo to help make ends meet. There's a few larger towns around here. They need live entertainment sometimes. I don't need a lot of money. I've saved some and I don't want to be a burden to you and Jeremy. . . I'll pay my own way, you'll see."

"Don't worry about that now. We're sitting pretty good, I'd say. At least, the house is ours free and clear. That's a big expense we don't have anymore. I'll get a job, too, if I have to . . . sell my artwork freelance like I used to. Made pretty fair money at it once. Maybe Ben would have some ideas where I could market some of it. I have so much right now I could sell. We'll make it," I said brightly.

For the first time in days, Jim seemed really happy as we sat up hatching out plans for our future. It was strange, I reflected later up in my room as I got ready for bed, that the longer we stayed in this house, the more we loved it — and regardless of the danger we knew existed here, the more we wanted to stay.

Maybe, I smiled into the dark as I pulled the covers up over my shoulders and lay down, the house had bewitched us all.

Maybe it had. All I knew, lying there in the dark half asleep, even after all that had happened, was that I never wanted to leave. At what point, I sleepily wondered, had it ceased to be, "am I staying or am I going" and become "I can never leave"? No, it just wasn't the invisible shield the house seemed to have against the thing in the woods, and no, it wasn't even the warning I had received that I had better not leave for fear of losing Jeremy. It was something rooted far deeper. Much deeper.

This house . . . it's this house . . . I fell asleep thinking about how much I had grown to love it.

CHAPTER EIGHTEEN

The rocks were gone. All of them. Jeremy was down on his knees feeling in the dark with his hands. He was sure he had piled them right here. He was sure . . . who could have taken them? The night shadows whispered around him and he shivered with the coolness that night had brought. He had to be very careful and quiet. He didn't want to wake his mom and uncle up. He'd caused them all enough trouble today.

Where were those confounded rocks?

"Charlie!" Jeremy hissed out into the night. "You fink . . . you took them back, didn't you? You Indian giver!" Jeremy finally came to the conclusion that the rocks were really gone . . . if they had ever existed at all. Now that was a thought to chew on. He perched on the top step and rubbed his tired eyes.

A breeze ruffled his fine hair and slapped his lightweight pajamas against his warm skin. It was so dark out. Children laughed on a distant wind.

What was out there? Had Charlie, like the sparkling rocks, been just a figment of his imagination? He mulled it over as he tried to conjure the pale face up again in his mind's eye. He drew a blank.

He couldn't remember what Charlie had looked like.

Very white, that he recalled. Blue eyes? Or green? Jeremy could neither remember if the pale boy had been short or tall, fat or thin. Even the sound of his voice and most of their conversations were lost to him. Maybe he had dreamed Charlie up out of his loneliness.

He bit his lip, fretting. No, Charlie had been there. Charlie was real. He couldn't forget that for a minute. Some inner sense warned him never to doubt that. He vividly remembered the fear. More laughter and voices rode the wind and brushed by his ears.

Jeremy sneaked back into the house and silently crept up the steps, still thinking about Charlie and the missing rocks. He suspected the whispers in the woods were evil . . . just like Charlie.

Just like Charlie.

Whose side was Charlie on anyway? That was a puzzle. The thing in the woods was evil. It had killed people. Charlie had tried to frighten him. He knew it was Charlie that had chased him home and tried to batter the door down. Charlie had stolen the rocks. Charlie was evil, too. He stood at the window in his room. A sudden wind rocked the pane. A face, or part of one, flickered in the darkness. Jeremy gasped and ran for bed, pulling the covers over his frightened eyes.

The wind retreated back to the cool woods. He was brooding. Silent. He had tried to get them and had failed. He had tried to lure them out and had failed. He had sent one of his own to lure the bait to him and enable him to catch the woman. It had all failed.

They always managed to escape!

He had tried to think . . . what was keeping him from them? He roared his summons and from under every bush and tree-trunk tomb came those lost souls he had worked so hard to capture and enslave in all the years. Charlie was just one among so many, many others. These were the ones too weak to resist his call, not strong with the *glow* like those in the house. The captive spectors came and floated

201

about him, each a light, pale essence of the puny creatures they had once been. He collected them like a crow collects shiny baubles.

He could taunt or torture them according to his whim. Sometimes he even promised to release them for services rendered, but never really did. He liked to see them squirm and beg as they lingered here in his hellish limbo, never able to die or be at peace. It was their punishment for being weak and their sentence for not obeying.

Evil. Yes, he was *evil.* He could roam the world and take what he wanted. So few could stand up to him that the search was everlasting.

One good one. One good essence could appease his hunger and boredom for a while. After all, what else did he have to exist for, but the hunt and the kill? To find and destroy goodness was the only reason he existed. That was why he was.

Without goodness to fight, he would cease to be.

Glowing hideously alone there in his nocturnal domain, he herded his ghostly pawns before him like cattle. If he could, he would have smiled, at the meek way they danced to his tunes. But evil has no smile but death. He was bored.

Sometimes he even forgot his own power. Sometimes he would forget for long periods of time what he was after or whom. The lethargy would eventually pass and he would go on as before as if only a moment had passed. A second was a year and a sigh, an eternity. Time meant nothing when one could never die.

He slept then. Pulling into himself to solve his problem. How to kill . . . *them.*

The woods sighed with the new peace and the trees embraced the dark sky as the world went to sleep.

CHAPTER NINETEEN

I had been dreaming something about Jonathan. I couldn't be quite sure what, because as sleep faded, so did its memory. But as my eyes accustomed themselves to the bright sunlight that dappled my room, there remained the familiar vision of Jonathan in his blue uniform. How many times I had seen him like that in all the years of our marriage. For a time after I awoke, I felt the old grief and loss as I looked at the empty pillow beside me.

What are you doing now, Jonathan? Are you happy? I would never know. He never talked to me anymore, not even on the phone. In fact, he hadn't even talked to Jeremy in so long I was beginning to worry.

The sense of loss only lasted a few minutes. Outside, the sun was shining and the birds were singing. It was too beautiful a day to be unhappy. I had faced my loneliness long ago and conquered it. A whole world lay out there. I had my son, Jim and . . . my home.

And Ben? A tiny voice chirped inside my head. It was a silly, premature thought and I didn't know what had put it in my mind. I climbed out of bed and went to stretch before the bay windows.

I had taken my grandmother's seance room for my own. I'd always loved those tall, beautiful windows. I had cleaned the room until it was spotless and painted in a happy yellow. I had hung my mother's old crucifix next to my dresser. Delicate lace curtains hung across the windows thin enough for me to see out and the sunshine to come in. At this height, the trees kept prying eyes out. I loved this room. I planned to fill it with books and my paintings make it my own miniature world.

Jeremy and Jim were still sleeping and I tip-toed to the bathroom and took a long, hot shower. It felt good on my cold skin because the mornings were still cool. Then I went downstairs to the kitchen.

I made a fresh pot of coffee and some bacon and eggs for myself, leaving everything out so that when the fellows came down I could make them some too.

Nothing terrible had happened the night before and even though I knew that before I turned the first page of the morning paper it was still a welcome relief. But still, the papers were full of the last murder and theories as to why he had been killed. The poor child's whole tiny life had been spread out for all to see. I slapped the paper shut and drank my coffee, happiness shattered. I knew there was more I could have done . . . there was more I could do, had to do.

But how?

I was so deep in thought I didn't see Jim when he came down. When I looked up he was smiling and he seemed happier than he had in days. So he had missed the band? Perhaps a change of scenery was just what he needed.

"How about a hot cup of coffee and some bacon and eggs?" I asked him, getting up to pour the coffee. Old habits died hard. I was so used to waiting on my men, that it just came natural. Jim sat down and picked up the paper, nodding at me. I saw a frown slide over his face as he caught the headlines, but he shook it off fairly fast and held out an empty cup to me with a smile. I filled it.

"Bacon and eggs sound good. I better take advantage of your home cooking while I can . . . it's back on the road again for me." He grimaced and rubbed his tummy like he was soon to be in pain. "I hate restaurant food, sis. I'm going to miss your cooking. Up early, aren't you?"

I threw a slab of bacon in the pan and turned the fire on underneath it. The pungent aroma drifted up to tantalize my nose. "It's so beautiful . . . and besides, I have a lot to do today. You're leaving and I wanted to send you off with a full stomach. And I'm going to enroll Jeremy in school." That was only half of it. If Jim knew what else I had planned for today, he'd never leave. I had to be careful of what I said. Jim was super sensitive to my moods. I had a hard time hiding anything from him. "I need an early start."

"Well, it's time the kid went back to school, especially after that escapade of his last night. He's got too much restless energy. School and homework is just what he needs. You think he'll go to our old school? DeHart, wasn't it?"

"Yes. I haven't seen another school anywhere around."

Jim was silent. We were both thinking about our old grade school. I could still see the flaking green walls and smell the antiseptic cleanliness of the place. I found myself remembering that one conference night when it had been so warm and we had all been innocent children still. I could still smell those night smells and hear the June bugs flinging themselves against the windows. We ran through the empty hallways waiting for our parents to come out from our classrooms and take us to the cookies and punch. I could still see the drab rooms with the childish pictures tacked up along the walls and the dark tile squares with the tiny white flecks that covered the long hallway.

It had been a huge, rambling brick building with a towering flag pole out front, with a perfect lawn and a gravel circle-drive that enclosed the whole place. I could still see all of us traipsing off to school on a crisp fall morning. We lugged our books and wasted time, not anxious to be trapped within four walls too quickly. Charlie would always be left behind, resentful with tears because we wouldn't wait up for him. We were too fast and we taunted him for it, calling him a slowpoke and playing childish pranks on the straggler.

Looking back, I felt shame at the way we had treated him.

One rainy morning we had hid in the apple orchard, and ambushed Charlie with rotten apples we had found on the ground. I had always regretted that. I could have stopped it. I was usually the one who did. But that time I had been carried away with the naughtiness of the moment; I saw Charlie's sad face again and a lump rose in my throat. Even after all these years! Yes, Charlie had been a cruel child, but we had been cruel to him as well. No wonder he had been the way he was.

The bacon was done and I broke the eggs gingerly into the hot pan. When they were done, I flipped them onto a plate and set them in front of my brother. The only brother left, the only family I had now except Jeremy. "I hope it's the way you like them." I had always overcooked Jonathan's eggs and he'd be so angry at me for it.

"They're great," he said and started to eat them.

"You'd eat anything," I bantered back, sitting down next to him with another cup of coffee. He'd filled out the short while he had been here. My cooking, I guessed. It made me feel sad that once he was gone again, he would grow thin and hollow-eyed. He never learned how to take care of himself. He still looked tired, but no longer starving.

"I might eat anything, sis, but you sure are a good cook. Don't let anybody tell you any different." It was a direct cut at my Jonathan and I knew it. Bless you, Jim, I thought. Still trying to mend my wounded pride any way you could. "That's why I'm coming back, to tell the truth."

"I bet."

"I mean it. You don't know what it's been like. I love good food, you know that. I'd do anything for a good juicy breaded porkchop like grandma used to make. Remember?"

"Yes." Her breaded porkchops had been legendary.

"You leaving this morning, then?"

"I better. It'll take me a couple of days to get there in my old truck. I don't want to push the thing too hard. It's on its last legs. And they need me by next Monday."

"You want to borrow my car, since you're coming back anyway? As little as I use the car, I could put up with your old truck for a while. It might not make the trip. I don't want you stranded God knows where. I mean, I want you to make it back here." I was worried that he wouldn't, somehow. There was no inner premonition or anything to worry me, but it was better to be safe.

He shook his head. "Thanks, but no thanks. She'll make it one more time. Then she can come home and retire. You need your car."

"As you like."

He flashed me a thoughtful look.

"Do you want me to stay? I don't have to go. If you have any doubts at all I can call them and tell them to find another guy!" I had no doubt he meant just what he said, but I couldn't make that decision for him.

"What about Rich and Beth's baby? What about the drummer and . . ."

He hung his head. "If you're sure it's all right for me to go. I know," he groaned, "I have to go. On the phone, Kyle was practically begging me. He's a proud guy, Kyle, so I know they're desperate. He even said if there was any other way out for them they wouldn't have bothered me."

"Then they don't know what's been going on here . . ." I supplied.

"No, they don't. To them, the biggest crisis is that job they're going to lose next week if I'm not there to bail them out. I felt trapped into helping them and I'm sorry now that I said I would help at all. I should stay here with you and Jeremy. To protect you." His face was dark and he nervously folded and refolded his napkin over and over as he watched me. There was conflict raging in his eyes and I fancied there was more going on inside him than I had been allowed to know. Jim had a secret and like Jeremy he wasn't going to tell me. Yet I'd be here when he was ready to confess everything. I'd be here, waiting.

"You don't need to protect me." I shook my head and cleared off the table. "You go. I'll be safe. Jeremy will be safe. Trust me."

He looked away into the distance and we both drank another cup of coffee together. Then he tapped me under the chin in the old familiar way and went upstairs to pack. When he came back downstairs, carrying his suitcase, Jeremy was trailing along in his footsteps.

I could tell right away that Jeremy didn't want his uncle to go. They were debating the issue loudly as they ambled back into the kitchen. I had to laugh at them. "Jeremy, stop bothering your uncle and sit down right here. I'm making your breakfast. Be done in a minute."

Jeremy ate, his eyes never leaving Jim's face. They had grown quite close since Jim had arrived. There was a strong bond between them.

"He won't be gone forever, sweetheart." I planted a kiss on the top of Jeremy's blond head. "You'll see, he'll be back before you know it."

Jeremy mumbled something I couldn't hear, his face suddenly angry. I asked him what was wrong and he'd only shake his head, refusing to answer.

Jim shrugged his shoulders in puzzlement. *Leave the child alone. He'll be fine.*

When I walked Jim to his truck, Jeremy didn't want to follow us outside.

"Leave him alone. He's just pouting," I told Jim, a little confused by the uncharacteristic way my son was behaving. He needed a good spanking, I thought. It didn't come to me until much later what was really going on, that there was a much stronger bond between the two than I had ever dreamed, and Jeremy was more than angry at what he thought of as a calculated betrayal.

"Goodbye, Jim." I smiled and waved as the old truck

drove out of sight. *Hurry back.*

I trudged back inside and looked at the dejected child still sitting at the kitchen table and thought he looked just like I felt. Now with the reality of my brother's departure, I wasn't quite as brave as when I had cheerfully told Jim to go.

I noticed the time. "Hurry up, sport," I told Jeremy. "I want to get you up to your new school early." It'd be easier on Jeremy if he could start school on time like the rest of the kids. It would be bad enough to be the new kid but to have to walk into a new class with all those curious eyes on him would be too much to put him through. Jeremy was shy around strangers. I remembered how I was when I was a child: shy and awkward, just like he was.

He went upstairs and dressed. When he came downstairs again he seemed resigned to it all. "Ready, Mom." He grinned. Out of his right pocket peeked something shiny and silver—the Slinky I had gotten him before we left the other place.

"And I imagine the other pocket's full of your matchbox cars, huh?" I threw my hands up in mock exaggeration.

"Mom, don't you want me to have friends?" he said.

"Oh, is that how you get friends these days . . . buy them?" I teased back as I pulled on my jacket and tugged my long hair free.

"No," he remarked sullenly heading for the car. "You share things, like toys, you know?" He scooted into the front seat and waited for me to get in.

I knew. I looked over at my son and I felt pride that he was mine, that he was as smart and generous as he was. He was some boy, my son.

The school brought back so many memories of my childhood that I had a difficult time keeping my eyes dry. The ivy still climbed up the front walls and they still hung the children's first attempts at art in the wide windows for everyone to see. I took Jeremy by the hand and led him down the empty halls to the principal's office. Despite my trouble, classes had already begun. The secretary asked polite questions about Jeremy's birthdate and recent shots. She didn't blink an eye when I mentioned my name. It was better that way.

When I left Jeremy in his classroom, out of the corner of my eye I saw a tiny girl just standing there watching me in the strangest way. I wouldn't have thought anything of it except that she seemed out of place. Why wasn't she in class and why was she just standing there? Then there was her clothes. Even from a distance you could tell her dress was torn and dirty. She had the biggest eyes, dark, and brooding. A small white face was framed by the longest dark braids I'd ever seen on a child. They hung down past her waist. I felt instantly uneasy at her watching me like that and I stopped the car with a lurch and turned to take one last look at her. Maybe she was in trouble. Maybe I could help her. I was feeling very peculiar . . . and suddenly she was gone. For a second, I couldn't believe it and I searched quickly with my eyes looking for her. She was nowhere.

I worried about it for a fraction of time and then shrugged. She'd run away. There was nothing I could do. But as I drove home, something darted across the edge of my mind over and over. Her pathetic image haunted me.

This had happened to me before and I was afraid I had had another warning. Perhaps the child was in danger somewhere and that was why I had seen her. I hoped it wasn't that. I wouldn't want anything to happen. I waited anxiously, but nothing came.

The first thing I noticed when I drove into my driveway was Ben's black motorcycle parked out front, then Ben himself. He was lounging nonchalantly on my front porch like he owned the place.

I got out of the car and walked up to him. He looked much better than the day before, rested and clean-shaven, he gave me a genuine smile.

"Good morning, Miss Sunshine."

I felt instantly on guard because I knew there was a reason for this visit. "Good morning, Ben." I walked past him and unlocked the door. He'd get around to telling me what he wanted in good time. It just felt funny because here we were alone and I had never been totally alone with him before. I hadn't been alone with another man, come to think of it, since Jonathan had left me. Unbelievable that at my age I could be shy, but I was.

"I needed to talk to you. I'm sorry I didn't call first. I just happened to be riding by and I thought I might as well stop."

"Oh, you just happened to be riding by. . . but you had to see me anyway, so you stopped even though I wasn't home and you decided to wait?"

"You got me." He admitted, sheepishly. He was standing very close to me. So close I could smell his after shave. "I was sent over here . . . not that I needed an excuse to want to come and see you. I would have sooner or later on a social call anyway. Remember you owe me a cup of coffee?" He grinned down at me as I shoved the battered door open gently.

"Just a little sooner than later, huh?" I grinned suspiciously back up at him as he followed me inside. I invited him into the kitchen and he sat down while I made us both a cup of coffee.

"I noticed that your brother's truck isn't here," he said.

"No. He had to rejoin his band in Michigan. They called last night after you had left . . . Jim's replacement was very ill and they needed him. He left just this morning."

"Oh. How long will he be gone?" Was it just idle curiosity on his part or intentional interest because of me, I mused, watching his handsome face.

"Just long enough to help them out of their problem and help them find another replacement, then he's coming home for good. He claims his traveling days are over. He wants a home and hearth."

"He's giving his music up?" Ben seemed surprised. I

wondered how much Jim had talked to him about it.

"Not really. He's always wanted to write music. He mentioned something about playing around here for money and spending most of his time on the writing part. If he settles down in one place, he can. Besides," I leveled with him, "he's worried about Jeremy and me here . . . alone." I didn't need to say anything more, Ben nodded understandingly. "Jeremy's in school right now," I stated.

"I don't blame Jim. I'm worried for both of you, too." There was something in his gaze for a second that I caught. Concern, maybe. Maybe something else. I wasn't sure. "So he'll be back?"

"Soon as he can." I sipped my coffee and waited for Ben to say what he had to say.

He didn't waste much time. "The reason I'm here, really, is that Captain Sinclair has asked me to talk to you about coming in officially on this case . . ."

"You told him about me!" I snapped, ready to protest his indiscretion.

"No." Ben's anger flared up to match mine. "Captain Sinclair's been a police officer here a long time. He connected this murder with your brother's murder thirteen years ago right off. And he knows you, Sarah. 'Home town girl with tragic background makes it big as psychic.' He's followed your career carefully through the years. I didn't say a thing to anybody. He's the one who insisted I come over and talk to you, since I already know you."

"Aha! I've forgotten what a really small town can be like. I guess the whole town knows you know us, then? There are spies everywhere." But I wasn't actually mad when I said it because in a small town everybody always seemed to know everything. Of course, the captain would know we had moved back into town since that murder. He might be very curious to why I had come back after all these years, and why another murder occured so soon afterwards. It had probably raised quite a few eyebrows. I shivered inwardly at the thought that I was no longer anonymous.

212

My reputation had caught up with me.

"I'm sorry, Ben. It isn't your fault. I just hate the thought of starting that whole damn circus again. I wanted this to be a fresh start." I lifted my chin and looked around the kitchen. There were still things I wanted to do here. The house was so old and so beautiful . . .

"He wants to see you in his office this morning, if possible." Ben laid a strong hand comfortingly over mine. I almost pulled it away and then I saw the look in his eyes. He was sorry, too. He no more wanted my whole sordid past splashed across the front page than I did. He was just trying to do his job. He wanted to make sure there were no more murders and that we were doing all we possibly could under the circumstances. He still wanted to believe that it could be stopped.

"So is this an official or unofficial visit you're paying?" It had crossed my mind that they wanted more from me than just my psychic abilities. They already had established connections between Charlie's murder and this latest one. "*I'm* not under suspicion, am I, Ben?" The thought frightened me more than a little. Could they arrest me for that? Suddenly the implications were staggering. "They don't think we had anything to do with the murder itself?" Terror had crept into my voice and Ben tried to set my mind at ease with his next words.

"No, I'm sure Captain Sinclair merely wants to talk to you. See if you can shed any light on what's happening or what might happen. But I'll tell you this, I don't think he holds much stock in this occult stuff. He's a pretty down-to-earth guy. And he's a tough cop, so don't let him scare you."

"You think it's my past that he wants to know about?"

"Some of it . . . he's one of the cops that talked to you after Charlie was killed. He remembers you very well."

"So that's the story, huh? He remembers me . . ." What had he thought all those years ago, confronted by a hysterical child who thought she knew more than all the grownups put together? He must have thought I was just plain touched. Which cop had he been? There had been a series of them after the first murder and then as the years went by there had been more—after all the successive murders. Their faces all blurred in my memory just like those horrible times had begun to. There was a lot that I didn't want to remember and my mind had mercifully locked it away so I wouldn't have to face it.

Ben hadn't said anything to my last comment so I knew about what to expect. "This isn't going to be a picnic for me, Ben." And when I visibly shuddered, his hand squeezed mine tightly as if he could give me some of his strenght. I'd need it. "I don't want to go . . . but I will." He seemed relieved that I understood. We both realized I had no choice.

In the eyes of the law I was innocent. In my heart, I was as guilty, I thought, as if I had killed that child myself. It was *me* that creature wanted, I was sure of that now. It was my own selfish fear of dying that kept this nightmare going. I fussed and twisted the gold ring on my hand. Had everyone who wore this ring been cursed by more than just the power to see the unseen? Was that thing its companion piece?

I should give it what it craved . . . me. Then it would all be over. How many more innocents would die if I didn't?

"That's a pretty ring, Sarah. You didn't have it on when I first met you." Was the observation a flattering one? Had he taken that much of me in on his first visit, or was this simple detective's attention to detail?

"Thank you. It belonged to my great-great-grandmother." I avoided the fact she had the power, too.

"You want to go now? You don't have to. Whenever it's convenient for you, the captain said."

"Might as well go now and get it over with."

"Afterwards, can I take you to lunch? It's the least I can do," he offered.

I hesitated, then smiled back at him. Why not? I thought.

214

I'm free. Jeremy's in school until four. The other reason I didn't admit to myself. I liked Ben. I felt safe with him. It was a good feeling after all this time of being alone. I had felt that way with Jonathan once. Why couldn't I have another chance? Isn't that what life is all about . . . second chances?

"Yes. Afterwards you can take me to lunch."

CHAPTER TWENTY

"Detective Raucher here tells me you're a pretty well-known psychic, Miss Towers." Captain Sinclair was trying to be pleasant. As a cop, he had long ago stopped trusting people. And he remembered me; that didn't help any. The whole interview was a strain on both of us. Though I didn't remember his face, something was unpleasantly familiar and I couldn't place my finger on it. He made me feel uneasy. He wasn't the type at all to believe in psychic insights and premonitions and therefore was openly wary of me. I could imagine just about what was running through his mind.

"Yes, I guess you could say that. I didn't plan it that way, though, you see."

Was it my imagination or did he seem to smile condescendingly at me then? I could tell he didn't believe my unwanted notoriousness.

"You're a home-town girl, am I right?" he went on.

"Yes. You know that, I've heard." I didn't want games. I was here for a reason; let's get on with it.

I hated this whole interrogation. What good could it go? If I told them the truth they wouldn't believe me anyway. One look at Captain Sinclair and I knew that . . .

Ben was sitting next to me trying not to interfere but it

wasn't easy at times. I was more than just a stranger or a suspect. I was his friend. Once in a while our eyes would make contact and he'd smile encouragement at me for what it was worth. It did help. I didn't feel so alone.

"Well." Captain Sinclair was speaking again. His bushy eyebrows lowered over his crafty, blue, intelligent eyes that belied his otherwise beefy appearance. He was going bald and his face was rough, as if he needed a shave. He wasn't a small man, by any means, but next to Ben he appeared much shorter. He had an ugly jagged scar down the left side of his face. I thought he must be a vain man. His dove gray three-piece suit was impeccably cut and spotless. A tiny silver chain glittered above the dark curly hair that peeked out from under his white shirt. His dress was in deep contrast to the gravelly voice that bellowed out around him. As he talked to me, his eyes shifted nervously around the room as if he was continually looking for something he had forgotten.

I had been in quite a few offices like this one. Sitting there discussing my painful childhood, I had a strong feeling of *déja vu*. The cigar smoke from the Captain's cigar, the desk loaded with forgotten reports and empty candy wrappers, the paper coffee cups and the bare grey walls that almost matched the captain's suit . . . they were all familiar. Everything here reminded me of Jonathan. It seemed ironic that even after Jonathan was long out of my life, I would still be part of this. Jonathan's world . . . Ben's world . . . my world since Charlie's untimely death. How many bizarre cases had I help to solve? I had journals packed away somewhere detailing every one of them. At one time I had even entertained the morbid idea of putting them into book form. It was just something else the divorce had helped to put off for a while.

"Well." The Captain began again. It seemed like he was having a hard time remembering what he wanted to say to me. "We usually don't go about solving our homicides quite like this, Miss Towers. But I'm a liberal man and I won't turn away any suggestion. Now, this case has us all pulling our hair out. There are no apparent motives and no real concrete clues. Whoever did it is extremely clever and extremely vicious.

"Then there's the connection between those murders concerning your brother and his friends thirteen years ago and this recent one ... too strong a connection to be completely ignored. Your psychic, er, power is just one reason why I asked you to join us today. Though anything you can offer in the way of aid will be appreciated and taken into consideration. The town's in an uproar over this particular murder and they expect us to do something about it. A lot of people remember your brother's murder and, let me tell you, they're afraid. Why, I even have mothers who want to keep their children home from school, for Pete's sake! A murder like this one can ruin a small town, Miss Towers. You know that?" He had thrust himself up from his chair and had walked heavily to the window that faced the street below.

"I'll help you as much as I can, Captain," I sighed. I meant it too. Any way I could—except for telling him the absolute truth. If Ben couldn't accept it, then I was doubly sure the Captain wouldn't.

"I'm glad you feel that way." The Captain suddenly smiled a toothy grin at me and walked back around the side of the desk. "Tell me about your brother's death. Tell me anything you might know about any of this." His eyes were alert. He was back in his own back yard when it came to facts.

So we talked about Charlie and his death. We talked about what had happened since then and the reasons I had come back here to live. I answered all his questions politely.

"Then you think these murders are being done by the same person even after all this time?" he finally said, aghast at my last statement.

"Yes. I'm sure of it." I looked over towards Ben and

caught him frowning.

"One of your intuitions?" the captain asked. I could tell he wasn't a true believer.

I nodded and he got up again and took something out of one of his drawers. I wasn't sure what it was until he stood right in front of me and dropped it into my hands. It was a scrap of someone's shirt. "The victim's?" I whispered hoarsely, my hands shaking as I caressed the bloodied fabric.

"Yes. Can you—see anything? This is usually the way you psychics find things out, isn't it?" He'd done his homework, I thought. And then suddenly the images came, stark and brutal. When it was all over, I was crying and shivering in Ben's arms.

The captain apologized but insisted that he wanted any feedback he could get from what I had seen. So I told him in a cold voice exactly what I had experienced. I told him about the dead child. For a second I saw suspicion fighting with acceptance in his beady eyes. He couldn't deny my gift, but he couldn't believe it a hundred percent, either. Nothing ever changes, I realized sadly.

"That's amazing . . . some of those things were strictly classified." He was writing something down in a notepad and staring at me in a puzzled manner. "Some of them I have to check up on." He moved nervously in his chair.

"I think she's gone through enough for now." Ben came to my rescue. He'd handed me a handkerchief to clean my smeary face with and turned to his captain then. "This isn't easy on her. She has a son of her own." He came to stand behind me. "This whole incident has been hard on her, dredging up all those past tragedies."

"O.K., Detective." Captain Sinclair flashed a meaningful look from one to the other of us as if he saw something we didn't. "I need to check out a couple of things." He closed his notebook with a loud snap, and then he strolled over to me.

"There's one last thing I need to ask you, Miss Towers."

"If I have the answer, Captain."

"You believe there will be another murder, don't you?"

I covered my eyes with my hands and spoke through clenched lips. "I'm afraid there may be more. But that's all. Except . . ." I had just remembered something. I looked up at him.

"Except what?" His face was white. He purposely looked away, twirling his wedding band tightly around his finger.

I related the incident with the girl and the long dark braids at the school. "I don't know if it means anything, but . . ."

He sighed and then smiled at me, getting up to escort us to his office door. "I'll have some of my boys try to find her. It can't hurt to check into it." In his own way, he was dismissing us. We'd given him a lot to chew on.

"Miss Towers, if there is anything else that comes to you later, or if you need anything, don't hesitate to contact us. That problem with your door yesterday that Ben has filed a report on—you could have more trouble." He handed me a card with his telephone number on it. I quickly dropped it in my purse.

I hadn't been much help to him and I knew it. But what could I have told him? It was a hopeless situation and the police couldn't help me just as I couldn't do much at this point. It wanted *me,* and it would kill until it got me.

I knew as we left the station that Captain Sinclair was still not a believer. I had the impression that he was one upset police officer who only was trying to stop these hideous child-murders, and I pitied him. But I had done what Ben had asked of me, no more and no less. I was exhausted.

"Lunch sounds good now," I said to Ben as we settled ourselves on his motorcycle. I had been surprised when he had suggested that we go to the station on it but now sitting behind him, holding on for dear life, the wind in my face, I was glad he had. Behind him I had time to think. In fact, I found it was soothing for me. My tensions seemed to fall away with the miles. We rode for a long time.

"Where are we going?" I finally yelled above the wind at him. My hair was lashing wildly against my face. I made a mental reminder to tie it back the next time we went for a ride like this. I'd have to remember a few other things the next time, too. In all my years, this was the first time I had ever ridden on a motorcycle. When Ben had first suggested it I had pulled back just a little but then thought what the heck? Ben was someone I could trust to drive carefully . . . why not enjoy it as much as I could?

My life might be a short one . . . why not enjoy it?

"To a special place I know of," Ben yelled back. His hair was concealed beneath his helmet and he was grinning like a little boy. For a while we had both forgotten all our troubles. "We'll be there in a few minutes."

Content, I leaned my head against his broad back and tried not to think of what I had seen back at the station when I had held that shirt. I tried to think about Ben and Jeremy in school . . . about my lovely home waiting for me.

But I kept seeing that little girl with the torn dress and the long braids. I'd close my eyes and she'd be there. I couldn't shake her.

We ate at a small cottage restaurant called Jenny's by a lake. When Ben told me the name as we stood out front, I felt the funniest sensation. That name meant something— or it would. I racked my brain trying to recall if I had been there or if I had known someone by that name that would account for it; I could not.

"Come on inside, Sarah." Ben smiled at me and taking my arm, led me inside to a dim quiet corner. Perhaps he thought I was still disoriented by what had happened with Captain Sinclair. I guess he was right. I still didn't feel all that hot.

He ordered the speciality of the house, shrimp creole, for both of us and it was delicious. At first, I was sure I wouldn't be able to eat it but Ben teased me until I laughed and after that the rest was easy.

Over that lunch I finally found the true Ben. He was gentle, sensitive, witty and companionable. By the time we climbed back on the bike and I wrapped my arms tightly around his slim waist, I was happy again.

"I'm going to take the long way home," he laughed as we bumped down the country road. "There is some scenery out this way you wouldn't believe. There's an old mill and this old farm house that's been empty for God-knows-how-long. I want you to see it." When he stopped, he took my hand and we climbed a steep hill. At the top we could look down on a sort of valley protected from the rest of the world. A huge crumbling structure squatted in the middle between three towering trees.

"Come on!" he yelled and started running down towards it. I kept up as best I could until we stood panting before it.

"What's this?" I gasped, holding my side. "It looks like it's ready to collapse."

"Very funny." His eyes had a dreamy look to them as he ran his fingers over the worn boards of the old house. "This is my dream house." He smiled shyly at me.

I wanted to laugh. It was only a shell. Not even my grandmother's old house had been this far gone. And yet, I tried to see through his eyes and smiled back up at him. "The land's beautiful, Ben."

He was staring into the distance. "Someday I want to own all of this." He spread his large hands around him. "Just think what it could look like with a little bit of work!"

"You mean a *lot* of work."

He turned intense eyes on me. "That barn you live in wasn't much better than this place before you moved in. Look at what you've done with that! It's beautiful."

I just looked at Ben. He was so like me. How long had he had his eye on this place?

"Why don't you buy it?" I surprised him by stating outright. "It looks like it's been empty for a long time." I studied the house. "Probably get it real cheap. They might even *give* it away." I laughed at the hungry look on his face.

"I'd take it in a minute!" he said seriously, "If I had the money."

"Have you ever asked about it . . . the price, I mean?" I asked as we walked back slowly to his bike.

"No. It's just a dream, that's all. I come here and wish I had it all. But I know I can't. Not right now. I don't want to . . . not until I have someone to share it with. My ex-wife would have hated it all the way out here."

"Your ex-wife?" I had never ever thought of the possibility.

"Yeah. She couldn't take being a cop's wife. She divorced me."

He turned me towards him and for a second I thought he was going to try to kiss me, but instead he only smiled and put the helmet—*his* helmet—on my head. He tucked my long hair up under it and waited until I was settled securely back on the seat before he swung his long leg over it and started the engine. Something about the way he had looked at me back there for a moment made me feel good. He was strong and I like that. "Why not buy it now and *then* find somebody to share your dream?" I asked. I was very aware of his body so close to mine.

"Not the right time, I suppose," he said above the loud roar of the engine as we took off. There was something in his manner that made me think he didn't want to talk about it for some reason. I knew when to take a hint so I didn't intrude further. I had found out more about him than I wanted. A divorced cop. A lonely man with a dream. I thought about it on the long ride home, even as we talked about trivial things. Maybe I had come too close to the secret person inside of him and he had pulled back from me. I could understand that better than he knew. We have many faces in our life and a few sides of ourselves we only want to show to those we care about—or love. Ben had many sides, I was starting to learn. There was more to Detective Ben Raucher than I had at first thought. I wondered what side he would show next.

"Ben, thank you for lunch and the ride. I loved both." It was a sincere compliment and I guess he knew that. We were standing on my porch suddenly speechless. He'd talked a mile a minute half the afternoon and suddenly he had nothing else to say. But it wasn't an uncomfortable silence that enthralled us now, rather a silence of contentment.

He looked down at me for the longest time and then gave me one last smile and a wink before he walked away. I watched him get back on his bike and ride away. We waved only when he was almost out of sight. Not a word had been said about when I would see him again, but we both knew I would.

Then reality hit home again. I turned and there was the battered door and all the doubts and fears about everything swept back over me like a flood. I remembered the images in the station house and I remembered running through the woods that night with Jim and hurting my leg. I heard the laughter in the woods and I saw as if through a veil Charlie's poor little mutilated body. Then his body turned into the other boy's body. Then, as I slumped down on the porch against the door fighting to control the visions and to keep from screaming out in horror, the image sparkled and shifted until it was the image of a *little dead girl* . . .

. . . with huge brown eyes that stared into nothing and long, dark braids.

I screamed then and I must have passed out, because when I opened my eyes next I was lying at the bottom of the porch steps on my stomach, my face in the grass. I had fainted. That had never happened before. I whimpered as I wiped my dirty face with a trembling hand. I was crying and I didn't even know why. I dragged myself to my knees and stumbled back up the front steps.

My hand touched the doorknob before I saw it. The door was covered with wet, dripping blood. It covered the whole splintered door and trailed down to where I had been lying in the grass. I looked down at my hands and was shocked to see that they were covered with blood. I couldn't hold it back anymore and I began to scream, long piercing wails that bled all the anger and shame out of me.

No one heard me. Everyone was too far away. As always, ever since I had been a child, I was alone in this. Alone. No one could help me, not even Ben.

In the end I crawled into the house and huddled on the kitchen floor and cried until I couldn't cry anymore. My face was all red, ugly and puffy but it didn't matter because I wasn't crying for myself any longer. I was crying for the child who was to die. Soon. And I couldn't stop it.

I finally wiped my tears with a bloody hand, and went to clean myself up. Crying had made me weak. I didn't look into the bathroom mirror as I walked past it, but shed my bloody clothes and stepped into the shower. I scrubbed until every trace of blood was gone. There were no cuts or bruises anywhere on my body; the blood had not come from me.

Before I went to pick Jeremy up from school, I washed down the splintered front door, until it was spotless. All the way to the school yard I prayed that Jeremy would be standing outside, waiting for me as we had agreed earlier. I prayed that he was even there at all. I prayed that he was still alive.

CHAPTER TWENTY-ONE

Jeremy was starting to get worried. School had been out for almost a half hour and his mother still wasn't anywhere to be seen. He was a little angry too. *She promised that she would be here.*

He didn't like standing all alone on the empty playground. For some reason the place gave him the chills. He was pretty sure, it was the same school that his mom and her brothers and sisters had gone to. He shuffled around in the gravel and dirt and finally went to sit on one of the lonely swings to wait.

School hadn't been so bad. He liked his teacher, but that creepy girl that sat three seats behind him kept staring at him all day! Everytime he turned around there she was, staring. He got tired of it and once, right before recess, he had deliberately looked back to catch her eye and had stuck his tongue out at her.

He was lucky he hadn't been caught by the teacher. But she deserved it! Why had she done that all day? He pushed out at the ground and started moving the swing in graceful arcs until he was flying high above the playground.

That's when he spotted her, hiding—or trying to—behind a tree gawking up at him. Suddenly all his anger, because of her staring and his mother's lateness, burst out and he jumped in mid-swing and galloped right at her. She screeched when she realized what he was doing and took off like a bullet. Jeremy easily caught up with her and flung her mercilessly to the ground. It was only when he stood planted above her watching her cry and rub her scraped knee that he felt guilty. It finally overwhelmed him and he knelt down beside her.

"I'm sorry! I'm so sorry! I didn't mean to hurt you . . . just scare you! Please, are you O.K? Please!" He took the edge of his shirt and tried to wipe her tears a little. He had never done anything so mean in his life. He was ashamed and he couldn't do enough for her to make up for it.

She wouldn't stop crying at first and he apologized at least a dozen times before she believed him and smiled warily at him through her tears. Finally, she trusted him enough to stop cowering like a beaten puppy at his feet. "It's all right," she blubbered, wiping her face with the back of her dirty hands. "I guess I had it coming." She had a funny way of talking, he noticed immediately. She slurred her words like a baby. He realized she had a slight speech defeat. Some of the kids called her a dummy and made fun of her.

She was a loner. She had no friends. When she gazed up at Jeremy there was such a hungry, sad glint in her pretty brown eyes that he couldn't stay mad at her. He grinned down at her funny little face and put out a hand to help her up. She had the longest braids he'd ever seen.

"My name's Jenny." She hiccoughed.

"Jeremy," he said.

"You're that boy that lives in that haunted house," she said.

"Who told you it's haunted?" Jeremy exclaimed indignantly, helping to brush her clothes off.

"My mom. She warned me never to talk to you or go near your place . . . said the devil would get me if I did." She embellished the story as she went. Both her parents worked and she was left to roam the streets alone most of the time.

She had learned to amuse herself; to make up stories when there was nothing else to keep her from getting bored.

"Why would they say that?"

"Well, ever since Timmy disappeared . . . last week, you know?" Her brown eyes were huge and shiny. She moved her small dirty hands as she talked. "Mom says it's 'cause you folks are cursed and you came back here just to do mischief. That's what my mom says. I'd get whupped for sure if she knew I was even *talking* to you." She'd listened to all her parents had had to say but she wasn't sure she believed all of it. The boy in front of her didn't look like a monster to her. In fact, he was kinda nice . . . now.

Jeremy started to walk away from her. She had to run to keep up with him. "I don't think it was very nice of your mother to say those things." She could tell he was angry. "None of them are true. Why does everybody hate us here?" Jeremy studied the thin, dirty-faced urchin behind him and he knew he'd have to settle for her. Girl or not, skinny and dirty, she was the only friend he seemed to have in this horrible place. She was someone, after all, to talk to. Someone who would listen and play with him.

"Sorry. . . it's just what people are saying." She gave him a brave grin showing two dimples at the corners of her mouth. "But I don't believe it. I like you."

He was genuinely grateful and reached out to touch her out of gratitude when she jumped and backed away from him.

He turned his small back on her and sat down, discouraged and lonely, at the base of the nearest tree. He stared up at the cloudy sky through the leaves that were just becoming green. He'd only touched her! Why couldn't he make friends in this silly old place? Oh, he knew about the murder. One of the kids had talked about it today in school. Everyone had known Timmy what's-his-name. What did it all have to do with his mom and him?

"Go away!" he ordered her, pouting, when she tried to sit down next to him. "Go away. . . I don't need you . . . I don't

228

need nobody!" He put his head in his arms and closed his eyes. Against his will a lump was rising in his throat. He hoped that if he ignored her long enough she'd just go away. He didn't want her to see him cry. He had some pride and she had hurt it. He didn't need a friend that badly.

A long time went by and then he peeked. She was still standing motionless above him, watching him curiously. "Are you O.K? I mean, I'm sorry I said all that stuff. I don't know what got into me. I didn't mean to hurt your feelings ... Jeremy?" she rattled on. No one could say that Jenny didn't have a heart. Sometimes it was too big for a little girl.

Jeremy couldn't stay mad at the only friend he had. He grinned and held out his hand to her. She touched it cautiously and smiled back. "Let's go and swing?" He stood up, walked tentatively back to the playground, and then turned to see if Jenny was coming. She smiled and ran to him. They took turns pushing each other.

"That's just stupid gossip about us and our house. It's not haunted. And Mom wouldn't hurt a fly. Why don't people here like us, Jenny?" He was swinging next to her now, both moving back and forth under their own power.

"Cause you're strangers, I guess."

Jeremy didn't feel like talking about the real truth, that his mom and her family had lived here a long time ago. No, they weren't strangers.

"They always say bad things about strangers." She went on to talk about the rest of the gossip and Jeremy listened quietly as they arched back up and then down on the swings through the air. ". . . since you came back it's all starting again," she finished.

"What's all started again?" Jeremy had caught that. What was that supposed to mean?

"The murders, silly!"

"Well, there! That shows how silly it all is. We have nothing to do with the murders or anything else." He said it but even as the words slid out, he seemed to remember something he had overheard one night when his mother

229

had been talking alone to his uncle. Jeremy was silent thinking of some of the things that had happened since they had come here. Mom's old place . . . Charlie. The door and . . .

"*I'm* not afraid of you, though," Jenny bragged. She focused those big soft eyes on him. The wind was making her long braids fly behind her. Her skinny legs were pumping crazily to just keep up with him.

"Thanks."

"You like to climb trees or fish?" she asked excitedly, slowing the swing down so he could hear her.

"Yeah—both."

"So do I. My dad takes me fishing sometimes, when he's not too busy. Maybe he'll take you, too."

Jeremy doubted it.

"We used to go fishing a lot." Her voice sounded sad and Jeremy's heart went out to her. "But now he says he don't have the time. Says he's got to work two jobs to pay all the bills Mom's running up all the time. But maybe he'll take us some Saturday. I'll ask."

Jeremy looked at her. He missed his dad, too.

"They fight an awful lot these days, Mom and Dad. I don't stay around when they do, though. They just yell at me and tell me to go away." She was talking in a whisper now and Jeremy could tell she was afraid. Of what? "I always sneak back home after it's all over. Or when dad goes to work. Mom's not so bad when she's alone . . . sometimes." It was that "sometimes" that worried Jeremy. He'd noticed the ugly bruises on her arms and he almost had asked about them. Now he was glad he hadn't. "They fight all the time now," she was saying wistfully, playing with her braids.

"You don't think they're going to get a divorce, do you?" The word struck terror into a child's heart. He wouldn't wish that on a dog.

"Oh, I don't think so." A second later. "Oh, I hope not! Who would take care of me?" She seemed upset.

230

"No problem. You could come live with us," he told her brightly.

The look she threw him said it all. "Not in that house."

"My Mom and Dad are divorced, you know. It's not so bad." He lied to her, not knowing why he had to say anything. "Don't let it happen if you can help it. I never see my dad any more."

"That's too bad," Jenny consoled him. She wouldn't mind that herself. When her father drank with her mother, they started yelling and screaming at her, and she wouldn't care if she ever saw either one of them again.

Jeremy jumped from the swing and decided to walk around front again. He was really getting worried about his mom. He could walk home, it wasn't too far . . . but his mom had said she would pick him up. Where was she?

"It's not so bad now. Mom's got a boyfriend already. A cop." Jeremy grinned mischievously.

She skipped along beside him, her pigtails bouncing.

"What else do you like to do?" he asked as he scanned the horizon for his mother's car. It had to be at least an hour since school let out.

"Well, I like to search for lost money and old empty bottles along the road and in the fields. The bottles you can turn in for two cents apiece. Sometimes I find a lot. Once I found a whole dollar bill!"

He almost laughed until he saw that she was perfectly serious. What a silly girl she was, looking for lost money and dirty bottles. It occurred to him that she must be very poor to have to do those things. "Lost money?"

"Yeah, people lose money out of their pockets or their kids do on their way to the store up there. You'll have to look with me some day."

"Sure, I will." He was busy looking for his mother.

"And we can climb the old treehouse in Sutter's field. You'd like that, I bet. It's real old."

Jeremy could hear a motor coming from far away and his eyes lit up as his mom's car finally came into view. He had all but forgotten Jenny standing somewhere behind him when he ran out to the street waving at his mom. "Here I am!" he yelled. "Mom . . . I was worried!" He ran up to the car and smiled at his mother, who smiled back. "Hey, mom? I got a friend I want you to meet . . ." He announced. But when he turned to grab Jenny's hand and introduce her there was no one behind him. She had vanished.

Heck! Jeremy thought, baffled, as he got into the car. She hadn't even said goodbye.

"I guess she couldn't wait. I guess she had to get home," was all Jeremy said.

"Oh." His mom seemed amused. Her mind must be on something else, he thought. "That's too bad. I'll have to meet her some other time, then."

"I guess so." But he wasn't sure. Jenny was a little strange. Maybe she was afraid of meeting his mother, after all those things she had said everyone was thinking about them. Girls were weird.

They drove home and he went upstairs to change clothes and get ready for supper.

Jenny stayed hidden behind the tree until they were out of sight. She wasn't sure why she had run away like that when Jeremy had wanted her to meet his mom.

Head down, she started the long journey home. She didn't really want to go there. Her dad would be drinking again and he'd be mean. And if her mom was at home, too . . . Jenny kicked viciously at the dirt as she walked down the road. She didn't want to go home. She was scared of her parents. They were always angry at her; always trying to get rid of her, always hitting her and saying she was bad. Jenny didn't think she was bad.

But they only did that when they were drinking. She had to be very careful around them then. It was best to just stay out of sight. She'd creep around the house like a mouse or a thief. If they didn't see her, they wouldn't beat her. There were still long ugly red welts all over her thin back from the last time.

It wasn't really their fault, Jenny lied to herself as she always did. They just had a lot of worries and when Jenny was bad they. . .

Jenny was afraid to go home, but it was getting dark and she had no place else to go. She hid outside the back door when she got there and listened to their angry voices battering back and forth inside. She huddled out in the dark, cold and hungry, and waited until they were quiet and it was very late. Then she sneaked inside and darted to her room where she jumped into bed.

She'd fooled them one more time.

CHAPTER TWENTY-TWO

Jim awoke gradually, sluggishly, as if he were moving in slow-motion. The dream world he was leaving behind had been his childhood again; innocent children with no hint of the shadows to come.

Jim lay in his bed and thought about the dream. His eyes were swollen and he was all tangled in his blankets. They had all been playing in the basement . . . no, that wasn't exactly how the dream had begun. He rubbed his puffy eyes. First, the scene had been barren of life, just the old, squeaky steps, the coal-burning furnace with its smoldering clinkers and the cold concrete floor were just there. It seemed to him that it was probably late fall, very chilly. It was raining outside. He could hear the drops pounding against the old house. The windows had streams of water cascading down the glass. It was warm in the basement, though, just as he always remembered it.

The overall atmosphere was one of sadness because he was viewing something he knew was long gone and the children long dead. And yet, it had been so long since he had seen them all that just being there filled him with an ambivalent joy. Like very old, dear friends he had missed them, and it was so good to see them again!

It was dark at first and he had to let his eyes get

accustomed to it. The old basement smelled of dampness and age peculiar to such places. The fire danced brilliantly in the furnace and intermittently illuminated the tiny hidden spaces and corners. The clinkers popped and he could feel the warmth pouring out in waves. How many times had Sarah and he taken shovels and dug out those unwanted hunks of fire-rocks and discarded them in the metal buckets?

The basement had always been full of old junk and furniture piled here and there. A long sheet-covered table lined one wall. It was a very old table. One of the tasks they hated the most was cleaning that basement. It seemed to take forever.

In the dream he finally heard voices coming to the top of the stairs. Then a ray of light sliced into the darkness and he heard someone say: "Darn, we'll have to straighten it up some before we can skate ... it's a real mess, Jimmy." Skinny legs covered in blue jeans appeared at the top of the stairs.

"Then we'll clean it up, sis. Is the broom up here and down there?" another voice replied. The voices were familiar. He heard scuffling up above him.

"I got the dustpan." Giggles poured down the steps and the hanging light bulb shed its dim light into the basement. The basement's old wooden rafters were covered with nails and floating spider webs. In the worst weather their mom would use the nails to string lines for her wash. "Let's get a move on," he heard his sister say, "or we'll never get to skate today."

He remembered that his sister had always been afraid of the basement as a child. She would never go down if there were no light. Once when she was very young and very bad, their mother had locked Sarah in the dark basement to teach her a lesson. She'd cried down there alone until Dad came home and brought her out. Sarah had never gotten over that. She had been afraid of the basement from then on.

A grownup Jim watched, fascinated, as the two children cleaned up the basement. They piled the jumk in neater, more compact piles in the distant corners, merely cleaning out a skating area. Jim smiled as he remembered.

"Can I skate, too?" Another timid voice piped in. It was Ann. Perched up on the top step, her big blue eyes pleading to be allowed to play with the bigger kids, she couldn't have been more than three years old. In her lap sat her teddy bear. She loved that thing more than anything else. "Can I?"

"Did you ever find the key to your skates, stupid?" Sarah asked.

"I think so . . . I'll go get it." And Ann was gone.

Jim always lost his skate key, too. Sarah was the smart one because she tied hers on a long string around her neck.

"Let's not wait for her. Let's skate," Jimmy selfishly demanded.

The look that spread across his sister's face was one he was well acquainted with. "You can skate, but me—I'm waiting. You know she can't put her skates on by herself. Someone has to help her. Go ahead and start without me."

Sarah couldn't stand to be mean to anyone.

Had he always been so selfish, he wondered. Was he still that selfish? He found himself wishing that he could go back and change things, go back and be a better person. He realized, now, how little he liked himself. He'd always been such a coward. He'd always been hateful towards the other children . . . especially Charlie. Poor Charlie.

The dream wound on as dreams do and soon all the kids were skating and laughing in the basement. Ann had found her key and was out there, too.

"Charlie! Come on down and skate!" Sarah yelled up to a boy about six or so.

Little Jimmy hissed to his sister, "We don't want him down here!"

Charlie sat pouting alone on the steps, his face in his hands. "Why it's the crybaby. . . you gonna cry for us now,

236

crybaby?" taunted young Jimmy. The words were as cruel as one child can be to another. Jim was ashamed for the child he had been.

"Leave him alone, Jimmy." Sarah skated up to the steps and reaching up, patted Charlie on the arm. "You can skate if you want to. Come on down." She threw a warning look towards her mean brother. *Leave him alone. Stop picking on him. He never means you any harm.*

Charlie was glaring hatefully back at his would-be attacker. There had been a silent feud between the two brothers from the very beginning. Why? Jim would never know now. No one would. All the children were dead.

"You can't . . . you're being punished for what you did! Get out of here! Or I'll call Mom!" small Jimmy yelled.

"Don'd do that!" Sarah began. She always felt sorry for that brat.

"I will. Charlie, get back upstairs. Leave us alone!"

"No, I won't . . . besides Mom knows I'm out of my room," Charlie said smugly. "She said I could get out." He smiled a sly smile. "Dad told her to." Typical. Mom would punish and Dad would give early reprieves. "I wanna skate!" he demanded.

Jimmy grumbled and skated away, ignoring them as Sarah helped Charlie on with his skates. But when Charlie started to skate, he'd come up fast behind the younger kids and make it dangerous to be anywhere near him.

It was then Jim remembered what the dream was coming to and what had happened next. He froze. He could feel the sweat trickling down his back already. One never forgot pain.

There was a shrill scream and then sobbing in one of the darkened corners. One of the children had fallen. One of the children had broken a leg . . .

How could Jim have forgotten that day? Or forgotten why Charlie had been punished? Because he had not wanted to remember it. There were many things about the past Jim had swept under the rug and conveniently forgotten.

Like the day Charlie had found the nest of baby birds and got jealous over the attention the find had received. Everyone was out scouting up tiny worms for the hungry creatures and everyone tiptoed around the rock garden so as not to scare them. Everyone "oohing" and "aahing" over them and saying how precious and cute they were. Charlie had found them and then had been forgotten. He hadn't liked that at all and so, as he figured it, since he had found the baby birds he had the right to do what he wanted with them. In a moment of ugly spite he had lifted his foot and crushed all of them, killed every one of them in front of his brothers' and sisters' eyes.

Sarah had cried as she buried the poor mashed piles of feathers Charlie had attacked. Charlie and the two of them had spent a day or two in their rooms for punishment. But the problem went deeper than that. Something in Charlie wasn't right . . . he was a cruel child. Punishment never seemed to bother him. And he always got even again. Charlie always had his revenge. He was a master at it.

That's what Jim had remembered . . . Charlie's revenge. Charlie had tripped Jim in the basement. Jim's leg had been broken in three places. Looking on after all those years, he could still feel the terrible pain. But it hadn't been just the broken leg that had hurt. As he sprawled, screaming on the cold floor of the basement that day he looked up through his tears of pain at Charlie and he had hurt more. That look of pleasure that played on Charlie's face had sunk in much deeper. His own little brother. If he could do such a thing at six years old, it horrified Jim to think of what he would do when he was sixteen.

Of course, Charlie had never quite made it to sixteen . . .

Jim's dream had shattered irreparably at the remembered pain and with great relief that he found himself tangled in his own bed and not on the basement floor. But the vision had left him shaken and weak.

He trudged into his motel bathroom. The reflected

238

image he saw in the tiny, cracked mirror was tired and unshaven. He looked a hell of a lot older than he was. He turned away from the mirror with self-loathing. He knew why he looked this way. Ghosts. Ghosts and vengeance that would never leave him alone.

For years he had been on the run. A desperate, mad dash for safety and utter forgetfulness. He had run when Charlie had died, run again when Leslie had been killed . . . and Jonathan, Ann, and Samantha. His mother and father . . . and each time, with his music and then the bands, he had run farther. Faster. But it still gnawed away at his brain and his soul.

He hung his head and one tear hit the basin as he tried to shave with shaky hands. He had run in his own way, too, when his sweet Amy had disappeared. Even though he would never admit it to any living soul but himself, not even dear Sarah, he had known all along what had probably happened to her. *It* had got her, too, just like all the rest.

It had taken her away.

Until a few years ago, he had tricked himself into believing first one fallacy and then another . . . anything but the bitter truth. No, that was too hard to swallow. And until a few years ago he hadn't really known what the game was or what it really wanted. Not until he had been back home had all the pieces finally fallen into place.

He knew now. And he knew how to stop it. There was only one way.

Wherever he went or whatever he did . . . that evil thing stalked him. It always found him. At the worst times, in the dark haunted nights or just at dawn when he would be lying awake remembering, he wished fervently that it would just kill him and get it over with. He couldn't sleep anymore, waiting for it to come for him; he couldn't think straight half the time and he'd long ago lost his appetite. He had become like a shadow of a man. A man wasn't supposed to be afraid of the dark and empty houses, of going home or cars or. . . life. But he was. Oh, he was always afraid. Afraid that he'd end up dead like all those children in the basement; more afraid that he'd never be allowed to die. To have to live like this the rest of his life! The *glow* was so faint . . . how much longer could he hold on?

Sometimes he thought he was crazy—those were the good times.

Somethings he went to pray late at night in a church. For what? No one ever answered his prayers. And yet, it seemed to help some. Peace of mind. He never had been very religious, not like Sarah; he smiled then, thinking of his sister. She was one of the reasons he didn't throw himself under a train—her and his cowardice.

He finished shaving and took a quick shower. Then he called Sarah to let her know he was all right and told her what was happening in the continuing search for his replacement. So far, he hadn't been able to even think of leaving the band until he had found them someone. The drummer's sickly mother had had a setback and was in a hospital. The bills were staggering. The doctor had informed Rich that Beth's baby could be twins . . . any day. How could he leave them in such a bind until a replacement had been found? There was no way out.

When he finished talking to his sister he lay back down on the bed and stared at the ceiling. *He should go home. He should be there with Sarah.* Who was he fooling? For the first in a long time he had not been lonely, back there in Sarah's home with her and Jeremy. Now, without them, he felt the loneliness more than ever.

From Sarah and Jeremy, his thoughts logically went back to his long lost Amy. "Oh, Amy!" he moaned into his pillow and let himself wallow for a while in the bitter misery of it all. How he missed her! How he had loved that woman.

Unable to stand being alone another black second, he dragged himself from his unmade bed and walked out of the room in search of one or more of the band members. He couldn't stand to be alone.

He grabbed his guitar from the corner and headed for Kyle's room down the hall. Halfway there, he had a creeping sensation down his back and spun around to glare into the dim hallway.

Was that something standing there? Was that. . . ? His heart turned cold like a hunk of ice in his chest and he dropped the guitar case in the middle of the hall. He barely made it to Kyle's room before the fear had turned him into a mindless idiot. Kyle had stared at him wondering, like all the guys were these days, what the hell had gotten into good old Jim.

Jim was shaking inside and praying. *Leave me alone! Please, leave us all alone . . .* for *it* was forever stalking him. Forever there. Forever evil.

"Hey old buddy! Take it easy," Kyle soothed Jim. "You look like you could use a cup of coffee. How about some breakfast? I'm starved."

"Sounds good to me," Jim said. Anything, as long as he wasn't alone. *It was too close. Too close.*

As they went to breakfast all Jim could think about was getting away. He had to get back to Sarah and Jeremy. He had to get back there now. *Now.* Before it was too late.

"I just had a call from Rich," Kyle said. "Beth's had her kid . . . kids, I should say. Two of them. A girl and a boy." Despite the happy news, he sounded as if there was something wrong.

"What's the matter?" Jim looked at Kyle's strained face and swallowed hard.

"I feel sorry for the guy. Beth came out real sick. Some kind of complications I can't even begin to explain. Doctor's mumbo jumbo, you know." Kyle went on talking about it but Jim wasn't really listening anymore. All he was aware of was the ropes that kept tightening around him, the trap that kept gripping him tighter . . . *Beth is sick. Beth is sick.* It would mean huge hospital bills. It would mean he couldn't go home yet. Not yet . . .

CHAPTER TWENTY-THREE

The weeks went by and life seemed to fall back into a normal routine again. I continued painting the house . . . and waiting. I waited for Jim's call every day to be sure he was still alive and well. I waited for another vision to tell me what was to happen, but there was nothing. I waited for Jeremy to come home from school every day. I waited for anything—anything at all—to happen and nothing did.

After a few weeks I began to feel lulled by the calm and as always I even found myself wondering if it had all really happened at all. Each morning as I got up and padded around in my sunny kitchen I said a prayer that nothing had happened the night or day before. No, I wasn't going to ask for trouble. It would come soon enough.

The days grew longer and warmer and I let some of the despair fall from my shoulders gladly. Ben always seemed to be around. An unspoken agreement had grown between us. We were more than friends and yet we weren't lovers. For now, that's all I wanted and all I would allow. The police department had put all their men on twenty-four hour call since that first murder and Ben was intimately involved with the case and spent most of his days and most of the nights in running down leads and searching. Searching for what, no one seemed to know. Ben was working too hard and that's what started the late night visits.

He knew I stayed up late. I loved to read or draw after Jeremy was safely tucked away in bed. I'd sit on the floor in the front room and make my macrame hangers or draw as I watched television. I wasn't really lonely. I had Jeremy sleeping upstairs and I had my home, even though I missed Jim. One night very late I heard a timid knock on my door and was relieved to see it was only a tired-looking Ben on my doorstep.

"May I come in for a while . . . and talk?" he asked. "I just got off duty and—well, I just thought you might like some company?"

I let him in and made him something to eat. We sat and talked for hours. That was how it started.

As the weeks went by he took to coming over a few nights a week. We'd talk or I'd fix him something to eat or we'd simply watch television together like an old married couple. But unlike two old married people, we were very aware of each other. Sometimes he would put his arms around me and sometimes he'd never touch me the whole night. Our relationship was comfortable, and I was content. I grew happy just hearing his late night knock, knowing he was there outside the door. I was happy just having him close and sharing things. I began to understand Ben better than any other man I had ever known—except Jim, perhaps. I knew I understood him a lot better than I had ever understood Jonathan. Jonathan had always seemed distant, even to me. He wasn't sensitive, like Ben was turning out to be. Maybe it had something to do with Ben and his dream farm out there on the other side of town. I knew what it was like to love a house, a home.

Ben never pushed me and he never made demands. One night he brought steak dinners for all of us because it was earlier than usual and he hoped Jeremy was still up to enjoy it. He had just gone to bed, but I called him down and he was able to eat some of it before sleep reclaimed him and Ben had to carry him back up to bed. One night

Ben brought donuts and another night he brought me flowers and candy. It began to be a game for us. He loved to bring me little gifts, and he'd make me guess what they were.

He had told me with a shy smile, it had been a long time since he had cared enough about someone to give things, and now he wanted to make up for lost time.

I realized I was getting in too deep when one night he didn't show up, nor the next two nights and I found myself missing him. How had it happened? A few months ago I thought there was never going to be another man for me. Just Jeremy and me. Just us two. I couldn't conceive loving anyone else. I couldn't conceive trusting anyone else. But here I was . . . missing Ben . . . another cop. Crazy, is what I was. Crazy.

Time passed quickly, almost too quickly.

It had gotten very warm at night. It was almost midsummer and the heat during the day was unbearable. I was glad that our home was one of those old gigantic houses with the high ceilings that stayed cool most of the day, like a cave. At night, Jeremy and I would go out and sit on the front porch or the porch above it like we had the first morning which now seemed so long ago. We'd sit and talk about the day and just be with each other until he went to bed. School was finally out and some nights I let him stay up considerably later than usual.

One night we were sitting on the front porch watching the rain, a light, soft warming rain that is always a joy to share with someone. It had been so long since anything unusual had happened that that part of our lives seemed far away and unreal. Tonight we were just enjoying the warm beautiful night and the rain.

Everything felt so normal.

"Is there enough room here on this porch for a tired old cop?" Ben's voice came from out of the dark, followed by his tall lanky figure.

"Sure! Sit right down here." Jeremy seemed pleased when he did just that.

I smiled at Ben in the dark and felt his hand lightly touch mine for just a moment or two. We didn't need words anymore.

It was nice to just sit there in the warm dark listening to Ben and Jeremy talk and listen to the rain, too. I was happy, I realized; at that moment I was really happy. I peered at Ben's animated face in the dark and my heart was content. I wondered if Ben felt the same way when he was here with us, too.

Later, when Jeremy was in bed asleep, Ben asked about Jim.

"I think he's all right—as far as I know. He calls me almost every day still—and yet," I hesitated, trying to put my feelings into some sort of order. "I think he's having a hard time up there."

"He wants to come home, and he can't. Most men, once they make that kind of a decision, find it hard to wait." Was he talking about Jim or himself? "It's not easy to do something you have to do out of duty, when you'd rather be doing something else. Any news about when he can come back?"

"None, so far. They keep trying out new guitarists but they haven't found one yet that's good enough or who will travel. Jim is really discouraged." I felt Ben's arm circle around me in the night. "But you don't care, do you?" I teased him. "You like having me for yourself, don't you?"

"I'd be a fool to say I didn't. Just look at us. We're all alone. Nice, isn't it?"

"Yes, it is," I replied simply and leaned my head on his shoulder. He was the reason I felt safe and I also knew that he was the reason Jim was sure I was all right. Ben was keeping an eye on us. Jim couldn't do better.

"Look! A falling star!" I exclaimed, pointing towards the velvet sky that was suddenly slashed with a streak of white light.

"Make a wish," Ben whispered in my ear and we both laughed softly. I listened as our laughter faded away on the still air.

"It's so pretty out," I whispered back. Ben's arms were strong and warm around me. I didn't want the moment to end. I loved rainy nights like this. The rain made the world smell so clean and fresh. On a night like this I felt like I owned the world. It was nice to have someone special to share things with.

I wasn't the only one who had a friend. I was sure that Jeremy had one, too. He was secretive about who it was and didn't want to talk about it. As long as he was home by dark and stayed away from the woods and the old ruins, I respected his privacy. He never talked about his friend and there were times I wasn't even sure he really had one, but he seemed happier. I'd catch him sneaking out of the house in the late afternoon with food packed away in his pockets or some of his little match box cars or toys. I couldn't help but think he was taking food to someone. "Don't go too far," I'd warn him as he would run outside.

He'd nod and wave as he ran out the door. At first I was afraid to even let him go outside but as the weeks went by uneventfully and some inner alert told me that everything was still safe, I allowed him more freedom. He was a healthy, growing child and I had no right to lock him in the house like a caged animal. Deep inside, I'd know when it was no longer safe. Then I would decide what to do.

I knew when the evil was sleeping.

CHAPTER TWENTY-FOUR

"I live here." Jenny pointed to a nondescript ranch style house with swaying trees surrounding it. There was a old beat up swing set in the back.

"Doesn't look like there's anybody home," Jeremy remarked casually. He ambled up to one of the filmy windows and peeked in. It was dark in there. He looked back at Jenny where she stood away from him. He had known Jenny for weeks now. While school was in session, she'd wait outside his house early in the morning, hiding behind a tree, and they'd walk to school together. It was an uneasy truce. She refused to meet his mother or to come any nearer his house. Jeremy was angry at her at first and then he just accepted the fact that she had been frightened by all the vicious rumors about the place being haunted. He dropped the whole subject. She hadn't shown him where she lived, until today.

"There never is. They're always at work," Jenny said coldly and almost added, but didn't, that she prefered it that way. That way she didn't get yelled at or beat on. It was when *they* were home that she was afraid to go home.

"Who fixes you something to eat? Aren't you lonely?" He felt sorry for poor Jenny. Her parents were always gone. They didn't seem to care about her much, he thought. They let her run around in dirty, torn clothes and she never had enough to eat. He had to sneak food out for her. What had she done before that? By the looks of her she was starved. Still too thin, her bony legs stuck out from her shorts like two pipe cleaners. Her face was all eyes.

"Well, I'm supposed to have a babysitter. She lives three doors down. Name's Donna. But she has this boyfriend . . . I don't see much of her. She just collects the money every week for watching me. I don't like her much."

It was a hot day and Jeremy wiped the sweat from his face. The shade felt cooler and he didn't want to move. "She doesn't need you, either?"

"Sometimes, if I time it right, I get a sandwich or two. If I'm late . . ." She used her skinny hands to indicate what she would have if she was late. Jeremy could only surmise what she meant.

"I have a key." She produced it proudly, pulling out something shiny that hung around her neck on a shoestring. A house key. "It's for the back door." She led him around to the back of the house and let them both in. "I stole it a long time ago because they lock me out sometimes. Oh, they don't mean to." She had seen that pitying look cross his face. She didn't want his pity; she didn't want anyone's pity. "This way I can just get in anytime I please." Her grin was wicked. She was thinking of all the times she had used the key to quietly let herself in when they were fighting. Then she'd creep silently to her bed and go to sleep without them even knowing she was there. If they didn't catch her, then they didn't get mad at her. It was the way her life just was and she had cleverly adapted to it. It was called survival.

"It's awful dark in here," Jeremy whispered as she gave him the grand tour of the place. He couldn't imagine living like Jenny did. He could see the dinginess of the place, and the filth. Dirt crunched under his feet and wherever he laid his hand it was dusty. He looked in the refrigerator. It was practically empty. What did they eat?

But there were bottles everywhere and empty cans of beer. What kind of parents were they? He fumed to himself. Jenny was left to fend for herself, and she was younger than he was. He was really glad he had his mother and Uncle Jim.

"We'd better leave now," she said suddenly. Her eyes kept darting towards the windows. "I couldn't begin to explain to them who you are . . . my mom's funny about you Towers. I could get a whipping for just talking to you." She was already out the door, impatiently waiting for a lagging Jeremy to follow. "I don't know what they'd do if they caught you here in our house."

"All right." Jeremy didn't think it was fair that they all thought mean things about his mom and him. What did they know? Who were they to condemn them just because they were new to the neighborhood and their name was Towers? Or his mom's name anyway. He thought Jenny was being over dramatic about the whole thing. No one could blame him for just being who he was, would they?

"I got some money," he said, trying to be cheerful as they walked away from her locked house. "How about getting some ice cream?"

Jenny brightened at the prospect of food. She was anxious to get as far away from home as possible and as fast as she could. If her mother came home now she'd be in trouble. She hadn't done the dishes or cleaned her room like she was supposed to each day. She had neglected to dust and sweep the kitchen floor. Oh, well, she made excuses as they ran towards the store, she'd do it later. Ice cream!

When Jeremy snuggled down in his clean bed that night, well fed and sleepy, he thought of Jenny. He hoped she had had supper and that things were all right with her. He felt uncomfortable somehow and he was worried about her for some reason. Then his thoughts came to rest on his Uncle Jim and he frowned in the dark.

The last thing he thought of before he drifted off to sleep

was that he also hoped his Uncle Jim was all right as well
But why he should think that, he didn't know.

CHAPTER TWENTY-FIVE

The night was going like so many, many nights before. Jim was an artist when it came right down to it and he usually loved playing to a good audience. He appreciated the excitement and the applause. The only thing he loved more than performing was writing songs . . . or maybe waking up in the old house to smell Sarah's bacon and fresh coffee.

The nightclub was dark. He couldn't see but three feet ahead of him because of the stage lights focused on him. But, by the roar, there was a big crowd out there, and they loved him tonight. He'd just started the third set, balancing and tuning his guitar on his knees. He looked out into the darkness and smiled. He'd miss this when it was all over. He'd been on the road with these guys almost seven years. A lot of good times, and some bad ones. His thoughts touched the sensitive memory of Amy and backed off like he had touched a smoldering coal . . . Amy, smiling through the crowd at him as he played . . . Amy waiting for the set to get done so she could steal a kiss . . . Amy helping pack up things when the night was over . . . Amy's funny little smile. Amy. Gone.

After she disappeared and he realized that she was gone forever, he'd almost grieved to death. He quit the band completely for a while and ran away from everything—music, life. He worked in a bottle factory and lived in a sor of self-made slum. For weeks he didn't eat, unless he ha to, and punished himself in every small way he could thin of just to feel pain.

It had been over a hundred and twenty degrees in tha factory during the day with all those machines. It had fel like hell and he had welcomed it. He worked like a devi and the lower class apes that worked with him thought h was a drug freak or something worse. He liked to work toc much and *nobody* liked to work that much. The job wa: monotonous. Looking back, he realized he might have diec in that rat hole if Rich hadn't come looking for him to bring him back to the band. He owed these guys a hell of a lot He'd never been so glad to be back up on stage in all hi life. Yet, at that moment, he knew his heart was back with Sarah and Jeremy.

He had to get back home. He had to. But when? More than anything in the world he just wanted to go home There was this something nibbling frantically at his subconscious mind . . . warning, begging him to return home . . . before it was too late.

But the guys needed him.

All of the other band members could sense Jim's restlessness and had commented on it. Jim remained tight lipped, told them small lies, while inside he wanted to scream *leave me alone!* They couldn't begin to understand about Evil. Real Evil.

Not like he did.

When the others strolled on the stage and he checked his mike one last time, he smiled at Rich and nodded. They went into their first song. Later in the set they would sneak in a few of Jim's own songs.

Like all groups that traveled, they had their share of admirers and groupies. There were always people hanging around. Nobody could ever say he was alone, but standing up there tonight facing that crowd and knowing what he

new, Jim felt exceedingly lonely. He wished he could talk
to Sarah about the strange occurrences he had been
experiencing; but not on the phone, it would only have
worried her more than she already was.

Half-way through the last set, he saw her. She was out in
the crowd with all the rowdies and tipsy bar hoppers. When
Jim first saw her watching him intently from a seat at the
bar, her eyes cool and her long hair hanging free, his heart
nearly fell to his feet. His first crazy impulse was to just
stop everything, drop his guitar and run out into the crowd
and throw his arms around her.

It was Amy!

Somehow he made it through the song and then as if he
had no will of his own, he stepped down from the stage,
laying the guitar aside, and walked into the crowd. He
heard the guys yelling at him as if from far away, but he
didn't stop. There was Amy. . . he had to get to her before
she disappeared again. He had to touch her — hold her! She
mustn't run away again! "Amy! Amy!" He thought he was
screaming her name, but in reality no sound passed his lips.

Suddenly, he was running towards her through the dark.
The surprised crowd seemed to melt in front of him. She
disappeared again.

"Amy!" He spun frantically, searching the faces, but
none of them were his Amy's. He could feel his heart
thundering in his chest and his palms were hot and sweaty.

Then he spied her standing in the doorway and he ran
toward her. He yelled to her but she didn't seem to hear. He
darted out into the parking lot, into the night. A full moon
glittered overhead. Where had she gone?

His truck! He shivered and ran towards it, remembering
how he had first met her. He remembered her smile, the
way she kissed him and her perfume. She was so close, he
could feel it!

He saw her smiling at him with that same old smile. She
was sitting inside his truck waiting for him. He couldn't
believe it! "Amy!" he breathed as he tore open the door

and looked into her eyes. He wanted to say a thousand things all at once but he couldn't say another word. He couldn't believe this was happening, not after all these long years, all the agony. He slid into the seat behind the steering wheel and tried to focus his eyes on the woman next to him.

Something was wrong! He was so dizzy. He couldn't remember where he was or what he was doing. He turned his haunted eyes on Amy's gentle face. "Amy?" He whispered reaching out to touch her.

But he touched nothing. A soft laugh rang out. Amy's laugh. He unconsciously turned the key and started up the engine. He started driving, musing vaguely as he watched the landscape go swiftly by; a night world of unreality.

He tried to talk to her but found he was so sleepy he couldn't seem to get the words out right. But she sat there, still smiling her old sweet smile. If this was a dream, he didn't want to wake up.

He never heard the guys screaming at him in the parking lot behind him, never saw Rich and Kyle jump into their own cars and follow him through the deserted streets trying to flag him down. Jim saw nothing. Jim felt nothing. But Amy was there beside him.

Jim knew he was going to die as the truck went careening off the road. He saw three trees coming towards the truck's lights. He heard the tires squealing. *I'm going to die. I'm going to die with Amy . . .* he thought. But when he turned heavy-lidded eyes towards her, he saw a face he didn't know, a shadow that wasn't there. *I'm going to die . . . and be with Amy.* He smiled over the steering wheel.

"No! No!" He finally snapped out of it, screaming. His hands gripped the steering wheel in terror as he felt the malevolent presence envelop him. *It* was gloating! *It* thought it had him. *It* was going to kill him! He'd let his guard down just one split second and it had sunk its bloody teeth in for the kill.

"God help me!" he begged, as the truck swerved all over

he road and he tried to keep from going through the windshield. "No!" he screamed, realizing the truck was completely out of control. It went careening wildly down the street as if it were driving itself; and he'd taken his foot off the accelerator!

Jim felt all the blood drain out of his face, even as he fought the demon that wanted his death. Like all the others . . . like all the children in the basement . . . was that why he had had that dream? Because he too was going to die?

He found himself thinking of Sarah and Jeremy and he could have almost sworn he heard the boy's voice far away, promising him that he would be safe; to just hang on and everything would be all right. It was so real, that voice, that Jim found himself answering in a whisper, praying, as he fought the wheel. *Yes. Yes.*

"Leave me alone . . . leave me alone! You bastard, you want my blood and you want my soul. You can't have either! You can't have either!" he screamed, and he thought of Jeremy . . . Jeremy.

Then the car seemed to leave the ground with a sickening roar and was flying towards a tree in front of him. Sobbing, he wrenched the wheel to the extreme right. He was drenched in sweat but he was shivering so badly he could hardly hold on to the wheel. He could suddenly see Jeremy's pale face before him.

Don't give up, Jim. If you don't give up it can't get you. I'll help you. Fight it . . . just fight it!

Jim fought it . . . for Jeremy . . . for Sarah.

Then she was by him again . . . sweet, serene Amy, smiling and laughing.

The truck smashed into a tree and bounced off to hit another in its path. Half the truck was ripped off right about where Amy was sitting. Terror-stricken, and half out of his mind with fear and pain, Jim tried to grab for her. It was too late. He watched in horror as the woman's head slammed hideously up against the windshield and then was propelled along with her mutilated body through the hole in the shattered glass. There was a whoosing sound and the body was gone.

"Amy!" he wept, clutching for her in vain as the truck came into full impact and Jim, mercilessly, passed out. "Amy!" His bloodied lips muttered one last time . . . "Amy!"

Jeremy awoke with a startled gasp. He sat up, his heart pounding like a hammer and his mouth tasting like it was full of cotton. Somebody called his name. It had sounded like somebody was calling for help.

It was still the middle of the night. He wondered exactly what time it was. A light breeze fluttered through the window and caressed his hot face.

What had happened?

He swung his bare feet over the edge of his bed and slipped to the floor. The wooden floor felt so cool to him. He still wasn't really awake, but he was drawn to the windows by an unheard summons and he stumbled as he walked. He pushed the billowing curtains recklessly aside and went down on his knees so he could prop his elbows on the window sill. The breeze was so sweet on his hot face. He gulped the night air as if he were starving for it and he waited. He had no idea for what. Just something. Then, he smelled roses, and a voice whispered as soft as starlight.

Something had called him to the window. Someone. His eyes grew accustomed to the dark and they were roaming the spaces outside. There was a soft light moving from one shape to another as he watched. Weaving. It seemed to almost evaporate and then a tiny dot reappeared and rapidly grew into a child-size glow.

Jeremy caught his breath and drew back from the window. He knew who it was! And he knew he didn't want to see him now, or ever! He still remembered the first time he had met him and what had happened . . .

"Charlie?" He tried to keep his voice from trembling. He was terrified that if the ghost didn't see what he wanted he would come in after him. "You're taking a big chance coming here, aren't you?" His head was crammed up against the screen as he shifted his eyes to the left and then the right following the glow. Then suddenly it was gone. "Charlie . . . I know it's you! Where are you?" Inside he hoped nothing would answer. He hoped Charlie would just go away and leave him alone. Yet . . . something had happened and Jeremy had an instinct that Charlie was part of it—whatever it was. He remembered the door and then he remembered the uncanny feeling he had had as he woke up. Charlie might know something. "Charlie?"

"Here." It was a faint whisper on the breeze, hardly there at all.

Jeremy swallowed hard as he looked up into Charlie's sorrowful eyes . . . eyes from the grave. "How do you do that?" He gulped. Charlie was hovering in mid-air. It was awesome.

Charlie didn't smile. He never smiled, maybe Charlie couldn't. "It's easy if you're dead, like me." Charlie had no humor in him. And he never changed. He looked the same as he had the last time. Except he had no cat.

It was so cold! Jeremy thought as his teeth began to chatter. There were icicles on the windows now. Jeremy backed up a little more. Charlie laughed hideously.

"Where's kitty?" Jeremy stuttered. Oh, why was he so frightened? He mustn't let Charlie know he was so frightened of him!

"Ooh . . . the cat, you mean?" Charlie seemed confused. Perhaps he had forgotten the cat. Then he said: "I don't like cats." Scowling. "I don't like *anything*."

That Jeremy believed.

Jeremy thought ghosts must get bored with only floating around to do. That was why they were probably so out of touch with things.

"What are you here for? What do you want?"

"To warn you." The ghost's face was a pale orb and Jeremy could see right through him.

"To warn me about what?" Jeremy was unsure. He

257

wanted to listen to Charlie and hear what he had to say and yet he also wished fervently that he could just run away and hide under the bed.

"Tell Sarah that Jim is hurt . . . Jim needs her."

For a second Jeremy was baffled. Just a second. "You mean my Uncle Jim?" he exclaimed, putting his hand to his mouth so he wouldn't cry out.

"My brother." The ghost nodded.

"Your . . . brother?" Jeremy repeated.

"My brother. I'm your uncle, too, remember?" He said it sadly, like it was a joke on him. On all of them. It did seem strange. It was hard to link this thing with real people. Jeremy frowned. Did Charlie have any loyalty left to any of them?

"I never really thought about it. Is Uncle Jim all right?"

There was no answer as the light faded. "Charlie! Is he all right!" Still no answer. Jeremy was shaking. Should he go downstairs and wake his mother up and tell her?

"Charlie! Don't play games. Please! Tell me!" Jeremy felt like crying. But Charlie was gone. Why had he come in the first place?

And then, as if it had been an afterthought, the wind moaned. *Do you know what it's like being dead? Having the earth thrown over you . . . do you know how lonely it is? She was my sister and she loved me a little . . . I owe her. I owe Jim. I hurt him once and I have always been sorry for that. I was so bad. So bad. I have debts to pay.*

It had been Charlie. But what did it mean? Jeremy had no idea. The dawn was coming in a cloud of pink and all the shadows were fleeing. Charlie was sorry. What did it matter now? Jeremy couldn't believe what was happening. Didn't people just die and go to heaven—or the other place? What was Charlie still doing here?

Jeremy's fingers touched the screen. His knees hurt from kneeling so long and he was cold. He didn't know what to do. Should he tell his mother about Charlie?

Would she believe him?

Do you know what it's like being dead? the ghost had asked him.

And how had he hurt Uncle Jim? Charlie had left so many puzzles. Jeremy turned from the window, sighing.

"You're dead, Charlie. You're dead." He said it aloud. "Why don't you just stay dead and stop scaring me?"

Jeremy got dressed and went downstairs. It was so early, he knew his mom wouldn't be up yet. He sat down in the front room and waited. He had to tell her about Charlie when she got up. He'd let her sleep, so she wouldn't be mad.

What was he going to tell her? What could they do? *What was going on anyway?*

When it was all over and the smoking truck sat crammed up against the tree in the coming daylight, Jim was still for a long time. He came to gradually, cradling his aching head in bloody hands. At first, he didn't know where he was or how he had gotten there but then, painfully, the memories came sifting back through the fog until he was sobbing. The worst tragedy was that he was alive.

Still alive for the torture to continue. Why hadn't he just died? No, no. He looked up at the ragged hole in the windshield and felt a great wave of sadness . . . that wasn't the way it was supposed to be. He knew that.

Amy!

With swollen eyes he stared at the empty seat next to him and then at the sharp fragments of glass scattered over everything. Had it really been Amy, or just a lure to get him outside and in the truck? Had Amy been a trap?

Had there even been an Amy to begin with?

His legs were hurting and when he tried to move them he cried out in anguish. Maybe he had broken something. Still in a haze of shock, he wanted to go outside and see if she was out there.. She might need his help. The truck was a smoking hulk, hardly recognizable as ever having been anything else but a lump of burnt metal. It could explode any second.

I have to get out of the truck . . . I have to find Amy!

He forced his bleeding legs to move and he fell from the seat to the hard ground with a loud cry. He pulled himself up by the door handle and fought off the wave of dizziness that soon engulfed him. His glasses had been smashed and lay in pieces in his lap. He brushed them away. Slowly, he hobbled to the front of the demolished truck and carefully combed every inch in front and around it, as best he could without his glasses; everything was blurry. The headlights were still glaring away into the trees and the horizon was dimly silhouetted by a salmon colored sky. Soon, it would be dawn.

He looked, his heart in his throat, his hands trembling as he stumbled around in the weeds searching for a body that wasn't there.

Even as he desperately peered into the gloom, he knew he wouldn't find her. Finally pain and weariness overcame him and he collapsed in a heap in the truck's dimming headlights.

The police found him a couple of hours later, unconscious. After they took him to the hospital and he was thoroughly examined and then released, he was taken to the police station to fill out an accident report. He had not been drunk as far as they could tell and no other car had been involved in the crash. They decided, after talking to him, that it would be useless to press any kind of charges. No real harm done except to the truck. When they gave him a ticket for reckless driving, he laughed very softly.

He never mentioned Amy. They wouldn't find a body anyway. There had never been a body, Jim was sure of that now. After he'd answered all their endless questions, he went outside to the lobby and with shaking fingers dialed Sarah's number.

"No, they aren't keeping me. No, no charges." He slumped against the wall, fending off the terrible dizziness. His mouth was dry and he could barely stand. He shut his tired eyes, everything spinning.

"Yes. I'm all right, I think." He told her about Amy, the truck, and the accident. Panic circled below the surface waiting to attack.

"Jim, please come home? Now. I think it's time. I don't want to lose you," she begged.

"Yes. I'm coming home now, Sarah. I've done more than my duty to the band. I've stayed on a lot longer than I had ever planned to. I don't care what they need or what they say. . . I'm coming home." His voice was adamant. "As soon as I can get my stuff into a suitcase, inform the other guys of my decision, I'll catch a bus home. I'll be on my way home today."

Sarah could read between the lines and she knew her brother was terrified. "Be careful," was all she said.

Jim hung up and called a taxi to take him back to his motel. He didn't look forward to telling the other guys he was running out on them, not under the circumstances. He didn't have any choice. He could no longer live the way he had been living all these years. The day had come to change. He'd been playing with fire long enough.

He should be dead. His time was up. As he packed his clothes nervously in his suitcase, he felt as if he had been given a short reprieve. He purposely refused to dwell on the accident or the woman that had never been. All of that had reopened a wound so painful and so deep that to dwell on it was to invite insanity or total disaster. He turned to face the door and there was a strange gleam in his tired eyes. It was time. Time to face what he had run from all his life . . . and longer.

CHAPTER TWENTY-SIX

I sat in the chair by the telephone for a long time after Jim's call. I couldn't believe what he had just told me. No, that was wrong . . . I *could* believe it. It all made sense now. He was coming home because *It* wanted him here.

Neither one of us could escape any longer.

I held my hands tightly together in my lap, just sitting there staring. I hadn't had a vision in weeks. I had almost been fooled into believing that we were normal people in a normal world again. So much for fantasies.

But thank God Jim was all right. Thank God he was finally coming home. "Our only hope, I think, is in our strength. Our strength," I whispered to no one.

It was dawn. I looked over at where Jeremy was curled up sleeping on the couch and wondered as I had when I had run down to answer the ringing phone, what he was doing sleeping down here. I went and perched next to him and looked down at him. It was too early to wake him and he must be really tired if the phone had failed to bring him to. I had known it was bad news even before I had lifted the receiver. When it rings like that in the middle of the night, I never want to answer it. What can it be but bad news?

I leaned back on the couch, careful not to disturb Jeremy. I'd ask him why he was down here when he awoke.

It could wait. I closed my eyes for just a second, my hand light on Jeremy's shoulder as if I could protect him and I fell asleep. It wasn't just that I was tired, though the call had taken a lot out of me—it was my way of escaping the moment.

"Mom?" Jeremy's voice was waking me. A small hand was shaking my shoulder insistently. "Wake up, Mom— who was on the phone?"

With much effort, I pryed my eyes open. The sunlight was blinding. I wondered how long I had been asleep. "Jeremy?"

"Mom . . . who was on the phone?" Jeremy's eyes were level with my own. He was peering down into my face with a worried frown.

I wasn't fully awake. "What phone? Who?" I said stupidly. Then the clouds started to lift. "Oh! The phone. It was Jim. He's coming home." I sat up, rubbing my eyes and yawning.

"Then he's all right!" Was that a sigh of relief I heard?

I sat up and look at my son. "How did you know I had a phone call? You were asleep." I didn't mention the rest of it.

"I just knew." He had that look on his face of someone who was wiser than you and mystified that you couldn't see it. His face was not a child's face in that instant. He seemed to be weighing something in his mind. "I know a lot more than you think I do. I know Uncle Jim's been hurt." Then in a whisper, "Charlie told me he was hurt. He said he was hurt, but all right. Or at least he *told* me he was all right." His child's face was clouded with heavy thought.

We were both silent for a minute.

When I found my tongue I really didn't know what to say. Bells were going off in my head. I felt sick to my stomach. *Charlie* . . .

"Charlie?" I pronounced the word cautiously, as if just by uttering the name, I would call up the dead child himself. God help me!

Jeremy turned his head away. His face was puffy from

sleep and his hair was all wispy in disarray. He was just a child. "You know . . . your brother Charlie. The one that's . . . *dead*." Jeremy turned huge hurting eyes on me and I took him wordlessly into my arms and stroked his hair. I loved my son so much but how could I protect him and save him from what was going to happen? It might happen anyway no matter what I did or didn't do.

As he told me about Charlie—everything—I was astounded. Frightened. It was that close to my son. *That close.* I hadn't seen what was in Jeremy before. I hadn't seen one of my own kind. If, truly, that's what he was. I couldn't be sure. I was afraid to be sure. And, God, how I pitied him if he were.

What did Charlie want? What was he up to? "Does this sort of thing happen often, son?" I asked him. I had to know.

"No. It never did until we moved here. You did say Uncle Jim was all right, he's coming home. . . ?"

"Yes. Uncle Jim's coming home." I smiled at him. "Come on, I'll throw you back into bed. It's Sunday and it's only six-thirty." I walked with him back up the stairs.

"When Uncle Jim gets home can we all go fishing?" he asked sleepily as I tucked him into bed. I was looking out the windows towards the distant woods and I was remembering Charlie and our old home. I was remembering all those other children now dead, too. I didn't hear him the first time he asked it, but I did the second. I pulled myself back to the present.

"Yes, we'll go fishing when Uncle Jim gets here." It was a strange request but I didn't question it. I was too tired and Jeremy was already half asleep. I could see Jim far away climbing on a bus and turning to wave at us. Charlie was there, too. I shook my head to dissolve the vision and looked down at Jeremy's innocent face.

I just couldn't believe I hadn't seen it sooner.

Jeremy had the gift . . .

I stood up to leave and something caught my eye

outside the window. I went closer to investigate. A scrap of bright cloth was caught on a twig and was waving like a banner against the skies. That was all it took to trigger the memories . . .

I was tunneling back through the years. How many I couldn't be sure. I was a spectator again, but yet I was part of what was unfolding right before my eyes as I looked outside the window. It was like a mirror into another world; another time.

There was only wilderness out there, the kind of wilderness this country must have known over a hundred and fifty years ago. There were no houses or towns, only desolation. In my vision I was suddenly down there among the trees that lined the creek. It was night, or early morning. I was walking towards the wagons, and the campfires that illuminated them. There were maybe seven of them, old covered wagons pioneers used to travel west. They sat around like huge beached whales with their ribs showing. I had seen hundreds of movies and pictures of the rugged men and women who lived in these traveling temporary homes out on the prairies, but this was different. I was touching these; they were as close to me as my own hand. I could see the grain of the wood and count the spokes of the mammoth wheels. I could hear the fear in the voices of the people who crowded around the blazing campfires.

I hid behind the nearest wagon, confused. I knew who I was and yet I was afraid they might see me and I could never in a million years explain myself. Since I had returned to Suncrest it was terrifying how vivid my psychic experiences had become. This sort of thing had happened before so I knew in time I could be able to go safely back into my own time. The campfires were crackling and far off in the woods I could hear a wolf baying at the moon. I was seeing something that I couldn't be seeing. What was I doing here? I shivered and looked down at my feet. There was snow on the ground and my feet were covered in some sort of fur boots. I was no longer dressed like Sarah. I had a long baggy skirt on covered with a thick, worn shawl. I was cold, shivering.

The dream was *too real* and for one riveting second I wondered if I had gone so far this time that I could never go back. Was I trapped here? I ached to turn and run home. But home didn't exist anymore.

I pressed myself up against the wagon as tightly as I could and when I had found my courage, I began to listen to the people on the other side. If I was here and I couldn't go back for a while this time, then I had better become familiar with the situation. There was a reason, I told myself calmly, that I was here. Now I should find out what it was. Maybe it was the key that would release me.

Of the five people huddled around the campfire, three were children. One was a very small child of about six and the other two were somewhat older. Two boys and a girl. There was a very old woman and another older man who appeared to be her son.

One of the children, the girl, was crying.

They were all terrified of something and at first I thought it might be Indians. There were three shafts sunk deeply into the side of the one wagon, the feathers brightly colored in the firelight. One of the other wagons was partly burned. Behind me I could hear low-pitched talk at one of the other campfires, but I was drawn to the family crouched before me. I could smell their terror. The wind snapped at the trees.

I moved closer to listen.

"It'll get us just like it got Edward! It'll get us . . ." The girl was weeping. Her eyes were glazed and wide. She seemed to be in shock because the tears were silent as they rolled down her thin face. The older boy patted her on the back to comfort her and all of them jumped at the sound of a branch crackling somewhere out in the dark. They were afraid of something out there in the woods—and it wasn't Indians.

"Hush, Becky!" the old woman warned. Her eyes shifted

nervously among the shadows. Her face was wrinkled like an old prune and she was shrunken into a lump of bones hovering above the warm fire. When she spoke her voice was like the croak of a frog out in the marshes in the night. "It will hear you! It'll get you!" she crackled down at the child. Even this far away, I could see the child jerk.

The older man threw the old woman a warning look and walked over to take the small girl in his arms. "It'll be all right. You'll see. Tomorrow morning we'll be away from this cursed place. Tomorrow we'll leave." He stared out at the darkness. He seemed to stare right at me and I saw the light glitter in his eyes. "Right after we bury Edward," he finished coldly.

The girl hid her face in her hands and her shoulders heaved.

Who was Edward? What had happened to him?

The wind howled around me and threw the wet snow up into my face. It was one of those terribly cold winter nights when your breath freezes almost before it gets out of your mouth. I glanced back at my home and there was nothing but the wilderness and the winter sky. When I looked back to the people I felt as if time had slid past unobserved. The children were all huddled together before the dying fire. The old woman was building it up again and licking her lips before the flames. They were all just waiting. They weren't going to sleep in the wagons. What were they afraid of?

It was then he saw me.

"Mandy? Is that you out there, girl?" He turned in the firelight and for a moment my heart lurched. He was a young version of my own father. Was he really seeing me?

I froze. Why didn't I wake up! What was this?

"Mandy!" he whispered loudly and started to walk towards me in that particular lumbering gait of his. Like father's . . .

He was close enough to touch me when he stopped. I wanted to cringe, but didn't.

"Mandy?" I repeated dumbly like a pet parrot. He could

see me. He had mistaken me for someone else.

"So you ran off. We've been looking everywhere for you. Thomas said you would come back. He did. Said, *Mandy knows the woods like the back of her hand. Nothing would hurt her out there in the woods. Why, that's her second home. Animals love her.* That's what he said, girl. Are you all right?" There was concern in his voice and something else . . . suspicion. "Well, leastways . . ." He smiled crookedly at me as if I should know him. "You're back safe. Come over to the fire and warm yourself a spell. Your brother's worried over you. Gave us all a fright, you did. You surely did."

"I don't . . ." The words hung suspended in the air as I said them because he had grabbed my wrist and was gently dragging me out of the dark and into the firelight. When his hand touched mine it was colder than ice. He grinned and his teeth were black. Hie eyes narrowed as a spark seemed to jump between us at his touch. I never finished what I was going to say, though I had no idea what I could have said. I didn't belong here. I would go back any second, so what did it all matter anyway? I only had to play the game a little longer . . .

The scream ripped his hand from mine. The woods were alive with that terrible laughter I remembered so well. The man dropped my hand in horror and ran towards the children around the fire. It was out there . . . and it was coming closer.

I watched as *it* came into the dying light and eyed its prey. In a panic I screamed as it took the smallest girl and slammed her helplessly against a tree. She fell to the snow-covered ground in a heap, never to move again. Like me. I tried, but already it was useless . . . everything, even the screams, were fading away back into the past and I felt the cold leaving my cheeks even as I started to run towards them. I had to help . . . fight it! I had to stop it. But I couldn't because I was going back.

It had turned on the boy now and he cowered down before it, not even trying to fight. A huge hulking hairy thing that seemed to be all fangs and fire. Its laughter rang like the cry of a banshee and it changed shapes as it tore at the huddled boy. Blood seeped and colored the snow. His cries mingled with the wolves howling in the night. I stood and watched in horror as he turned pleading eyes on me to help . . . *Jimmy's eyes. Jimmy's face.* I screamed.

The creature spun on me letting the boy go, and I felt fangs sink into my arm. The pain was so great, I only saw the boy escaping through the trees in a pain-filled haze.

He was running away, leaving us all. Running away to save himself . . . and I was to die in his place. I closed my eyes and felt the claws closing into my neck and I didn't feel anything. Things were shifting, breaking up like clouds . . . was this what death was like?

I barely felt the cold snow on my face as I was thrown to the ground and I remembered what it was like . . . dying. The blood and the final surrender. *It* laughed hideously above me, its eyes like coals. This had happened before. Why was I reliving it all again?

It all faded away into the night. The creature, the bleeding children in the snow around the old wagons and then the night itself fused into twilight and then daylight again. Jimmy's pain-filled eyes were all that remained to haunt me.

I awoke in my bed, trembling. How I had gotten there from Jeremy's room I'll never know. I don't want to know. Sunlight was shining brightly across my bed and I was so glad to be back that I cried. I was always weak after a vision, but later, as I dragged myself downstairs to the kitchen to make some hot tea, I knew that *that* had not been just a vision. It had been a warning or a message of some kind. . . . As I heated the water, I realized tea wasn't what I needed . . . I needed help.

I don't know what made me look, but I did. And there, vividly red and fresh on my upper right arm were claw marks . . . already old healed scars, but there. I traced them

lightly with my fingers and cringed.
  They had never been there before.

CHAPTER TWENTY-SEVEN

"Do you know anyone named Jenny?"

Jeremy looked at me as if I had gone crazy. My question took him by surprise, but he got over it fast.

"Yes. Come to think of it, I do." His eyes were a blank.

"Oh, my God . . ." I said in shock.

It was very late the next night. I had been on pins and needles all day waiting to hear that Jim was safely on his way home. I'd called Ben early in the day and left messages. He was out on a case and wouldn't be back until later, they told me. I was still waiting to hear from him. If I could just talk to Ben about everything, I would feel a lot better.

About an hour before it had exploded into my mind. I knew the next victim, and when it was going to happen. It wasn't exactly a vision, it was just a strong suggestion . . . the girl with the long braids in front of the school. I'd known it all along but it hadn't been completely concrete. I also knew the girl's name . . . Jenny.

"She's my friend." He sat down on the edge of a chair, sensitive to my mood. Jim was in trouble and unreachable. Now I was asking about his little friend. "How did you know her name? I never talked about her. She's afraid of you. She's afraid of everybody. Her parents don't take care of her and they beat her. She heard rumors about us and this house . . . she hid from you all the time. Are you mad at me because I kept her a secret?" I could hear the clock ticking away behind us and I wondered how much time she had. How much any of us had. "She promised she'd never talk to me again if I snitched on her," he added in a weak defense, and sighed at the look I gave him.

"No." I took his hands in mine and looked into his worried eyes. "I'm not mad at you. Where does she live?"

It was the direct question that scared him.

"There's something wrong, isn't there? Something to do with Jenny." His hands tightened on mine. "Is Jenny in trouble?"

"I don't know that for sure, but yes, something is wrong. Something to do with a little skinny girl with long dark hair. She wore them in braids."

"How did you know that? You've seen her?" His eyes opened further.

"Yes. I've seen her." My voice chilled even my own son. How could I tell him that his friend was going to die, was maybe dying even at this moment out in the woods?

"In one of your dreams, wasn't it?" He knew. He understood. "She's in danger."

I smiled sadly up at him and nodded. "I have to call the police . . . before it's too late. Where does she live?" I got up to dial the number. I couldn't wait for Ben any longer. Jenny might be extreme danger this very moment and every second was wasting precious time. I had to try to save her, no matter what the police would think. I realized it would be in all the papers if I came out in the open like this, right smack in the spotlight again. The weirdos would start bothering me again.

I wouldn't be able to hide after this.

I tried to stay calm as I talked into the phone. I had to try and save Jenny's life, there were no two ways about it. I couldn't stand by and let another innocent child die if I could prevent it. And, thank God, this time I could do something about it. If it wasn't too late.

"Captain Sinclair . . . this is Sarah Towers." And out it all came.

When I hung up the phone I looked at Jeremy. His face was pale and he was trembling like a frail leaf in the wind. "Can I go look for her?" he begged. "Can we go find her now? Please?"

"No. We'll let the police handle this. It's very dangerous."

"Is Charlie doing this?" Now he was angry. He was trying to understand something way beyond him and there weren't enough words to explain away his fear.

"No. Not Charlie."

He didn't probe any further. He walked over to the window and pulled the drapes apart, pressing his face against the glass so I wouldn't see the tears. I'd given the police her address and told Captain Sinclair everything I knew. I told him to hurry. He'd been surprised to hear from me, especially like this. But he listened to every word I had said and had briskly signed off with a quick thanks. I wasn't sure if he had believed me. I went to stand beside Jeremy.

A short while later we heard the sirens crying across town through the night.

"They gonna save Jenny?" he asked.

"I hope so." But my heart was in turmoil. I knew something the rest of them didn't. That *thing* had never been beaten before, not that I could remember. I wanted to run out into the night and find Jenny, save her myself. I wanted to do something!

But I was afraid. I was afraid to leave Jeremy, afraid to go out there and face that thing I had hated and feared since I was a tiny child. Afraid of the thing I had seen in my vision last night.

Jeremy was scratching at the glass making terrible scraping noises that set my teeth on edge. "She doesn't deserve to die . . . she never had *anything*, Mom. Poor Jenny, she never had anybody to love her." He was crying and I had to firmly put my hand on his shoulder because for a second I was afraid that he was going to just run out wildly into the night and try to find her.

"Don't. It won't do any good," I said through gritted teeth.

"How do we know, unless we try? Mom!" His words died on the stillness around us and then bounced back to haunt us over and over. I didn't have time to answer before the sirens got so loud I couldn't speak above them. They were growing into a great roar—and then there was silence.

When the loud knocking came at the front door both of us jumped.

CHAPTER TWENTY-EIGHT

Jenny had been sent to bed very early that night. She had been punished for some silly thing or another. She couldn't remember quite what, really. They were always doing that to her, though. They just didn't want her around. They wanted her out of the way so they could be alone with their bottles. She didn't mind. They'd started fighting again, so she sneaked outside to play.

Her mom was furious at her dad for spending too much money on something or other. He hadn't gone to work again that morning, either, which had made her even angrier. Jenny knew he'd stayed in bed half the day after her mother had gone to work waiting on tables. Jenny knew he'd had another one of those mysterious headaches he always got when he drank too much the night before.

When her mother had come home a little while ago, she hadn't been too happy at seeing him home and all those empty bottles lying all over the place. That's when the yelling and the screaming had begun. Jenny could have recited the scene that was to follow word by word. It was always the same. Clever Jenny, she knew the ropes and she stayed out of their sight, out of their range of fire.

She'd hid outside beneath the window, until it got dark. She grew afraid of the dark, and tried to sneak past them to her room. That's when she had made her mistake. They were busy throwing things at each other and there was plenty of noise. But it was worth the risk because ever since that boy Timmy had been killed, Jenny imagined this monster out there in the woods that loved to eat little children. That's what had happened to poor old Timmy — that kid-eating monster had had him for dinner. She wrapped her skinny arms tightly around her body and tiptoed cautiously through the kitchen and into the hall. She could see her parents in the next room yelling at each other. Her mother's face was red and angry and her father was pretending not to hear her. They were too close to the door. She'd never get past them to her room, where they thought she was sleeping.

Silently, she slipped back into the kitchen and pryed the refrigerator open enough to get her hand inside. She didn't want to open it so wide that the light would alert them to her actions. She was hungry. They'd sent her to bed with supper again. She spied two wrinkled apples in the back and reached for them. Better than nothing; at least they would stop her stomach from growling.

She was tired of being hungry. Jeremy was so lucky he didn't have two parents. All they did was fight and send you to bed without supper. There were times since she had met Jeremy that she wished she was his real sister. That she could live with them. But, she thought quickly, not in that house! She wasn't sure what she'd do about that problem. Well, it didn't make any difference . . . she *wasn't* one of them. She went back to the door, the apples tight in her hands. Her parents were still fighting and she sighed and slid down to the floor by the door to wait. Sooner or later they would pass out. Then she could get back to her room and go to bed.

A long time went by. Jenny quietly devoured her apples and waited. She catnapped against the wall whenever the shouting subsided, but was rudely awakened by further outbursts. Finally, they seemed to calm down. They turned the television up and got interested in some show.

Jenny made her move. All she'd have to do was sneak around the corner behind their backs and run into her room. It should have been easy since their eyes were glued to the television set, but nothing seemed easy for Jenny these days.

"Now what's this? What are you up to, brat?" Her mother turned just as Jenny got half-way across the back of the front room and caught her. She jumped up and grabbed her by the nape of the neck like a reckless kitten. "Got ya! Where have you been, young lady?" Her mother's speech was slurred, her eyes angry, and hateful. The eyes told Jenny the whole story. She'd get a beating no matter what she said or did. She'd just better accept it and get it over with. At least, afterwards, she could cry herself to sleep. Her eyes slid urgently towards her father for help, but there was no help from a drunkard. He didn't even seem to know what was going on, much less care about it. He smiled his dull smile at her over her head and Jenny knew she was lost.

"You little sneak!" Her mother started to hit at her. Jenny closed her eyes and tried to protect herself as best she could until the rain of blows were over. It was all she could do. "Naughty child . . . running all over the neighborhood like some little thief! What have you been up to? No, good, I bet!"

"Nothing, mama. I haven't done nothing!" Jenny whimpered and tried to keep from crying. If she cried, it would always please her mother and she'd stop sooner. But Jenny had little of anything but pride. Pride was all she had left and so she kept the tears inside and bore a beating until her mother let her go.

"You need to be taught a good lesson. You'll get some discipline in ya, or else you'll grow up just plain bad. *Bad!*" Her mother let go of her neck but was still glaring at her. Jenny simply nodded and tried to slink away. Please, let her forget me like she usually does!

Jenny tried not to hate them. They had so many problems and that was why they drank too much. When they weren't drinking they weren't so bad. After all, they were her parents. But there were times, more frequent lately, when they didn't seem to know when to stop hurting her, when they would beat her too hard and draw blood. She could almost forget not to hate them then.

"She needs to be taught a real lesson, George," she heard her mother whine from the front room as she cowered in her bed, sniffling. Her arms and back ached from the beating and suddenly she was more afraid than she had ever been.

"I'll tell you what she needs, George—a good beating with a broomstick, that's it. An old-fashioned whipping. That'll put her in her place. Imagine her sneaking out of her room like that! I'll teach her."

Jenny was shaking as she waited in the dark room for her mother to come after her with the stick. She'd been beaten once with that stick and it was bad. It wasn't going to happen again. She wouldn't allow it.

"Ha, here's the stick. I'll show that little brat who's boss."

Jenny scrambled from her bed like it was on fire and ran to her window. She swiftly climbed out into the dark night without a moment's hesitation or a look back.

What had she done that was so wrong? She tried to stay out of their way, but somehow that wasn't enough anymore. They hated her. They wanted her *dead*! There was no other explanation. She was like a tiny caged animal beaten over and over and now the cage was open. She ran.

She ran out into the cool night, hesitating one second as she heard her mother back in her empty room screaming for her to come back and take her punishment, and then her mind settled on a destination ... Jeremy's house. Haunted or not, that's where she was going to go. She knew Jeremy would take care of her. She flew down the driveway and out across her yard, panting as she ran, so afraid they would catch her before she could get to Jeremy's. They would be so mad at her if they caught her!

She ran down the empty streets and through the darkened yards that lay silent in the night world. It was a long way to Jeremy's house, though, and she was already tired and bruised from the beating. She'd have to go through part of the woods.

She was limping by the time she had gone half-way. Her foot slipped and she stumbled, twisting her ankle. It hurt like the dickens, but she knew she couldn't stop right here in the woods, alone, and at night. There was Timmy to think about. He'd gone out and never came back.

Only desperation could have gotten her out here alone at night. There were trees everywhere, and it was so dark she couldn't see her hands in front of her face. Yet, she kept on running.

The trees! They were everywhere . . . moving! One of them seemed to be loping clumsily, slowly separating itself from the other surrounding shadows. It started directly towards her! Its huge leafy arms reached for her as if it wanted to embrace her.

At first, she stood there staring up at it in shock. Then as it came nearer she heard the growls it was making and its laughter on the night breeze. Jenny started to scream. Too late, she tried to run away, but it grabbed her and lifted her like a twig from the ground. Up . . . Up . . . So high she could not even see the ground. Then it dropped her.

She tried to crawl away like a wounded animal. Her left leg had snapped and she dragged it, whimpering. She instinctively knew that there was no use in wasting her breath in pleading. She needed all her energy to get away from *it*. She didn't even dare think about what it was or why it was doing this to her. A vague idea flitted past that maybe this was what had happened to Timmy.

It got her again and lifted her up, up. This time she never recovered from the fall. She didn't hear the laughter and she didn't feel the claws or the teeth. Jenny felt nothing. Jenny would never feel anything again. Her grave was dead leaves.

It loomed over her broken body. Something as big as the sky, with fangs and claws and red coals for eyes. She had died too easily for it. It had been robbed of its sport. It was angry.

CHAPTER TWENTY-NINE

"I'll have patrolman Henderson stay here and watch the boy." Captain Sinclair's face was grave. He was in uniform this time and I hardly recognized him when he had first knocked on the door. He didn't waste time in being polite or asking redundant questions.

"Do you have any idea where she may be right now?" he'd asked right off the bat when he'd faced me across the threshold. I had the strangest feeling that he really didn't believe anything I'd say.

I started to shake my head, then suddenly an image came so strongly that I had to steady myself by laying a hand on the door frame. "Yes, I know where she is!" I tried not to look at Jeremy as I quickly got a coat while the Captain waited at the door.

"Mom, I want to go with you!" Jeremy burst out, taking my hand and refusing to let go. "I know where she lives. I can help."

I still didn't look him in the eyes. If I would have, he'd have known instantly. I could tell him later when it was all over and I would be here to comfort him. "No, son. I have to do this alone."

"But Mom!"

"I said no." Now I took his face into my hands and tilted

his chin up so I could see him better. "It's too dangerous out there. Do you understand what I'm saying?"

His eyes clouded, his mouth quivering as he nodded his head in the appropriate response. I wondered what he was thinking at that moment. "I have to go. Do what the officer tells you to do and don't give him any trouble, you hear?"

He merely nodded.

"Let's go." I turned back to Captain Sinclair. As we walked down the porch in the dark I didn't look back once at Jeremy standing in the doorway. My mouth was dry and I felt like I was going back in time, back to the night my brother had died all those years ago.

There were two patrol cars in front of my house. One had its lights silently going and the door was open. I slid in and waited until the Captain was seated and we were on our way. Then I let the misery and weariness wash over me.

"She's dead, Captain. So there's no hurry." The words struggled through my lips. I looked straight ahead so I don't know how he reacted.

"How do you know?"

"I know. I saw her in one of my visions right before we left the house." I put my hand up and covered my face so he wouldn't see my tears. "I think I saw her so clearly because she's linked to my son . . . she was his friend. Only I never knew he'd become friends with the girl in my visions. The girl had long braids." I turned my face to the window, trying to wipe the tears away. "Jeremy knew her all along. She was afraid of me and my reputation, and the house. She forbade him to tell me about her. I guess she was afraid I was some kind of witch. I never put two and two together and saw the possibilities. I was having those visions because the girl was close to me—through Jeremy. She's dead and I could have prevented it. I didn't try hard enough."

My riding partner was silent. "Don't blame yourself," he said gruffly. He was a man not used to emotion, a man of steel on the outside with a soft heart he didn't want anyone o know about. "Where are we going?" he finally asked, totally ignorant of my distraught state of mind. In this case, was glad he was. After all, this was his job. This was going o be hard enough without acting like an hysterical woman on top of it all.

I briefly explained where the vision had taken place. I remembered the exact location all too well. He turned to look at me directly then and something clicked in his eyes. Maybe he was remembering something, too. My record, probably. He called in to the station and asked for a backup. Soon there were other sirens calling across the night, all heading for the same destination. "For the little girl's sake, Miss Towers, let's hope this time you're wrong."

The woods were wet and very dark. The moon was hidden and no light shone through the clouds. The only lights shining on the tiny bloody body half covered with leaves were the police's spotlights and headlights. The domes of light revolved silently and the squadcars sat like cold sentinels in a large circle. When we had first found the body, more cars had been called in.

I sat quietly in one of them and watched the scene with bitter tears in my eyes. How I wished Jim was here, or Ben. Someone I could cry in front of and not be ashamed. Everyone scurrying around out there was a stranger to me. Not one friendly face anywhere. I sighed. They were all busy examining the scene and putting things in small plastic bags to take away in their cars. There were camera men and curious thrill seekers ghoulishly poking around. I'd had cameras pushed in my face too many times and microphones shoved at me since the discovery had been made a few hours ago. I was tired and sick—I wanted to go home. But they weren't done with me yet. Captain Sinclair was out there somewhere and he had asked me to wait for him. He'd take me home. I wondered if a stop at the police station was to be first. I squinted at my watch in the pale light. It was after two.

I would never forget that corpse lying out there, and I

could feel *its* malevolent presence still lingering out beyond the trees. Waiting and gloating. Playing *its* hellish games. In some ways I almost wished *it* would show itself to everyone out there so I could stop being the only insane person. I was sick of the secret I harbored and the truth that was too unspeakable to mention and too hard to be believed. The Captain was going to ask more questions and I wasn't sure how I was going to answer them. I had led them right to the body.

It was out there somewhere. I kept expecting it to come storming out any second to claim me, like it had Jenny. I didn't care anymore if it did. With me dead the murders would end. It would all end. Then maybe Jeremy and Jim had a chance to live.

I got out of the car and started to walk. The night was cool and when I got so far away that the squadcars' lights were just flashing circles in the distance, I turned to look back. It was like a scene from a nightmare. I turned again and kept walking deeper into the woods. I didn't know what I was doing anymore. It filled me with terror just to remember that thing in my vision last night and yet I was drawn by something far stronger. Something wanted me to come into the woods. Something was calling me. I could hear nothing else. It would be so easy to end it all.

"Sarah!" I was grabbed from behind and two strong arms encircled me. "What are you doing! Where do you think you're going?" The voice was angry, but relieved.

"Ben!" I stared up into his worried face and then collapsed into his arms, sobbing. I was so glad he was there. "I was running away," I mumbled, when I gained control again. I just wanted to snuggle into his embrace and never think of another thing again. I wanted the world, the murders and the past to all just fade away and never come back. I couldn't bear it anymore.

"It isn't your fault, Sarah," Ben told me as we walked back to his squadcar. He'd been on duty and in the middle of a burglary stake-out. This was his first chance to get

284

away. He'd been frantic when he'd learned about the little girl's death and my involvement, especially when he had found out that I had tried to call him so many times that day. I had really needed him, and he hadn't been there for me. "You couldn't have stopped this from happening." He looked over to where the body was being carted away on a stretcher. I followed his gaze and shuddered. "You tried, but couldn't. It isn't your fault," he repeated staunchly. "Stop punishing yourself. Don't worry, we'll catch this thing eventually . . . whoever or whatever it is. We've got every man on it and they're calling in specialists to help."

"They won't find it," I said in a whisper.

Ben only held me closer.

"They took pictures. I'm going to be in all the papers tomorrow." I said the words without feeling, like it didn't really matter to me. But Ben understood what I was going through. My life wouldn't be my own anymore. They wouldn't leave me alone — not after this.

Captain Sinclair sauntered up then and nodded at Ben. Then he turned to me. "We have some reports to fill out. Could I have some of your time, Miss Towers? It won't take long, I promise. I realize it's late and you've had a hard time of it." We all knew that he meant the media and the unwanted attention. He wasn't a hard man, no matter what anyone else thought. He was just doing his job.

"All right. Let's go." I was going to help in any way I could. Ben smiled at me and took my hand. Everything was going to be all right, the smile said.

If he only knew.

CHAPTER THIRTY

When the dawn eased the blackness into pale grey, Jim picked up his suitcase and his guitar and checked out of the motel. He was tired and his steps showed it. The bus station wasn't very far away—he wasn't about to get into another car, so he refused all rides from the other band members. He wasn't about to put any of their lives in danger. It was a long dusty walk and it was starting to get warm already. He made a quick stop at a donut shop and got a cup of coffee and a few jelly donuts. He ate them on the way. It wasn't easy with a suitcase and a guitar, but he managed. It was the first thing he'd eaten since the accident.

He got to the bus stop and sat down under a tree to finish his breakfast while he waited. Siteston was a small, insignificant sort of town that didn't really have what you could call a bus station. It was just a place on the highway where you could catch any lone bus heading in one direction or the other. . . if you were lucky and it wasn't too late. After about an hour he knew that his bus was late.

Jim tried not to think about the accident. It was better if he didn't think, or else the fear crept in with razor-sharp teeth . . . and he wasn't strong.

"I'm coming, Jeremy." He muttered the words under his

breath as his eyes scanned the highway under the relentless glare of the sun. Where was that damn bus? He grumbled various phrases as he walked out to the very edge of the highway and stared down it. No bus. So he went back to sit under the tree. He wouldn't allow himself to get too comfortable. He wouldn't allow himself to fall asleep, even though it was peaceful and cool here in the shade. It was going to be a scorcher today. This was turning out to be one hell of a summer and it had just begun. He closed his eyes for just a second and caught himself. He couldn't fall asleep.

He had to get home to Sarah and Jeremy. He wished there was a telephone so he could try to call them again. He wouldn't admit how worried he was. How many times he had tried to call home since the accident—ten? Twenty? He'd lost count. It was always busy, or rang but was never answered. He refused to go crazy over it. He'd simply get home in one piece and see what the hell was going on. He'd sent a telegram to them just this morning telling them he was all right and on his way home. Safe.

A tiny dot appeared floating on the horizon in the heat waves. It was growing larger. "About time," he mumbled, realizing that he didn't have much of that at this point. Jumping up, he gathered all his stuff and went running to the edge of the road to flag it down. It mustn't leave him behind.

The bus came to a sighing halt amidst a great cloud of dust and gravel as the brakes took hold. Another few inches and it would have literally run him down. The driver must be crazy! Jim dusted his jeans off angrily and climbed aboard. He heard the door slide shut with an escape of air and his eyes happened to skim back past them and outside to the line of trees he had just vacated. The heat waves were dancing out there among the foliage in the lazy eddies that teased the dust. Something moved out there among the trees. As the bus lurched away, Jim could have sworn he had seen—no, it couldn't be . . .

It looked like a small boy waving at him. Goodbye. Goodbye.

Stunned, Jim paid his fare to the driver and tried not to act conspicuous as he made his way back to a seat. Yet, his eyes remained riveted to that spot where he had just seen something. A small unknown child had waved at him. He racked his memory. Why had that gesture bothered him? Why? Now there was no one there. Nothing.

He stuck his suitcase and his guitar on the seat next to him. He was so tired, he fought to keep his eyes open. Slumping in the seat, he couldn't help but want to be lulled to sleep by the bouncing of the bus as it made its way down the highway. He thought the driver was going a little too fast.

It wouldn't hurt to get a little shut-eye. He was on a bus filled with people. *No.* He rubbed his eyes, sat up straighter and lit a cigarette. The bus bumped along as he watched out the window.

They passed a carnival, one of those small neighborhood ones. People were laughing, smiling, and spending their money. Children were prancing everywhere. There was a musical carousel with all its brightly painted wooden horses doing its laps.

Sarah had always loved carousels. Jim could see her out there among that crowd; a tiny girl with braids and freckles riding the wooden horses around and around to calliope music. They used to ride the giant ferris wheel and the wild roller coaster high into the night sky. It had been magic. Sarah had always loved the thrills but he had always held back, a little afraid of being off safe ground. She would coax him into riding with her and he'd sit frozen next to her, clinging to her arm as if he would surely fall if her dared let go. They'd laboriously climb the tracks until they reached the very top. He'd hold his breath until he'd almost pass out because he'd forget to breathe.

"Please, sis. Don't rock this thing," he'd stutter, shivering with fright. He was petrified to move an inch in their precarious perch. He'd sit rigidly, looking neither to the left nor the right, so afraid the swinging seat would start to move. He couldn't bear that. "Don't move so much, Sarah!" How was it that she could always lead him to such folly? With her at his side, they had been such daredevils.

"Stop moving!"

"It's not me, Jimmy," she replied every time indignantly. "It's the wind. See?" She'd laugh then and tease him, throwing up her hands without holding onto anything. "Take your hands away from your face, you silly goose. How can you see anything?" She'd try to pry cotton-candied fingers away from his eyes.

"I don't *want* to see anything."

"We're at the top! Look, Jimmy! You are not going to fall, believe me."

"Don't!" he'd hiss back at her.

"Look!"

"No. Leave me alone!"

Sitting there on that bus, he could still smell the cloying aroma of pink cotton candy . . . tantalizing hotdogs with their tangy mustard smell and pickle relish heaped over the whole mess. The wheel would lurch and sway as each new person got on below until they too were at the top. His stomach would be lurching, too.

"Look. There's snotty old Leslie and her new boyfriend!" Sarah would giggle and point down at their older sister. "Down there—see—by the dart game." Against his will he would peak. "And look . . . there's our house over there." She'd rattle on excitedly while he was trying his best not to throw up. "Can you see it?" She'd prod him mercilessly, sending his heart into a tailspin.

The whole world would be spinning down below them in swirling lights and breathtaking colors like a mystical kaleidescope. He couldn't make out a darn thing, he was shaking so bad. "I don't see our house," he'd grumbled and glue his fingers back promptly over his eyes. "Stop this thing and let me off. Let me off! I don't want to play anymore."

Wasn't it still like that?

Then they would go in the spookhouse. Jim sighed. In his mind the laughter of those visits now turned to real screams of fear and terror. . . the screams of Charlie and all those others. And they were all running through those cursed woods fleeing some huge black hulking obsenity that always caught them and tore them to pieces.

"I'm sorry, Sarah! I'm sorry," Jim whispered in the dimness of the back of the bus. "I can't help you. I tried . . . I can't!" The words were so fragile no one else heard him. Desperate words, prompted by extreme guilt.

He hadn't been able to help any of them. He was a coward. He hung his head and there was sorrow in his face.

It was his turn now.

The very fact that he was finally ready to give up so Sarah and Jeremy and the others could live, might be the very reason he might never make it home. He gazed at his sunken reflection in the dirty bus window. *It* might not let him make it home.

Did anything matter anymore?

Jim was haunted by too many dead faces. Charlie's. Leslie's. Amy's . . . his parents'. For the first time he admitted that he had *always known* about that entity in the woods and what it craved. He'd *always known* why they all had to die. He had never told Sarah, though. He'd never told a soul. No guts. Since that first time all those years ago . . . that terrible summer's night out in the fields with Sarah. Oh, he had known it was out there. *He'd always known.* So when he'd run away and let Sarah go into those accursed woods alone, he knew what she was up against. But he had been too frightened to warn her—or any of the rest of them—because if they hadn't have died, *he would have.*

So simple the way the game was played. The entity demanded sacrifices; needed young souls and craved blood. *It was either them or him.*

All he had to do was keep his mouth shut, and bear the

290

guilt. Or let poor Sarah keep believing she was the reason they were all dying. Jim hated himself.

He was sick of it. Sick of running and sick of watching the dying. Now it was time to end it. He had lost the game. The thought put a faint smile on his lips for the first time in years. He spied his face in the dirty window and suddenly it was Charlie's pitiful face grinning back at him, content at last. Jimmy was coming home.

Going back home was the first step. Sarah and Jeremy would live.

The bus bounced all over the road at full speed but Jim was so exhausted that he still kept dozing off. He'd be on the road at least two more grueling days and he hadn't slept since the accident. Why he kept thinking of it as an accident, he didn't know. It had simply been the card that called in all the players; the game's over. *Allie. Allie . . . all in free! All come home free. Come home.*

He wasn't so stupid that he'd stop along the way in some flea-bitten motel for a much-needed rest. He might never get home to throw in his ace. A nagging thought kept occurring to him; maybe it wanted *all* of them and wouldn't settle for it to end this way. That wasn't an improbable concept. It had played dirty before, so he wouldn't stop anywhere that he didn't have to.

When a couple of hours later the bus pulled into a rest stop and everyone clamored off in a herd for the restrooms and the snack bar, Jim propped his legs up on the back of the seat before him and stayed behind. He wasn't hungry. He had candy bars in his guitar case and he munched on them.

By the time the bus pulled out onto the highway again the sun was going down and there was a chill in the air. Only a few of the original riders were still on the bus. Most of them had gotten off at different stops during the long day. A large city was right ahead. Jim could see its lights twinkling in the fading light as they flew around a curve in the road.

Damn that bus driver! He was still driving way too fast, Jim thought. They should be pickier about their drivers. This one could get them all killed. There was no longer a smile on Jim's thin lips. He felt funny. Watched. The hair on the back of his neck was standing on end as he glared out the window into the coming night.

It was watching with ancient cunning eyes. It had watched him board the bus all those miles back and it had followed the bus's weaving trail down the narrow curving roads. It rode the wind and skimmed the tree tops like a shimmering grey mist that at times was visible and at times, when the sun was brightest, was not. It was only coasting . . . gloating over the people in the moving vehicle below.

It was keeping an eye on its quarry.

Greedily, it glided in lower over the speeding bus and cast a huge shadow. It could hardly wait to see him suffer as he was going to suffer this time. It had plans. Yes, the man would suffer like the man had made him suffer all those centuries ago. Revenge would be so sweet.

They must all die this time. None must escape. It was not the rules of their game, but the hatred was so strong it seemed not to have had a beginning or a reason. But the reason was buried deep in the bowels of its memory and far back in time. Revenge. Always revenge for what had happened all those centuries ago. It had started out that way in the beginning . . . but now? He had crossed him and humiliated him so much and they would all be made to pay and suffer for his crimes — forever.

One punishment — one life of punishment wasn't enough for what he had done! Now . . . what was it the man had done? He couldn't really remember . . .

Did it matter? No. It just loved to kill now. That was all. It just loved to kill. From century to century, the man and his loved ones were the link that forever led him on.

The bus careened dangerously around a sharp curve

292

throwing gravel and squealing half-bald tires as the thing in the clouds flew down close to it. The shadow passed over Jim's face as he sat staring out the window. Alarm filled his face as he peered out and upwards towards the sky; and then it went as white as marble.

But there wasn't anything up there except the darkening sky and the fleecy clouds that trailed through it. Nothing to panic over, he calmed himself and settled back into the hard seat. Besides, he was safe in a crowd.

He knew that was a lie.

There wasn't much time. There was a small notebook in his hands and he began to write in it hurriedly, as he had so many times before. The tiny book was full of his barely legible scribbling. He frowned and bit his pencil, then went back to writing. It was a journal he had started after Amy had disappeared.

When everything was over, the journal would go to Sarah. He had to explain—it was the very least he could do for her. He owed her that much. He took a second away from his work to look out the window again. Still nothing. Anyone seeing him for the first time at that moment would have said he was a man haunted. You could see it in his thin, strained face. His head bobbed over the journal as he wrote about the woman he had thought was Amy in the truck—just another trick. There were so many things in his journal that had been very difficult to put down in words.

Cautiously, making sure no one was watching him too closely, he wrote the words: *I think I have found the answer to our problems. I think I know how to rid us and the world of this evil thing. I pray to God that I am right. I cannot let Sarah and Jeremy die. I have had enough of death and fear. The Evil belongs in hell and I must do what has to be done to get it back there. I owe this to Amy and all the others. I must . . .*

Someone had just flopped down beside him and Jim stopped writing and put the little book back in his pocket with a sigh. He had hoped he might finish what he had to

293

say before he was interrupted.

The man who sat down next to him was middle aged and bald. He was chewing on a cigar. "Jesus!" the man swore as the bus started up with a big jerk and accelerated so abruptly that he almost landed in Jim's lap as they hit a bump in the road. "Who taught that creep to drive? Change that. Whoever told him he could drive was nuts, he can't!" Then the guy threw a look at Jim and raised his eyebrows. "Is he this bad all the time?"

"So far, yes," Jim replied dryly, looking back at the stranger. "Don't worry, it gets worse. He's just warming up now."

The man settled himself in the seat and muttered something to himself under his breath. Then he sighed and opened the newspaper he had clutched in his hand. Jim couldn't help but see the headlines on the page he started to read.

PSYCHIC PREDICTS SECOND CHILD MURDER

Jim instantly recoiled but he couldn't keep himself from peeking over to read more. It was Sarah all right. Old photos of her were splattered all over the front page along with smaller dismal photos of the two victims.

Jim felt sick. It wasn't just the fact that Sarah's whole life was being dissected and spread all over the front page, but there had been another innocent child butchered. It was all there in black and white—grisly in detail.

Jim closed his eyes and his head swam with pain and guilt. He was the cause of this. He knew Sarah blamed herself. All those stories their grandmother had told them about rings and power. Sarah must have believed it was the price she paid for her "gift."

And what must Sarah be going through right now?

"You all right, kid?" the man next to him said. "Can I help you? Here, take a sip of my coffee. It's almost cold but it might help." The man sitting beside him pushed a paper cup at him.

Jim accepted the cup without a word and drained it as

the man told him to do. It did help. He was very thirsty all of a sudden. "Thanks—I'm all right. Just been on this bus too long, you know?"

The bus lurched again going around a turn and the man nodded conspiratorially. "On this bus, I can see what you mean."

Jim smiled at him and then turned his head towards the window. He wished the man would mind his own business and leave him alone. Suddenly his throat closed up and he developed a terrible headache. His vision blurred and he leaned his forehead against the window. He had to get home. My God, what Sarah must be going through now! He had to get there and be with her, help her.

He had to stop this thing before someone else died. The bus continued to speed through the night and out of sheer exhaustion and worry, Jim drifted into a fitful sleep. A sleep filled with memories that weren't all from *one lifetime*.

CHAPTER THIRTY-ONE

I thought I knew what it was going to be like. I remembered those last years in Benchley. Yet nothing had prepared me for this. The phone started to ring early the next morning, waking me from a sleep riddled with corpses and people I had once loved, now all dead and gone. At first I thought the phone was just part of my dreams. Unfortunately, I found out soon enough it wasn't. I stumbled downstairs in my nightgown and answered it.

People kept phoning, wanting advice, help in finding missing loved ones, or wanting me to solve all their problems or solve crimes that had been off the books for years. Some just wanted their palms read. Those were the nice calls. Some were cranks wanting to know why I was killing those little children or why I was lying. They called me witch and worse.

When I couldn't stomach it anymore, I simply stuffed the phone under the chair cushion; taking it off the cradle, risking a missed call from either Ben or Jim. Everything was fresh in my mind from the horrors of last night and I was so worried about Jim, I almost put the receiver back on. I knew it wouldn't do any good. It would just ring all the time anyway—and all the wrong people. Not Jim. I wondered where my brother was now and why he hadn't called in three days. Was he still alive? I didn't know, and it scared me. I couldn't see the future when I really needed to, so what good was my "gift"?

My world had turned into a vicious nightmare again and I felt trapped and helpless. If Jim was only here . . .

Someone threw a brick wrapped in newspapers through my window. I stooped down in shock and picked it up after I had nervously looked out just in time to see a green Pontiac speed down the road and out of sight. So much for good neighbors. I unwrapped the newspaper from around the brick, holding my breath. Maybe it was a bomb. It was worse. My face was all over the front pages, as well as pictures from the horror out in the woods last night and other things, things that they must have stayed up all night digging for. My whole past history was there. All about my family and . . .

Clutching the paper to my breast I slumped down in the chair right on top of the phone. I couldn't believe how sordid everything appeared to be. No wonder one of my neighbors had thrown a present through my window. I was a celebrity! Now everyone would know about me. Everyone would know where to find me.

After a while I walked into the kitchen and made a pot of coffee. I needed to talk to Ben. What I really needed was to sleep this whole mess off somewhere for a couple of years, but I knew that was impossible. I had promised to help the police and help them I would.

I had fallen into quicksand and there was no longer any easy way out.

Jeremy's feet padded down the stairs a short while later and I smiled sadly at him as he ambled into the kitchen. "Are you hungry? How about some hot chocolate?" Bribes. My son was devastated over Jenny's death and not even hot chocolate could make him smile back at me. He'd been asleep when I'd come home in the early morning hours last night and I hadn't a chance to tell him that she was dead. One look at his serious face, though, and I knew *he* knew. It only made sense that he would know that. She had been his friend.

"That sounds fine, Mom," he said listlessly and sat down in the chair next to me. The incriminating newspapers were still spread all over the table and I tried to lay my startled hands over them so he wouldn't see. I didn't have to bother. He sat there dazed just staring out the window, not noticing anything. When I set the cup and a few pieces of buttered toast before him he didn't even touch them.

"Jeremy?"

He turned and looked directly at me with such a tortured look in his eyes that I only had to hold out my arms and he was in them, his head up against my shoulder as he cried soundlessly. I could feel the tears through my blouse, hot on my skin.

"She never hurt anybody, Mom! She never had nothing or nobody until I became her friend. Who would hurt Jenny?" He sobbed into my shoulder as I rocked him.

"Something very evil, honey." I replied quietly. I didn't know what else to say. I could never expect him to understand what even I couldn't understand.

"You said last night it wasn't Charlie . . . then who was it?" he demanded, looking up at me, his face suddenly hot with anger.

I sighed. I didn't answer. I couldn't. Inside there was this strange premonition that if he knew too much, he, too, would be doomed.

"That thing in the woods did it, didn't it?" There was a subdued quality in his tone but I could tell he was deadly serious. It was time for the truth now.

"Yes. I think it is there now. I think it . . ." I was going to say killed Jenny but I couldn't get the words out. I kept seeing that pitiful body lying there all torn and bloody among the wet leaves. The image overpowered me and we sat there in silence, both thinking our own private thoughts. It was terrible if he could see what I was seeing. I only hoped he couldn't.

"Mom?" he asked meekly after he had stopped crying. "Do I have to go to the police station and tell them about Jenny and me now? I mean, that we were friends and all. About how bad her family was to her. All that?"

It was the first time I had heard anything about any of that and Jeremy told me all about her parents and the way they had mistreated her. No doubt the police would try to place the blame for what had happened in some way on her parents. After all, they would probably point out, she was an abused child anyway. Maybe her parents had just gone too far this time. I could hear it now and I knew with certainty that that was how they would hide the real truth. No need to start a panic in the area if a plausible scapegoat could be found.

I told Jeremy that he didn't have to go to the police station but that maybe someone would come here to ask him some questions later. Right now, as Ben had informed me when he left me at my door this morning, the police would have their hands full searching the immediate crime scene and gleaning it for clues.

They would find nothing.

I had told them all I knew and the Captain had stared at me as if I were just plain crazy. No one had to tell me to stay in town and no one had to tell me that psychic or not, I was their prime suspect. I knew too much. I didn't blame any of them—it was hard to swallow that some *thing* in the woods was killing innocent children just because it liked to. The Captain was a realistic man. Wouldn't it be a fitting punishment for me, I had thought cynically, if they accused me of the crime and it went to trial?

I decided to try to reach Ben again, but got no answer at his place and then, hesitantly, I dialed the station and was politely told that Detective Raucher was on duty and at that time unreachable.

When I couldn't stand it any longer I took the phone out from under the cushion and set it back on the table where it belonged, the receiver back in its cradle. It didn't ring for a few minutes and then the whole thing began all over again The phone went back under the cushion.

No telling what Jim would think if he tried to call and couldn't get through.

It was understandable that when someone knocked on the door I ran to it hoping it was finally Jim. It wasn't.

I shook my head, not believing what I was seeing. Then it all came back. Everything, and I know my face went cold like my heart.

Jonathan!

"What do you want?" I immediately blurted out in a tiny voice. It was like seeing a ghost. No, it was worse. Once this man had been my whole life and now, as I studied him standing there nervously in front of me after so long, I could feel absolutely nothing but impatience and indifference. He was no longer part of our world—by his own choice—so what was he doing here in my new life? Just as my heart had begun to heal from his mistreatment, here he was back again to reopen old wounds. How could anyone be so cruel? I put on a fake smile and stared at him as if he were Santa Claus come too early—like on Halloween.

"I saw the papers . . ." The four words said it all.

I sighed aloud and opened the door so he could come in. I felt stiff all over and searching his strange, yet familiar face, I tried to read his intentions. The square jaw was set firm, his eyes were steely and bottomless. I remembered that look: a mingling of anger and impatience that always came off as arrogance. He had always been the kind of man who took what he wanted and never cared who got hurt in the process.

"Well?" I stood inside the door glaring at him, my hands on my hips. This was the stuff of my wildest fantasies . . . Jonathan before me again after all this time. Jonathan here. I could reach out and touch him. Jonathan, my son's father. Jonathan, whom I had always loved and been faithful to. Jonathan, who hadn't been faithful to me. Loving Jonathan. Hateful Jonathan.

I felt nothing. He was an annoyance, that was all, something that no longer belonged here. I wished I could snap my fingers and have him vanish. As the realization washed over me, a great burden was lifted from my heart. I wanted to laugh with relief. It no longer hurt. I was free.

"When I heard about your connection with this murder, Sarah, you can imagine, well — it came as a sort of shock." He was smiling coldly at me, looking right through me as if I wasn't there. Typical. If something was distasteful to him, he pretended it didn't exist. "I'm worried about my son." He leveled his cold blue eyes at me and his jaw worked under his skin. I had surprised him with my indifference and he was trying to get back at me. I knew the procedure too well to fall for it. He was trying to bluff me into giving myself away. The problem was, though, that he no longer knew who I was. I was not the weak-willed woman he had left.

"That's strange. You've never worried about him before, *Jonathan*." I stressed his name and smiled sweetly up into his empty face. Why hadn't I seen it before? He wasn't handsome *or* sensitive. Watching him now I was amazed at how different reality was from fantasy. Jonathan was shorter than I remembered, and a little . . . pudgy. Nothing like Ben. I had forgotten, too, how pretentious Jonathan was. It was hard keeping a straight face.

"I've always worried about my son," he threw back indignantly, turning to take in his surroundings. I saw his eyes narrow as he let them rove around my home, probably filing every little sordid detail away in that clinical mind of his for further dissection and later criticism. I resented it as much as I resented his being here. He turned back to me. "Where is he?" It came out like an order, not a simple question. I resented that, too. How dare he!

"If you were so worried about your son, why did you leave us?" I hated myself the moment I said it, but it was too late and the harm was done. I knew I had meant the words as I said them but the funny thing was that I really didn't care anymore. Another surprise.

His blue eyes flashed at me and then a sadness seemed to invade their depths. It was then I felt sorry for him. He had loved Jeremy, too, once. Of course, he would miss him. Wouldn't I, if it was the other way around?

So in the end, I nodded and smiled sincerely at him for the first time. "Truce?" I asked and he nodded back, a ghost of a smile playing on his lips.

There wasn't enough of anything left in either one of us even to keep the hate alive for very long. Each one of us, then, had come to terms with ourselves and our actions long ago. "There's nothing to worry about," I said softly as he followed me meekly into the kitchen.

I didn't have to announce him. Jeremy with a squeal of delight was out of his chair and in his father's arms in two seconds flat, laughing and talking a mile a minute as if his father had never left or hurt us in any way. I felt tears come to my eyes, for what once had been and could never be again. All of us together as a family. We had all gone separate paths and there was no going back. Ever.

But seeing them so happy together made me happy as well, if only for a short time.

"Why are you here, Jonathan? Really?"

He looked up at me as he hugged his son. "I'd like to take Jeremy back with me . . . if I may. For a while." His eyes were soft now, not cold as before, and there was a terrible pleading in them. "After all that's happened, Sarah, I'm afraid for him to stay here until that maniac is caught."

He was perfectly serious.

I stared at him. Anything else I might have expected, but not this. I had been prepared to fight his hate or his arrogance, but this pity I felt for him, I could not fight. He loved Jeremy. Whatever reason he had for staying away from his son for so long, no longer mattered. He loved him as much as I did.

Only he didn't understand. He didn't understand anything! Something inside of me cried that I should stop it all now. I should simply tell him no and kill it before it grew.

Jeremy would never be allowed to leave here. *It* wouldn't allow it. And yet . . .

"Sarah, for God's sake! Can't you see it's dangerous for him to stay here? With that maniac out there killing children?" His eyes said even more. *And you're involved in the case and now everyone knows it. Because of you, and what you're doing, Jeremy isn't safe anymore!* It was there in his eyes for me to see.

"Let me take him home with me," he begged, standing up with Jeremy in his arms. Jeremy was looking at both of us, torn between us, his eyes large and puzzled.

"For how long?" I gulped, my heart racing almost as fast as my mind. Was it possible that Jeremy could get away safely? Surely nothing could happen as long as his father had him? Surely, it only wanted *me*? If I stayed . . . couldn't he go? *If I stayed . . .*

"Until this nut is caught or until it's safe," Jonathan stated. His eyes were fever bright and his voice was quick. He was really concerned. He really cared. "Then I'll bring him back. I promise. I miss him so much, Sarah." I thought he was going to say something else, but he didn't and I would never know what it might have been. For a moment I almost wished there would have been something else and then it, too, passed. We lived in two different worlds now, and mine was a very troubled and dangerous one at this time. Maybe Jeremy could escape. That was the best solution.

It only wanted *me*, after all.

I didn't let my confusion stop me. I made the decision and then locked it in.

"All right. I agree. It's about time he goes with you for a visit." I touched his arm and felt sad that he stiffened as I did. "But, Jonathan, only until everything's under control or I think it's safe for him to come home. Do you understand?"

"I understand, Sarah." The voice was the same as I remembered it, the face, even the way he hugged Jeremy close to him, yet he wasn't my Jonathan anymore. There

303

were so many subtle changes that I had to constantly remind myself that he was Jonathan at all. "You're coming to visit with me for a while, son, how would you like that?"

Jeremy turned questioning eyes towards me and I smiled, nodding. "You go."

"But, Mom—what if you need me?" he asked.

"I won't. I'll be fine." What was so wrong about Jeremy going with his father for a simple visit? He would come back. He wasn't leaving for good, I told myself. It was about time that his father spent some time with him . . . *and he would be safe with his father.*

I sent Jeremy upstairs to get some of his clothes together, saying I would help in a minute. "Why have you stayed away from him so long? It's been months," I asked him when our son had left the room. I tried not to accuse him but I could hear the words coming out harshly anyway.

"You moved so far away. What was I supposed to do? Fly down every weekend? Remember, I'm not rich." He was instantly on the defensive and I decided it just wasn't worth it.

"A telephone call doesn't cost as much as a plane ticket," I said bitterly and went upstairs to help Jeremy pack. I didn't give him a chance to answer and I knew I was being unfair but that man standing back there silent was someone I once trusted.

There were no easy answers. Jonathan no doubt had his reasons for what he had done, but I would never know or understand them, and he would never enlighten me now. I was sure of that. Either he wouldn't or couldn't.

Jeremy was stuffing his clothes into my old suitcase. "Everything'll be wrinkled if you do it like that," I told him, and took over. Trancelike, I neatly refolded everything he would need for a few days. Too much had happened in the last few days and I felt as if I were in shock. Jenny's death. The newspapers.

Jonathan was downstairs waiting to take Jeremy away with him. I shook my head trying to clear it. Was this really

304

happening? Was Jonathan really going to take my Jeremy?

"That enough, Mom," Jeremy protested. "I'm not going away for a year. I'll be back in a few days, right?" My son touched my hand and smiled up at me as he sat on the edge of his bed. Just a short while ago he had shed tears for his dead friend. I steeled myself against emotion or selfishness. I didn't want him to go, I knew that, but he had to. It would be much safer for him to be away from this place. It would get his mind off Jenny's death . . . and most of all, he needed his father right now. He had missed him terribly these last few months. He had never hid it that well from me. I didn't realize until now what seeing him again really meant to Jeremy. I had to let him go.

When he was all ready I walked back downstairs with him, my hand on his skinny shoulder. I hugged him. "I'll miss you so much, son." I said, my voice muffled in his shoulder. I didn't want to let him go. I walked with them to Jonathan's car.

"You'll telephone me every day, won't you?" I made him promise. As he got into the car I felt as if my heart were going with him. There was a feeling of endings, as if nothing would ever be the same again.

Jonathan threw me a frozen smile as he started up the car. Jeremy turned to wave at me through the window, trying not to cry. I could stop him still, I thought frantically as the car started to move away. I walked along beside the car as it backed slowly down the driveway. I had a sickening premonition that somehow this wasn't right. How could I let Jeremy out of my sight? How could I be sure he would be safe? But then, how could I take care of him when I couldn't even guarantee my own safety? I lightly touched the scars on my arm.

The car's shiny paint glinted in the sunlight and I stood and waved as it pulled away from me and gathered speed. Jonathan was intent on his driving. I saw him turn and smile down at our son. My heart grew so heavy, I gasped and clutched myself. The car soon disappeared down the road and into the sun.

Dazed, I looked around me and then at my empty arms. I stifled a cry of loneliness and trudged back alone into our home. Without Jeremy, it wasn't a home. It was only a house again. It had all happened too swiftly . . . Jonathan's arrival and then their departure. I was numb.

I shouldn't have let Jeremy go. But it was too late. It was done and for whatever reason I had let it happen there was no changing it now. He'd said he'd call every day and I could always just have Jonathan bring him back. *Or could I?* That thought nagged me as I fixed myself a good strong cup of coffee and tried to get myself together. I was lost without my son and that knowledge shocked me. Had I come to depend on him that much, that I couldn't bear him out of my sight?

Maybe it was best he had gone, then.

The day moved on like any other day, yet the house was full of echoes and shadows that pulled at me and made me anxious and weary. So many times I found myself in Jeremy's emtpy room just staring at his things as if he had died and not just gone away for a short visit. I found myself wondering if I had dreamed everything, as if I couldn't believe what I had done. I knew it was pure silliness. There had to be something wrong with me. It was probably strain over what had happened and the fact that I missed my son, that's all. It just seemed strange to have him gone when he'd been so close all these months. Not to mention the shock of seeing Jonathan again. That had taken all the wind out of my sails all right.

I ripped into the house with a vengeance. I cleaned everything I could lay my hands on and pushed all my fears and unpleasant thoughts out of my mind. Jeremy was fine. He was with his father. He was safe. Accept it and forget it. Calm down.

I tried calling Ben again and when the phone started ringing like crazy and it wasn't Jim or Ben, I fled the house. I drove to the store and walked around windowshopping like a zombie for hours, trying to act oblivious to the stares and finger pointing of people who connected me with the face on the front page. I finally put on a pair of sunglasses and wrapped a scarf around my hair. I wasn't ready to go home. I couldn't.

When it started to get dark I reluctantly went back and tried to call Ben yet again. I felt guilty that I hadn't been there all day to receive the call from Jim I knew should come at any moment. I wondered where he was and why he hadn't phoned.

I was never so glad to see Ben as I was that evening when he showed up looking worried and tired. I ran straight into his arms.

"What a welcome! I should come over more often." Then he pushed me away to study my face. "You'd better tell me now—what's wrong? You look terrible." There was gentleness in his eyes and concern and I told him about Jonathan and about sending Jeremy away.

He held me in his arms and never answered me when I asked him in a whisper if I had done the right thing. He only stroked my hair and held me tighter.

CHAPTER THIRTY-TWO

The bus jostled its tired passengers mercilessly through the long night. Jim dozed periodically or stared out the window into the night, thinking. He calculated that he should be home in a couple of hours, if nothing happened. It would be none too soon for him. He had this hunch that they weren't alone out there on this dark highway—something was following them.

But Jim, like a hounded rabbit, was so tired he no longer cared. If he was meant to make it, he would. That was all there was to it. His face was thin and drawn and the man beside him thought he was sick. That was fine with Jim. The guy left him pretty much alone.

His friends, anyone his life touched lately, had a way of coming to harm—or death. But there was nothing new about that. It had happened before. Jim didn't want to talk to anyone. They were safer that way.

When he first noticed the big white Buick, it was trying to pass the bus, beeping its horn and flashing its headlights as if it were in a frantic hurry to get somewhere. Jim remembered thinking idly that it was going too damn fast and when it finally passed the bus on a dangerous curve, it came too close to them for comfort. "What the hell . . .?" Jim sat up and blinked as it sped by in a white flash.

Another inch and it would have left white paint all over the side of the bus. Then it was gone.

"That car was really moving, huh?" the man next to Jim remarked.

"Yeah." For some reason Jim couldn't forget the white Buick. It had looked so familiar . . .

An hour went by, and he drifted back and forth between sleep and consciousness. Out of the corner of his eye he caught a white flash. It was the white car again! That car had passed them so fast and so many miles ago, it should have been in Alaska by now. How could it be right behind them gaining and crowding them again? It had be a similar car. He was tired, and that explained that.

The white Buick honked wildly and then passed them just as the other one had a while ago. Very close. Too close, Jim fumed, staring outside the window as the tail lights disappeared again up ahead of them. Something slithered deep in his memory and Jim's hands nervously clutched the seat ahead of him. What was there about the car that bothered him so?

"That car . . ." he started to say to the guy next to him and then looked over before he finished. The man was fast asleep, so he wouldn't have seen it whiz by so recklessly.

It started to rain outside, a fine drizzle that was lightly tapping on the roof and the windows. He could see the wind slapping at the trees. He had unconsciously been waiting and so he wasn't even very surprised when the car reappeared behind them a few miles further down the road. There was a funny buzzing in his head as he followed its progress. This time it didn't pass them right away. It drew up alongside the bus and maintained the same speed for a long time.

It was the same car. The inside was all shadows, so Jim couldn't see who was driving it. It suddenly crashed into the side of the bus and then bounced away again, still keeping pace alongside as before. The whole bus jolted slightly.

"What the hell does that idiot think he's doing!" The bus driver yelled.

The man next to Jim was wide awake now and his eyes were open in shock as he watched the car head in for another hit. The bus lurched and people began to scream.

"If he keeps that up, he'll force us off the road!" The bus driver swore, yanking the wheel to the left as the car made contact again. He fought to keep the bus on the road. "That nut's gonna cause an accident if he don't cut it out! SHIT!" The bus swerved precariously near the edge of the road. Nothing lay beyond it but blackness drenched with rain.

By then the bus was in pandemonium. The passengers were either clinging like leeches to their seats or rolling all over the floors, everyone yelling and crying as the bus bumped down the road at break neck speed. The white Buick persistantly knocked against the bus again and again. Jim was tossed violently back against the seat, but he wasn't screaming like the others. He had finally realized where he had seen that Buick—it had been his mother and father's car many, many years ago. Not one like it—but the *exact same car.*

He shoved his way up to the front of the bus and shouted into the driver's ear, "Stop the bus! Stop it right now!" He grabbed the man's fat shoulders and shook them. The movement of the bus threw him to the floor but he pulled himself back up. "Stop it . . . it's *me* they want!"

"Listen, buddy. I'd damn well like to stop this bus, but they're too damn close. They'd ram us for sure *right* into the river down there." The driver's fat face was beaded with sweat, his shirt stained with dark, wet patches. His beefy arms fought with the wheel. "I'm not stoppin'. Not on your life, buddy! If I stop now, we'll go over the edge for sure! Get down!"

"I know who they are . . . what they want. Stop the bus and let me off and no one else will get hurt, please!" Jim said hoarsely, but it was no use. The man was frozen at the wheel, acting only by raw instinct. He was being chased, so

310

he ran. The bus was picking up speed. Peering out the window, Jim couldn't see how the driver was still on the road anyway—he couldn't see a damn thing. It was a miracle the driver could.

"I can't stop!" the driver hissed, his eyes glued to the road. Jim was forcefully propelled to the door as the driver spun the wheel hard to avoid the car, suddenly in their path. He'd hit his head pretty hard and was numbed when he put his hand up and it came away with blood all over it. The whole side of his face was bleeding. The sound of screeching brakes and the screams of panic-stricken people rose into a cacophony that peaked as the bus narrowly missed the edge of the road and a thirty-foot drop.

Desperate, Jim got up and, grabbing the wheel, slammed his foot over the driver's on the brake. They fought for a few wild, dizzying seconds then the bus careened with a sickening crash into an embankment on the other side of the road. People were tossed against the windows and thrown to the floor in heaps. The silence was deafening. Smoke engulfed the whole bus. Jim had been dumped on the floor again and knocked out cold.

When he finally came to, he had no idea how long he had been out. It could have been minutes or hours. The only hint he had was that it was still dark. He woke to eerie silence and propped himself up on an elbow to survey the damage. So far he was the only one moving. "My God . . ." he moaned, staring around at the murky forms that littered the bus like corpses. The driver was still slumped over the wheel, seemingly unconscious.

What had happened to the car?

He didn't know what drew him, but he crawled weakly over to the door, that hung open, and fell outside into the wet grass. He took a deep breath of cool air and tried to stop his head from spinning. How many were dead in there? And it would all be his fault . . .

"I can't take it anymore," he whispered, looking back up

into the blank windows of the bus. There was blood all over him and burying his face in his hands, he cried, "I give up!" He yelled into the woods, "Anything you want!" He released a long sigh of defeat. *"You win!"* There was a great hush as he spoke. Something stirred in the wind and seemed to gasp. The darkness was silent. Jim didn't move for a long time.

"Jim?" The voice surprised him and made him glance up with a start. It was a child's voice. "Jim, what's the matter?" A gentle, caring voice.

It took Jim an eternity to understand. "Charlie?" he asked softly as his eyes grew wide . . . Charlie, as he had looked so many years ago as a small child. He was standing patiently above him in the twilight of dawn, smiling at him and clutching that mangy old cat of his, the one he had slammed the door on by accident and lopped off part of its tail . . .

Jim's mouth went dry. *But Charlie was dead! Charlie was . . .*

"Oh, it's me," Charlie chuckled then, petting his cat and looking amused.

"Charlie! My God! Where did you come from?" *You're dead,* he thought but didn't say aloud. Instead he groaned, "What do you want?" He started to tremble all over . . . did this mean that he was dead, too, then? He jerked his head around and closely studied the smoking hulk of the bus behind him. *Was he dead, and just didn't know it yet?*

"Oh, Jim, are you hurt?" The small ghost reached out its pale hand towards Jim as if to comfort him, but Jim recoiled in fright.

"Don't touch me!" he screamed, breaking the silence shirlly. Jim stood up unsteadily and propped himself against the trunk of a tree. His eyes never left Charlie. "Am I dead, too?" There was cold sweat beaded all over his face. "I don't feel dead," he stuttered, running his hands over his arms. The blood had dried on his face and hands; he wasn't bleeding anymore. That must mean something. He felt haken, bruised and sore, but not dead. Charlie was laughing at him and he gaped in amazement at the ghost.

Jim had seen a lot of terrible things in his life, had been aware of existences that most people would never experience in their limited lifetimes—but this took the cake . . . he had never thought that he'd see Charlie again! Not in this lifetime . . . not in any.

"You want *me* to tell *you* if you're *dead* or not?" Charlie laughed again.

Jim put up his hand as if to ward off evil. "No! I don't want to know!"

"What do you think?" Charlie was floating there stroking his stiff cat in long, soft strokes and it made Jim's hair literally stand on end just to watch him.

"I don't really know." He eyed him suspiciously sideways. "I don't feel dead." He mulled over the notion that he might be insane. No, that wasn't likely. He felt too normal to be insane. "You're not real!" His eyes narrowed and he glared down at Charlie. "I'm hallucinating this whole thing . . . it's a mirage."

Charlie shook his head and started to walk away.

Jim closed his eyes and prayed when he opened them again, he'd be sane again. It didn't work. "This isn't happening."

"Stubborn!" Charlie chortled. "You're a silly goose, Jimmy. Just like always!" The child had stopped at a distance and was looking back at Jim from behind a tall tree.

"Go away!" Jim moaned and slid back down to the ground at the base of the tree where he hid his head in his hands.

"I can't go away. I came here to help you, Jimmy. I wasn't very nice to you when I was *there*, so I owe you something. You and Sarah were my favorites and now she needs us. I can help." The eerie voice was serious but Jim sensed fear there, too. What could a ghost be afraid of, he pondered.

Jim looked at the phantom differently now as his mind

313

started to click. "How can you help?" he asked.

"I can help you save Sarah and her son." The ghost smiled. "I like Jeremy. He's funny."

"How can you help me save them?" Jim licked his fevered lips. He was so thirsty all of a sudden.

"I know what to do to keep them from having to die that's all." The ghost shook its head pitifully.

"How?" Jim felt the beginning of panic and then he remembered the promise he had made on the bus. He would let no more die if his death would appease the entity. He had conceded the game and forfeited his survival.

"I know how to trick the thing in the woods . . . I know how to fool it." Charlie's pale face screwed up in ugly hate that had fermented in a damp grave. "Silly Jimmy . . you know what I'm talking about, don't you?"

Yes, Jim knew. He muffled a sigh and nodded his head tiredly at Charlie.

There was a yearning glowing in Charlie's eyes that Jim had never seen in them when the child had been alive. Compassion. The apparition reached out for Jim again and this time Jim didn't recoil. The touch was solid and it took Jim by surprise, but it was cold, so cold. They smiled knowingly at each other, Jim thinking that he still couldn't believe he was standing there talking to a ghost. He kept expecting to blink and find Charlie gone.

"I'm really here." Charlie said, hurt.

"You want to see something?" he said excitedly, taking Jim by the hand and pulling him along. Jim's heart seemed to freeze at his touch.

"What?" He hadn't needed to ask because he had been looking beyond the child and he was drawn along by the shock of what he saw. "It can't be! We're at least an hour or so away from Suncrest," he shouted, yet even as he mouthed the thought he knew that what he had meant to say was that they were years away from what he was seeing now, not mere miles. There before him amidst the trees and the lengthing shadows was something right out of his

314

past—his old house as it looked twenty years ago. It was as if he had been transported back into time and he was back home . . . his real home. It was utterly unbelievable.

"Nothing's changed . . . it's as if I'd never grown up," Jim whispered to himself in total bewilderment. He heard Charlie laugh softly beside him. The old brick house was alive again with lights and noises, the familiar noises a loving happy family had made twenty years ago. In the coming dawn, shadows moved across the windows. The smell of morning bacon lingered on the air. There were people in there getting ready to start the day, going to school and to work . . . he could heard children quarreling and laughing upstairs just like it had been back then. The memories were so poignant, he could hardly stand to face them.

Jim stood there shaking, yet fascinated. This was the way it had been—once. This was where all the love had been. This was where they had been happy. He wanted to walk into that house again and never come out. Maybe he would find the peace he had been seeking for so long. Charlie seemed to read his mind. "It's *home*, Jimmy . . . you're *home*." The ghost was smiling up at Jim, but when Jim looked into those empty orbs he felt a chill in his bones. Charlie belonged in his grave. It sharply brought him back to reality. He looked at the house again. This all belonged to the past. It was over. *All of them were dead!*

He could look but not touch. He could long but not have.

"I'm in hell, is where I am," Jim whispered. Children were tumbling out of the house now, all scrubbed and dressed for school. They skipped past him so close that he marveled they couldn't see him. Why, he could just reach out and touch them. Jonathan, Leslie and a very young Sarah. They had their school books tucked under their arms and soon they were out of sight. Jim wanted to follow them so badly . . . anything, just so he wouldn't lose them again. He desperately wanted to belong again, to be a carefree, innocent child again.

"Is it so bad, Jimmy, coming home?" Charlie crooned, his voice mesmerizing in its gentleness.

"No," Jim said in a daze. Then why, he wondered, did he feel so cold? His head was numb and his thoughts were all muddled. The pungent scent of fresh roses was over powering. It remained so sweet, it made his head swim. He watched in suppressed horror as the past swirled around him. He kept thinking, *this is real. This is not a dream, it's real.*

Time sped by crazily in this dead world. Suddenly darkness arrived like a giant curtain and took away the light. He saw two children climb stealthily out of one of the forbidden upstairs windows and scoot down the edge of the roof. They shimmied down the old tree like monkeys and escaped into the fields. He could hear their giggles for a long time. It was Sarah and himself. With bated breath, he waited for the lone, frightened child to come slinking back, escaping from something evil in the woods that he had known all along was there. Jim watched in utter shame as the cowardly child sneaked back into the dark house, leaving his sister along and vulnerable out there. A scream rose on the night wind and a terrified small girl came running back, breathing heavily, and collapsed on the porch in the shadows. He heard her crying. He heard the voice that she had heard that fateful night and his blood went cold. Suddenly Jim understood everything . . . he remembered.

He could block it no longer.

Jim turned to Charlie who had been patiently waiting for just that. Their eyes met and Jim knew he was crying. It had been a long hard road and he was almost relieved that the burden wasn't his alone anymore. "So that car back there . . ." he asked softly. "That was Mother and Father, wasn't it? It was really them."

Charlie nodded his head. "Yes. But they weren't trying to hurt you, Jimmy! They weren't trying to hurt anybody, eally. They loved you a lot."

The eyes reflected just a hint of old jealousy and then it
vas gone. The eyes were empty again. "They only wanted
ou to *stop*. I had to see you, you know. We've got to help
arah and Jeremy, you see. I promised . . ." Charlie said
ravely. "I promised."

Jim was confused. "But they wrecked the bus; they
night have hurt innocent people!" He looked back
owards the still smoking bus. "They could all be dead back
here. I don't know for sure. Why did they have to do that?"

Charlie merely shrugged. "Go back, you'll see, no one's
eally hurt. It was just a trick to get you here so I could
how you this . . . so you'd remember," Charlie explained.
You have to go back anyway. You have to warn Sarah. You
now what to do, now, don't you?" Charlie said.

"I know." Jim hoped Charlie was right about no one
eing hurt on the bus. "Will I ever see them again?"

Charlie knew Jim was talking about their parents.
Charlie lowered his eyes and answered, "They're here with
ll of us. They'll be here when you come back. I don't see
hem very often, but *you* will." His voice sounded sad and
im again wondered just how much he could trust Charlie.
He had never been trustworthy in life. It was a gamble Jim
ad to take. As bad as the odds were, he didn't have much
hoice.

"Never mind them!" the phantom suddenly burst out.
I'm going to help you and Sarah—not them! We haven't
nuch time. Please!"

Charlie took Jim's hand again and led him quickly back
o the smashed bus. Everyone was reviving inside and Jim
ighed aloud with relief. Charlie had been right; everyone
vas moving around and griping up a storm.

"You were right, Charlie." But when Jim turned to thank
he ghost, there was nothing there. He was alone. Charlie
vas gone and the sun was coming up in a blaze of glory.
The night had sped by.

Charlie had done what he had been told not to do. He

had redeemed himself. The ghostly child watched from distance as Jim went back to the bus. He smiled sadly an let out a haunted sigh.

"You getting back on the bus, or not?" The bus doors flev open in front of Jim.

Startled, Jim looked up into the burly bus driver impatient face. The man was unharmed. It was a miracle Jim thought.

"Well, are you coming, or not?" the bus driver yelle down at him as he continued to gawk and not move. " you are, you better get your butt on this bus, pronto! I'r getting the hell out of here. No little dent's gonna stop m from keeping my schedule, you better believe it!"

Jim climbed back on the bus and the driver closed th door. The driver rammed the bus in reverse, and with a lou crunching sound disengaged it from the tree where it ha lodged. It was a wonder the bus could still run. As Jir stumbled back to his seat he noticed, too, that all th passengers seemed strangely unaffected by the whol incident. They had all pulled themselves together amaz ingly fast and they acted as if nothing had really happene at all. It was strange.

But Jim was so numb from what had happened to hin that he didn't pick up on much at that point. He was too tired. Everyone seemed O.K. and he was so happy to se them that way, that he refused to question the reason behind it. He fell into his seat, checking to see if his guita and suitcase were still there under the seat. They were Leaning his aching head against the window pane, h closed his eyes and tried to keep his stomach where i belonged. He felt slightly sick. *God, Charlie and tha house . . .*

He didn't notice how the rest of the trip went; or hov quiet everyone was . . . or that the bus driver never onc said another word to anyone.

He had to get home to Sarah, to warn her not to le Jeremy out of her sight, not even for a moment and not fo any reason. Jim found he couldn't keep his eyes open. He kept drifting off into a deep sleep where Charlie and all the rest of them were waiting for him. He didn't want to come back, but he knew he had to. He had to get back home to help Sarah . . .

Jim slept the rest of the trip and somehow, in a stupor, felt the driver shake him when it was time for him to get off. Someone was handing him his suitcase and his guitar and helping him get off the bus into the sunlight before he even realized it. "Hey, wait a minute!" Jim squinted into the strong light and tried to figure out where he was and what he was doing here. He was in a daze. "What about the accident?" He hollered as the bus drove out of sight. "What about the reports and things . . ." His voice trailed off, baffled. What about the police?

Jim was left standing alone at the side of the road. He wasn't far from home. He got his bearings and started off. Plodding along the road, lugging his stuff, he had to remind himself to put one foot in front of another. He was still so tired and sick, he could hardly walk. Maybe he had been hurt in that accident after all, and just didn't know it.

His mind kept going back to that bus and the accident. Something wasn't right—he knew that. But for some reason he didn't seem to care.

The whole thing had been darn peculiar. Maybe when he got to Sarah's he'd talk to Ben about it. Yes, that's what he'd do. If no one else was going to report it, he would just have to. A real upstanding citizen.

Jim kept walking. He felt strange, but that didn't matter. He was almost there. He was almost home.

CHAPTER THIRTY-THREE

Ben had left Sarah's house that night with disturbed feelings over what he had learned. Call it a sixth sense for trouble or simply a veteran cop's intuition, he didn't like the way things were shaping up. Just the fact that she had let Jeremy out of her sight so soon after that last murder left him incredulous. Not to mention her ex-husband showing up unannounced like he had, being completely out of character. It just didn't sit right. Why did he choose to show up now, of all times? Sarah had explained it all to him and he had let her believe that everything was all right. She had enough on her mind right now without all his suspicions dumped on her shoulders, too.

As soon as he was able, without arousing her interest, he made some excuse about checking up on her brother's bus schedule and got away. He hadn't lied, really, just didn't tell her everything. He got to the police station and not only checked some of the bus arrivals and any information concerning Jim, but put out an alert for Jonathan's blue Toyota.

It didn't take very long for them to find it. "Detective Raucher?" One of the men handed him a computer sheet and copies of a routine report filed just a short time ago in a neighboring area. "Is this what you were looking for?" The

320

man was a pleasant enough guy. He'd worked there for over two years and had hopes of being a detective, too, someday. He had always respected Detective Raucher for his professionalism. He was shocked, then, when the Detective's face went white and he dropped the file as if it had been a hot potato. "Can I help, sir?" The young man asked.

"Are these reports correct?" Ben almost yelled at the man.

"Yes, sir . . . as far as it's gone." The man was baffled over the Detective's abrupt change of manner. "But if you want, I can run another check. Pull in the men who were on duty and question them on the report." He was only trying to help, not realizing that there wasn't anything he could do. Ben had half-expected what he had found in the report, but he was still shocked.

"No. There's nothing else . . ." Ben hesitated and then slapping the papers down violently on the desk, his face lit up. "Yes . . . you can do something else for me. Get those men on the phone for me and I'll take it from there." Ben's mind was working overtime. He lightly drummed his fingers on the desk the whole time he was on the phone with officer Hartford and then officer Snell. When he had gleaned all the pertinent facts, as well as those often overlooked, he went in search of the Captain.

Captain Sinclair's eyebrows shot up when he saw Ben coming so purposefully towards his office. "What's wrong, Ben? I'd know that look anywhere." He smiled grimly and offered him a seat. Ben was too nervous to accept.

"I want a search party rounded up immediately for the whole damn area," Ben intoned grimly right off the bat. "I just read the report on that abandoned car found this evening over in Shattley Terrace . . . I know who it belongs to. They might be on foot or they might be in danger and I want men out there combing that damn woods before . . ."

"Hold on there a second, Raucher." The Captain held up his hand and stood up. Now he was really worried. Ben

Raucher usually never went off half-cocked like this unless something big was in the works. "What is this all about?"

Ben finally allowed himself to calm down a little and he slumped into the chair and faced his Captain. "I mean here we are faced with a series of particularly brutal murders and along comes Sarah's ex-husband who has just decided out of the blue to take Jeremy for a visit. He hadn't seen or even contacted the boy for months and suddenly he wants to play parent. But . . ." Ben's eyes clouded up and his fists clenched. "He picked up the boy six hours ago and never got back home. Sarah was worried so I ran some checks: that's his blue Toyota we found empty five hours ago, still running with the lights on, the horn stuck and not a sign of him or the boy. Something's wrong and I have this horrible hunch that if we don't find them pretty damn soon, there might be nothing left to find . . . alive, that is. The car was found only miles away from the last murder scene." The last words fell like a bomb. Both men knew the odds were already stacked against them. They stared across the desk at each other.

"The experts think this thing may be an animal of some kind. The coroner swears it's a wild bear because of the teeth and claw marks on both victims." Captain Sinclair was talking more to himself than to Ben. He didn't want to face another one of those tiny mutilated bodies, not so soon—not ever again. He had a soft heart for kids, something few of the other officers were aware of. But Ben knew his weakness and he felt sorry for the man . . . but there was a job to do and they had to do it. They had to prevent the next murder.

"Sarah says it isn't an animal." Ben said softly.

The Captain was picking up his cap and putting out his cigar in the ashtray. "What do you think it is?" he asked.

"I don't know," Ben replied truthfully and he wasn't lying. He didn't know what it was, only that it had to be stopped. "But we have to hurry. They've been out there in the woods in the dark for hours . . ." Worry was etched over

322

his face and the Captain nodded. He lifted up the phone and sent out his orders, barking commands as they went out the door. The station came alive.

"Does he have a gun?"

"The boy's father?" Ben still couldn't stand to say the guy's name. Because of Sarah and the way he felt about her he couldn't help but dislike the man for what he'd done to them. "I suppose so, he's a police officer."

"Then he can protect himself if he has to," he said.

Ben stared at him and shook his head. Both of them had seen the victims in the woods and knew how ineffective a mere gun might turn out to be against it whatever it was. "I don't think a gun will help much."

"A gun always helps. What does Miss Towers say about all this?" the older man asked as they stopped in front of Ben's desk so he could put his gun on. He had rarely had to use it since he had joined the force. He usually never had cause to carry one. Now, he had more than enough reason. He took it out of the drawer.

"Nothing. She doesn't know Jeremy and his father are missing yet." He glanced up as someone moved by the desk. Some of the other officers were aware of the emergency by instinct and were milling around waiting for some kind of orders. Ben saw determination spread over the Captain's face as he talked briefly to the men and told them what he wanted done. It was something he'd often seen on the older man's countenance and it had an effect on all of them. There was silence, none of the usual joking that normally went on.

"I thought . . ." Captain Sinclair had finished and was talking to Ben. The men were scattering to do what they had to do. "We'd call her in to help."

He meant Sarah.

"Under the circumstances, we don't have a choice," Ben remarked. "She has the right to know that her son is missing." It would destroy her to learn about Jeremy. She wouldn't be much good to them after that.

323

"I'm going to call her right now," Ben sighed and started to pick up the phone when someone handed him a piece of paper. Captain Sinclair watched him read it calmly and set it down on the desk. Ben continued to stare at the paper until the Captain couldn't stand it any longer and snatched it up himself. Neither man spoke. Ben cursed under his breath and finally after what seemed like a long time, reached out and dialed the phone.

"Sarah?"

"Oh, thank God! Ben! What's wrong?" By the trembling of her voice Ben suspected the worse. "No . . . don't say it! Something's happened to my son." It was a statement and not a question. She knew. Somehow, she knew. Ben agonized for her . . . it must be a terrible thing to know things that you weren't supposed to know.

"How do you know that?" he asked it before he could stop himself. He had never fully accepted her psychic gifts. He'd been a skeptic all his life and he was never one to change overnight.

"You wouldn't believe me if I told you." Her voice dragged and he thought she sounded like someone on the verge of a breakdown. He'd seen stronger women break over less. "Let's just say something that began a long time ago has finally come true." Sarah didn't have time to explain. "Never mind. What's happened?"

"We're not sure . . . only that your ex-husband's car was found abandoned and empty over five hours ago . . ."

"In the woods." She said it for him. She was frantic now. How could she tell him that her Grandmother had *told* her just before he called that Jeremy was alone and lost in the woods? *That he was going to die* unless she could get to him. Sarah had been devastated by the vision and had almost gone into hysterics. It was only the sure knowledge that her son would die if she didn't find him—and soon—that kept her from giving in to that weakness. Then Ben had called and she had known exactly what he would say.

"And I have something to tell you, too," Sarah continued and Ben could hear the strain in her tone. "Jonathan is dead."

Ben swallowed. He could think of absolutely nothing to say. "Sarah . . . I'll be right over." The world had collapsed all in one afternoon and Ben felt like tearing his hair out. There was more, but he didn't have the courage or the heart to tell her about it. It could wait until they found her son. Sarah might not make it if he told her what he had just found out. It could wait. Nothing could change what had already happened but a small boy still had a chance to live if they worked swiftly. She didn't reply, and he hung up the phone.

Then he told the Captain what Sarah had said.

"We don't have much time, then. We'll pick her up on the way in the squadcar, Raucher. Come on." Captain Sinclair led the way outside. Some of the other officers had already been dispatched to the area where the car had been found. Others called in and then followed their car as they drove away into the dark.

Ben was uncomfortably aware that they didn't have a snowball's chance in hell of finding the boy unless a miracle occured. What would that do to Sarah? He didn't want to think about it. The whole ride to Sarah's house Ben and the Captain talked strategy. There was little they could do but send out search parties and pray.

Sarah was waiting for them in front of her house, shivering though the night was warm. Ben took her into his arms and was surprised when she tore away from him. "We have to hurry!" She whispered and when he caught a look at her face he saw it was red from crying. Yet her eyes were cold and full of anger. He helped her get into the car next to Captain Sinclair and they drove where she told them.

Ben's heart was so heavy with what he was keeping from her, that he could barely stand to look directly at her. He took her hand and listened as she talked. She knew where they were going and what she was doing.

Captain Sinclair only asked a few questions and drove the rest of the time listening to Sarah.

How long would it take til the newspapers got a hold of this tidbit? Ben fretted, holding Sarah's cold hand tightly. Those newspaper people were like vultures. They could smell fresh carrion before it hit the ground.

"Here. Here!" Sarah cried suddenly. "Stop here!" Captain Sinclair stopped the car and Sarah jumped out and started running.

"Sarah! Wait!" Ben yelled after her in vain as she disappeared into the night, then followed her. Help was on its way and it was too dangerous for them to go out there alone before it arrived. But he knew nothing would stop Sarah. She was a mother looking for her child.

He grabbed her by the arm and shook her. He held her as she cried in the car's headlights. The Captain left them alone.

When they came back to the car, all her tears were shed. They could hear sirens coming closer and Sarah's eyes were wild. What was taking them so long? "I have to look for them now," she kept repeating, turning frightened eyes toward the silent woods.

They didn't have much time.

"What was the boy wearing when they left?" Captain Sinclair asked her as they all walked together to where Jonathan's blue Toyota sat empty and forlorn.

Sarah stared at him. "Bluejeans . . . yellow shirt . . . does it matter?" My God, she thought, did it matter at all? She peered into the empty car. No blood anywhere; no Jeremy, no Jonathan. "I want to start looking now!" she exploded. "Why are we waiting?"

"For help to arrive. Listen, Sarah, we can't go out into those woods alone with—something out there. We need back-up help. What good are we to Jeremy if we're dead?"

"I can't just stand around here looking at that car! I have to do something!" Her eyes traveled through the dark woods and she remembered that other more recent night in

326

these woods when Jenny had been found. She choked on the thought. *Jeremy!* "I have to look for him! Let me go!"

"Where?" Ben threw up his hands. He wished those damn others would get there before Sarah went completely mad.

Sarah put her hands to her face. "We must look someplace ... *deep*. Someplace where there is *dirt ... water. Oh, my God!*" She wept, trying hard to control her emotions. She had to stay calm or she couldn't help her son.

"Anything else?" Ben gently prodded. Anything to keep her mind occupied until help arrived. He could hear the sirens very clear and loud now. They were close. The night noises were eerie all around them. The trees were shaking around them in the wind and there was no moon. It was pitch black. Dead souls seemed to moan as dry leaves crunched under their feet. Sarah stood there silhouetted in the night and Ben mulled over the thought that he had just been through all this before. Jenny's murder was still fresh in all three minds as they solemnly waited on the edge of the woods.

His cohorts were urgently trying to pin that murder on the girl's worthless parents, but so far, there was no real proof that could securely link them to it. There was no proof or concrete clues to link the murder to anyone or anything else, either. Again, they were stumped and they didn't like it.

Captain Sinclair studied Sarah's worried face next to him. "Do you *see* anything?" His voice was barely audible over the noisy katydids and the rustling of the leaves above them.

"No. *I see nothing.*" A plea in the night for help. The old curse was ever present, she thought helplessly. When she had to save someone she loved ... there was nothing! Impulsively she grabbed the ring and viciously tearing it from her hand, threw it into the darkness. No more. No more!

She relived moment by moment the conversation she had had with her Grandmother before Ben and the Captain had picked her up. She had been so frightened for Jeremy and Jonathan she had thought her heart would burst with it. She'd cried out to the house to help her. . . anyone. *Help me!* And her Grandmother had spoken to her in her thoughts.

Jeremy is still alive, Sarah-child . . . take heart. Jeremy is still alive but he lies in his grave, waiting . . . In the woods, alone. Jonathan is dead, so do not worry for him. Find your son. It is all I can do . . . for I must go now. My job is done. I have protected you as best I knew how and now you must protect yourself. Go to the woods . . . he will be there to help you.

Sarah had cried out when she had heard that Jonathan was dead but she hadn't shed a tear because she had realized that Jeremy, too, could die. She wasn't going to let that happen! "Why can't *you* help me? When I need you most, you leave me alone. Why won't you help me save Jeremy? *Please!*" Sarah had closed her eyes in agony when the house remained silent.

It couldn't have her son!

"Who will be there to help me?" She suddenly remembered her Grandmother's last words. "*Who?*"

There had been no answer and she finally gave up. Then Ben had called and the rest of the puzzle fell into place. Now she knew who had been protecting them all this time . . . her Grandmother. But what would happen now that she was gone?

When Ben had called she had thought that was who her Grandmother had meant when she had told her someone would help her. It had to be Ben!

Now Sarah waited, shivering as she gazed over the woods, knowing her son was out there waiting for her to come and save him, to protect him as she had always done all his life. The knowledge that she had sent him to this end herself by letting him leave in the first place was almost more than she could bear. Ben saw her anguish and put his arms firmly around her.

"They'll be here very soon. Have patience," he told her in a whisper. But he wasn't sure anyone could help now. Sarah had said Jonathan was already dead.

He handed her to Captain Sinclair so she couldn't follow him and walked into the woods a short way, past the empty car. The brush, he noticed was all trampled in a large area behind it. He used his flashlight and traced the flattened path deeper into the woods.

The light flew across the body first and Ben, as seasoned as he was, had to keep himself from crying out when he saw it. It was a man's body, mutilated and bloody, or what was left of it. But it wasn't the grisly sight that had brought bile into his throat; no, it was the look on the dead man's pitiful face . . . a look of such complete horror and disbelief that it would be branded on Ben's memory forever.

Sarah had come up behind him, silently. It wasn't until he heard the sobs that he turned around and saw her. Then it was too late for him to hide what lay at his feet.

She had found Jonathan, too.

CHAPTER THIRTY-FOUR

Sure it was late, Jim mused, as he knocked on Sarah's door for the third time, but shouldn't someone be home? "Is anyone here?" he shouted at the locked door. He fumbled in his pockets, searching for the key that Sarah had given him the last time he was home. When he found it, he poked around until it fit into the hole and he pushed the door open. He walked in and set his suitcase and guitar down by the couch. It felt so good to come home again. He'd never have believed it would affect him this way.

"Sarah? Jeremy?" he called out, hoping they were just busy upstairs or somewhere. No answer. Nothing but heavy silence greeted him. He sat down in the chair for a second. He was so weary. That walk had been the final straw. Why did he feel so rotten?

After he rested for a few minutes and still no one showed up he went upstairs seeking them. He found only an empty house. No Sarah and no Jeremy. He checked Sarah's bulletin board for a message or something. She knew he was coming. Why would she just go off like this without leaving some kind of note? It wasn't like his sister at all.

He began to think about everything that had happened and he grew increasingly worried as he stood there in the kitchen watching the darkness outside. The coffee pot was still plugged in and he poured himself a hot cup of coffee and sat down to drink it. It was tasteless to him, and he couldn't finish it. He hadn't eaten in almost three days but he wasn't in the least bit hungry. He didn't dwell on it because he was worried about Sarah.

Where were they?

In the front room there were newspapers and he glanced at them lying on the floor. He found the brick and the broken window. Something evil seemed to permeate everything around him and as he stared at the brick in his hand he *knew* where they were. Something deep down inside of him knew just as if they had left a written note addressed to him. The air in the room seemed to vibrate and it was as if he were already out in the woods awaiting his punishment. He had accepted what was to be so why was he hesitating? It was time.

He would forfeit his life in exchange for theirs. A gnawing doubt crept upon him and he went white. What if what he did made no difference any longer? What if he had guessed wrong and that monster out there decided not to play the game fairly this time? What if they *all* had to die . . .

Were Sarah and Jeremy already dead, or out there trapped and suffering? The thought stunned Jim momentarily and then anger flooded in. He threw the brick out the open door and ran outside and started running for the place where his old home used to stand. He hadn't been there in so many years he was afraid he had forgotten the way. But even in the dark his feet seemed to know where to go. Some things you never forget.

For the first time in many lives, Jim wasn't a coward. For the first time in *his* life, he was running towards trouble and not away from it. Sarah and Jeremy mattered! Nothing else in the whole damn world mattered but them!

If Sarah and the boy died, he'd have no reason for living anyway. A grim smile spread across his lined face as he ran down the old roads to where he had once lived. He even recalled a few short cuts through yards and a field. And he ran faster, his heart became a lump of stone in his breast at the terrible suspicions that were fighting in his mind. He wasn't going to be left alone. Until that moment he had never seen how much Sarah's presence had meant to him. He had taken all the other deaths as they had come. But if Sarah died *again,* so did he.

As he jumped a spiked fence and scurried around some houses that shone with lights, he tried to keep from thinking. Yet the memories burst into his thoughts anyway. He saw his family again as they had been. He heard Charlie crying in the field when he had been a child; Leslie talking about what she dreamed of being when she grew up; and he saw his mother's bright eyes and soft smile again. His father's laughter haunted him as he ran, panting harder as he fought the tears of bitter truth. So many had died because of him and the worst crime was that he had let poor Sarah carry the guilt all these years without uttering a word.

Now they might both be—he gulped and smothered a cry at the terrible images that slunk across his mind. He scurried up a steep hill on his hands and knees, grabbing at trees along the way. The houses were behind him and now he was going into the woods. He easily jumped the same gullies that had been bottomless to him when he had been a small child. There was no light anywhere and he had to almost feel his way through the closing trees, but he never slowed down.

He fancied he heard Jeremy crying off in the distance . . . crying in fear and pain and it drove Jim mad. He fell into a creek and clawed his way out of the fetid water to climb up the slippery muddy bank and keep going. *Don't stop. Don't stop,* his heart kept telling him. Jeremy's whimpering grew louder and Jim's heart ached at the sound.

A branch flew out of nowhere and cut him across the face. There was no pain and when he wiped his face with the back of his hand there was no blood. He kept on running. When he fell, he pulled himself up again as the forest watched and laughed silently. He kept running towards the sounds . . .

And the woods watched . . .

"Mom . . . Mom . . ." Jeremy kept saying the words over and over in the dark until they dissolved into a whimper that became almost too soft to hear. He lay crumpled and broken in the cold dirty water at the bottom of a deep hole or a well. He wasn't sure. He only knew that he hurt. He had stopped crying hours ago but he still felt the puffiness and fever that the tears had caused. He was so afraid that if he made too much noise that *thing* would hear him and come for him. He wasn't sure if it was still out there looking for him or even if it had followed him after it had . . .

He covered his face with his hands to stifle the sobs and his whole body shook, sending ripples through the water. Again he tried to sit up, to crawl up out of the water, but his fingers were numb from clinging to the stony sides and he had already pulled out every weed or protruding rock that he could have hung on to. There was nothing but slime and his fingers slid down the sides and his body fell back into the mud and water.

Exhausted, he seemed to fade in and out of consciousness not aware sometimes of where he was or what he had seen in the last hours. He welcomed those blank moments. Anything just so he wouldn't have to remember what that *thing had done to his father*. He gasped, terrified at the loud noise he had made. His eyes flew up to the darker circle of an opening above him. He could see pin pricks of stars and he inhaled the fresh night air. If he breathed too deeply he could smell the stale water and the slime so close by and he could still smell the blood—his father's blood, splattered all over his body.

No! He must stay still and quiet. He must! Quivering with fright, he willed himself not to continue crying like a scared baby. If he cried, that monster would tear him to

333

pieces just like it had done to his father! No, he mustn't let that happen. He knew in his heart that if he only could hold out long enough—stay calm and patient—Ben or his mother would come and save him.

He could still hear his father's screams. Jeremy couldn't help himself and he began to cry again, silently, as he remembered how he had tried to help his father. But it hadn't worked. He was too *little* and that *thing* was too big and strong . . . *and it had huge teeth and sharp claws.* He had been tossed aside like a rag when his father had started firing his gun. And he had finally run away to hide from the *thing* when his father's screams and yells had died away and Jeremy had known that his father was dead. Sobbing, he had obeyed his father's last words to run and hide. He'd run faster than he'd ever run before and all the while he had sensed the *thing coming behind him* after it had finished with his father. Jeremy had heard its laughter and felt it breathing down his neck in the night. He had run and fallen into this hole.

And now, he whimpered in pain and frustration at the bottom of it, praying that he was hidden well enough so that that monster couldn't find and kill him, too. If it found him, he didn't have a chance. His father had had a gun and the bullets hadn't even slowed the thing down.

Ben would find him! Someone, his mother, or Jim, would come and save him before that thing found him. *They had to.*

Jeremy tried to avoid thinking about his father's death, but no matter how hard he tried, the sorrow wouldn't release him. He wanted to escape this horrible hole and be in his mother's arms. What would happen if no one found him down here? He couldn't shout or cry because he didn't want to attract the thing that killed his father. Yet, if he didn't make some kind of noise, how would they know where he was?

Terrified, he looked around his tiny prison and began to think about how he could die there. How long would it take

334

if no one found him? Moaning very low into his arms, he tried to move his left leg again. The pain almost made him scream. It hurt so bad! Maybe it was sprained or broken or something. His shoulder hurt, too, but not half as bad as his leg.

Time dragged by and he leaned back against the bumpy sides of the hole and listened to the forest. If he could hold on until daylight, maybe then that *thing* might be gone. Then he could yell for help and someone would hear him. If there was anyone out there even looking for him . . .

He wondered if they even knew he was missing yet. How could they? He was supposed to be with his father . . . *safe with his father, now dead.* He buried his scraped and dirty face in his arms and whimpered again. He was never going to get out. He was going to die, all alone, and it would be days before they found his body. By then, the *thing* would have found and eaten him. Overwhelmed, he finally passed out from shock and exhaustion.

When he awoke, it was to the sound of someone murmuring his name from up above. His heart jumped with joy until he saw who it was. *Charlie!* He instantly froze. Was that *thing* with Charlie! Had Charlie found him only to alert *it* to where he was hiding?

"Jeremy, are you down there?" The ghostly wail found him cringing down in the bottom of the hole.

If he was very quiet, the ghost might go away and leave him alone, Jeremy thought frantically. He didn't reply and instead, tried to curl up into a tighter ball to hide. *Go away, Charlie! Don't let him see me!*

"Jeremy! I know you're down there. I can *see* you!" Charlie chuckled up above him, peering into the dark pit. "Come on, answer me . . . I won't give you away, I promise! I've come to help you. Don't you want to get out of there before he finds you?" The ghost laughed and Jeremy shivered because he knew who he was. "I can help you!" There was a pause and then the ghost said coaxingly, "I helped your Uncle Jim."

Jeremy couldn't stop himself from saying something back now. *Uncle Jim!* What did Charlie mean about helping Uncle Jim? "I'm here," he croaked, and stared hard up at the dead boy. "How did you help Uncle Jim?" he demanded.

"I told him you needed him. Right away. He's looking for you now," the ghost bragged.

Jeremy smiled in the dark. He was going to be saved! "You mean you did that for me?" He had to admit he was flabbergasted. Why would Charlie help him?

"Why not? I told you once that I liked you. I don't want nothing bad happening to you . . . you're her son." The voice droned on as smooth as silk and Jeremy felt uneasy because the ghost was being too nice. He smelled a rat somewhere. He couldn't trust Charlie for some reason but neither could he put his finger on why he mistrusted him, he just did.

"Thank you, Charlie," Jeremy said humbly. "When is he coming to get me out of here?" He asked, licking his lips nervously. He had this idea that he didn't have much time either way. He knew he was grasping at straws by depending on Charlie; but there didn't seem to be anyone else around to depend on. "Where's Uncle Jim?" Jeremy recalled vaguely that Uncle Jim had had an accident and had been coming home.

"He's coming now. I just saw him. He'll be here any minute." Then the giggles started. "If I don't go get him to show him where you are, he might not find you. I'll lead him here."

Alarm bells went off in Jeremy's head. Was this one of Charlie's mean tricks? Jeremy's heart sank as deep as the hole he was in. He wanted to cry, plead with Charlie to help him, but something inside him—pride perhaps—warned him that it wouldn't do any good. If Charlie was playing a game with him, he had better learn how to play along real fast or he might just die and rot away like an old sponge. He felt like one already, all soaked and crusted with dirt down in a hole full of water. He was deathly afraid of spiders, bugs and snakes. He'd already killed lots of big hairy spiders that he found crawling along the slimy walls—he'd closed his eyes and squashed their soft fuzzy bodies under his flattened palms with a grunt of disgust. Anything, just so they wouldn't crawl all over him or bite him. Remembering, he felt sick.

"You're gonna bring him here, aren't you?" Jeremy breathed in and held it, fearful he would start crying any second. Charlie would laugh at him then, he knew it.

"Maybe."

"Charlie! Please? You can't leave me down here!"

Charlie was quiet for a long time and Jeremy thought for a terrible few minutes that he had just left him there. He tried to pull himself up a little and his eyes searched the darkness above sharply.

"Hush!" A hiss from above. "Don't move! I'll come back." There was a whoosh of cold air around him and Jeremy sensed that the ghost was no longer there. His heart was racing again. Had *it* come back? What was happening?

Maybe Charlie really *had* gone to fetch Uncle Jim. *Oh, please,* Jeremy prayed as he waited for something to happen. *Please, Charlie, come back and bring Uncle Jim.*

The minutes ticked by and Jeremy was just about to give up. He didn't care anymore . . . he was going to die anyway. He couldn't trust Charlie. What a food he had been to even think of it! Charlie belonged to that *thing* in the woods and was his enemy, not his friend. At this very moment Charlie was probably bringing that evil thing with the teeth and burning eyes to get him!

Where had Charlie been when that door had been busted? And where had Charlie been when Jenny had had to die . . . and his father? Those thoughts plagued Jeremy until he thought he would simply die from fear of not knowing.

"Jeremy?" The voice was back and so was Charlie. "You still down there?"

"Of course I am! Where else would I go? I'm *trapped* down here," Jeremy said, a little miffed at the ghost's denseness. "Are you going to help me or not? I don't feel so good."

Charlie wasn't listening to him. "I had to leave like that because it's very close now. I was afraid it would see me here talking to you. I'd be punished for sure." The voice was petrified. Charlie's fear was catching and Jeremy found himself biting his lips so he wouldn't cry out in desperation.

"*It's* here?" Jeremy cried.

"*No!* Not now. But it was close. Too close. I'm not supposed to be helping any of you and if it finds out it'll hurt me bad. But I'm going to help you get out anyway. *I promised!*" he went on, and the way he said it gave Jeremy heart.

But how could you hurt a dead person? Jeremy's head was spinning.

It was plain to see that Charlie was very afraid of it, too. That knowledge only increased Jeremy's terror.

"What is that *thing?*" Jeremy gasped.

"It's evil and it's bad and it's killed everybody I've ever loved," Charlie said softly. "And you can't hurt it or run away from it. But you can try. I hate it! I'm going to get back at it, too, by helping you to get away. I'll fix him." The ghost chuckled softly to himself this time, still clearly afraid. "It wants you and her badly. . . and I'm going to help you fool it. You'll see!"

"It killed my father. . ." Jeremy sniffled. He hated it too. "Why does it want to hurt all of us? What have we ever done to it?"

"It was something Jim did to it a long, long time ago, I think, and it still hates him . . . it's vowed eternal vengeance on Jim and everyone he cares about. It's become a game."

"Why won't it leave us alone?" Jeremy exclaimed.

"When it hates—it hates forever. I have to go now . . ."

"Wait! What about me?" Jeremy was frightened. Was Charlie going to leave him anyway?

"No, I have to go . . . to bring Jim here. I have to hurry. We don't have much time!" Charlie hissed and then was gone again.

Down in the wet hole, hopeless, Jeremy began to sob again; and this time he didn't care who or what heard him. He wasn't going to get out of this alive, he knew it. Charlie wouldn't come back and Jim wouldn't find him. He'd die here in this hole!

A long time passed and Jeremy had about given up. Then he heard someone up above him calling his name. It was Uncle Jim!

"Jeremy! Are you all right? Are you down there?" Jim yelled, clutching the sides of the old well, searching the darkness below him. He'd been so surprised when Charlie had led him here to where he said Jeremy was hurt and trapped down in the old well. Jim had thrashed through the woods like a madman following the ghost to get to Jeremy, so afraid he'd be too late and find the boy dead.

For some reason, he knew there wasn't much time but he didn't know why he felt that. He could sense the evil in the forest all around them, glowering and gloating and waiting . . . perhaps it was watching them at this very moment. He had been just as leary and apprehensive of Charlie the second time as he had been the first, except that he wasn't really afraid of him anymore.

"Uncle Jim! Yes, I'm down here. I'm O.K.—I think." He wasn't going to be a crybaby, not now. He could tell Uncle Jim he was hurt later, once he got out of this mess. "I'm so glad you're here! You found me!" Jeremy shouted back up the well, so happy, he cried. Nothing could hurt him as long as his Uncle Jim was here to protect him. He was safe.

"Thank God! How did you get in there?" Jim helplessly looked around for something to get Jeremy out of the hole with. He could see nothing he could use. He needed rope.

"I . . . was with my father. He was taking me home with him for a visit. Mom thought I would be safer away from here. Oh, Jim it killed my father!" Jeremy's voice gave out and Jim couldn't believe what he had just said.

"It killed your father?" Jonathan dead?

"Yes. I ran away from it and fell down this hole." The boy's voice trembled and he sighed in pain. "I was so afraid it would get me like it did him. *I couldn't help him*." It was a hopeless whisper of guilt.

Jim squeezed his eyes shut in agony. How many more would have to suffer and die before the score was even? He had never liked Jonathan, it was true, but then that was no reason to wish the man harm; he had been Jeremy's father. God! What the child had gone through. "Jeremy," Jim spoke tenderly, "don't think about that now. Let's just get you out of there. Hold on a second, I have to find something to pull you out with."

Jeremy, relieved to put everything into his Uncle's capable hands, seemed to deflate, collapsing into a cold lump huddled in a black corner. Below ground as he was, Jeremy couldn't see the fog starting to roll in high above the ground . . . but Jim did. He sensed it before he saw it. Billows of grey and black wispy smoke began to seep into the area around him and the well.

Jim walked around the top of the hole, urgently pushing aside leaves and branches. There must be a rope somewhere to go with the bucket he'd already discovered. The fog was creeping in thicker every moment and Jim knew time was almost up. He had to get Jeremy out of there *now!*

He finally settled for stripping a long branch off a nearby tree.

He dragged it over to the mouth of the well and called down to his nephew, "I'm going to drop this tree limb down there, Jeremy . . . let me know if it's long enough to reach the bottom, all right?" he yelled down hoarsely. The strain of the last few days and what had happened to him had all taken their toll; every muscle ached and cried in his body. It was a wonder he was still on his feet. "So watch out—here it comes!"

Jeremy couldn't tell him that he couldn't move; that he was hurt. His pride wouldn't let him complain. When the limb came crashing down just above him, dangling just inches above his head, he couldn't even lift himself up to grab it. His legs refused to hold his weight, no matter how badly he wanted to he just couldn't get up.

"Uncle Jim, it's *not long enough!* I can't *reach* it!" His voice was close to breaking. He was so weak . . . and he couldn't feel his legs anymore. They were probably all wrinkled up like a prune from being in the water so long. "Jim?" His words were tiny and Jim wasn't sure he had heard them right at first. "I can't move."

Jim cursed his stupidity to himself. Jeremy had hurt himself in the fall. After all it had to be a good twelve foot drop down there. "You're hurt?" He viciously yanked the limb up and out of the well's opening and peered over the edge into the black pit. Jeremy's voice floated softly up to him.

"Yes . . ."

"Why didn't you tell me!" Jim shook his head in aggravation. "What hurts?"

"My legs. I can't move them," Jeremy whimpered.

"Damn!" Jim fully realized what that meant. He'd have to find some way to climb down into the well to get him out. He shifted his gaze to the towering trees that all but concealed by the fog now. *It* was very close. If he went down the well he'd be at *it's* mercy.

It could trap both of them down there.

He grimly pursed his cold lips and went to find another branch. He didn't have time to go on a wild goose chase for anything as convenient as a rope. A branch, longer this time than the last one, would have to do. It was either that or both of them were as good as dead. That alternative didn't seem to bother Jim in the least. For the first time in his life he put someone else above himself. He could die, it didn't matter one way or another. But he was determined to see Jeremy free and safe, if it was the last thing he ever did see!

"Don't cry, son. It's all right. I'm coming to get you." Jim didn't know why he happened to glance up right at that moment—maybe a whisper behind him—but he did. Charlie stood silently beside him, watching him with dead eyes. He had brought him here to Jeremy and then just disappeared. Jim wasn't sorry he had, either. Charlie gave him the creeps. Now he was back.

The ghost smiled at him and held out his hands. There was a longing in his eyes that even the grave couldn't hide. Remorse. In his hands he held a tangled, frayed rope.

Astonished, Jim reached out for it and Charlie faded away into the darkness like he had never been there at all.

Thanks, Charlie. . . .

You're welcome, Jimmy . . . the words echoed hauntingly on the empty air. Charlie had kept his promise.

Jim turned back to the hole and tying the rope onto a nearby tree trunk he lowered himself swiftly into the hole. He splashed down next to Jeremy in the dark and took him into his arms. "Oh, Jeremy, thank God you're all right!" There was tears in his eyes that no one else could see.

"Uncle Jim . . . you're so cold!" Jeremy said, as he hugged him back.

The child must really be frozen, Jim worried to himself. "Now let's get the hell out of this place," Jim said, attempting an optimistic laugh. It came out very hollow.

"You got a deal!" Jeremy stuttered, shaking. Jim thought he was in shock. He couldn't blame the kid. No telling how long he had been down here in this filthy hole. Any length of time would have been too long, Jim thought.

"Good. Wrap your arms around me tight—that's it—and hold on. We're going up." Jim grabbed the boy, careful of his hurt legs, and started back up the rope. It was dark, and the walls were so slimy his boots kept sliding away from them. He ground his teeth in silent anger. With Jeremy's added weight and the condition he was already in, it was a nearly impossible climb.

He kept getting half way up and then his arms would give out and down they'd slip again. But he didn't give up. He couldn't . . . *something was coming through the forest. Something was stalking them . . . coming for them.*

Frantically, Jim forced himself not to give up, to try harder . . . pull harder! He gritted his teeth and bit back the agony of his screaming muscles and kept digging his boots in.

He stoically kept placing one hand over another on the rope, wheezing with exertion and fear. He had to get them out of here, before it was too late. Up above him the wind was starting to howl and taunt at their efforts to escape the hungry well. Jeremy clung to him like a leech. He was so still he thought the boy had fainted.

Jim's feet slipped out from under him one more time and he felt the water at the bottom of well lapping at his boots. Cursing and sweating, he panted at the bottom while he regained his strength to try again.

This time they made it.

He hung onto the rim of the well with weak fingers, unable to hold out a moment longer and then suddenly pulled both Jeremy and himself up into the night, with one final heave. He laid Jeremy down on the soft grass and stretched out next to him. He allowed himself to rest only for a few precious seconds and then righted himself to wobbly feet. "We have to get away from here, Jeremy. We can't stop now."

The woods were alive with tortured cries and a living, breathing evil swirled all around them. Jim faced the source and smiled. Strange, he was no longer afraid . . . only for Jeremy, not for himself. He wondered what it meant. He had a sensation of being in limbo, as if he were in a trance. He bent down and scooped Jeremy up in his arms.

All his strength had miraculously returned. The boy was groaning.

"Uncle Jim? . . . It's coming . . . it's coming to get us just

343

like it did Dad. Don't let it get me!" Jeremy begged clinging tighter and muffling his fear in Jim's shoulder "Don't let it get me!"

"I won't, Jeremy. Trust me. It's not going to get you, I promise." Jim eyes glowed with a fevered intensity as he turned to face his age-old nemesis. There was a smile on his lips.

CHAPTER THIRTY-FIVE

You disobeyed me!

The thing screamed at the tiny, cowering shadow as it rushed down on it. It was so angry, even blood wouldn't assuage his fury. It knew no blood could be spilled from the poor being that skimmed the darkened woods before him. The frightened shade was trying to escape a fate worse than death. He had already met that. Charlie had been dead a long time . . . but he could still be punished; it had a way of exacting its ounce of blood regardless. It had its ways. It could let the wretched creature relive his own death or it could seal the being into a pocket of time beneath one of the trees in the forest where the poor thing could whimper to eternity. It would serve him right!

Charlie squealed and dodged the huge black hulk one more time.

"You helped them!" it roared, in its wind-tunnel voice. "You warned them when you knew it would help them slip through again . . . you betrayed me! And you shall pay for it! I shall lock you up in a tiny hole away from the world—forever! I shall send you to your cold grave and there you shall remain."

Wailing, Charlie fled to the farthest end of the woods and tried to hide among the grass that fringed the creek. It found him and growled down at him. Charlie then tried to merge with the sky and the wind. He was found. He flowed with the dirty water of the creek, his misty face pressed to the surface of the water as it lashed down the riverbed. And when that didn't work, he tried to melt into nothingness and became a thin wisp of blue smoke ... but each time It found Charlie and laughed its hideous laugh.

"I didn't betray you! I wouldn't betray you!" Charlie whined and screamed and tried to lie his way out but it didn't work.

"Don't lie ... I saw you. I see everything! You helped them!"

Charlie thought of the dank grave and the eternal loneliness. Charlie couldn't stand to be alone! "Don't punish me!" he begged, as the evil surrounded him and his screams rose to the moonless sky. "I'll do anything you want — just don't lock me away again! Please ..."

Then his cries were gone, lost like the wisp of smoke he pretended to be. The woods were left in peace again. But there was a chill in the air that helped to tempt the leaves to the ground where only a moment before, they had clung green and fresh to forest boughs. Now the leaves were bright with the color of fresh blood.

CHAPTER THIRTY-SIX

"Jeremy!" I cried out to Ben. "I hear Jeremy! He's calling." The sounds were coming from somewhere in the woods. I was frantic, wringing my hands in agony as I listened to the cries of my child. "I can't wait for help any longer, Ben! I have to go help him! Please!" I became hysterical as I clawed at Ben when he tried to hold me back. The woods were whispering beyond the squadcar's headlights. Ben had been cradling me in his arms, hiding me from Jonathan's gruesome body, discarded in the wet grass at our feet. Captain Sinclair was talking softly into his car radio, asking for help.

Why wasn't any of the backup here yet?

Ben heard it too. "We don't know what's out there," he warned me, gripping me tighter.

"*Jeremy's* out there!" I screamed and tore myself away from him as another wail hit the night air.

"Sarah! Wait . . ."

I heard him tramping along behind me through the woods. "Jeremy!" I shouted as I ran, cupping my hands around my mouth to send it further ahead of me. My son was out there . . . in danger! My son! I ran crashing through the tall trees, sobbing. My blood had turned to ice in my veins. "I'm coming, son . . . I'm coming!" I gasped as I pushed myself away from a tree with my hands. Faster . . . I must run faster, my mind screamed.

This had happened before. I was aware of that as I ran to save my son's life. This had all happened many times before! It was so dark that I was running blind. The moon was hiding behind the pillars of clouds as if it didn't want to be witness to what occurred down in the woods. Thorns tore at my hands and face as I ran towards the child's screams . . . as long as he was screaming, he was still alive.

Time was standing still. It was that night that summer so long ago and I was running from something evil. It was that night again, but this time I was running towards it. I bumped into a tree, righted myself, and ran on. It had all begun that night—was this the way it had always been meant to end? How had it ended all those times before?

I could hear Ben shouting behind me somewhere. I had lost him. I had never meant to. He must be frantic trying to find me again. He could hear the screams and the unearthly snarls out there, too.

Twice I stumbled and fell to my knees. Once I thought Ben had caught up to me, but when I glanced back, there was nothing, so I kept on going.

"Jeremy!" I shrieked in terror as I came out into the clearing. It was the same place I had first sensed the evil all those years ago. Now it seemed like yesterday, except there was a different cast of characters. And now I was no longer that innocent, unknowing child—I had seen too much and I knew too much.

Jeremy was screaming at the top of his lungs at the tall hulking creature that was hovering over him. Standing there, I froze for a minute, as I stared up at the gigantic shadow that seemed to dwarf the entire forest. There was a fleeting impression of long tapering claws, wicked fangs, and glaring, vicious eyes that burned holes into the night. Then I saw Jim . . .

"Jimmy!" I whispered disbelievingly. "Watch out!" I screamed because it was crouched over him . . . but he walked towards it! Jeremy yelled as the shadow merged with Jim. I lunged at Jeremy, tackling him to the ground to get him out of the way. We rolled over and over together in the grass and when I looked up again both Jim and the thing were gone. Only one wail of anguish rent the air and then slowly it trailed away into the night, moving off until it was only a memory of a whimper. But that cry, I knew, would live forever in my ears and would haunt me to the day I died. Not a death cry. . . a cry of victory.

It had taken Jim! My brother was gone. But something else was missing, too. *It was gone!*

Shaking with relief, I rocked my child in my arms, as we sprawled on the ground crying. When I closed my eyes to shut off the tears, I could still see Jim's face before me in that last terrible moment. He had been smiling at me, and he had waved. Goodbye . . . poor sweet Jimmy. Goodbye. Where was he now?

"Mom! Mom!" Jeremy snuggled in my arms and cried.

"It's all right now, son," I soothed him, stroking his damp head. He was soaked. I looked up to see Ben over me, reaching out for both of us. The look in his eyes was indescribable. I smiled up at him weakly and touched his hand, still cradling my son in my lap in the dark. I had lost so many, but I still had him.

"Uncle Jim helped me, Mom. He found me in the hole and got me out . . . he helped me . . . but it got him, too. Just like Dad . . . it got him, too!" Jeremy sobbed, looking up into our faces. He moaned and hid his eyes.

Ben had stooped down beside us and behind him I could see Captain Sinclair coming, huffing and puffing from the long run. The cry of sirens were now everywhere. Help had come. I wanted to laugh. Too late. Always too late. Now Jim was dead, too.

"Hell . . . did you see that thing!" Ben exploded, his face drained and his eyes huge as he stared into the woods. "Did you *see* that!" Then he seemed to have heard what Jeremy said for the first time. "What did he just say about his Uncle

Jim?" His voice sounded peculiar. He took Jeremy's face in his hands gently and tilted it up to look into his eyes. "What was that you just said about your Uncle Jim?" Our eyes met and there was the strangest glimmer in the depths of his.

Jeremy told him what he had said again but added to it this time; about how his Uncle Jim had arrived just in time and pulled him out of the hole and saved him from that *thing*. His voice was trembling. I looked up into Ben's eyes. Something was wrong. Very wrong.

But Ben didn't say anything. Instead, he checked Jeremy's legs where Jeremy claimed they hurt. "It was probably the fall . . . he might have broken something," he said to me, taking Jeremy into his arms from mine. "Let's get him to a hospital, Sarah. We can talk about all this after he's checked in." Jeremy was moaning in his arms and I wasn't about to object. My son looked very pale to me and there wasn't anything else I could do here. They were gone.

As I watched Ben walk away towards the car with Jeremy in his arms, I felt the hush of the woods; the peace. I knew somehow, looking out through the waiting trees as I followed them, that whatever had been out there; whatever had stalked my family and me all these years, was gone. Truly gone forever. It had finally gotten what it had come for so long ago. I still found it hard to believe that *Jim* had been the one it had wanted, and that I had never seen it before.

It was gone. And the smell of roses was everywhere . . .

I got into the car next to Ben. After a few hushed words with the Captain, who stayed behind to take care of the body, we left. They would search, I thought looking back through the forest, but they would never find it. It was no longer here. *It* had gone back to wherever it had come from. My heart was numb over Jonathan's and Jim's deaths, but I still had my son and, squeezing his arm tightly as he lay in my lap, I was so grateful for that. *It* could have taken all three—or even more. I turned to look at Ben's serious profile as we drove away. He turned the siren on and we sped to the nearest hospital. There was something on his mind and I knew I would find out soon enough. Jeremy had to be taken care of first.

The emergency room was very crowded for such a small town. They all knew Ben and soon Jeremy was whisked away to one of the back rooms to be examined. Ben and I sat in the waiting room under the bright lights. He held my hand firmly and let me lay my head on his shoulder. My mind kept repeating the events of the day and I couldn't even talk.

We waited.

Ben was silent for a long time and when he finally spoke to me, it startled me. "Sarah . . . I have to tell you something, but I don't know exactly how to go about it . . ."

His grip on my hand grew tighter and I looked at Ben. What else could happen? There wasn't anything that would hurt me more than I'd already been hurt. My ex-husband was dead and I had never meant him any harm. It seemed ironic that Jonathan's fears of his own death had, indeed, come true; and indirectly at my hands. Jonathan had been right to run away from me. Maybe he had known all along that I would be the cause of his death. I didn't blame him for running, even if he had broken my heart and Jeremy's. Poor Jonathan.

Then there was Jimmy, my sweet Jimmy who had never hurt anyone—dead too. And why was I still alive?

"All right . . . I'm ready. You can tell me anything." I could say the words so easily but inside of me a tiny voice was saying, but please, nothing bad. No more bad news.

"Jeremy said his Uncle Jim saved him. He said he pulled him from that well and protected him from that monstrosity that had killed his father." Ben was very subdued and he wouldn't look me in the eyes. I stiffened instinctively and tried to catch his gaze. He was still stalling.

"Spit it out, Ben. I'm a big girl, I can take it." I tried a weak smile.

"Did *you* see Jim out there tonight?" he suddenly asked.

It was such an unusual question that I tried to catch my breath before I could answer it.

"Yes. I saw my brother," I replied carefully. "But just for a second or two before he . . . disappeared." I was crying softly again but I didn't realize it until the drops fell on my hands and Ben's, large and warm. "He was helping Jeremy."

"Are you sure it was *Jim*?"

"Why, yes!" My voice came out harsh. Why was he grilling me like this? I wondered. "It *was* Jim."

"*I* didn't *see* him. I didn't *see* anyone or anything except that huge obscenity." He still couldn't believe he'd seen what he'd seen, I could tell by his expression. "*I didn't see him.*" He repeated it as if he were in shock.

"What are you getting at?" I asked finally.

"I should have told you this sooner, Sarah. But compared to a missing child and a dead man out in the woods, it didn't seem so important that I tell you right then. It could have pushed you over the edge."

"Ben!" He was garbling it all so badly I could hardly grasp what he was trying to say. "*What is it?*"

"You couldn't have seen Jim out there in the woods tonight! He's been *dead since this afternoon.*"

The words bit into me like vicious teeth and wouldn't let go. "Dead?" I whispered, not understanding. "Jim was already dead when I saw him? But that's impossible." Even as I said it I knew better. My grandmother and Charlie had both been dead for many years and yet I had talked to my grandmother just a few hours ago . . . nothing was impossible, not to me. "How?" I merely asked.

"There was an accident about an hour away from here. Everyone on the bus was either hurt or killed outright . . . Jim never regained consciousness. I'm sorry, Sarah. I'd sent out an A.P.B. on him this evening right before you were picked up and I got this information back. I would have told you sooner but I just couldn't bring myself to lay that on your shoulders when you were so upset over Jeremy's disappearance, you understand? I was trying to protect you." The look in his eyes was pathetic. I squeezed his hand reassuringly. Poor Ben.

"It's all right, Ben. It had to be. That's why I loved my brother so—I knew our time was short."

I looked away towards the rooms where they had taken my son and I said a silent prayer. *Please let everything be all right!* "You did what you thought would be best at the time." I smiled sadly at him. It had been quite a shock but so had been seeing Jim disappear back there in those woods. "There wasn't anything that could have been done to stop what happened, anyway. It wouldn't have made any difference one way or another."

Ben hugged me and it wasn't very long before a doctor came out in search of us. "You're the boy's mother?" He was brisk, businesslike.

"Yes." I shifted my eyes to Ben.

"He's going to be all right. He's got a bad break in that left leg of his, but he's a healthy child and it shouldn't take too long to mend. I've set it and he's already out for the night. So don't worry, he's fine."

"Thank you, doctor." I smiled, sagging against Ben in relief. I watched as the man in white walked away, already busy with other patients. Together, Ben and I went to see Jeremy. We stood for a long time over his sleeping form.

Everything was going to be fine. Fine. Ben wrapped strong arms around me and led me out of the hospital because I couldn't seem to walk too well myself. I was numb from everything. Then he took me home.

And for the first time in my life since that long ago summer's night, I wasn't afraid. There was no longer anything to be afraid of.

Jim had taken care of everything.

CHAPTER THIRTY-SEVEN

It was November 28, and it would have been Jim's twenty-eighth birthday. I breathed deeply of the crisp wintry air and thought about my brother. It was mild out today, compared to the last two weeks. Cabin fever had hit me with a vengeance after the snow began to melt and I found myself walking around the old neighborhood a lot lately. A week ago we'd had twelve inches of snow and temperatures down below zero, but today was mild; the kind of day where you just love to get outside and enjoy the clean, chilly air and the cold sun. I could feel its feeble warmth through my warm winter coat. My hands were covered by red mittens Jim had given me a few Christmases ago. I touched them to my cold face and walked faster.

The snow was piled everywhere in tall, frozen heaps along the side of the road and my boots left light footprints on the tightly packed powder on the road. I followed a tire track for a long time until it ran out and I had to wade through virgin territory.

I trudged the old familiar path to where I had grown up. I looked out across the empty white fields and tried to locate the treacherous hidden gullies that I knew lurked out there under the snow. I wasn't afraid any longer of the memories or the ghosts that had once dwelt here. The evil was gone forever . . . and, so too, were all the ghosts. My family—all of them—were finally at rest.

The trees that fringed the woods were like bent fingers against the bright sky. There were no voices anymore. No laughter. Nothing. It was just an empty woods now, as the house ruins were just loose rubble and cracked bricks scattered about on an empty piece of land. The cherry tree was just a cherry tree.

The wind came up as I strolled by my childhood home. I smiled wistfully. There were many good memories here, too. All I had to do was hold on to those instead of all the bad ones, and let time do its healing.

There was the hill all of us children used to tumble down in old cardboard boxes. There were the summer days and nights playing out in these fields. They had been good days, those days. Jim had loved them as much as I had. We'd go hunting in the twilight for the elusive fireflies, catching them gleefully in our hands only to let them go again. Jim could never stand to hurt anything small and defenseless. Looking out over the snow covered scene, I could still feel the blanket of soft warm summer nights speckled with tiny, twinkling lights. So beautiful.

I walked deep into the field towards the woods, unafraid for the first time in many years. Little white puffs of frozen air escaped my lips. Thanksgiving was close. I was going to make a huge turkey for us. Ben was coming, too. But, of course, he was always there anyway. I should marry the guy and make it legal, I thought, amused. It was sort of a joke between us. He'd asked me to marry him at least twenty times in the last few months. Ambling along, I stuffed my hands into my pockets and began to whistle a nameless melody as my mind drifted.

Years fell away and I was with Jonathan, long before all the troubles clouded our lives. Jeremy was a baby gurgling happily in Jonathan's arms. Before the baby had been born, we had stayed up all night in the labor room, Jonathan and

I, playing cards to while the long hours away. Jonathan had been so sweet to me. When I first held our son, I had been so content. I had everything, I thought. It was funny what life did to you.

Jonathan must have known for a long time that he was going to die. Some people do. Perhaps that was the real reason he had left us. He'd thought he'd missed out on life in some way and was trying to catch up . . . or maybe he thought that in running away from me, he would be permitted to live. It just hadn't worked out that way, though. No man can escape his destiny. I, more than anyone, knew that.

At first, I had experienced terrible guilt over these deaths. I had nightmares and couldn't sleep. I'd wake up screaming, blaming and punishing myself until I was sick. Until one day Ben pushed me in front of a mirror and forced me to take a good look at myself. I was a wreck! Thin as a rail with dark circles around my eyes that made me look like a raccoon.

"You're starving yourself," Ben exclaimed, making me look. "What will Jeremy and I do if you waste away to nothing?" There was pity and anger in his voice, and in his eyes as he took me into his arms and held me while I finally cried. Cried all my guilt away. . . and all the ghosts.

"Don't rush me, Ben." I laid my fingers softly over his lips before he could utter another word. "Give me time."

"You've had enough time. You have to live now." He looked deep into my eyes. "It wasn't your fault that they all had to die. Don't punish yourself, Sarah. Jim wouldn't want that and it won't bring any of them back." He was quiet for a while as he held me. "At least there'll be no more murders. You and Jeremy are safe. Take comfort in that," he told me.

From that moment on, I pulled myself together and went back to living. There was Jeremy. There was Ben. I had never been meant to stop what had happened. We had been spared because of Jim's love. I had to make something out of our lives to make his sacrifice mean something; to make some sense out of all the deaths.

But I wasn't the same Sarah as before. Against Ben's better judgement I decided to accept the psychic gift I had been given. I would help anyone I could. I helped the police on any case they brought me. I had gained overnight fame by Jenny's murder, and now I welcomed the tons of mail with open arms. I answered every letter myself and helped wherever I could. There was really so little I could usually do, but I tried. Even the unbelievable amount of hate mail didn't stop me from doing what I had to do. I would laugh at the mailman. He'd drop the bags of mail off about ten feet away from the house and dash off, he was that frightened of me. I felt sorry for the man but I couldn't help but laugh at him. There were always those people who were afraid of what they didn't understand.

But I knew this was the price I had to pay. I had been allowed to live for a reason . . . and this was it.

And then there was my new popularity.

Ben had placed some of my artwork weeks ago in a few select art galleries. Now, everything was suddenly selling like hotcakes. The galleries were begging for more. Ben was pleased. I was skeptical.

"It's just my name they want," I told Ben sadly. "Not my pictures. I'm a celebrity now. That's all. They could care less how good I really am. I'm a freak and they can buy a piece of me for a few bucks to hang on their very own wall."

"Sarah! You can't really mean that. It's your pictures they want. You're a good artist. You have a special talent. They'd have snatched up your stuff anyway. Don't be so hard on yourself." He laughed and kissed me lightly on the nose.

Sweet, caring Ben. I hoped he was right. I wanted to be cherished as a true artist, not some kind of a new craze.

I'd been walking for hours and my feet and hands were freezing, but I didn't really want to go home yet. I was thinking about Jim's journal. I had found it lying on the nightstand right after his death. I had been surprised when I had found it. But it dissolved a lot of my guilt and it explained why we had been cursed.

It was a message to me, I knew it, the minute I picked it up and stared uncomprehendingly at the scribbled pages. It was Jim's handwriting, that I didn't doubt. I read it, and at last understood everything I had never been allowed to understand before.

I finally knew why they had all died.

I finally had some insight into what that *thing* in the woods had really been.

. . . *That summer night. The night my sister Sarah had seen it in the woods and run home crying . . . I had first known it was back again. Back again! It will never leave me in peace, no matter how many lives I escape to; no matter how hard I try to hide—it finds me! I should kill myself now and end all the misery I know will soon begin, but I am such a coward. How can I kill myself? How can a child kill himself? Maybe it will go away this time. Maybe, it won't find me this time. Maybe, it won't hurt anyone . . . this time.*

That had been written by an adult Jimmy reaching back into his haunted childhood, trying to find some comfort in his confessions. I felt sick as I read page after page. Of course, I almost knew what happened next. How Jim must have suffered knowing all along that *he* was the cause!

The demon—for that's what it is, sis—still wants to punish me for disturbing its sleep so long, long ago. Lifetimes ago. I will put these words down here, now, hoping that someday you will read them and try to understand, but most of all, forgive me for all the harm I have done you and those I loved. I was a coward; and that has been my curse and also my excuse all these terrible years. I could have ended it so many times by just admitting defeat and giving it my body and soul. But I was afraid of dying forever. The others never lost their souls as I will if I give in to it. I kept playing for time, Sarah, believe me! Playing for time to yet find a way to defeat it and to regain all those who had been lost to it over all these years . . . all these centuries.

Oh, it started so long ago and the story is so . . . bear with me dear Sarah, and I will try to make you see why I had to do what I did all these years.

At that part of the diary, the words had become wild and hard to read. But, fighting back the tears, I took a deep breath and read on. My Jimmy had been in agony when he wrote these words and the very nature of my gift seemed to lock into that misery and it swirled around me pricking and biting at me. My hands were shaking.

Sarah! We live over and over. Forever. It is true, believe me because I know. I have — we all have — lived many times before and I wasn't always as wise or cowardly as you know me to be in this sorrowful life just past. Many lifetimes ago I sought to answer the greatest questions of the universe. I have always doubted that God existed and in my earlier foolish existence I once took it upon myself (how arrogant!) to find out which was truly the stronger—good or evil. I was such a fanatic that I was sure good would always prevail in the end, no matter what. What a fool I was! It never occurred to me that good doesn't always win; that my arrogance in itself would weaken me and my cause; that sometimes man aids the evil by the imperfection in himself. That evil can be stronger sometimes. I was a monk, a man of foolish righteousness and ego, in the first life. The Devil and his minions were pawns, I thought, to be moved and toyed with by my infinite control and link with the Almighty. So I called up a demon by the old art of black magic and woke it from its slumber. I yanked it from hell, out into the unsuspecting world where its evil increased tenfold! I had been so sure I could handle it, defeat it, and send it whimpering back to the fires with its tail between its legs . . . oh, how wrong I was! I couldn't beat it and in the end I couldn't even control it. I couldn't send it back where it belonged; where it wanted to go. It haunted me, begging first, then growing angrier and angrier at my folly. In the end, coward that I was, I ran away from it and it stalked me. Like a tracer, it could track me down if it came close enough to me. The glow of my talent of magic shone bright, and no matter how hard I fought to diminish it with the tiny powers I had left at my disposal, would always give me away. Yes, not all my powers from the old days had died . . . at times, as you know now, I could still keep it at bay. I could still at times keep it confused long enough to get away — but my powers faded over the lifetimes. Finally, I couldn't even protect you and the boy any longer and I knew it was only a matter of time before it would take you or him . . . and, Sarah, that I couldn't allow. We lived so many lives together. I always ran. You and the others of my lives were allowed to suffer. In all these centuries, I never gave myself to it. That's all it ever wanted. Had I but faced it years and centuries ago, all those lifetimes of killing would never have been. I know you've seen them in your visions. I know. Do you see now what I have had to live with? When I could no longer protect you or myself I knew I had to give it its revenge, give it what it craved or it would never stop killing. There wasn't any more time . . . I had to take it back to hell with me; it is my punishment for my arrogance.

The next page was dated the same day Jenny had died and by his handwriting I could tell that Jim had known about it. I read on, my face draining of color at what I found.

. . . Charlie knew about the demon even before it came to claim him. He always knew what it wanted. I think that was why he hated me so in life . . . and in death. He still blames me for the limbo he exists in. I have heard his voice many times and I have seen him. Yes, Sarah, Jeremy is not the only one that Charlie appears to. I am followed constantly by the tormented child that was once Charlie. The demon has used him where he could never use the others because — how can I say this — there are people who are marked when they enter this life with the sign of evil. They know each other. Oh, it isn't their fault. Charlie wasn't completely evil, Sarah

360

. . . it's just that he had so little good in him. That's why he hated me. He knew what I was. He knew what he was. He never belonged here with us. It had been a mistake. He heard the demon's call and thought it would give him power, too. He was wrong. Evil cannot ever be trusted. Charlie . . . poor Charlie! How he wanted to be special! How he wanted love, but he couldn't outbalance the bad inside himself and so he was doomed . .

Here the writing broke off. The next entry was strange.

. . . I have thought so much about Charlie these last few days. I have seen him so often. He is trying to warn me—tell me something . . .

A few pages later: *Charlie! I would never have believed it! He has promised to help us . . . he has promised! He wants to redeem himself . . .*

Perhaps, I thought sadly, Charlie *had* redeemed himself. I prayed he'd find peace. Thank you, Charlie.

I puzzled over that last entry that was written on the final day of Jim's life. What he had meant. What had happened? That entry was merely a few desperate pleas for help and forgiveness: *It has killed so many people I love and I still haven't found the courage to end this hell called my life! I am responsible! I am to blame . . . It only wants me to submit and give up my life. It only wants me.*

. . . but if I do give in . . . what good will it really do? Will it just begin all over again, anyway? I don't think I can stand to face another life. I really loved my family. I always loved all my families. Why won't it leave me the hell alone? Why won't it be appeased and let me live in peace . . .

. . . if only I could have just a little more time to find out how to beat it. How to defeat its evilness and send it back to hell where it belongs forever and still save myself. If only I had more time. Only empty, frightened words. He had always known it would have to end the way it had ended . . .

I cried at his tormented words. He had never found the answer and the hideous evil had trailed him finally to his own final death. No more lives; no more evil. I wasn't angry at Jim for all the death he had brought to us. No one blames the rabbit hounded by the dog pack, if it tries to escape, to stay alive. After all, according to the diary, Jim knew that his death would probably only begin the horror all over again from a new start. He had nothing to lose, and nothing to gain. He had been playing for time. I wondered what had happened to him those last few days that had made him give up? Why had he finally given in?

The answer, I knew, as I read the last few paragraphs of the sad little book, lay with Jeremy and myself. For some reason, he wouldn't or couldn't allow us to die in his place . . . he'd sacrificed himself. My poor, sweet Jimmy . . .

. . . *when you read this, Sarah* . . . He had written on that last page in a calm handwriting, calmer than most of the previous pages could attest to. . . .*it will be all over. I cannot let you and Jeremy die. I cannot let anyone else die. I know how to stop it. It is futile to keep going on like this. You and your son are special and I owe this to you, to our family. I will always love you all. Do not forget me, Sarah. And don't hold what I have done against me. I have always been a coward. Perhaps, that is why it never stopped hurting . . . I'm sorry, Sarah. Forgive me . . .*

I closed the book with tenderness. So none of it had been my fault.

I prayed that now *it* was satisfied and was gone for good—at least, from this life. I also prayed that Jim had found peace and that he had not really lost his soul. I smiled; if you looked at it one way, Jim had won. He'd won against his cowardice. He'd beaten it at its own game. Forever's evil had lost its eternity. It was small comfort, but it was better than nothing. He'd saved us. Love had been stronger than evil. That was a victory.

Forgive me, Sarah.

I put the diary away somewhere safe. I never wanted to see it again.

I forgive you, Jimmy, I thought, finally smiling. I love

362

you! I'll miss you . . .
As I missed all of them.

CHAPTER THIRTY-EIGHT

I'd been walking around the old place for hours. My hands and feet were numb but I didn't want to go home yet. Jeremy wouldn't be home from school for a while and Ben was coming over later. It was his day off.

I was just turning to go back home about a half-hour later when I saw Jeremy running towards me at breakneck speed. He grinned widely at me and waved. I waved back. How had he found me? I didn't need to answer that. I had been here every day since Jim and Jonathan had died . . . *no, gone away.* No one ever really dies, I thought. They just go away. They just weren't here any longer, and some day I knew I would join them. We'd all be together again.

Sarah! We live over and over again . . .

"Mom! Here you are." His eyes were sparkling.

"You're a real bloodhound lately, aren't you?" I teased him, giving him a swift hug.

"Someone's got to keep an eye on you when Ben ain't here." It was a private joke with us these days. Jeremy had become increasingly fond of Ben lately. Ben had been good for him, too. When I saw them roughhousing or doing something together I was reminded of Jeremy's father. Ben was his substitute. But it didn't really matter, as long as Jeremy was happy. He'd had a hard time of it.

"Who's going to keep an eye on *you*?"

"You will." Always the same answer. Jeremy smiled.

"How's your leg?" I asked him, looking down at the leg that had been in the cast for such a long time. I still worried about it. It had been a bad break and I was always cautioning him about it. "Don't do this; don't do that." He rarely listened. The cut on his face had left a scar. We all had scars.

"Ah, Mom, it's fine. It's been fine for ages."

"If you say so. When did you get home from school?"

"Just a little bit ago. Can I come along with you while you walk?" he asked.

"Sure, for a little while." But my mind was already far away again . . . remembering.

Jeremy looked over at me. "Mom?"

"Yes?" We were walking away from my old home with all its poignant memories and tragedies, heading back to our own. I was content knowing we would soon be there, safe and warm. I smiled, thinking of Ben.

"He's happy, you know?"

"Who's happy?" I asked, looking for cars as we crossed the street. But a chill had traveled up my spine. Of course I knew who he was talking about.

"Uncle Jim," Jeremy replied. "He helped me; he saved my life. He's happy he did that. Don't worry about him, Mom. He's not lonely." Jeremy turned those eyes towards me that were so much like Jimmy's had been. Eyes exactly like Jimmy's, I reflected. *Too much like Jimmy's* . . .

"No. He's not lonely," I said with a cheery smile and ruffled his hair. The whole family was with him, how could he be lonely? He had been forgiven. *He's at peace like Charlie.* I felt it deep inside.

"I'll race you home!" I cried and started running. I couldn't beat my son, I knew. He doubled back to tell me to hurry. Ben was waiting for me at the house.

"Now you've taken up running, huh?" Ben chuckled as I panted up to him in the street in front of our home. "How many miles you up to?"

"Very funny!" I huffed, doubled over from the strain of running all that way. "Boy, am I out of shape!"

"I don't think so," Ben said with a grin. He was sitting easily astride his bike, watching me tenderly. I thought sure he was going to ask me to marry him—again. He had almost every day the last two months and I had smilingly refused, but we both knew it was only a matter of time before he wore me down. He was impossible! He even rode his motorcycle in this weather. Now *that* was crazy, but he loved it.

"Ben." I nodded towards Jeremy and shook my head. Ben laughed.

"You want to take a ride with me?" he suddenly said brightly. There was a light in his eyes that I had seen before many times, but this time I knew he was up to something.

Ben couldn't hide anything from me.

"Well," I looked longingly at the warm house. "I'm really cold . . . how about a cup of hot chocolate first?" I tried to tempt him but he didn't buy it. "You really expect me to ride on that thing in this kind of weather?" I laughed.

"Please? A short ride? Jeremy can go in and watch television. We won't be long, I promise. I want to show you something." His eyes begged.

"All right." I laughed back and watched Jeremy run into the house to wait. It was as if he were in on it or something. He'd never agree so easily otherwise. I got on the bike behind Ben and hung on as we took off down the street. We did pretty well on the snow-packed street.

I knew where we were going before we were half-way there—Ben's dream place. He pulled the bike up onto the side of the road, the same place he had all those months ago in the summer. It seemed like an eternity ago. I was shivering. "Heck of a way to travel in the winter!" I indicated the bike and let Ben rub my hands between his until I could feel them again. "Why don't you buy yourself a car?"

"A car?" He turned to me and took my hand and we started to walk across the ground before us. "I had one of those once . . . ate too much gas."

"Ben?" I waited for him to say what he apparently wanted to say.

"Yep, it ate too much gas and I've got to cut corners any way I can now." He was serious, but in the corner of his eyes lurked a smile.

"Why?" I squeezed his hand hard. "Stop teasing me!"

"Why? I need all the money I can get my hands on to help pay the mortgage on this place . . ."

"You *didn't*!" I cried, happy that I was hearing what I hoped I would hear. What other reason did he have for bringing me out here in the dead of winter?

"I *did*. I bought this place today. It took every penny I had saved. More. But it was worth it. It can be our vacation spot. Our get-away-from-it-all spot for weekends and such. Or maybe, someday, we'll all just move out here . . . You can even have a horse out here, Sarah." He was smiling down at me now and he kissed me lightly on the tip of my nose.

There wasn't any need for words. We just stood there and looked at his dream ranch and held each other tightly against the wind.

After a while, he kissed me. "I'm ready for that hot chocolate now. Then afterwards, how about a nice hot supper at an expensive restaurant—my treat? All three of us."

"Can you afford it?" I laughed, nodding at his property. "I'm starved. You won't get by cheap."

"Well, it's only money," he said and laughed. "The best things in life are free."

We walked back to the bike and I got on behind him. The sun was starting to go down and it was suddenly very cold. I leaned my head up against his strong back as we fought the wind and I thought to myself how true his words had been. The best things were free, but sometimes you had to pay a terrible price to get them. Love never died and that made it worth it all.

On the way back I thought of my family, every one of them, but this time I smiled into the wind holding tightly to Ben as we went home. I would never forget all the love they had given me so long ago. All of them . . . in all our lives.

I would never forget in a thousand years.